PRAISE FOR

"Kitty Johnson's *Five Winters* features such a warm, relatable protagonist in Beth and is a wonderful story about finding yourself—and love, of course! I very much enjoyed this read."

—Emily Stone, author of *Always, in December*

"This book is such a tonic. Entertaining characters, a heartwarming storyline, and an ending guaranteed to make you smile."

—Imogen Clark, bestselling author of *Impossible to Forget*

"Told in a fresh and original voice, *Five Winters* is a moving and hopeful study of one woman's quest for love and motherhood. Readers will adore Beth and cheer for her all the way. Kitty Johnson's book follows the tradition of all the best Christmas books: it gives you that warm feeling that, if you try hard enough, you can make all your dreams come true."

—Anita Hughes, author of *A Magical New York Christmas*

PRICKLY COMPANY

ALSO BY KITTY JOHNSON

Five Winters

PRICKLY COMPANY

a novel

KITTY JOHNSON

LAKE UNION
PUBLISHING

Text copyright © 2024 by Margaret K Johnson
All rights reserved.

Published by Lake Union Publishing, Seattle

www.apub.com

Amazon, the Amazon logo, and Lake Union Publishing are trademarks of Amazon.com, Inc., or its affiliates.

ISBN-13: 9781662518089 (paperback)
ISBN-13: 9781662518072 (digital)

Cover design and illustration by Cassie Gonzales
Cover image: © Mashmuh / Shutterstock; © Parkheta / Shutterstock; © Lina Melnik / Shutterstock; © Lana Brow / Shutterstock; © amana images inc. / Alamy

Printed in the United States of America

For wildlife saviours everywhere. You're all amazing.

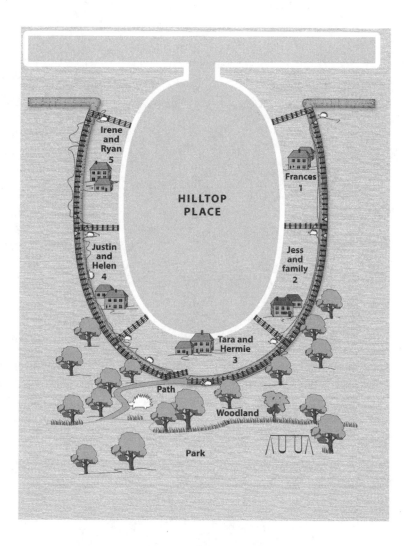

1

The hedgehogs had lived on the land surrounding Hilltop Place since before the city was a smudge on the horizon, and the only contact hedgehogs had with humans was when they came to hunt them for their meat. Hunting forays aside, the land was a hedgehog paradise, with leaf-shedding trees and soil rich with worms, beetles, and juicy slugs.

Nowadays, although humans bought their meat from the super-market and had given up their hedgehog-hunting ways, life still wasn't easy for the snuffling, shuffling creatures. Apart from a few pockets of woodland, the area had been developed, and the hedgehogs were forced to search for food in gardens, where they often encountered fences. Lots of fences.

What the hedgehogs needed was a more natural environment, espe-cially with autumn on the horizon—a time of gathering in and feeding up as they prepared to hibernate over winter.

The hedgehogs didn't know it, as they squeezed under gates and negotiated concrete planters, but a champion was about to emerge. A champion whose efforts would unwittingly change the lives of all the residents of Hilltop Place, and not just the prickly ones.

It wasn't only the hedgehogs in Hilltop Place who were busily gath-ering in and storing up as summer galloped to its close. The humans were focused on satisfying their deepest cravings too. Some craved a new car or a piece of expensive jewellery. One even longed for a reason to carry on. But Jess Crawford, who lived at Number Two, longed to welcome a second child into her family.

As any hedgehog will tell you, things are never straightforward. Just as you discover a juicy cache of earthworms and it seems as if your most deep-seated desires are going to be satisfied, some human will open their back door to let the dog out, or another hedgehog will come barging along and shove you right out of the way to gobble up the worms themselves.

If the hedgehogs needed to make sure they ate enough food to get them through the long months of hibernation, Jess Crawford needed to find the strength to start a new, positive chapter of her life. For even with the sense of purpose and fulfillment she got from caring for Stella, her daughter, Jess still felt, metaphorically speaking, as if each of the two miscarriages she'd experienced since Stella's birth had carved away a little more of her flesh, leaving her angled and hollowed out. As if the space the babies had taken up inside her might never be filled again.

But all that was about to change. For tomorrow, the son she had longed for, for so long, would arrive. And this evening, as hedgehogs roamed unseen outside in the warmth of the August night, Jess put on a sexy, silky nightdress instead of the comfortable cotton one she favoured, determined to make love to her husband, Michael, by way of celebration.

They hadn't done anything remotely sexual for some months. The stress of the adoption process, coming hard on the heels of sex dictated by ovulation kits, had led to a sexual desert. And with one-year-old Toby arriving the next day, it felt somehow important to make the most of this last night before they were thrown once again into the chaos—a fulfilling chaos, but chaos nevertheless—of nappy changing and getting used to a new being.

So Jess got into bed and rubbed against Michael's naked body, smoothing one hand down his back and nuzzling a line of kisses down his neck. But Michael, while not completely unresponsive, shifted ever so slightly away from her.

"Sorry, love, I'm a bit tired tonight. You are too, aren't you? You were nodding and snoring in front of the telly just now."

It was true, she had been. Complete, no doubt, with the tiniest bit of open-mouthed drooling. It was no wonder Michael wasn't feeling sexy.

"I just think this might be our last opportunity for a bit, that's all. You remember what it was like when Stella was a baby. We didn't have sex for months."

As Michael gently stroked her back, Jess remembered the way they'd once clung to each other. How he'd pressed every particle of himself against her in an explosion of the senses, neither of them wanting to accept that they were two instead of one.

Now, even though her hand was still gliding towards his buttocks, seeking to pull him against her, Jess was secretly glad he wasn't up for it. Quite happy to accept any reassurances that it was okay not to want sex. She was tired. And preoccupied. But it also saddened her that she felt relieved.

"He's almost two, though, isn't he?" Michael said, his deep voice rumbling through the space between them. "Not a baby. You won't be breastfeeding him. He'll sleep through the night once he's settled in with us."

"D'you really think so?"

"I do. Come on, let's get some sleep." He snapped off the light. "Everything's going to be fine."

As if you could *will* something to be fine just by saying it. And as Jess lay sleepless beside him, thinking longingly of her comfortable cotton nightdress, she was struck by a sudden thunderbolt of doubt.

Are we doing the right thing? she wanted to ask, but Michael was already drifting into sleep. And in any case, that wasn't really what she wanted to know.

Right from the start, she'd been the driving force in this process. It had been her saying, *"Let's have another baby."* Michael saying, *"Are you sure? Things were pretty rough with Stella. I feel like we've only just come out the other side."* Her flapping her hand as if his doubts meant nothing. *"We've learnt what to do now, haven't we? It'll be fine."*

She had surged on to spearhead the "Let's get pregnant campaign," one Michael had gone along with, performing when required to do so, commiserating each month when her period arrived. Rejoicing with her when she fell pregnant. Grieving with her when she miscarried. Agreeing when she decided not to put her body through any more trauma and to adopt instead. Going through the ordeal of the social workers' scrutiny alongside her. The high stress of the adoption panel.

But deep down, Jess had always known Michael would have been quite content to stop at Stella. To enjoy that one experience of parenthood and to not have any more children. So the question that really burnt in Jess's mind, the question destined to keep her awake through the night and leave her limp and ill prepared for the momentous day when she welcomed her brand-new son, was, *Is this what Michael really wants?*

But how could she ask that? For the past few years, she had been pushing boulders up a steep hill, and now they were piled up in a perfect mound. The wrong answer would bring the whole lot of them toppling, bashing, bouncing, and bruising as they cascaded around her ankles.

No, the opportunity to ask questions had long passed. After all, there had been plenty of time for Michael to object if he'd wanted to. And he hadn't. Because he wanted her to be happy. And she would be. How could she not be? Toby was arriving tomorrow. Her son was arriving tomorrow! A brother for Stella. Their family would, at long last, be complete.

2

Jess couldn't believe it the next morning when she woke to find Michael dressing in his business suit as usual.

"Where are you going? Toby's arriving at ten."

"I just want to put an hour in. Answer a few emails and get the ball rolling on a few things. Don't worry, I'll be back in plenty of time."

Minutes later, he left, and Jess slid her feet into her slippers, tied her robe, and tried not to let his reluctance to take the whole day off work mean anything.

"Mummy, why are stars twinkly?" Stella came into the bathroom while Jess was having a wee, as instantly switched on and awake as always.

"I don't know, darling," Jess said, flushing. "We'll have to ask Mr. Google. Or Daddy when he comes home. Come here and get kissed. What d'you want for breakfast? Snap crackle or toast?"

"Toast. Toast, toast, toast! With honey and jam."

"You can't have honey and jam, sweetheart."

"Why not? It will be super yummy."

Jess sighed. Why not, indeed? Just this once.

"All right. You can have honey and jam if you promise to get dressed by yourself afterwards. Mummy's got some things to do before Toby arrives. Okay?"

Stella nodded. "Okay, Mummy. Can I put the bread in the toaster?"

"All right."

With breakfast done and Stella in her bedroom, hopefully keeping her promise to get dressed by herself, Jess drifted into the nursery. There really wasn't anything else to do to get ready for Toby, not practically, anyway. She just liked being in the nursery. Imagining Toby in his cot, smiling up at her when she came in, arms stretched up, ready to be lifted out.

The cot was new. Michael hadn't wanted to buy a new one—she'd seen it on his face. *"The kid's nearly two years old. He won't be in a cot for much longer, Jess."*

Jess had pretended not to notice. Michael was a man, so he didn't understand. Toby'd had a difficult start to life, removed from his parents as a young baby due to their drug addiction, fostered out to two different couples. The poor little mite deserved everything to be perfect. And it was. Crib. Fish mobile. Blue curtains with pictures of clouds and rainbows. A shelf of age-appropriate picture books.

"Mummy! I want to wear my crown," Stella called from her bedroom.

"Well, you can if you want to."

"But I can't find it!"

Jess sighed, reluctantly turning her back on the perfect room. "Okay, coming," she said. But before she could get very far, there was a knock at the front door. Surely it couldn't be the social worker with Toby, already? They weren't due for another hour.

Stella dashed from her bedroom. "Is it my new brother, Mummy?"

"I'm not sure. You wait up here, and I'll go and see."

But there was no way her headstrong daughter would miss being part of any welcoming committee, crown on her head or not, so when Jess opened the door, Stella was right alongside her in her princess finery.

"It's a man, Mummy," she announced.

She was right; it was. A man with muscular, tattooed arms and shaggy, uncut hair. With an expression bordering on hostile on his face.

In a wheelchair, with a cardboard box balanced on his lap. In short, as different from social worker Linda as it was possible for anyone to get.

"Hello," Jess said, instinctively taking Stella's hand. "Can I help you?"

She saw him notice the protective gesture. Had just enough time to wonder whether the hostility radiating from him was actually defensiveness.

And then he said, "Hi, I'm Ryan. Irene Tindall's son. I'm afraid . . . Well, I think this might be yours?"

Jess hadn't realised overbearing Irene Tindall, who lived at the end of the close, even had a son. Or rather, Irene may well have told her, but she was so intense that Jess tended to be too busy thinking of excuses to get away whenever Irene engaged her in conversation.

"Oh," she said, thinking he must have taken a parcel in for them. "Thanks." And she reached out to take it from his lap. Only as she did, the lid flapped open. Frowning at whoever had sent an unsecured parcel, Jess started to pull the flap open further.

"No," the man said quickly. "Don't open it here."

But it was too late. Jess had already seen the horror of what was inside. Stripey, Stella's cat, face frozen hideously in death in an expression of terror, his beautiful coat matted with blood and grit.

"Let me see, Mummy. I want to see!" Stella clawed at Jess's arm, trying to get the box down to her eye level.

"No!" Jess shouted at her, gripping the box, backing away from the front door. "Thank you," she said to Irene's son. "Thank you for . . ." Her voice trailed off.

He nodded, backing his wheelchair up. "Sorry."

Jess went inside, blinking to hold back the tears, kicking the door closed with her foot.

"Mummy?" Stella said, a terrible note of suspicion in her voice. "Let me see!" She clung to Jess's arm, jumping up, trying to see inside the box all the way along the hall to the kitchen.

"Stop it, Stella!" Jess snapped, panicking as the box listed, almost depositing Stripey Cat onto the carpet, ghastly staring eyes and blood-drenched fur and all.

Stella, who wasn't used to being shouted at, dropped her hand from Jess's arm, plonked herself down on the carpet, and began to wail.

"Mummy will be back in a minute, sweetheart," Jess said belatedly, trying to inject some reassurance into her voice, continuing on to the kitchen, resting the box and its gruesome contents on the corner of the draining board as she fumbled for the door key on the hook.

Outside in the garden, with the sound of Stella's cries issuing from the house, Jess searched helplessly for somewhere to put the box until it could be dealt with. The only place out of Stella's reach were the shelves Michael had put up recently for his plant cuttings and seed trays. She stretched up—with Stripey seeming to weigh twice as much dead as alive—to lodge the box between two plant pots. As she did so, she accidentally dislodged one of them, sending soil and tender leaves cascading down over her legs.

She stepped back, treading in a deposit of poo lying on the patio. Great. That was just what she needed. Some animal had been pooing on the patio on a regular basis lately. At first she'd suspected Stripey, but now she wasn't so sure. Anyway, she would soon find out, wouldn't she? Because Stripey Cat wasn't going to poo anywhere ever again.

Tears came, and she reached into her back pocket for her phone. Thank God she had put it there so she could call Michael to come home and help deal with all this.

"Shit," Michael said when she told him what had happened. "Today of all days. Poor Stripey."

Poor Stripey, indeed. Stella had adored him. They all had. He'd been such a character, with his habit of hiding behind a fence or low wall and jumping out to surprise them. He hadn't deserved to have his life end the way that frozen look of terror was testament to.

Jess could hear someone speaking to Michael in the background. He sounded busy.

"Can you come home?" She wasn't sure what she would do if he said no. Scream, probably. And file for divorce later.

"Of course. Give me five minutes."

"Okay, he's in a box on one of the shelves outside."

Jess ended the call and went back inside, kicking off her poo-encrusted shoes and leaving them outside, scooping Stella up from the hall floor, and taking her into the front room to cradle her on her knee, away from any possible sightings of Michael digging a hole in the flower border. He'd go through the side gate, wouldn't he? She ought to have thought to suggest it. But wait, was the side gate even unlocked? She wasn't sure. There was nothing she could do about it now, though.

"*Shh*, baby," she crooned into Stella's feather-down blonde curls. "*Shh.*"

"You were mean to me, M-mummy," Stella sobbed, her arms creeping around Jess's neck anyway.

"I know. Sorry, baby. Mummy was a bit worried about something."

"Where's Stripey Cat?"

Jess sighed, moving so she could look her daughter in the face. "Well, you know how Great-Grandma really liked playing with Stripey before she went to heaven?"

Stella nodded, as quick as ever. "Has Stripey gone to see Great-Grandma?"

"Yes, sweetheart, he has. I think . . . I think perhaps he thought Great-Grandma might be lonely without us all, so he went to play with her."

More tears fell from Stella's eyes. *Bugger.* She'd taken it too far. *Well done, Jess. Well done.*

"But I will be lonely without Stripey," she said.

"Oh no, not when you have Mummy and Daddy," Jess said with more conviction than she felt, picturing the cat fast asleep on Stella's bed in the crook of her bent knee. Or sometimes, even on her pillow. "And don't forget your new baby brother is coming today. We'll never let you be lonely, my darling."

Stella put her thumb in her mouth and sucked silently for a moment while Jess stroked her hair. Then she said, "I don't want a new baby brother. I want Stripey back."

Jess pulled Stella close. "Toby hasn't got a family, sweet pea," she said. "We've talked about this, haven't we? He needs a mummy and a daddy. And I know he's really looking forward to having a big sister. He's never had a sister before."

"But, Mummy, he can go to another family where they have a little girl to be his sister. I just want you and Daddy and Stripey Cat."

Jess squeezed her eyes tightly shut, suddenly feeling unequal to the task of explaining that it was too late. That Stripey Cat was gone forever, and even if they wanted to change their minds about Toby being a part of their lives, he was already on his way in social worker Linda's car.

"I think that would make Toby and Great-Grandma very sad," Jess said. "You wouldn't want to make anyone sad, would you?"

Stella began to cry again. "But I'm sad," she protested. "Very, very sad."

"Oh, baby," Jess said. "I know you are. I'm so sorry."

They sat holding each other, Stella's small frame shuddering as she sobbed, until they heard the sound of Michael's key in the lock. The side gate must have been locked.

Instantly, Stella slid off Jess's lap and rushed at full pelt into the hall to see her daddy. "Daddy! Stripey Cat's gone to see Great-Grandma in heaven and Mummy says he can't come back anymore, and I don't want to have a baby brother and it's not fair!"

Jess went out to the hallway to find Stella clinging to her father like a little monkey.

"Stella, honey," he said after a minute or two of soothing her, "Daddy's got to go and do something. You stay with Mummy for a little while, okay?"

But Stella only clung on even tighter. "No, Daddy, no."

"I'll do it later," Michael mouthed to Jess over the little girl's head, but Jess shook her head. Stripey needed to be dealt with now. She couldn't risk Stella seeing him. Or God forbid, Toby. So leaving Stella sobbing in Michael's arms, Jess went back outside, put on her pooey shoes, and headed for the shed to find a spade.

As well as garden tools, the shed was filled with the carefree paraphernalia of family fun: A blue, inflatable paddling pool. A set of floral sun loungers for lazy days. A kite with a multicoloured tail. A bright-red sledge bought for the two days of snow they'd had in the four years of Stella's life. Objects that spoke of happy days, quite incongruous for the way this one was turning out so far.

Michael had recently dug over one of the flower borders with a view to turning it into a vegetable patch, so Jess began digging there, hoping it would be easier to just make a hole deep enough for a grave in freshly dug earth.

As she dug, she tried really hard not to think about her two babies. But how could she not? Neither of them had a grave to mark their passing because they hadn't been full term. Nobody at the hospital had mentioned where the babies went, but Jess knew their unformed bodies had very likely been disposed of unceremoniously.

Her poor babies. As she dug, Jess wept for them all. For her babies. For herself and Michael. For Stripey Cat and poor, bereft Stella. But oh God, this was no good. She'd have to pull herself together quickly if she were going to face Linda, the social worker. To carry on perpetuating the lies she'd told in her desperation to have another child. That she'd finished grieving for her lost babies. The babies she dreamt about most nights. Brooded and wondered about. Would they have been good at sports? Art? Invented a cure for a rare disease?

"*How did you feel when the hospital told you how much of a miracle Stella's birth was?*" Linda had asked. "*When they told you you'd very likely never carry a baby to term again?*"

"*How the hell do you think I felt?*" she'd wanted to snarl at Linda.

But instead, she'd taken a deep breath. Smiled a sad smile. Told Linda she'd been very sad about it at first, but then she and Michael had experienced a profound sense of gratitude that they had Stella. That over the weeks, they'd become convinced adoption was for them. That they wanted to offer a child a life of happiness. To make a difference to someone.

Linda had listened to this speech, her head tipped to one side consideringly. Then she'd nodded and made copious notes. At the time, Jess didn't have any idea whether she'd managed to convince her. But she must have done, because their application to adopt was accepted, and their little boy would arrive today. And she was thankful for that. Very thankful.

The hole was deep enough now. It was time to take poor, battered Stripey from the box.

Jess hesitated, reluctant to see the cat's tortured body again. How Linda had hated him. It hadn't been personal, not really. Linda just hadn't been a cat person. And Stripey seemed to sense that, during the long months of interminable interviews, inevitably trying to jump onto her lap and clawing her skirt or her tights in the process.

Oh, Stripey Cat.

Because he had been her friend and the love of her daughter's life, Jess forced herself to reach into the box to lift out Stripey's hideously cold body, paying him the respect his place in their family warranted, rather than taking the easy option of upending the box into the hole. She stood for a moment, silently thanking him for all the joy he'd brought them in his two short years of life. Then she filled the hole in, stamped the soil down, and replaced the spade in the shed.

When she went inside, she found Michael and Stella seated at the kitchen table, painting. Drawing and painting were Stella's absolute favourite things to do, and as well as the pictures displayed on the fridge, in Stella's bedroom, and ad hoc around the house, Jess and Michael kept a special folder for her work. The folder was so full it was practically bursting at the seams. From Stella's choice of orange and white, Jess guessed she was painting Stripey Cat. At least she had stopped crying.

"Sorry," Michael mouthed to Jess, reaching out to give her arm a sympathetic stroke.

Jess shrugged, smiling sadly as she turned away to wash the soil from her hands. As she dried them, she glanced at the clock. Nine forty-five. Linda would arrive soon. There was no time to have a shower or, better still, a bath. She'd have to make do with splashing cold water on her face. But first she must have a coffee. The stronger the better.

"Do you want a coffee?" she asked Michael.

"I'll make it," he said. "You go and get changed."

She looked down at her dress—chosen for the occasion for her by Stella. *Shit.* It was smeared with dirt.

"No, Mummy," Stella said. "Wear that dress."

"Silly Mummy's gone and made it all dirty," she said. "What am I like, eh? I'll wear my pink one with the flowers. You like it too, don't you?"

"Not as much as that one," Stella said, but she kept her head bent, concentrating on her drawing, and Jess thanked God, her lucky stars, or whatever it was that had suddenly reported for duty after being markedly absent while Stripey Cat was crossing the road.

"You're such a good artist," she said as she passed Stella on her way to the door. "That's a lovely picture."

"It's for Toby," Stella explained. "So he can see what Stripey Cat looks like."

Instantly, Jess felt choked up all over again. "What a lovely idea."

~

Jess was about to scrub the dirt from beneath her fingernails when the knock on the door came. No time. They were early.

She smoothed her dress and hurried down the stairs, arriving in the hallway at the same time as Michael and Stella. Stella bravely clutched her painting of Stripey Cat, one freshly painted orange stripe dripping down to the edge of the paper. Jess wanted to hug her close, but there was no time. Michael opened the door, and there stood Linda, holding Toby's hand.

"Here he is," Michael said brightly. "Hello, Toby."

For a moment, Toby stayed frozen to the spot, tucked in against Linda's leg, his dark eyes shy and watchful. But as soon as Linda said, "Aren't you going to say hello to your new mummy and daddy?" he dropped Linda's hand and propelled himself towards Jess like a torpedo, shoving Stella—and her picture—right out of the way.

"Mama," he said, his solid body colliding with her leg. "Mama."

3

Toby's little body was shaking with emotion. She could feel it against her leg. Poor little mite. She reached down to touch his head. "Shall we all go into the kitchen and get a nice drink?" she said, trying to stand up straight.

Linda stepped towards Toby with her hand outstretched. "Come on, Toby, let Mama walk."

Somehow, they all managed to make it to the kitchen. Only to find Stella's painting paraphernalia all over the table.

"Sorry," said Michael. "I'll get this cleared up."

But Stella began to wail. "No, Daddy. I want to do another painting of Stripey. This one's all spoiled."

And she shot a look of such dislike in Toby's direction that Jess felt compelled to whisper to Linda, "Stella's cat got run over this morning." But Stella heard what she said and began to cry all over again, and everything in Jess ached with a need to comfort her. But Toby was still clutching at her leg, and short of dragging him along like a ball and chain, she couldn't move closer to Stella.

As the sobs of both children filled the kitchen, Jess wanted to say to Linda, *Would you mind terribly going away again and coming back another day, when things have calmed down?* Only, of course, there was no other day. Linda was here to bring Toby to them now.

By the evening, Jess was beyond exhausted. She hadn't had a minute to herself all day. Toby had refused to settle down for a nap and had continued to follow her everywhere, speaking mostly in baby language and protesting whenever Michael tried to help with him. Now they sat in the sitting room, watching a game show on TV.

Jess had Toby cradled in her arms, his dark head cushioned against her breast and her shoulder. His eyes were closed, and his impossibly long eyelashes flickered as he tried to stay awake, one leg kicking now and then into the air. But finally, the leg stilled, and Jess sensed he was asleep.

She thought of his mother, wondering whether she'd ever held him like this. Whether it had been agony to give up such a perfect child. For he *was* perfect, especially in sleep, with those long, dark eyelashes and that rosebud mouth. The solid warmth of him. Had his mother gazed down at him before he was taken? Committing every detail of his face to memory? Or had she been cold, emotionless, unaffected?

Just the way Jess felt herself.

No, that wasn't quite true. Jess felt affected. Deeply affected. Just not in the way she had expected. The way she was supposed to feel. She certainly hadn't fallen in love yet. But it had been only a matter of hours, after all. There was no need for the spiraling sense of panic she felt swimming around inside her.

The game show finished. "Time for bed, Stella Bella," Michael said.

"Carry me, Daddy," she said, rubbing her eyes, clearly exhausted.

"You go with Mummy. I think I'll have to carry Toby up. He's fast asleep."

He came over, and Jess gratefully relinquished her hold on Toby, reaching out for Stella's hand. But halfway up the stairs, Toby woke up and, taking one look at Michael, began to scream, flailing about in his arms, trying to get free.

"Don't do that, mate," Michael said. "You'll fall and hurt yourself. Mama's just here, look."

"Mama! Mama!" Toby cried, inconsolable, forcing Jess to let go of Stella's hand to take him from Michael.

By the time Jess had changed his soiled nappy and settled him down to sleep, Michael had finished reading Stella her bedtime story, and her light was out.

"You don't think we've made a mistake, do you?" she asked when she joined him in bed, unable to believe she was even thinking the question, let alone voicing it out loud. Michael had been there for every appointment with the social worker, answering question after difficult question. But it had been Jess's primeval clamouring to have another baby which had brought Toby to them.

Toby wasn't a baby; perhaps that was the trouble. She couldn't hold him in her arms the way she'd imagined holding her own babies. The babies who had died.

Toby's hair was soft, yes, but it wasn't the indescribably soft fuzz of a newborn. When Stella had been a baby, Jess couldn't get enough of the smell of her, cradling her against her throat, stroking her head, and drinking her in through her senses.

"Of course we haven't made a mistake," Michael said. "It was always going to be a bit of a fraught day, wasn't it? Even without Stripey. The poor kid's suffered so many losses already. Give it time. It will all come good, you'll see. Things just need to settle down."

"I'm sure you're right," Jess said, snuggling in against Michael and losing the opportunity to explain how claustrophobic she'd felt all day with Toby's determined little arms clinging to her. How strange it felt to carry out the most fundamental tasks for him. That he didn't *smell* like them. Like family. That all day she'd felt a distance between herself and Stella she couldn't bridge with Toby there in the way.

∼

Two mornings later, Jess was up before dawn with a cup of coffee— instant because it was quieter to make—sipping it at the dining room table, looking out at the grey garden. A movement caught her eye—a fox going about its business, its head low, slinking behind the greenhouse, where they'd once had a chicken pen. Did it come every night to see if the chicken pen had magically returned?

Jess hadn't woken early enough to see the fox since she'd stopped breastfeeding Stella. But now she remembered the carnage of feathers she'd found that last time. The snapped-off heads and beaks.

"No more," she'd said to Michael. "I know how much you like your fresh eggs, but I can't do this again." His bowed head had shown his disappointment, but he'd nodded and gone off to B&Q to buy the greenhouse.

Jess closed her eyes, almost falling asleep with the mug in her hand after the last few broken nights. Ever since Stripey had died, Stella had been having nightmares. And as soon as she started screaming, Toby woke up. Which meant Michael had to go and comfort Stella so that Jess could settle the little boy down again. The night before, it had taken hours of reading to him. Singing to him. Stroking his hair. But Toby had just lain in his cot watching her, resisting sleep, clinging to her hand, as if he feared she'd vanish into thin air. Eventually, against his will, his eyes had begun to close, his grip on her hand slackening. She'd waited five minutes. Ten. And then she'd crept from the room, only to find Stella starfished on her side of the double bed next to Michael, forcing Jess to go to Stella's bed. Where she had lain sleepless, thinking how different it felt to do all those things to soothe a child to sleep when he wasn't her flesh and blood. It was hard enough to go against the instinct of sleep when you loved and adored your child. But a stranger . . .

Toby wouldn't always be a stranger, though. She would come to love him. Wouldn't she?

Jess's eyes closed. There was a sudden crash as her coffee cup smashed on the floor. *Shit!* It wasn't her scalded toes that made Jess gasp with horror. It was the fear that this precious, private time would be broken by a lost voice calling to her from upstairs. *"Mama? Mama?"*

No voice came. Jess felt such intense relief that she covered her face with her hands and wept, surrounded by broken pieces of crockery. And suddenly she wished, when she had put her adoption plan to Michael, that he had turned to look at her the way she'd looked at him after the chicken slaughter. That he'd said, "No more. I know how much you want another child, but I can't do all this again."

In her mind, she pictured herself nodding. Accepting his decision. Going out and buying . . . what? What was the equivalent of replacing a chicken coop with a greenhouse? A new car? A camper van? Something to take Stella for adventures in, instead of someone—an unwanted brother—who would cause her misery? For Stella was miserable. The nightmares were a testament to that. And every time Jess tried to comfort her, there was Toby, demanding something from her. In the way.

4

One particularly fine male hedgehog—let's call him Augustus—was in the habit of starting his evening's wanderings in the garden at the back of Number Five. It wasn't that Number Five held the richest pickings; that honour went to Number One, the garden belonging to Frances Mathews, a widow with wild-bomb hair. Since her husband's untimely death twelve years ago, Frances had allowed her garden to become as wild as her appearance. It was chock-full of worms and grubs and tasty roots, with an abundance of leaf piles for a hedgehog to curl up in.

Augustus chose Number Five because he'd been born there, in a now-filled hole beneath the garden shed. Not that he remembered his mother or anything about his days as a hoglet. Starting at Number Five just felt safe to Augustus, that was all, and he was too busy sniffing out food, nose to ground, to wonder why.

But recently, things had changed at Number Five. Augustus always waited until it was quite dark before he ventured into the garden, but for the past few weeks, no matter how late he left it, the garden at Number Five didn't darken. A light blazed out from a downstairs window long into the night, and sometimes Augustus even saw a tiny glow of fire moving through the darkness close to the house. This glow of fire was always accompanied by a dark shadow and the rumble of something moving across the paving stones.

The first time Augustus experienced the terrifying rumbling sound, he'd curled his body up into a tight ball, right there on the garden path.

Fortunately, all the other hedgehogs had been in different gardens, so they hadn't witnessed this humiliation, and after a while, when nothing happened, Augustus unfurled himself. The glowing light took its shadow back into the house, and Augustus realised both the light and strange sound belonged to a human.

~

The human was Ryan Tindall, only son of Irene. Ryan had returned to the parental fold after an abysmal year which included the implosion of his marriage, followed by a terrorist land mine which put him in a wheelchair and left doubt about whether he would ever walk again. There were some things Ryan couldn't do at the moment, confined to a wheelchair as he was, and there were some things Ryan had stopped doing earlier in his life which his current situation made him want to do fiercely. Smoking being one of them. And it was smoking Ryan had been doing when Augustus first encountered him in the garden. Out on the patio, where he had trundled himself in his chair through the doors from the dining room, where he currently slept. Not that Ryan got much sleep these days. His mind was far too full of jumbled, depressing thoughts. And even if he did drift off, a maelstrom of remembered screams and blasted-away body parts soon jolted him awake again.

No, sleep was overrated at the moment. But then, so was being awake. Just look at what had happened the morning he'd found the dead cat. He'd woken feeling determined. With a goal. Admittedly, that goal had been to get himself as far as the corner shop for the cigarettes his mother moaned so much about buying for him, but it was a goal, nevertheless. And the minute he'd got out onto the street, what had happened? A lost delivery driver had swung his van into the road to turn around and had run over a ginger cat.

Ryan had seen the cat before. For some reason, it liked to sit on the post of the wall at the end of his mother's drive. Not being a cat lover, his mother always shooed it off when she saw it, but Ryan enjoyed the way the large cat yawned and jumped unhurriedly down, stalking away, tail up, taking his own good time. The cat had style.

Only this morning, the cat had been out in the road when the delivery driver had roared into Hilltop Place, causing Ryan to call out as the speeding tyres made impact with the handsome mass of fur and muscle. Last week he'd seen a dead hedgehog in the road—a sickening enough sight, squashed as flat as a cow pat. But Ryan hadn't seen the hedgehog alive, so its death hadn't affected him so much. Whereas the ginger cat—fuck-you personality and all—had been alive one moment and dead the next, transformed in a matter of seconds from graceful cat about town into a pile of gore-splattered, stripey fur.

Jesus. He couldn't leave the poor thing there to be run over by the next car that came along. He'd have to move him. With his useless legs, that wouldn't be easy. Far easier just to tell the owners so they could deal with the body themselves. Easier, but not very kind. No, he had to get the body off the road.

His mother was out. She almost always was out since she'd retired. Not that she'd have wanted to help, anyway. Ryan could already picture the slight upward turn of her mouth when she found out the cat wouldn't be adorning her wall and trampling her bedding plants to have a poo any longer. She'd never been an animal lover.

Wheeling his chair into the road, Ryan drew alongside the stricken cat. Before he'd even tried, he knew he wouldn't be able to reach it. If he couldn't reach to put his own socks on, he couldn't reach to pick a dead cat off the road. The cat had a sparkly collar. As far as he knew, the cat lived at Number Two. There was a kid there, wasn't there? A little girl, about four years old. *Shit.* He couldn't risk her seeing her pet like this.

He'd need a box. That wasn't difficult. The dining room remained filled with boxes from his move. Most of them still held his belongings, but there were a couple of empty ones. He could use one of them. But how to pick the cat up? His mother had given him a litter picker to pick up small objects he dropped, but a litter picker wouldn't cut it with a dead cat. A gardening tool from the shed perhaps? If he could reach far enough into the shed from the doorway. Because his wheelchair sure as hell wouldn't fit in there.

Turning in the road, Ryan used his upper-body strength to manoeuvre quickly back up his mother's drive and round the side of the house to the back garden, heading for the shed. Opening the door, Ryan peered into the darkness. He could see a garden rake, a pair of hedging shears, and a broom. The broom wouldn't be much use. But the rake maybe? Straining, Ryan reached for it, almost sending it flying, but managed to grab it before it could topple out of reach. Reversing one-handed out of the shed, Ryan left the door open and made for the side passage, only to quickly realise he couldn't get up there with the rake balanced across his legs like a tightrope walker's balance pole. Turning the long-handled tool with difficulty, he managed to shove it through the space beneath one of the armrests and propelled himself forwards, the rake looking like some strange sort of jousting weapon.

He was almost back at the front of the house when he remembered he needed a box. *Jeez.* How was he going to get into the dining room to get that with the rake in position as if he were fucking Sir Lancelot or Saint George? In the end, he used the rake to drag an empty cardboard box from beside the bed. When he had it within range, he managed to lift it onto his lap. It took several minutes to reposition the rake with the box in the way on his lap, but finally he managed it. Then he headed back out onto the street. The whole obtain-a-rake-and-a-box-and-get-back-to-the-dead-cat operation had taken around ten minutes and left him sweaty and exhausted. And the cat wasn't even in the box yet.

By the time he'd managed to scoop the cat up and get it—grossly staring at him—into the box, Ryan's muscles were shaking. He sat with his eyes closed for a moment, taking a series of deep breaths. Then, straining, he managed to reach the box to close the lid flaps. But there was no way on earth he was going to be able to get the box onto his lap, not with the rake or the broom, or even with the sodding garden shears. Why hadn't he thought this through?

Short of a miracle to get him up and walking again, only another human being was going to be able to help him pick up the box. Which meant he would have to do what he should have done in the first place and tell the cat's owners. At least he had the cat's body in the box now so it wouldn't get squashed by a vehicle, but he still felt bad about it. As well as endlessly frustrated about not being able to complete the task he'd set himself. He was useless. Completely useless.

"Excuse me, do you need any help?"

He turned to see the blonde woman his mother was always complaining about while twitching the curtain, giving a running commentary about visitors, inconsiderate car parking, and letting her kid run wild. Ryan had seen the woman come and go in her flashy car but had never actually met her in person. Toni? Tara?

Now Ryan appraised her, his practised eye judging that she was around thirty-three, or possibly older, just well maintained. She wore a short dress and high heels with heavy, well-applied makeup. Obviously on her way out somewhere more interesting than the local supermarket.

Could he ask her to lift the box onto his lap without telling her what's in it?

"What's in the box?"

Ryan looked round to see a girl of about nine or ten years old by his side. He'd been so busy looking at the woman, he hadn't noticed her.

"It's just a delivery." He looked back up at the woman. "Yes, please, some help would be great, if you don't mind. If you could just lift the box onto my lap?"

The woman looked from the box to the rake and back at him again but made no comment. "Sure." She clip-clopped over with a sashay of her hips, calling to the kid, "Get in the car, Hermie."

"It might be a bit heavy," he warned as the blonde bent to lift the box.

She smiled up at him, a lopsided, flirty smile he suspected she used reflexively. "That's okay. I'm a big girl. Blimey, you weren't lying, were you? What have you got in here? Bricks?"

Ryan smiled but didn't answer. Seconds later, she'd positioned the box on his lap. Her face was close to his. Too close. He could see the lines accentuated by face powder, and he readjusted her age in his mind. Forty, perhaps. But pretty. Or would be with a bit less makeup.

"Thank you. I appreciate it."

"No problem." She stuck out her hand. "I'm Tara, by the way."

"Ryan."

"Irene's son?"

"Yes, that's right."

"Nice to meet you, Ryan."

"Mum, we're going to be late," the child called from the car.

Ryan saw a quickly concealed flicker of irritation cross Tara's face. "Just coming, sweetheart." She hitched her shoulder bag further onto her shoulder and began to back away. "Well, I'll leave you to your . . . delivery, then," she said.

"Thanks again for your help."

That same reflexive smile. "Anytime, Ryan."

He wheeled himself out of the way so she could reverse out of her driveway, returning the little wave she gave him as she drove off, carefully avoiding the rake. Shit, he should have asked her to move it onto the pavement. Someone would get a puncture if they ran over it. But he'd have to deal with that problem later. First, he had to get this dead cat delivered to Number Two before it cut off the circulation in his useless bloody legs.

The doorbell was out of reach. Of course it was. Nobody designed doorbells with wheelchair users in mind. A fact that had never once entered Ryan's head in all his previous non-wheelchair-using years.

He spotted a garden cane in the flower border, supporting a late-blooming rose. Ryan tugged it out and used it to depress the doorbell. As the rose flopped beside him, he heard the bell's strident summons sound out in the house.

The door opened. A tall woman with long dark hair and the greenest eyes he'd ever seen looked out at him, her eyebrows lifting slightly when she saw him brandishing the garden cane. She held the hand of a little girl wearing a princess outfit. The reason why he'd wanted to hide the cat in the box in the first place.

He let the garden cane drop to the ground. "Hi," he said. "I'm Ryan, Irene Tindall's son. I'm afraid . . . Well, I think this might be yours?"

"Oh," the woman said. "Thanks."

Before he could say anything else, she'd reached out to take the box from his lap. As the box moved, one of the lid flaps flipped open.

"No," he said quickly. "Don't open it here."

But it was too late. The sudden horror in those green eyes told him she'd seen her cat's hideously frozen face. The beautiful ginger fur coat matted with blood and grit.

The princess girl was clawing at her mother's arm. "Let me see, Mummy. I want to see!"

"No!" the woman shouted at her, gripping the box, backing away from him into the house.

She thanked Ryan, he mumbled something back, and then he beat a hasty retreat.

Jesus. That had gone well. Not. What an idiot. If he hadn't been so set on achieving something—anything—he'd have realised he should have put the cat in the box and gone round to Number Two with a note. That way the woman could have collected it at a good time.

If there was ever a good time to collect a squashed pet.

God, he needed a cigarette. Unfortunately, it was highly unlikely he'd make it to the shop and back now. Not after expending all that effort. Better get that rake off the road and go back to bed for a rest.

By the time he'd gone to collect the litter picker and used it to drag the rake behind him along the passageway, he was thoroughly exhausted. And more depressed than ever. Hauling himself onto his bed, he lay on his back and thought of the horrible suspicion dawning on the little girl's face. He wondered what her name was. What the woman's name was. Couldn't remember whether his mother had told him. If she had, he hadn't listened. She banged on about the neighbours a lot.

Was the girl sobbing her heart out now? Had the woman told her about the cat?

He'd wanted to buy his son a pet once. A kitten. Annie, his wife, had said no. That it would get run over and that would break Eric's heart. As far as Ryan could see, Eric's heart had been broken by the fact that he couldn't have the thing he wanted most in the world. *"He'll soon forget about it,"* Annie had said. Which was very likely exactly what she thought about Ryan's sudden disappearance from his life. *"He'll soon forget about you."*

On impulse, Ryan reached for his phone from the bedside table and dialed Annie's number.

"What d'you want, Ryan?" she asked when she answered, sounding irritable. "We're just leaving for Eric's dentist appointment. I told you he had one this morning."

"I just wanted to speak to him."

"Well, you can't now. We'll be late. Call back later, okay?"

He wanted to argue. To plead. *"Just let me say hello, at least . . ."* But it was too late, anyway. Annie had gone.

The front door slammed. He heard his mother call to him. "Ryan?"

Seconds later, she poked her head round the door. "You haven't forgotten that physiotherapy appointment today, have you?"

He had, and his face showed it.

"Oh, Ryan. I know you've had a tough time, but if you don't try to help yourself, then nobody can help you, can they?"

"I know. You've said before." About a thousand times.

"Well, it's true, isn't it?" She sighed. "Come on now, stiff upper lip. All this will pass. Time's a great healer, you know."

"Don't tell me," he said bitterly. "There'll soon be light at the end of the tunnel?"

She gave a brisk nod. "Exactly. Now, up you get. I'll make you a cup of tea."

Tea. His mother's answer to everything. Never mind that he preferred coffee.

5

Frances stood in her kitchen, looking through the window at her garden, drinking from her chipped coffee mug. It was her favourite way to start the day. There was always something to notice, whatever the weather. This morning the sky was full of fluffy white clouds, and Frances smiled as she looked at them, thinking they looked as if they were made of cotton wool.

The time Frances woke up varied. These days, she didn't have any rigid schedule to adhere to—she was free to follow the patterns of the seasons, the way the hedgehogs did. No need for rigid routines of shopping, ironing, and housework because it didn't matter to Frances whether her house was clean or dirty, just so long as it wasn't so dirty she was liable to catch something. The kitchen could probably do with a good going-over, she supposed. The cast-iron frying pan she kept hanging on the wall looked a bit dusty, for example, and she did like to keep that nice. She'd get to it soon. When it suited her.

Some people might find the freedom of being able to do what you wanted when you wanted slightly challenging, but Frances generally enjoyed making her life up as she went along. Reacting rather than planning. Doing absolutely nothing all day if she felt like it. Spending two solid hours lounging on the patio, gazing up into the trees, absorbing the colours of the rustling leaves. Frances had invented mindfulness before it was a thing. She lived and breathed it. True, from time to time she did feel a little isolated, but no company was definitely better than bad company.

Right on cue, somebody knocked on the front door. Without even looking, Frances guessed it would be Irene, from Number Five. Had to be. Nobody except the Sainsbury's delivery guy ever knocked, and he came on Friday mornings. Today was Tuesday. Frances's meter readings were taken automatically because she had a smart meter. She rarely had parcels delivered, because who would send anything to her? Cold callers were discouraged by the large BEWARE, GUARD DOGS sign her late husband had put up to deter them over fifteen years ago. No, it would be busybody Irene all right; no doubt about that. Frances guessed she could ignore her, but Irene was such a conscientious busybody that she might assume Frances was lying dead on the floor, being eaten by the mythical guard dog, if she didn't answer.

"Good morning, Frances, how are you? I was beginning to think you weren't in."

"No, I'm still here," said Frances, aware of Irene's gaze on her chipped coffee mug and her floppy-arsed trackie bottoms. Irene herself was dressed as she normally was: as if she were about to attend a garden party and all she had left to do was to put on her hat. Fussy blouse, swingy skirt, tights, and court shoes. How she managed to have a son like Ryan, Frances didn't know. And how Ryan put up with living with her since his accident, she had even less a clue about.

"How's your son?" she asked now. "It must be a worry for you, seeing him at such a low ebb. Had the rug well and truly pulled away from him, hasn't he, poor sod."

Irene looked taken aback. Frances knew she'd probably come round because she assumed Frances was a poor widow who needed a kind soul to look out for her. That she hadn't expected poor, pathetic Frances to ask about *her* welfare. And she probably hadn't liked the swearing either.

"How kind of you to think of him," Irene said. "He is experiencing some dark times, there's no doubt about that. But we all do, don't we? Life is never trouble-free. We have to make up our minds to help ourselves. That's what I'm always telling him."

Frances bet she was. Poor bloke.

"Did you want to come in? The kettle's not long boiled."

Another glance at Frances's coffee mug. "Actually, I've only recently had a cup of tea, thanks very much. But I will come in for a moment, if that's all right?" She held up a carrier bag. "I hope you don't mind, but I picked out one or two bargains I thought you might be interested in from the charity shop I volunteer at. I thought you might like to rummage through. We get some awfully good things. Far too good not to have a second life. Some things are brand new."

Lady-fucking-Bountiful. Coming round here with her assumptions and cast-off clothes, like someone from a Jane Austen novel, visiting the poor.

"How good of you. Well, come on in, take a pew. I'll have a good old rummage."

Irene smiled—a smile of smug self-congratulation that turned Frances's stomach. Five minutes later, Frances had picked out a pair of trousers which had clearly once belonged to an office worker, a velvet evening top in a shade of deep purple, a bright-blue blazer, and a wide-brimmed straw hat.

"These will be perfect," she told Irene. "Thank you very much."

Irene smiled the smug smile again. "I'm so glad."

They sat in what had once been the dining room, but which Frances now used as her main living room, looking out onto the garden as it did. The patio doors were open, giving a perfect view of the unpruned shrubs and the once-pristine lawn, now evolved into a weed patch.

Frances struggled not to laugh as she watched Irene trying not to show her horror. As if it were perfectly natural to have ivy tendrils reaching into the room from the washing-line post.

"I can recommend an excellent gardener if you're interested, Frances." Irene kept her tone carefully casual, as if it were no skin off her nose whether Frances took her recommendation. No doubt she'd had a conversation with the Hedgeses at Number Four. Or Mr. and Mrs. Neat, as Frances called them. She'd heard Justin Hedges grumbling about her overgrown frontage while washing his car the previous week. It had been a hot day, and Frances had taken refuge in the shadier front room for her afternoon nap, so she'd heard them, loud and clear, through the open window.

"It's a disgrace. I've a good mind to report it to the council. Bloody woman should be served with an antisocial-behaviour order."

"Justin, *shh*. She might hear you," his wife said.

"Good. Might stir her into doing something about it. Poor Trevor would be turning in his grave if he could see how she's let her property go."

Of course, that was why it bothered Justin. Irene too. Irene and Justin had lived here when Trevor was alive. Trevor, with his passion for mowing and hedge-clipping.

"Frances?"

Frances realised she hadn't responded to Irene's offer yet. "That's kind of you," she said. "But I rather like the garden as it is, actually."

"Do you?" Irene couldn't quite hide her incredulity.

Frances nodded. "I do. Come on, let me show you."

She got to her feet and headed through the french doors, giving Irene little choice but to follow. Out on the patio, Frances stood, surveying her domain. "Close your eyes," she invited Irene. "Listen. Hear the breeze in the copper beech trees? Better than music, I always think. Like water whispering over little rocks in a stream." And the sparrows chattering in the hedge. A magpie cawing to its mate. "You see? It's magical. Brimming over with life."

"But where do you peg your washing out?" Irene asked, looking as if she thought any magic wielded by the garden would be of the black, rather than the white, variety.

Frances shrugged. "I don't have much washing. And what little I do have fits on an airer. I regularly get foxes visiting, you know. Hedgehogs too. And all the birds, of course."

"I knew there were hedgehogs around because there was a squashed one on the road the other week. But I didn't know about the foxes." Irene shuddered. "I shouldn't want any foxes visiting my garden. Nasty, smelly creatures."

But Frances had stopped listening when Irene had mentioned the squashed hedgehog. "What did the hedgehog look like, do you know?" she asked.

Irene frowned at her. "Well, flat, I suppose. It was Ryan who found it. I didn't see it myself, but I think it had been well and truly run over."

"Was it large or small? Where, exactly, was it?"

Irene seemed to reel back from her interrogation. "I honestly don't know. You'd have to ask Ryan." She looked at her watch, no doubt thinking that good deeds were all very well, but there was a limit to the amount of time one had to devote to them. Especially when the person you were trying to help was acting all demented about a squashed hedgehog.

"Well, I'd better get off. There's a parish council committee meeting soon. I'm so glad the clothes were of use. Take care, won't you?"

Clip-clop, and Lady Bountiful was gone, leaving Frances worrying about the dead hedgehog. One of her regular visitors hadn't been around lately. Had it been him, squashed in the road?

Sighing, the golden tinge gone from her morning, Frances headed back inside, her mood lightening only when she saw the pile of donated clothing on the battered sofa. She knew exactly what she would do— make a scarecrow. Not for the back garden, but the front. To be displayed where anyone intent on visiting could see it, including Irene. That way, maybe she'd be left in peace.

6

"Stella, wait!"

Stella had run on ahead to the park entrance. Normally, Jess would have held her hand, and Stella would skip and chatter beside her, but today Jess was pushing Toby in the buggy, so she didn't have a free hand.

"Stella!"

The park—which could be tantalisingly viewed from Hilltop Place beyond a band of fenced-off trees—was only a short walk away, and she and Stella had walked there literally hundreds of times before. Stella wasn't going to suddenly veer into the road and get squashed like poor Stripey Cat. It was the first time they'd been out of the house in days, so she had a lot of pent-up energy to run off, that was all. She was a sensible girl who always looked both ways when they crossed the road.

Only nothing was like it always had been, was it? Toby's arrival had changed everything. Stella hadn't quite been herself since Toby arrived—none of them had—and Jess couldn't shake off her anxiety about her daughter doing something unpredictable.

When Stella turned into the park and disappeared from view, Jess felt a sudden panic and sped, half running along the pavement.

"Mama!" Toby wailed, and glancing down, she saw his little hands gripping the sides of the buggy as if he feared he'd be catapulted out any moment.

"It's all right, Toby," she said, trying to sound reassuring, her voice bouncing up and down with her steps. "We're just catching up with Stella. It's a game. See if you can spot her before Mama does."

But Toby didn't seem to think the game was fun at all, and by the time they reached the park, he was crying loud tears of distress, his mouth wide open on a wail, tears and snot streaming down his face. Stella had always liked it when Jess had run with the buggy, shouting, "Faster, Mummy. Faster!"

But Stella hadn't been torn from her parents and foster parents, uprooted like an unwanted weed. Stella had been loved and cared for from Day One. Even on difficult days when she had croup.

"*Shh*, Toby, I'll get you out in a moment," Jess said, her eyes flicking desperately over the bamboo and the bushes as they hurried past, searching for any trace of Stella's bright-red raincoat.

The play equipment came into view. Stella wasn't on the slide set into the hill. Jess saw no trace of her near the swings. Or in the tunnel made of twisted willow branches. There was no sign of her anywhere.

"Stella!" Jess called desperately over the sound of Toby's hysterical wailing. "Stella!"

"Over here," came a woman's voice. "On the witch's hat."

Thank God. Cutting awkwardly across the sandpit, Jess pushed the buggy through the willow tunnel to emerge at the circle of tyres with the cone climber roundabout in the centre. And there stood Stella in her bright-red raincoat, far higher up on the rope rungs than Jess had ever allowed her to go before, with an older girl standing on the ground and spinning the roundabout with all her strength while a woman—presumably her mother, and also presumably the person who had just called out to Jess—sat on one of the upturned tyres, placidly watching.

"Stella, be careful!" Jess called, seeing her daughter's face whizz past, unsure whether she was enjoying the thrill of the illicitly fast ride.

"Relax. She's loving it," the woman told her, and glancing over, Jess saw her stub out a cigarette on the side of the tyre.

Jess's attempt at a smile didn't quite succeed, and she turned back to look at Stella. "Hold on tight, Stella," she said.

"I am, Mummy." The irritation in Stella's voice relaxed Jess a bit. If her daughter was irritated, then she wasn't afraid.

"She's fine," the unknown woman said. "Unlike your little boy. Wow. He could win a screaming competition, that one."

Returning her attention to Toby, Jess crouched to unsnap his restraining straps, pulling him out of the buggy and cradling him close to her. "There, it's all right, Toby. *Shh. Shh.*"

She stood up and swung her body slightly to rock him, feeling his slight frame shuddering against her, the wetness of his tears quickly soaking through her shirt.

The woman got up from the tyre and came over. "I'm Tara. I think we both live in Hilltop Place? I moved in around three weeks ago. I saw you getting in the car once with your husband. Well, I assume he was your husband. Good-looking guy, dark hair?"

The woman—Tara—held out her hand for Jess to shake. She had full makeup on and perfectly manicured nails. Jess couldn't remember whether she'd even brushed her hair that morning. Probably not. She certainly hadn't taken a shower.

"Oh, hello," she said abstractedly, shaking Tara's hand while at the same time looking up at Stella, who, it seemed to her, was starting to look a little green.

"Would you mind asking your daughter to stop pushing? I think mine might want to get off now."

Tara glanced casually over and laughed. "I see what you mean. She does look as if she's going to puke, doesn't she? Hermie, stop pushing."

Hermie ignored her mother and carried right on.

"Hermie," Tara shouted at her, "pack it in. Now. Or else."

Hermie gave the roundabout one last shove, putting every bit of her strength into it, then skipped off to clamber onto one of the tyres.

Jess went over to the roundabout to try to slow it down, clutching Toby to her chest with her free hand. By the time Stella had climbed off, Jess was sweating and absolutely desperate to take her jacket off. It was a warm day, much warmer than she had anticipated, but to remove her jacket she'd have to prise Toby's fingers away from her shirt, which would only make him scream harder. And the world already felt like one big scream.

"Are you all right?" she asked Stella when she was on the ground again. "Shall we go over to the swings?"

The woman—Tara—seemed to think Jess was speaking to her. "Good idea. Come on, Brat Face. Let's go."

Hermie leapt down from the tyre without answering and began to run across the grass. Holding on to Toby with one hand, Jess dragged the buggy along behind her with the other, praying that Stella wouldn't trip as she ran towards the swings after Hermie. A cut knee on top of everything else would be just too much to bear.

"Careful, Stella," she called, half stumbling herself.

"Watch it," laughed Tara. "You'll go ass over tit if you're not careful. Want me to push that for you?" She indicated the buggy.

"Oh, yes, please."

"Or better still, dump it here. No one's going to steal it, are they?"

She was probably right, but even so, Jess didn't want to abandon the brand-new buggy in the middle of nowhere. Besides, she had all the things she might need for Toby in the changing bag stowed in the bottom of it.

"No, I'd better bring it."

Tara sighed. "Okay, I'll push it. Bloody things. I always hated them. Weaned Hermie off one as soon as I possibly could."

Toby's crying had calmed slightly now, his head dropping with exhaustion against Jess's breasts. Every now and then he gave a hiccup of distress, a plaintive sob escaping from his mouth and making his whole frame vibrate.

"Always sound as if their whole world has ended, don't they—kids?" Tara said, inclining her head in Toby's direction.

Jess's back ached. And her shoulders. Her arms. Toby felt like a boulder strapped to her chest. A big boulder she had voluntarily gone to a quarry and asked to be chipped out of the rock for her with a pickax.

"Well," she said, "it has, in a way."

Tara frowned, the sudden sharp focus of her expression making Jess regret having said anything.

"He's only just become a part of our family. We're adopting him."

Tara didn't say anything. She didn't have to. Her expression said it all. *Bloody hell. Are you out of your mind?* Jess looked quickly away, over at Stella, afraid of what her expression might hold, lowering her cheek to the softness of Toby's hair the way she could remember doing to Stella when she'd been his age. Nothing. Absolutely nothing. The sensation of something soft against her cheek, but that was all. No stirring of emotions, no surge of joy. No feeling that all was right with the world the way she'd felt with Stella.

"I was here first," she heard Hermie say.

"But I can't reach the other swing!" wailed Stella.

"Not my problem."

"What's going on, girls?" Jess asked.

But as she and Tara drew nearer, she could see. Some little vandal had thrown the other swing over the top rail several times, with the result being that it hung on its chains too high off the ground for Stella to climb onto.

"Don't be selfish, Hermie," said Tara. "Let the little kid have that one."

"I'm not a little kid," Stella retorted, but her voice quavered, and Jess knew tears weren't very far away.

"You mustn't speak to Hermie's mum like that, Stella," Jess began to say, but Tara swept on.

"No, she's right, she's not a little kid. Except if you compare her with my great hulk of a girl. Get off, Hermie, or there'll be no pizza for tea."

Hermie succumbed to pizza power with bad grace, climbing down and pushing the empty swing so hard Jess feared it would hit Stella in the face.

"Look out, Stella," Jess cried, reaching out to yank her daughter aside in the nick of time.

The combination of Jess's sudden movement and her cry woke Toby up. His eyes flicked open, his expression frightened and lost, and he began to wail all over again.

"Now look what you've done," Tara said to her daughter. "He's only just quieted down. Just for that, you won't get any pizza, anyway."

Now Hermie started crying, though judging by the way she kicked the swing frame, the tears came as a result of blind fury, not hurt feelings.

As Hermie and Toby wailed, Stella climbed up onto the vacant swing. "Mummy, push me," she commanded.

With Hermie looking resentfully on, swiping tears away with the back of her hand, and with Toby clutched to her chest, Jess pushed. God, she'd thought a trip out to the park would do them all good, but it had turned into a disaster. They should have stayed at home instead and . . . what? Watched more TV? Read more books? Had more squabbling matches because Stella didn't want to share any of her toys with Toby?

"Do you think you'd be able to climb up onto the other swing if you stood on Toby's buggy, Hermie?" she suggested. Then she quickly looked at Tara. "That is, if your mummy thinks it's safe?"

But Hermie had already pushed the buggy into position and was clambering up. The buggy began to move.

"Oh," said Jess quickly, "perhaps you'd better put the brake on first?"

Too late. Hermie was up on the swing seat, disaster averted, moving her strong legs to propel herself and smashing straight into the buggy as she moved forward.

Tara laughed. "She's a determined little bugger, my daughter. I'll give her that."

"Push, Mummy," Stella said. "Push."

"If you learned to do it yourself, your mum could put your brother in one of the baby swings. Plus, it would be much more fun."

"He's not my brother," said Stella with a pout.

Oh, God. Jess turned quickly away, heading for the baby swings and placing Toby carefully into the nearest one. He looked uncertain at first, his dark eyes exuding panic, hands extended towards her the way they seemed to have permanently been ever since his arrival.

"Move your legs back when you're moving backwards, and forwards when you're moving forwards," Jess could hear Tara instructing Stella. "That's it. You've got it."

Glancing round, Jess saw Stella's face break into a smile. "I'm doing it, Mummy," she said. "I'm doing it!"

"Well done," Jess said, wishing she'd thought to teach Stella how to swing herself.

Returning her attention to Toby, she caught hold of the front of the swing, pulling it towards her before letting let go. As Toby swung away from her, the panic in his eyes increased. Stella smiled encouragingly at him. "Where's that Toby gone? Oh, there he is!" Still with the same open-mouthed smile, she pushed the swing gently away from her again. And then, miracle of miracles, Toby smiled back. A full, gummy smile of pleasure at the unfamiliar sensation of moving through the air.

"He likes it, doesn't he?" said Tara.

"He seems to."

"That's a relief."

Jess didn't reply. The encouraging smile was frozen on her face as she watched Toby in the swing, his own smile waxing and waning as he absorbed everything, his dark eyes constantly on her. It was curious, how detached she felt. Curious and awful. What was wrong with her? How could she fail to be moved by the sight of a neglected little boy enjoying his first experience on a swing? He looked so cute with his chubby little fingers clutching the metal bar in front of him, the gentle breeze from the movement of the swing ruffling his dark curls. That gummy grin. Those chocolate eyes. Her brain recognised his cuteness but refused to send any messages to her heart to respond. As if she were frozen inside.

"Mind you," Tara was saying, "we'll have to go soon anyway. My boyfriend's coming round."

"He's not your boyfriend, he's your fancy man," said Hermie.

Jess looked over at her. Hermie stood up on the swing now, flexing her legs to make it go faster.

"Hey, you," said Tara, "don't quote your grandmother." Only she didn't sound that annoyed, not really.

Oh, God, Jess needed to get out of the park. To speak to somebody other than the children or Michael, or this strange woman. Gina. She would ring her friend Gina. She always gave good advice. Though Jess couldn't really imagine what Gina would say about this situation. After all, she more than anyone had listened to Jess's longings for another child, and now Jess had one.

Perhaps it was just a case of "Fake it till you make it"? Perhaps if she pretended to love Toby, she suddenly would? God only knew the poor little bugger had been through enough in his short life. He deserved to be loved.

She stretched her mouth again. "Look at you, Toby. You're flying!"

"He's not, Mummy," Stella said, sounding grumpy. "I'm going much higher than that!"

Beside her, Tara laughed. "Oh dear. Do I detect a touch of the green-eyed monster?"

Jess looked over and saw that Stella was swinging very high. Too high. And not only that, she looked as if she might try to stand up on it the way Hermie was.

"Stella!" Jess shrieked, an ugly sound that ripped Toby immediately out of the blissful world of the motion of the swing.

It was time to go home.

7

It was the first time Ryan had brought Eric to the park. To any park since he'd been in a wheelchair. He'd done a practice run on this one the previous day to make sure his wheelchair could cope with it. It would, just so long as Eric didn't wander off too far. Because there was no way Ryan could easily follow him if he ran off to the grassy areas.

"Remember, mate," he said. "Keep to the paved areas, okay?"

"Grandma lets me go everywhere," Eric replied, sounding sulky.

Grandma wasn't in a sodding wheelchair. "Grandma couldn't make it with us today, mate. I'm sure she'll come along another time, though. It's only that Dad's stupid wheelchair won't let me go on the grass, so I can't come with you."

"I can go on my own," Eric said scornfully. "I'm eight."

"I'm sure you could, but that might not be safe, okay? And besides, this is our 'boys together' trip, right? We can't be boys together if you're in one place and I'm in another."

God, he was making heavy weather of this. He was wary of upsetting Eric, that was why. It had taken so much persistence and effort to get Annie to agree to let him spend time alone with his son. No doubt she thought the two of them were watching TV together or playing with the assortment of toys Ryan's mother kept for Eric. But the boy had grown bored five minutes after Annie had left and demanded to come to the park. Ryan could hardly blame him—it was a sunny day. Who wanted to play with charity-shop toys when you could run about in the fresh air? The trouble was, Ryan couldn't run about, could he? Which meant he had to make Eric agree to stay on the paved areas. But if he wanted his cooperation, he had to do it in a way that wouldn't antagonise him.

"D'you want a ride on my wheelchair?" he offered, thinking it might give Eric a thrill.

But Eric started to run ahead. "No, I'll race you." And off he went.

They were on a slope—the play equipment was at the bottom of the slope and slightly to the right. So as Ryan followed his son downhill, he applied his brakes a touch to make sure he didn't catch Eric up. Eric turned, his laughter floating back to him.

"Ha ha, I'm beating you, Dad!"

"You certainly are," Ryan called back with a smile, remembering the ease he and Eric had had with each other before work had taken Ryan away too often. Before Annie had told him it was over and another man had become a father figure to his boy. Before the act of violence that had put Ryan in a wheelchair.

A woman came into view, pushing a buggy up the slope towards him, a little girl trailing behind her. Ryan slowed, calling, "Wait for me, Eric." But Eric didn't heed him, continuing on.

But maybe Eric hadn't heard him, because as the woman drew closer, Ryan could hear the sound of a child—the child in the buggy—screaming its head off. Then Ryan realised that the woman was the owner of the dead cat. The woman with the green eyes he'd unintentionally traumatised.

Ryan stopped his chair as she drew near, and she pushed the buggy onto the grass to get round him. "Hello."

She looked haunted as she glanced his way. He wasn't sure if she was attempting to smile or not. If she was, it was a dismal failure. "Hi."

She gave him a nod, then turned to look at the little girl behind her. "Come on, Stella, hurry up."

The little girl put a spurt on. Ryan waited for her to go around, trying to look past her to see where Eric was. The girl drew level.

"Mummy," she said, "is that the man who killed Stripey Cat?"

The woman looked distraught and horribly embarrassed. "No, sweetheart. He just found Stripey. Didn't you?"

Ryan nodded. "Yes, he was lying in the road, near my house. I'm so sorry."

Tears ran down the little girl's face. The boy in the buggy was still screaming his head off. Ryan felt hugely sorry for the woman, having to deal with all this. He also very badly wanted to move on and leave them behind. Life was hard enough without taking on other people's sorrows as well.

"Come on, Stella. Let the man get past, please. Let's go home and get some hot chocolate. I'll put marshmallows on yours, just the way you like it."

"Will Toby get marshmallows too?"

"No, I think there's only enough left for one."

Satisfied, the little girl smiled and skipped past him up the slope.

Ryan began to carry on down the path.

The woman's voice followed him. "Thank you for bringing our cat to the house. I was too shocked to say much at the time, but . . . thank you."

He turned his head to look at her, but he had traveled too far to see her expression properly any longer. "That's okay. Bye."

"Bye."

He continued on down the hill, the desperation he'd seen on the woman's face still on his mind, even as the noise of the child's screams grew fainter. His mother was always telling him he wasn't the only person on the planet to be suffering. It always sounded like some sort of cross between a pep talk and a lecture, but it seemed she was right. If anyone was suffering, this woman was.

"Dad," Eric called to him from further ahead, by the basket swing. "Come on!"

"Coming," Ryan said, his hands pumping at the wheels.

A woman was sitting by the swings. The same woman who'd helped him with the box. Tara. Great. Now he'd have to be sociable.

"Hello again."

Ryan manoeuvred his wheelchair into place, watching Eric run over to the swings. "Hi."

A girl who looked a bit older than Eric was on the other swing, standing up, swinging really high through the air. As high as he'd always swung himself as a kid.

"Dad, I can't get up," Eric called over to him. "The swing's too high."

"Some little sod's vandalised it," the woman told him.

Great. And he could do nothing about it, stuck in this bloody chair.

Before he could give Eric this bad news, the woman called over to the girl standing on the swing.

"Hermie, let the boy go on that swing, please."

"But that's not fair," the girl complained. "I only just got on it."

"It's all right," Ryan said quickly. "Eric can go on something else until your daughter's finished. Can't you, Eric?"

Eric didn't look too happy about that suggestion. "I suppose."

"No, it's okay. Hermie's been on the swings for ages now. She can go on something else. Get off, Hermie. Go on the slides or something."

"They're all wet."

"A little bit of water won't kill you. Come on, let Eric go on the swing."

The girl got off with obvious bad grace, giving the swing a huge shove as she did so Eric had to wait until it had slowed down enough to get on it.

"Thank you," Ryan called after Hermie as she slunk off in the direction of the slide. "That was very kind of you."

"Hermie, the man's speaking to you," the woman said, but her daughter ignored her.

The woman shook her head. "Apologies. She can be a bit grumpy sometimes."

"Can't we all?" said Ryan, hoping the woman would follow her daughter over to the slide. But she gave no sign of doing any such thing.

Eric moved his legs back and forth to get the swing moving. Ryan wondered who'd taught him that. Hopefully not Jimmy, Annie's new boyfriend. But then would he have taught Eric, even if it hadn't been for the land mine? Probably not. He'd probably have been off somewhere, working.

"I don't think your mother approves of me much," Tara said suddenly.

Ryan looked at her warily, wondering what to say to that. *My mother doesn't approve of me either? She doesn't approve of anyone unless they fit into her narrow idea of how people should be?*

"I'm sure that's not . . ."

"Oh, I think it is." Tara laughed. "It's okay, I don't care. She's entitled to her opinions. Live and let live, I say."

Eric looked bored. Ryan had hoped they'd chat together while he was on the swing. That he could subtly steer the conversation round to Jimmy and get some reassurance that Eric wasn't becoming too close to him. He hadn't planned on having his ear nailed to the floor by someone who looked as if she'd spent an hour in front of the mirror getting ready for a trip to the park.

"So how did you end up in a wheelchair?" Tara asked.

Ryan's shocked gaze swept away from his son to look directly at her.

She laughed. "Sorry, I'm afraid I tend to just open my mouth and say what I'm thinking. But then I suppose you have enough of people avoiding the subject, don't you?"

Since Ryan had pretty much been holed up at his mother's house after being discharged from hospital, he hadn't encountered many people he'd had to offer an explanation to.

"It was an accident abroad," he lied, twisting the truth, using a tone of voice he hoped would avert any further questions.

"That's bad luck. You certainly don't expect anything like that to happen when you go off on holiday, do you?"

He hadn't been on holiday; he'd been working. And it had been a land mine, not a traffic accident. But he didn't want to tell her that. He didn't want to tell her anything. And now the bloody memories were crowding back in. Not that they were ever very far away. They were like shadowy vultures, waiting to swoop in whenever he let his guard down. The mingled smells of burning—a poisonous cocktail of fuel, tyres, and flesh. Gunshots. Screaming. Flashes of colour. Red-hot pain. Then merciful blackness.

"I'm going to the slide, Dad," Eric said, jumping off the swing.

"Tell that daughter of mine we've got to go home now," Tara said. She turned to Ryan. "My boyfriend's coming round soon."

Ah. Hence the makeup.

"That's nice."

"Have you got a girlfriend? Or a boyfriend?"

Christ on a bike. She certainly did say exactly what was in her head.

Glimpsing his expression, she laughed. "There I go again. Just ignore me." She stood up, shouting to her daughter. "Come on, Hermie."

Looking over, Ryan saw the girl was playing with Eric now, chasing him over the sand at the bottom of the slide. Judging by the way Eric was squealing, he appeared to be enjoying it, racing up the slope to the top of the slide and scooting down again with Hermie in hot pursuit.

"Hermie!"

"What?"

"We've got to go."

"Do we have to?" Hermie called back.

"Yes. We'll be late."

"I want to stay and play with Eric."

Tara opened her mouth to yell back, then hesitated, glancing at Ryan. He knew immediately what she had in mind.

"Eric and I won't be here much longer either. My mother has something planned for us."

Got to get back to Mummy? he half expected her to say.

"Come on, Hermie!" she shouted instead. "Now!"

And finally, the girl traipsed over, shoulders slumped like a teenager banned from smoking, Eric in her wake.

"Well," said Tara, "it was nice to meet you properly, Ryan. You too, Eric. Drop round to ours whenever you like, won't you?"

"Can we come now?" asked Eric.

Tara laughed. "Well, not now, I'm afraid. My boyfriend's coming round. But soon, definitely. Come on, Hermie."

Together they headed off in the opposite direction to the exit, towards the trees between the park and the houses.

"You're going the wrong way!" Eric called after them.

The woman looked back, tapping the side of her nose. "We've got our own secret entrance. But it's top secret, so don't go telling, will you?"

"I won't," Eric replied earnestly.

She gave a final wave; then she and Hermie headed to the fence, which, Ryan saw, had a hole at the bottom big enough for someone to get through. Soon the two of them were climbing up the slope through the belt of trees and going through a small gate at the top, presumably to their garden.

"That's so cool. Can we make a passageway from Grandma's garden?"

"Grandma's garden doesn't face this way," Ryan said. "And besides, I don't think she'd want a hole in her fence, do you?"

Eric sighed, the sound expressing his frustration with a world entirely filled with grown-up killjoys. "Can we go back and watch TV now?"

Ryan sighed, giving up. "All right."

It was hard work, getting back up the slope. Ryan was panting by the time they reached the top, and Eric asked, "Dad, can we play football when you're better and walking again?"

Ryan stopped, his heart racing, leaning forward to put the wheelchair brake on so he didn't go careering backwards down the path. How the heck was it possible that his son thought him walking was a certainty? A strong possibility, even? Had he been so absorbed in self-pity he'd forgotten to make sure Eric was fully informed of the facts? Surely Annie would have told him. He couldn't believe Annie hadn't told him.

"I'm not altogether sure I am going to be able to walk again, son," he said, his voice cracking. "I'm going to try really hard to, I promise . . . but look, if it turns out that I . . . can't, we can always go and watch football together. I'll buy us a season ticket. That'll be cool, right? And you can have a burger or a pie, whatever you like. A team hat and scarf. A whole team football kit."

Eric stared at him, his expression so blank Ryan had no idea what was going on in his mind.

"Okay, Dad," he said at last, turning away. "I've already got a kit, though; Jimmy got it for me. I can always play football with him if you can't."

8

It only took Jess and Stella five minutes to walk back from the park, even with Stella stopping every now and then to pick up interesting leaves or to stroke the soft green moss on top of a garden wall. Ever since she'd learnt to walk, Stella had always wanted to examine the small details of her surroundings—a habit that could be frustrating if they were in a hurry to get somewhere. But today Jess happily indulged her daughter because—joy of joys—Toby had fallen asleep in the buggy, worn out, no doubt, by emotion.

"Can we leave him outside, Mummy?" Stella asked when they got back to the house.

It was tempting, because there was a distinct risk of Toby waking when Jess bumped the buggy up the front step. But the front gardens in Hilltop Place were open plan, unfenced, so it wouldn't be safe. And besides, Toby would probably be terrified if he woke up out there alone.

"We'd better not. But let's be very quiet, okay?"

"Okay, Mummy," Stella whispered, tiptoeing along with comically exaggerated steps.

Jess smiled at her. "That's very good tiptoeing, darling."

Stella put a finger to her lips. "*Shh*, Mummy. We've got to whisper."

"Okay," Jess whispered back, and they smiled at each other, coconspirators.

"Can I watch TV?" Stella asked when they were inside, still in a stage whisper.

Normally, on a sunny day such as this, Jess wouldn't let Stella watch TV until later, encouraging her to do creative activities instead. But today she had a deep craving for a chat with Gina, so she said, "Yes, all right. I'll get you a drink in a minute. I just want to phone Auntie Gina."

She kissed Stella on the top of the head, then watched her run off to the sitting room as if she were afraid Jess might change her mind. Smiling after her, Jess reversed the buggy carefully into the hallway, watching for signs of Toby stirring. So far, so good. He was still asleep, leaning against the side of the buggy, mouth slightly open, face slightly flushed. He looked hot, actually. But he'd be all right there, just for a little bit, while she called Gina.

Inching past the buggy, Jess took her phone from her bag and made for the kitchen, opening the back door and stepping into the garden.

Gina answered after only a few rings. "Hi, Jess."

"Gina, hi."

"Oh, sweetie, it's so good of you to check on me. But I can't speak now. The hearse has just arrived to take us to the church."

Shit. Of course. It was Gina's mother's funeral today. The fact that she had forgotten something so important was a clear sign of how self-obsessed she had become lately.

"Well, I . . . I just wanted you to know I was thinking about you. I'm so sorry I can't be there."

"No, no, that's all right. You know I quite understand. But look, I've got to go now, okay? Speak soon."

"Yes. I love you."

"I love you too."

Gina ended the call, and Jess stood there on the patio with closed eyes, wondering how she could have forgotten that her best friend had to bury her beloved mother today. Kind, generous Sheila, taken overnight by an aneurism. Thank God Gina hadn't realised Jess had forgotten. She would have been so hurt.

A cry reached her from the house. Toby was awake. Moving reluctantly, Jess turned and went inside, pausing in the kitchen to make drinks, because once Toby latched himself onto her hip again, she wouldn't easily be able to do anything.

By the time she reached him, he was red-faced and distraught, his cheeks streaked with tears, his chest arched up against the restraining buggy straps.

"It's all right, Toby," she said, bending to unclip him. "Mama's here. *Shh.*"

Lifting him onto her hip, Jess went into the kitchen to fetch Stella's drink, Toby screaming inconsolably all the while. When she went into the sitting room, she found Stella watching a news bulletin instead of a children's programme. The screen was filled with images of trees on fire as far as the eye could see, a woman talking about hundreds of homes that had been destroyed. The dreadful forest fires currently taking place in Australia.

"What are you watching this for, Stella?" Jess said, grabbing the remote control from the floor and quickly changing the channel.

"Will our house get burnt down, Mummy?"

If Jess had been able to hear the nuances of her daughter's voice over Toby's screams, she might have realised Stella felt shocked and tearful about what she'd just seen on screen. But tired as she was, her patience stretched to its limits, Jess just snapped, "No, of course it won't. Don't be silly, Stella."

And then she had two children crying their heads off, and Jess just wanted to put Toby down on the sofa next to Stella and go upstairs to have a good old cry herself.

9

"I can't understand why you let Stella watch that news report," Michael said to Jess later in bed. "The poor kid's going to have nightmares about burning to death."

Stella had gone on and on about the fires while Michael got her ready for bed, telling him in detail about pets burnt alive and people who had only just managed to get out before their houses had gone up in flames.

Guilt made Jess speak impatiently. "I was dealing with Toby at the time. I thought she was watching children's TV. I can't see through walls, can I?"

"All right, all right. I'm just saying it means even less sleep for us if she has nightmares, that's all."

Less sleep? What did Michael know about less sleep? He might stir when Toby woke up in the night, but he was always fast asleep when Jess eventually crawled back to bed. Though that was hardly Michael's fault, was it? He'd tried to help at night when Toby first arrived, but Toby just wouldn't have it. As soon as he realised it was Michael, not Jess, he screamed so loudly he ended up waking Stella too. Sometimes Jess wondered whether something had happened to him that they didn't know about. Something to make him wary of men.

"I'm sorry," Jess said, snuggling against Michael by way of apology. "It just feels as if bad things keep happening, you know? Stripey Cat, Gina's mum dying, the forest fires, Toby . . ."

Michael shifted slightly in bed to look at her. "Toby's not a bad thing, though, is he? He's only been with us a few weeks. It's bound to take him some time to settle, poor kid. And for us to love him the way we love Stella."

Looking into her husband's face, Jess felt the distance between them grow even wider. *"Adopting Toby was a big, fat mistake,"* she wanted to say. *"How can you not see that? And why the hell can't you tell how desperate and overwhelmed I am?"*

She and Michael had been together for ten years. Ten years. Surely that was long enough for a bit of mind reading? Or for him to pick up on her body language, at the very least. Not only did she not love Toby, sometimes she didn't even like him very much. Sometimes she wanted to tear his clinging little hands off her and shut herself in the bedroom to get away from him. Push the chest of drawers in front of the door and pile ten pillows on her head so she couldn't hear his screams.

Michael kissed the top of her head. "Everything will turn out all right. You'll see. Toby just needs to know he's here for good and we're not going to send him away, and Stella just needs to know we still love her just as much as ever. That's all. Look, I've got to work late the next two nights, but then I'm all yours. We'll do something together as a family at the weekend."

"You've got to work late? Oh, Michael."

"I have to, sorry. That new account I told you about."

He had told her. She'd forgotten.

"Don't look like that." He sighed. "Look, I hate to say it, but you were the one who pushed to adopt, weren't you? I always said it wouldn't be easy, but you were so determined."

Jess thought once again about Michael's chickens. Wished once again that he'd said no. For Stella was miserable. And so was Jess.

10

Tara stood in front of the hall mirror to brush her hair and touch up her lipstick. James would arrive any minute; he was nothing if not punctual.

"Are you going on your Xbox?" she asked Hermie as she trudged up the stairs.

Her daughter shrugged. "Dunno."

"Well, if you do, make sure you wear your headphones."

"It's a headset, Mum."

"Whatever. Wear them. It. And no shouting at your friends, okay?"

Hermie went into her bedroom and slammed the door without replying. Tara sighed. Her life would be a lot easier if James and Hermie got on. Hermie loathed and detested James, and James could barely bring himself to look at Hermie, let alone speak to her. She looked too much like her father, that was the trouble. Her father, Tony, who happened to be James's former best friend.

Not that it should make him feel guilty after so long, surely? It was water well and truly under the bridge, especially since Tony and his new wife had relocated to France. These days, Hermie's contact with Tony only consisted of Christmas and birthday presents. So much time had passed she barely remembered him any longer.

Sighing, Tara took a deep breath and let it out, arranging a smile on her lips. James always seemed to know if she had something on her mind, and she couldn't afford to irritate him. She had a pile of bills waiting to be paid.

A key turned in the lock, and there he stood, tall and devastatingly attractive despite the slightly thinning hair and the beginnings of a paunch above his trouser belt, expensively dressed and smelling of the aftershave she'd bought him for Christmas. The aftershave his wife thought he'd bought for himself.

"Hi, you." She took hold of his lapels, just as she always did, and pulled herself up to kiss him.

"Hello, you," he said, kissing her back.

He looked down, frowning. "Your shoes are dirty."

"We just got back from the park. Sorry." She quickly kicked them off. "Anyway, we don't need shoes where we're going, do we?"

"How do you know?" he asked, kissing her neck. "I might fancy you in nothing but high heels."

She giggled, hoping he wouldn't leave visible love bites. "Do you want me to trample you in them?"

"No, just have them waving in the air while I pound into you."

Lyrical language had never been James's strong point. "I think we can do something about that. I've got a pair in the bedroom. Come on." She took hold of his tie, pulling him towards the stairs, making sure to wiggle as she preceded him, her laugh playful and full of promise.

"Whatever's that?" James asked, pausing on the landing.

The sound of machine-gun fire issued from Hermie's room. Despite Tara's instructions, Hermie was playing her Xbox without her headset on, probably in a deliberate ploy to kill the mood. And already it was working. James reached out to grab his tie back, his brow furrowing.

"Don't worry. I'll sort it." She pushed her bedroom door open. "You go on in."

He moved past her, his body language telling her he wasn't pleased. That she'd have to work hard to get him back in a good mood again.

Angrily, she pushed Hermie's door open. "Get downstairs now," she hissed.

"I thought you wanted me to play on my Xbox?"

"I changed my mind. Go and watch TV. Now, Hermie. Or no pizza for a month."

Hermie gave a hideous-looking alien one final blast with her machine gun before tossing the expensive controller down. Then she flounced from the room and stomped downstairs. Seconds later, the TV was blasting out—far too loudly—from the living room. Tara was tempted to go and tell her to turn the volume down but decided it would take too long.

Positioning the smile back on her face, she went into the bedroom, where she found James lying on the bed—fully clothed, including his shoes—his hands pillowing his head. He looked exactly how she'd known he would—disgruntled and out of sorts. Things never worked well between them during the school holidays.

Tara climbed on top of him, carefully rubbing her breasts against his chest, one hand reaching for his trouser zip. "*Ooh,* I've missed you," she breathed. "I want you so badly it hurts."

"Ought she to be playing such violent games?" he asked. "She's on that thing far too much if you ask me. Cressida and I limit the boys' screen time."

Well, bully for you and fucking Cressida. Tara bit back the retort and slid her hand into James's trousers. James's body felt tense. She could tell he was trying to resist her ministrations. She also knew he would be unlikely to hold out for long.

She was right.

Afterwards, they lay side by side on top of the duvet, breathing heavily.

"I never did get a chance to put on those high heels," she said.

James frowned. "You were probably distracted by the machine-gun fire," he said.

Shit. Why had she had to remind him? "I could put them on now."

James looked at his watch and rolled away from her. "I've got a meeting in half an hour. I'll have to go."

She pouted, propping herself on one elbow to give him a good view of her still-perky breasts. "Next time, then."

He turned his back to her as he pulled up his trousers. "That won't be for a while," he said. "We're holidaying in the Seychelles before the boys go back to school."

It was becoming harder and harder for her to keep her smile intact. "Lovely. I hope you have a nice time."

"Don't be like that," he said, picking up on her disappointment. "You knew what you were getting into."

She hadn't, though, not at first. She'd believed him when he said he'd leave his wife. These days, not only did she not believe it but she was also no longer sure she wanted it to happen. Devastatingly attractive or not, sometimes she thought she ought to have stuck with Tony.

And she still hadn't asked for the money for the bills.

"I was thinking I might look for a full-time job," she said, continuing quickly before he could comment. "Although obviously it's tricky. I don't want to make it more difficult for us to meet up."

"I'm sure we'd still be able to sort something out," he said, doing up his tie. "Good idea. Fuel bills are rocketing."

"And council tax bills. Honestly, I can't understand how it can cost so much to empty a few bins."

He looked at her. "Well, this is all very scintillating, darling, but I have to get to my meeting. I'll see you next month."

And he was off, without a kiss, a backward glance, anything. All hints ignored. *Bloody hell.* She might actually have to get a full-time job.

11

Something had seriously riled his mother, Ryan thought. If she'd been the smashing-plates-against-the-wall type, there'd be a pile of broken crockery fit for a Greek restaurant by now. Instead, she bashed the cereal bowls about in the sink as she washed them up, her shoulders so tense they practically reached her earlobes.

It was very tempting to come out with something sarcastic, like *What's the matter? Was there a typo in the parish council minutes? Did someone try to discuss something that wasn't on the agenda?* But he restrained himself with difficulty, saying instead, "Everything all right?"

"No, it's not. That insufferable woman has done her best to humiliate me, when all I did was try to help her."

Irene stabbed her rubber-glove-encased finger towards the window. "Frances! I took some clothes I thought she might like round to her, and she's had the nerve to put them on a scarecrow in her front garden. As if she even needs a scarecrow when her front garden's a weed patch. It's downright insulting. If she didn't want them, why didn't she just say so?"

Stretch his upper body as much as he liked, Ryan couldn't get himself high enough to see out the window. Curious, he wheeled himself away to take a look.

"Don't let her see you gawping," his mother shouted after him, but he ignored her, letting himself out onto the patio and continuing round the side of the house to the front, where he caught sight of the scarecrow right away by Frances's front door.

Ryan grinned, stopping to take in the scarecrow's full splendour. Constructed out of a garden fork with a broom handle secured across it for the arms, it was dressed in smart grey trousers and a stylish blue jacket with something sparkly beneath. Its face was made of what looked like a stuffed pillowcase, and it sported a wide-brimmed straw hat. As he pushed himself closer, Ryan could see it had features drawn on in black marker pen. And that the scarecrow was unmistakably winking. All that Frances had left out were the hands. Which was a pity, really, since if she'd given the creature fingers, no doubt the middle one would have been stuck in the air to say *Screw you*.

It was magnificent. Ryan began to laugh. Then he remembered that his mother was most likely still watching out of the window and stopped himself.

She was waiting for him when he wheeled himself back through the patio doors, duster in her hand, swishing up imaginary dust. "I bet you thought it was funny, didn't you?"

"Well, it is quite creative."

"It's humiliating, that's what it is. But I can't expect you to understand that."

Ryan's amusement vanished. "Since I've only been able to deal with my own piss and shit for the last two weeks, I think I understand the concept of humiliation quite well, actually."

She glared. "There's no need to be crude."

"Of course, sorry. Silly me. Bodily functions are a no-go zone, aren't they?"

She whipped the duster over his bedside table. "Not everything is about you, Ryan. Other people have feelings too."

"Well, perhaps Frances has feelings about being pitied by the neighbours."

"I wasn't pitying her."

"What message did you mean to send by taking her a bag of donated clothes, then? That her clothes are shit?"

"You always have deliberately misunderstood and twisted anything I say or do. Even as a boy. But you aren't eight years old any longer. It's time you accepted that."

She stalked out. Seconds later he heard the vacuum cleaner start up, its bee-buzzing noise sounding louder than usual. Angry. Resentful. The way he'd felt most of the time since he'd come back to live here.

Ryan closed his eyes, breathing deeply in an effort to calm down. When that didn't work, he gave up and wheeled his way back outside to head for Frances's house.

She must have seen him coming, because the front door opened before he knocked. "Hello, Ryan."

It must have been ten or twelve years since he'd last spoken with her, he supposed. Before the explosion and its aftermath, his visits to his mother had been limited to quick sweeps in and out from wherever he'd been in the world, sometimes with Annie and Eric, sometimes not. He hadn't had time for neighbourly catch-ups.

Frances looked more crumpled than he remembered. Not just her clothes, but her face too. As if she left it untidily on the chair next to her bed at night, along with her discarded T-shirt. Her hair was longer than he'd ever seen it, as well, and greyer. A bristly mane of mottled red and grey that didn't look as if it saw a hairbrush very often. The Frances he remembered with the magnificent cascade of auburn hair and the ready smile seemed to be long gone. This Frances looked more like Miss Haversham in Charles Dickens's *Great Expectations*. If Miss Haversham had worn jogging bottoms.

"How are you? I was sorry to hear about your accident."

She sounded sincere but unpitying. A winning combination that didn't get his back up. "Thanks. My general health is slowly improving. Or so they tell me. How are you?"

She folded her arms across her chest. "In your mother's bad books, I imagine."

He smiled. "Just a bit, yes."

"Childish of me to make the scarecrow, I suppose."

62

He shrugged. "Fun, though, I imagine. And it's a truly amazing scarecrow. But d'you mind if we take it down? Only, things are a bit tense at home at the moment anyway, so . . ." He wasn't sure why he'd said that. Wished he hadn't when Frances gave him a sharp look.

"Of course we can. Help me, would you?"

He liked that she thought he could be of help, despite the chair. Most people just assumed he was useless.

So together they dismantled the scarecrow—pole, garden fork, Lurex top, and stuffed pillowcase face and all. And after Frances had piled most of it onto his lap, she led the way round the side of the house to the back garden through a slatted side gate, the bottom of which was kicked in, leaving a rough hole.

"Has someone tried to burgle you?"

She looked down. "What? You mean that hole? No, I did it myself. So my hedgehogs can come and go. I get lots of them visiting, you know. Every night. I feed them. Your mother said you found a dead one in the road last week."

"I did, yes. Poor thing."

Her face reddened. She looked suddenly ferocious. "It's because everyone puts bloody fences up in their gardens. It forces the hedgehogs to go out onto the street to get about, and it's not bloody fair. They were here long before we were, poor little buggers." She looked at him, abruptly switching subjects. "Bit difficult living with your mother, then, is it?"

He shrugged again. "Well, I don't imagine I'm the easiest person to live with at the moment."

She nodded. "Understandable, given the shit you're dealing with. Will you ever walk again?"

"They're not sure."

"Better get good at using that wheelchair, then, just in case. Not easy, though, is it? I was in one after an op a few years back. It was a nightmare. Never realised how tough it was getting about in one, before that. You constantly have to think your way around things, don't you?

Like the hedgehogs have to when they find another new fence, or when people hoover up all their leaves so there's nowhere for the poor little buggers to hibernate."

Frances had always been passionate about wildlife, he remembered. As a teenager, he'd once found a bird with a broken wing. She'd taken it in and nursed it back to health. Then she'd invited him back to see her release it. He could still remember the conflict of emotions as he'd watched it fly off—joy that the bird had healed and could continue its life. Sorrow that he couldn't visit it any longer.

"I heard something about hedgehogs on the radio the other day," he told her. "On *Woman's Hour*, I think."

She smiled at him. "In the habit of listening to *Woman's Hour*, are you?"

He shrugged. "These days, I listen to anything that comes on." It was true. He always kept the radio on in the background. Either that or the television. Right through the night, sometimes, much to his mother's annoyance. "Anyway, they had a woman on talking about a local hedgehog highway scheme she'd set up. All the community agreed to work together—leaving gaps under fences and gates, leaving areas of their garden wild. Even putting out feeding stations and what she called 'hedgehog hotels.' She's got cameras outside so she can watch their comings and goings too. Apparently, the hedgehogs are really thriving."

While he'd been speaking, Frances had become transformed. She looked as if he'd described a miracle to her—a visitation by the Virgin Mary or the archangel Gabriel. She clasped her hands together as if shaking hands with herself, her eyes wide and glowing, and a huge smile dawned on her face.

"Oh, that's a fantastic idea, Ryan! Absolutely fantastic! Come in, come in. I'll make you a cup of coffee while you tell me all about it."

"We can listen to a recording of the programme on my phone, if you like," he said, trundling after her towards the house.

She bent down suddenly to kiss him—a great big smackeroo of a kiss on his cheek—quite unable to contain her absolute rapture for a second longer.

"Steady on," he said, laughter in his voice. "The feature only lasted five minutes or so."

"Five minutes that will change my life!" Frances pronounced, practically dancing into the house. "Not to mention the hedgehogs' lives. I'm so glad I made that scarecrow. If I hadn't, you might not have come over today. And if you hadn't come over today, you might have forgotten about the radio programme. Come on, come on. What d'you want? Tea or coffee? I'm afraid I haven't got any milk. Oh, I'm so happy, I can't tell you."

12

Hedgehog mothers take care of their babies for around eight weeks before leaving them to their own devices. In that time, they're devoted mothers, lying on their sides to allow the hoglets to suckle, temporarily setting aside their nocturnal ways to venture from their nests during the risky daylight hours to find something to eat while their babies sleep. If the hedgehog family is left alone, all is usually well. But should their nest be disturbed—either by humans or a prowling male hedgehog—it can spell disaster; the mother hedgehog may abandon her babies. Or, in certain circumstances, even eat them.

After several weeks of taking care of Toby, Jess wasn't thinking of taking such drastic action. But she was starting to feel distinctly desperate. The little boy was as clingy as ever, sleeping as badly as ever, and Jess wasn't sure how she could carry on if something didn't change. Which was why, this particular morning, she called Linda, the social worker, to try to explain the situation. It felt wrong to speak about Toby with him sprawled on the sofa, head in her lap, but he was out for the count.

"Tell her about how difficult it's been," Michael had urged her on his way out that morning. "That's what she's there for."

But five minutes into their conversation, Jess hadn't mentioned her feelings of claustrophobia and despair at all. Of how she dreaded Toby waking up. She was too worried that if she did, Social Services would come straight round to take Toby back. And despite everything, she didn't want that. She just wanted to make the adoption work. To feel differently about it all.

"So it seems as if you're worried that Toby isn't bonding with Michael. How does Michael feel about that?"

How did Michael feel about that? Not particularly bothered, seemed to be the answer. But she could hardly say that. Could she?

"He just says these things take time and we need to be patient. But Toby's reaction to him is so . . . well, extreme, I was wondering what might be behind it. Whether you knew of anything."

A sigh. "There were no issues with his foster parents that I'm aware of, but Mr. Cook is a shift worker, so it's possible Toby didn't have much contact with him. Would it be helpful if I arranged for Michael to attend some training sessions, do you think?"

Oh, yes, Michael would be very pleased if he came home from work to discover she'd committed him to that.

"No, no . . . at least, not now. I'm sure things will settle down." She wasn't.

"Your husband's right, you know. These things do take time. Let's speak again in a week, shall we? And Jess, try not to worry. Toby's obviously bonded well with you, which is fantastic."

But I haven't bonded with him, she wanted to shout, only the words couldn't get past the barrage of stacked-up tears in her throat, and in any case, the social worker mentioned she had to get to a meeting and said goodbye.

At least it was Friday. Tomorrow Michael would be home, and they planned to go to the Dinosaur Park. He would see firsthand how difficult Toby was. Or maybe Toby wouldn't be difficult, and they'd have fun. Miracles sometimes happened, right?

~

The morning of the Dinosaur Park trip, Stella came downstairs dressed in her swimming costume.

"Why on earth are you wearing that?" Jess asked, already worn out at 9:00 a.m. from a long period of wakefulness with Toby in the night.

Stella's eyes flashed. They'd been doing a lot of that lately. Her easygoing daughter had developed an attitude. "Because of the Splash Area, Mummy," she said as if Jess were a complete imbecile. "I want to go in there first."

Jess's heart sank. It was the first weekend in September, and autumn appeared to have kicked in overnight. The temperature was verging on chilly, and she wouldn't be surprised if it rained later. Who was she kidding? Of course it would rain for this all-important trip.

"Why don't you wear your swimming costume under your clothes, sweet pea?" Michael said. "Come on, I'll help you. You could wear your unicorn jumper. I'm sure the dinosaurs would like to meet a unicorn."

"Daddy," Stella said, scurrying up the stairs, "they aren't real dinosaurs."

"Aren't they?" Michael said in mock surprise, shooting a smile in Jess's direction.

"No!" laughed Stella. "Silly Daddy!"

Pushing Toby's arms into his coat sleeves, Jess sighed. Another tantrum diverted. Clever Daddy. Except they'd still have to deal with it when they got to the Dinosaur Park, wouldn't they? No, that was negative. Surely Michael would think of some distraction or other to avert a crisis when they got to the park.

Determinedly, she plastered a smile on her face. "There you are, Toby. You're all ready to meet some dinosaurs."

She wasn't surprised when Toby looked wary. After all, he might not even know what dinosaurs were. But he would love the Dinosaur Park. Stella had, at his age. All children loved the Dinosaur Park.

"I'll put Toby in his car seat," she called up to Michael.

"All right. We won't be long. Miss Stella's just choosing her trousers."

The air outside felt damp. Not quite raining, not quite even drizzling. More like a sponge absorbing cold water. Hopefully, it would be a while before it reached saturation point. If the rain held off until lunchtime, they'd be in the indoor play area anyway.

Opening the car door, Jess placed Toby in the car seat, keeping up a running commentary. "That's it, let's put your arm through here. Clip you in. There, you're good to go, all the way to the Dinosaur Park . . ." It was what she'd always done with Stella, talked to her constantly, which was probably why her daughter had such a good vocabulary for her age.

So why did it feel as if she were acting? Self-consciously speaking lines that sounded rehearsed?

Jess straightened, moving her face away from Toby, ready to close the car door. He gave a little cry of loss, and she glanced back towards the house irritably. "It's all right, little man. Mama's just here." How long did it take to choose a pair of flipping trousers, for goodness' sake? Sometimes Michael could be way too indulgent with Stella. It was just as well it wouldn't be him who got her ready when she started school on Monday.

A sudden pang squeezed her heart. Stella, starting school. How would it feel to say goodbye to her? To turn away with Toby, knowing it would just be the two of them until three o'clock?

"Hello, Jess."

Looking up, Jess saw Frances beyond the car with Irene's son, Ryan. The man Stella had accused of killing Stripey Cat.

"Oh, hello." She moved towards them, down the drive. Instantly, Toby's whimpers of loss became real crying. She glanced back.

"We won't keep you," Frances said. "I can see you're just on your way out."

Michael emerged from the house with Stella, at long last. Jess decided to leave him to deal with Toby and moved further down the drive towards the visitors.

"No," she said, "that's all right. It takes us forever to get ready to go anywhere. We're off to the Dinosaur Park." She glanced in Ryan's direction, wondering if he'd ever taken his son there. Whether he could even drive these days. Why she hadn't noticed, the other day in the park, what an incredible shade of blue his eyes were.

He was looking straight back at her. So far, he hadn't spoken. The moment stretched on.

"We're here about an animal that's not extinct," Frances went on. "At least, not yet, anyway. But it is endangered, very endangered. And we want to do something to protect it, don't we, Ryan?"

He nodded. "Frances is referring to our local hedgehog community," he explained.

"I am," Frances swept on. "I don't know if any visit your garden?"

"I'm not sure, to be honest. They're nocturnal, aren't they? I don't generally go out in the garden at night." She frowned, remembering. "But we do get poo on the patio sometimes. I always put it down to our cat, but it's still been appearing since . . ."

Unnoticed, Stella had joined her. At exactly the wrong time. "Our cat's dead," she announced, glaring in Ryan's direction.

"Oh, I'm so sorry to hear that, sweetie," said Frances. "That is sad."

"Yes," said Stella, her eyes filling with tears. "It's very, very sad. I miss him this much." She spread her arms out as far as they would go to illustrate the point. "A car ran him over."

"Roads are very dangerous," Frances said. "For all animals. That's why we want to set up the hedgehog project we've come to talk to your mummy and daddy about. To protect them." She straightened to look at Jess. "It's called a hedgehog highway. Ryan heard about it on the radio."

Behind Jess, Toby's cries had become screams. It took a great deal of willpower not to turn round, but she could hear Michael attempting to soothe him, so she forced herself to keep looking in Frances's direction.

"Hilltop Place is perfect for one. The idea is that we all agree to leave gaps under gates and in fences so the hedgehogs can come and go as they please without needing to go out into the road. And you can set up feeding stations for them, and cameras so you can watch them eating. How do the cameras work in the dark, Ryan? I can't remember what you said."

"They're infrared," he said, still looking at Jess. "Why don't we leave one of your letters with Jess, Frances?"

"Oh, yes," said Frances. "I forgot about the letters. It's all explained here. We're delivering one to everyone in the road. You can ring me up when you've read it. Or pop round for a cup of tea."

"Oh," Jess said distractedly. "All right."

Ryan took a piece of paper from his lap and held it out. Jess stepped forwards, her fingers accidentally brushing his as she took it from him. Behind her, Toby's cries were getting louder.

"Sorry," Michael called. "I think we'll have to get going. Somebody's not going to settle until the car's moving."

Ryan began to reverse his wheelchair. "No problem. Have a nice day out."

"It's all in the letter," Frances said.

"I'll look at it as soon as we get home," Jess promised, giving them a wave.

"What was all that about?" Michael asked once she'd climbed into the car.

"Saving hedgehogs." Jess got travel sick if she tried to read in the car, so she shoved the letter into the glove compartment to read later.

Never mind saving hedgehogs, they needed to focus on saving their sanity. For despite the fact that they were all now in the car, Toby was still crying.

"We'll soon be there, Toby," Michael said brightly. "You're going to love it!"

Jess bloody hoped so.

13

"I couldn't tell whether Jess was interested or not," Frances said as they watched the family drive away.

"I think she was a bit distracted," Ryan said.

"Yes. That little boy certainly wasn't happy, was he? I don't know how parents stand it; I really don't."

"You never wanted children yourself, then?" He wasn't sure why he was asking. Wished he hadn't when he saw the expression on Frances's face.

"No. Trevor never wanted them. Maybe I should have put up more of a fuss, eh? Now that he's gone and it's just me on my lonesome? Oh, well, we can't plan for everything in life. And they'd probably be round every week, nagging me about my house being a mess. Anyway, where next? The new lady at Number Three or Helen and Justin?"

"Doesn't really matter, does it?"

"I suppose not. Though I always think Helen and Justin disapprove of me. A bit like your mum. No offense intended."

"None taken."

Ryan hadn't mentioned the hedgehog-highway idea to his mother yet. He would have to, of course—Frances had taken it for granted that he would. Probably thought he already had. Irene's response was a foregone conclusion, though. *"Nasty, smelly hedgehogs, pooing everywhere, digging up the flowerbeds."*

"Let's speak to the lady at Number Three first," Frances said. "I don't know her name; I haven't met her properly yet."

"Tara. We've met a couple of times."

"Fabulous," said Frances. "Let's go!"

~

Tara came to the door wearing a red, silky robe. She looked different somehow—prettier—and he realised it was because she wasn't wearing any makeup.

"Good morning. I'm Frances from Number One," Frances said. "I believe you know Ryan from Number Five?"

"Indeed I do. Goodness, you're both out and about early, aren't you? You've caught me just about to get in the bath." She turned to call behind her. "Hermie, turn the taps off for me, will you?"

"We won't keep you very long, dear," said Frances, and proceeded to launch into the hedgehog-highway spiel.

"It sounds like a delightful idea," Tara said after she'd finished. "Though I really shouldn't make any holes in any fences without speaking to the landlord first, and he's away for a while, I'm afraid."

"Oh," said Frances, "I didn't realise you rented."

"Well, the landlord's a sort of . . . friend."

Something about her expression caused Ryan to replace the word *friend* with *lover*. The boyfriend she'd rushed off to meet the other day, no doubt.

"Well, anyway, I'm having a meeting about the project at my house next week—all the information's in the letter. If you'd like to come along, you can find out all about it so you're ready to tell your landlord when he gets back."

"Sounds perfect. Count me in. Shall I bring a bottle? We could turn it into a party. Toast the hedgehogs." She burst out laughing, putting a hand up to her mouth. "Oh, God, that makes it sound as if I'm planning to barbecue the poor things, doesn't it?"

She turned her head, listening. "Look, I'd better go. I don't think my daughter's turned off the bath taps. The house will get flooded out. See you both soon."

The door closed. Shortly afterwards, they heard her shouting angrily as she pounded up the stairs.

Frances and Ryan exchanged glances. *"Hmm,"* said Frances. "I'll put her down as a possible, I think. Right. Helen and Justin next."

Helen opened the door to Number Four, wearing the same type of yellow rubber gloves Ryan's mother favoured when she did house-work. But there the similarity ended. His mother wore skirts—always. And beige tights and blouses. Like a throwback to another era, with a starched hairstyle to match. Helen wore skinny jeans with a soft, over-large shirt tied in a knot at her waist. Her long hair cascaded over her shoulders, and she was wearing glasses—the sexy sort—purple, with wings. She looked like a librarian on her day off, which, Ryan knew, was exactly what she was.

"Oh," she said. "Hello, Ryan. Hello, Frances."

"Hello, dear. Sorry to bother you. We're here to tell you about a project we're hoping to set up in the close, if you have a few minutes?"

Helen smiled. "Of course. Anything to get me out of dusting. Come in; I'll put the kettle on." She looked dubiously at Ryan's wheel-chair. "Or we could sit outside if that's better?"

"Outside would be perfect," Frances said.

Helen slipped off her rubber gloves. "Okay, you go round. I'll unlock the gate."

Seated at a table on the patio, Ryan could feel Frances scrutinis-ing the Hedgeses' immaculate, high-fenced garden disapprovingly. The lawn was bowling-green perfect, complete with stripes. The bedding plants were laid out in neat ranks in the borders, any weeds had been plucked out in their first seconds of life, and the shrubs were pruned so severely that Ryan got the feeling they wouldn't dare to shed any leaves, even in the strongest of winds. The gate Helen had let them in through stood high and robust with no gap beneath it. In short, this garden was the very opposite of a hedgehog-friendly garden. As pleasant a hostess as Helen was, Ryan anticipated a hard sell to come.

As before, he let Frances outline the proposal, which she did in her impassioned way, her eyes alight, her hands moving to illustrate her point. He examined her as she spoke, wondering why this was so important to her. She loved wildlife, he got that. But something—his journalistic instinct, perhaps, or the fact that he was currently, if unwillingly, thrashing about in the emotional soup of his own life—told him there was more behind it. Had she been floundering about, searching for a cause ever since her husband died? Was this her attempt to rise from the ashes of grief? He wasn't sure. He didn't even know why he cared. Didn't want to care. He wasn't a journalist any longer, was he? Couldn't do his job while he was up shit creek and in this sodding chair, living with his mother.

Ever since the explosion, he'd been wallowing, closing himself off from medical advice and his mother's platitudes and pep talks. *"It'll all come out in the wash; you'll see. Tomorrow's another day. For goodness' sake, Ryan. Anyone would think you were the only one to have suffered a bit of bad luck."* Et cetera. If alcohol hadn't reacted so badly with his—essential—medication, he'd have blotted it all out with booze. And now his curiosity and journalistic instincts had sprung to life, like a green shoot from a patch of hard-baked ground.

"Gosh," said Helen, her hands clasped in front of her on the table. "It sounds fantastic, it really does." Her words didn't match her expression. Her words said *yes*, but the frown on her face said *no*.

Frances didn't seem to notice. She clapped her hands together so enthusiastically she almost upset her teacup. "Oh, I'm so glad you think so. The more of us who are on board, the more successful the project will be. I hope you'll be able to attend the meeting at my house on Thursday evening?"

"Well, I'll have to consult with my husband, of course, but we'll certainly try to, yes."

Ryan's phone rang. He took it from his pocket. "Excuse me," he said, wheeling himself off a little way before he answered. But he was pretty sure everyone could hear his mother's strident voice.

"Ryan, the physiotherapist is here for your appointment. Wherever are you? She's a busy woman. And you can hardly afford to miss an appointment, can you?"

"I'm on my way." He ended the call, turning his chair to face them. "Sorry, I've got to go. Nice to see you, Helen. Thank you for the tea. See you both on Thursday."

"Thank you for all your help, Ryan," Frances called after him.

"No problem."

14

The trip to the Dinosaur Park was a dismal failure. Predictably, Stella raced directly to the splash area the minute they arrived, ripping her outer clothes off and running straight into the water sprays in her swimsuit, squealing with delight. Nothing anyone could say would get her out. Short of dragging her out physically, they had to leave her in there until, again predictably, she emerged shivering and bad-tempered, half an hour later.

Jess, who had spent the majority of this time with Toby in the adjacent children's play area in case he was tempted to join his new sister, was irritated with Michael, holding him responsible for Stella's shivering distress. Surely he could have found some way to get her to see reason? Now they had to go to the indoor play area full of screaming kids so Stella could warm up, and since Stella always insisted that her father accompany her at all times in the indoor play area, that meant that, once again, Jess had sole charge of Toby.

It was curious—and frustrating—that Toby seemed to have no idea how to play on any of the equipment. Toby seemed bewildered by the ball pool and afraid of the age-appropriate, padded climbing frame and tunnels. Hadn't his foster parents ever brought him to a place like this? It didn't seem like it. But then there was so much they didn't know about Toby. So much they would probably never know about Toby.

In the end, Jess abandoned her attempts to interest him and sat in the café area with him on her lap, where he sat gazing into her eyes, putting a curious hand out to her hair, which she had forgotten to tie back, or playing with her fingers. As if she were some sort of toy. Or as if he were claiming her. Making her his.

Jess thought back to other visits to the Dinosaur Park. She, Stella, and Michael tearing side by side down three adjacent slides, squealing. Joyful. Carefree. It was probably in part a false memory. No doubt there had been some tantrums, sulky demands for ice cream, sudden rain showers, scuffed knees, or tears. But Jess genuinely didn't remember any of those, or at least, not clearly. She remembered fun. Family. A feeling of being united. Not isolated and on the edge. Forgotten.

Oh, for God's sake. What was wrong with her? It almost felt as if she were suffering from postnatal depression. Only she hadn't given birth, so she couldn't be, could she? She just needed to pull herself together.

When they finally ventured outdoors again, the huge model dinosaurs made Toby cling to Jess in fear. The roaring, animated dinosaur made him scream with terror. He would only dig in the sand for dinosaur bones if Jess dug right alongside him, and he cried when Stella tried to join in, causing Stella to complain, "Toby's mean, Mummy. He won't share!"

"He's only one, darling," Jess responded automatically, but really, she just wanted to leave the sandpit and walk off into the woods that fringed the park. To escape.

~

By Monday morning, the feeling hadn't gone away, but with this being Stella's first day at school, Jess did her very best to put her misery aside. All these years later, she could still remember her own first day at school, or, at least, she felt as if she could, because her mother had told her about it so often. How excited she'd been. How proud and emotional her mother had felt at the school gates, saying goodbye.

"Look how smart and grown-up you look," she said, standing in front of her long mirror with Stella, doing her best to ignore Toby calling for her from his bedroom.

Stella beamed at her. "I do, don't I, Mummy?"

Jess kissed the top of her head. "You really do."

After breakfast, they walked to the school, Jess doing her best to push the buggy one-handed so she could hold Stella's hand and chat to her in a happy voice about the day.

Perhaps feeling a bit left out, Toby started grizzling. By the time they reached the school, his grumbles had turned into full-blown cries. Up until then, Stella had been skipping along happily, talking about what she thought her teacher would be like, which friends from play group she would see, what games they might play. But by the time they reached the school gates, she was frowning.

"Mummy," she said, "can we give Toby back?"

And Jess felt such a pang of guilty recognition and empathy she reacted by speaking harshly. "That's a wicked thing to say, Stella. Of course we can't give Toby back. He's part of our family now."

Whereupon Stella burst into noisy tears, right there outside the school gate, sobbing, "But I d-don't like him, Mummy."

And Jess—appalled by how she had snapped at her daughter on this, her all-important first day at school—crouched down and pulled her into a hug, tears filling her own eyes.

"It will be all right, darling, you'll see. Mummy's sorry she snapped."

Only would it? Be all right?

Thankfully, Stella seemed to have forgotten all about the drama by the end of the school day when Jess went to collect her. She had made a new best friend—a best friend with a little dog the friend's mother had brought with her to the school. Even Toby smiled while Stella fawned over the fluffy white dog sporting a sparkly pink harness. The only part of the Dinosaur Park trip Toby had appeared to enjoy was when they rode in an open truck out into a field to watch a pair of collies rounding up sheep.

Maybe it was the memory of Toby bouncing with excitement, his arms outstretched towards the dogs, that gave Michael the idea. Either that or a complete brain meltdown. Because when he came back from work that day, he wasn't alone. He had a puppy with him. A black-and-white, fluffy, totally adorable puppy he and Jess hadn't had a whiff of a conversation about.

"What is that?" Jess asked.

"A puppy," Michael said, parting the fleece blanket it was cosied up in to reveal a completely cute black-and-white face.

"I can see that. But why? Why have you got a puppy?"

He looked shamefaced. "Well, Pete at work's dog had a litter a few months back—I told you, I think? Anyway, this one was left. And I just thought it would . . . you know, help Stella and Toby to bond. He liked the dogs at the Dinosaur Park on Saturday, didn't he? And Stella's still missing Stripey Cat, so . . ."

Jess could feel panic rising up within her. "We can't have a dog, Michael. How can we possibly have a dog?"

"I'll do everything. I'll get up early and walk him before work."

"But you won't be here during the day, will you, you stupid man!" she wanted to shout. *"Get it out of this house now!"* But it was too late. Stella ran down the hallway to launch herself at her daddy and stopped, frozen with rapture at the sight of the wriggling bundle in his arms.

"Oh, Daddy, oh, Daddy! Is he ours? Can we keep him? Oh, Daddy!"

Shit.

By bedtime, the dog—which Stella had named Patch—had weed on the carpet and the kitchen floor at least ten times, chewed the back of one of Jess's shoes, and stolen all their hearts. Even Jess's. For how could she not succumb? She loved all animals, and this black-and-white fluff ball with a white patch over one eye was playing like a demon one minute and passed out asleep the next, tiny tail wrapped adorably over his face.

But at 11:00 p.m., Jess and Michael lay in bed, exhausted, having dealt with Stella's heartbreak that the puppy couldn't sleep with her in her bed, listening to it barking in utter bewilderment and loss at being alone for the first time in its life. And Jess wanted to cry right along with it.

"Whatever possessed you?" she asked Michael, unable to keep the sheer despair from her voice.

"I just wanted to make the kids happy, that's all," he said sniffily. "It's hardly a crime, is it?" He sighed. "Look, the first night is bound to be hard. But he'll soon get used to being away from the litter, you'll see."

But by 1:00 a.m. the puppy was in their bed.

15

Since they're nocturnal creatures, hedgehogs use their keen sense of smell to identify food sources. It can be frustrating in the extreme when their noses detect a tasty morsel just behind a gate or fence which they are unable to squeeze through. The human habit of sealing off their properties—as was the case with Justin and Helen Hedges' garden—is a constant obstacle to hedgehogs getting enough to eat. Which is why, once a hedgehog highway has been established and functions well, the hedgehogs experience a heady sense of relief, as they can focus their attention on foraging for food without having to take time-consuming—and at times, dangerous—detours in order to reach a tasty tidbit or two.

Since Toby's arrival, Jess had felt every bit as restricted and confined as those hedgehogs blocked by fences, gates, and brick walls. On the evening of Frances's meeting, she could hardly believe she was leaving the house without her new son. But Michael had said he'd be able to cope, so she'd left, turning her back on Toby's cries, on Stella's demands that she help her paint a picture, on the dog chewing yet another shoe. It was tempting to run, even though Frances's house was only just across the road.

The invitation directed guests to go through the side gate to the back garden. Frances had propped the gate open with a brick, and Jess could hear voices coming from the garden. She wasn't the first to arrive, then.

She halted at the open gate—not because she was nervous about joining everyone, but because the temptation to turn tail and go somewhere else, to do something else with this golden nugget of time alone—was so strong. But then she heard a sound behind her—the sound of wheels on tarmac. And a deep voice said, "Hi."

Ryan.

She turned to look over her shoulder at him. "Hi. How are you?"

"Well, this is the most exciting thing to happen to me this week, so I'll leave you to draw your own conclusions."

She saw a smile in his eyes. "Me too."

He grinned. "Better make the most of it, then, hadn't we?"

"Yes," she agreed, turning her back on whatever other exciting thing she might have done—A trip to the coast for a windswept walk? Late-night shopping, to treat herself to new clothes? A child-free supermarket run?—and walked through the open gate.

Tara and Frances sat on fold-down chairs at a rickety-looking table positioned amongst the weeds sprouting through the cracks on the patio. At a distance, Jess could see Tara's daughter—Hermie—thrashing through the weeds with a long stick, having an adventure.

"Hello, Jess. Hello, Ryan," Frances welcomed them. And to Jess's surprise—and Ryan's too, by the look of it—she bent to kiss Ryan on the cheek.

Jess felt oddly moved by the gesture. She hadn't realised the two of them knew each other that well. She and Michael had lived in Hilltop Place for three years and hadn't really got to know anybody beyond exchanging a few words about the weather or bin-collection dates.

Oh, God. She was getting emotional. For God's sake. It had only been a friendly peck on the cheek.

Frances approached her. "Hello, dear," she said, and then she gave Jess a kiss and a little hug too, and Jess had to hold her arms rigid to stop herself from clinging to Frances.

Fortunately, Frances didn't seem to notice, and Jess swallowed, hugging her arms about herself, sensing Ryan looking in her direction. Probably trying to work out what the hell was wrong with her.

But it was Tara who spoke to her, while Frances said something to Ryan. "I should take a seat. I'm not sure there'll be enough for everybody. Latecomers will probably end up sitting on upturned plant pots."

Jess gave her a jerky nod, accompanied by a fragile smile. "I don't mind a plant pot," she said, taking one, feeling the hard terracotta beneath her buttocks, and remembering too late that she was wearing pale trousers.

"Mum!" Hermie shouted from the bottom of the garden. "I've found a giant brown slug!"

"Well, you make sure you leave it exactly where it is," Tara shouted back.

"My daughter should have been a boy," she said with a shudder. "Imagine wanting to pick up a slug. Shame you didn't bring your little girl. She might have been a good influence. Didn't she want to come?"

She had. Vehemently. Jess ought to have brought her so Michael could spend some time on his own with Toby. But her own need for some time alone had won out.

"She was painting a picture," she told Tara. Which was almost the truth. Stella had been painting a picture. Right up until she'd learned Jess was going to the meeting, whereupon she'd abandoned her brush and paints and gone to fetch her shoes.

"Don't touch that little stone, will you, dear?" Frances called down the garden to Hermie.

Tara straightened, peering down the garden. "Stone? What stone?"

"It's a decorative stone with a fossil in it. I found it on a trip to the North Norfolk Coast. I put it there to remember my husband by."

"I can't see it."

"Well, yes, it is a little overgrown down there, I suppose. I know it's there, though. It's rather precious to me."

"Hermie," Tara bawled, "stay away from any big stones, okay?"

"Okay, Mum."

"Sorry we're late," said a male voice from the passageway.

Jess looked up to see Justin Hedges with his wife, Helen, bringing up the rear behind him. She'd never really had the opportunity to speak to Justin properly; the only time she saw him outside his house was when he mowed the lawn, or washed and hoovered his car in the driveway, both noisy activities which precluded conversation, even if she'd wanted to engage him in conversation, which she hadn't. The neatness of his garden and the pristine shine of his expensive car always made Jess feel inadequate.

"Hello, everyone. Thank you so much for the invitation, Frances. How good to have everyone gathered together like this. Helen, sweetie, I think there's a free seat at the table?"

Mr. Smarm. All honeyed words and let's-do-business smiles, while his gaze raked the garden and seemed to dismiss it as a bomb site that needed to be bulldozed.

"How charming. I never thought of plant pots as seats. They'll be on *Gardener's World* before we know it."

Justin delivered this to Jess out of the side of his mouth. She knew he expected her to giggle or smile sarcastically in response. She did neither. "It's very good of Frances to have us all here," she said instead, wishing it were easier to move plant pots about like chairs. He was invading her space.

"Of course, of course. We'd have offered our garden, had we known about it. We've just replaced our outdoor furniture, haven't we, sweetie? Fully waterproof and very comfortable."

"Sweetie" smiled. "Yes. Justin surprised me with it for my birthday."

"What a romantic gift," Tara teased, and Jess stifled a smile.

"Good relationships are about more than hearts and flowers, aren't they?" Justin replied.

"Lemonade, tea, or coffee?" Frances asked.

She took everyone's orders and came back with a tray of drinks in an odd assortment of cups and glasses. Jess strongly suspected that Justin would either leave his lemonade untouched or feed it to the patio weeds.

"Right," said Frances, taking her place at the head of the table and picking up her notes. "Thank you so much for coming today. I appreciate it. Hedgehogs mean a lot to me, you see. Well, they ought to mean a lot to everyone, not just me, because they're part of this country's heritage, aren't they? And their numbers have been dwindling for a very long time. Henry the Eighth didn't help, with those stupid laws he introduced, the Destruction of Crows Act and the . . . Now, let me see, what was the other one? I've got it written down here somewhere."

More than one person looked puzzled as Frances put her glasses on the end of her nose and leafed through her pages of notes.

"Here it is," Frances said eventually, finding the relevant piece of paper. "The Preservation of Grain Act. Everyone had to hunt down any wildlife that might eat crops. Hedgehogs included—"

"When was this exactly, Frances?" interrupted Tara.

Frances shuffled through her papers. "1532. There were several years of drought, you see, so it was the law. Any villages that didn't kill enough animals got a stiff fine. Anyway, of course, it was all rubbish. Hedgehogs don't eat grain. Neither did many of the other animals they slaughtered—foxes, kingfishers, adders, polecats, and badgers, to name just a few. And this went on for two hundred years. So much slaughter." Frances looked round at her audience. "Can you imagine? Bounties paid for half a million hedgehogs. Half a million! And even when they weren't killing them for money, they ate them. They used to press their poor little bodies into clay to get the spines off. Can you imagine?"

There was a stunned silence. Justin shifted impatiently in his seat. Catching his eye, Frances pressed on. "Anyway, in the 1950s, there were around thirty-five million hedgehogs in the UK. Now there are only about a million. If we don't act now, they'll be gone. Extinct. Caput. No more hedgehogs."

"Why don't you tell us what we can do, Frances?" prompted Ryan, and Frances put her notes down on the table with obvious relief.

"Well, that's why I asked you all round here this evening. To tell you more about hedgehog highways and to ask you to help me set one up. Hilltop Place is a perfect location for it."

"It's an odd name for something meant to preserve them, don't you think?" chipped in Tara. "I associate the word *highway* with fast cars. And fast cars are the last thing hedgehogs need, aren't they?"

Frances frowned. "I think the word *highway* was just used because it's something that helps you get from place to place quickly. That's the idea of a hedgehog highway—to allow a hedgehog to come and go from garden to garden without having to deal with obstacles like fences and locked gates."

"What they need is to evolve so they don't roll into a ball in the middle of the road," Tara said, shuddering. "I hate seeing their squashed little bodies everywhere."

"Evolution takes a long time," Ryan said. "And from what Frances is saying, hedgehogs haven't got that."

"They haven't. Like I said, if we don't act now, it will be too late. And we're at fault, with our cars and our over-cared-for gardens. Housing developments going up everywhere with keep-out fences."

Frances glared in Justin and Helen's direction. Jess stepped in quickly before they could notice. "So what can we do, Frances?"

Frances took a deep breath. Nodded. "Yes, of course. Sorry, it's just something I feel very passionate about. Well, in essence, we'd need to agree not to use anything that might be poisonous to hedgehogs, like slug pellets. To leave some corners of our gardens uncultivated. Not to sweep up every single dropped leaf, so the hedgehogs have somewhere to hibernate, and most importantly, to leave spaces at the bottom of fences and gates for them to pass through. It's about finding a way for us to live side by side with these creatures. And the benefits to us of doing all this—apart from the satisfaction of doing the right thing, of course—is the joy of having regular hedgehog visitors. Some people put out feeding stations, and hedgehog hotels. They even turn the holes in fences into decorative gateways. It's fantastic for the children."

"We don't have children," Justin said.

Frances looked impatient. "Neither do I. But I still care about them. We all live in a world where children exist, don't we? We all pay towards schools and nurseries, whether we have children or not. Children are our future, after all."

"Let's try to focus, shall we?" Justin said, looking at his watch. "Helen and I can't stay that long. I don't happen to believe people without children should automatically have to pay to keep schools running, but if we go down that route of discussion, we'll never get anything agreed."

A noise reached them from the street. A child, screaming loudly. Everyone looked up. Jess knew exactly who the child was, even before Stella came running down the passageway and round the side of the house.

"Hello, Mummy. Toby wouldn't stop screaming, so Daddy said we should all come here. And Mummy, what's that girl doing? Can I play with her?"

Not waiting for Jess's response, Stella ran straight down the garden to join Hermie and was soon thrashing about in the weeds with her own stick. Seconds later, Michael appeared with a squirming, screaming Toby clasped awkwardly in his arms.

"Mama! Mama! *Mama!*" Seeing Jess, Toby wriggled even more vigorously, and Jess quickly got to her feet, almost overturning the plant pot in the process, reaching for him.

By the time she'd soothed him enough to tune in again, Frances was saying, "The point is, people have all the power these days, don't they? Human beings, concreting over woodland, dropping litter, manicuring their lawns with nail-scissor precision. Wildlife hasn't got a chance. And it deserves a chance, it really does. Animals are just as important as us. More important than us. This land belonged to them first!"

"Frances," enquired Tara with a smile, "are you sure you didn't put vodka in the lemonade?"

Frances turned on her, indignant. "Why d'you say that? Because I'm speaking passionately about something?"

"It was just a little joke, darling."

"But that's what people do, isn't it? Joke about the things that are important or unpleasant to face. *'Oh, look at that squashed hedgehog in the road. Anyone fancy pancakes for tea?'* Nobody thinks about the poor starving hoglets back in the nest, waiting for a mother who will never come back to suckle them. Hedgehog extinction isn't a laughing matter. It's a real threat. All I'm asking you to do is leave a gap here and there so the poor creatures can come and go without having to go on the road. A few leaves, or a few weeds, left in a corner of your garden to give them somewhere to nest. A ramp leading out of your pond, if you've got one, in case they accidentally fall into it. I'm going to put food out for them. Ryan's going to help me make a feeding station, aren't you, Ryan? But you don't have to go that far. There are plenty of worms for hedgehogs to forage for if the whole garden isn't regimented to the point of . . . of . . ." Frances broke off, unable to think of anything adequate to describe such a horror.

"We're happy to make a hole in our gate, aren't we, Michael?" Jess said, wanting to say something to make Frances feel better, because she looked as if she might burst into tears.

"Well, yes, just as long as it's not big enough for the puppy to get through." Michael smiled round at everyone. "We just got the most gorgeous border collie pup."

Oh yes, the puppy. Jess had forgotten the puppy. She bloody well hoped Michael had shut Patch away somewhere; otherwise there wouldn't be an unchewed shoe left in the house.

Frances frowned. "Well, if you have a dog, your garden probably won't be suitable for the highway project, after all," she said. "That's very disappointing."

"Hedgehogs are nocturnal, though, aren't they? The dog won't be out at night," said Michael.

Oh yes? Was he going to take Patch up the road for a final wee before bedtime, then?

"I'll talk to my landlord," Tara said. "I'm sure he'll agree. He usually does what I want him to do."

"If it will help, I'll write a piece for the newspaper about what we're trying to do," offered Ryan. "I think they'd be interested, especially after we've got the cameras set up and there's footage to view. We might be able to get people in the next street to sign up to the project too."

Frances's frown disappeared. "That would be wonderful, Ryan. Do you really think they'd print a story?"

Something flickered across Ryan's face. Something that made Jess want to find out what had happened to him.

"I think I should be able to persuade them, yes."

Frances beamed round at everyone with renewed energy. "That would be fantastic, wouldn't it? We'll be a glowing example of a successful community project. Perhaps we could get the parish council involved. Order some leaflets from a hedgehog rescue charity and run education events at the community centre. Get a guest speaker to come and talk!" She clapped her hands together. "Oh, it will be amazing! Now, anyone for more lemonade?"

Toby was asleep in Jess's arms. The plant pot was digging into her buttocks. She daren't move in case she disturbed him, but it was well worth putting up with the discomfort to have some peace.

"Frances certainly is very passionate about this," she said to Ryan.

He sighed. "She is, yes. It's infectious."

Jess looked at him. He sounded reluctant, somehow. Almost as if he didn't want to be infected by Frances's enthusiasm.

He met her gaze. Shrugged. "Don't worry about me. I'm just a miserable, cynical git. It's been a while since I felt passionate about anything. I might just as well jump on Frances's bandwagon as anything else. What about you? I don't suppose you have time for passions with two kids to look after?"

Jess looked down at Toby's sleeping face. "Your kids are supposed to be your passion if you're a mother, aren't they? That's how it's always been with Stella." A little pause. "And now there's Toby too." Another pause. "Not forgetting the dog."

16

Something was clearly wrong with Jess. Ryan could sense it, one victim to another. It was the kid. The boy in her arms. She'd sounded authentic, speaking about her daughter, but her voice had flattened when she mentioned Toby. And the dog. Like they were burdens.

The boy literally looked like a burden at the moment. Her arms must be killing her, holding him like that. Ryan could still remember what a dead weight Eric had been at that age when he fell asleep. Why didn't that husband of hers notice? Take a turn, instead of chat, chat, chat to Helen, completely oblivious to his wife's discomfort?

Still, who was he to criticise? He'd been exactly the same himself. Prioritising work over everything else, leaving his wife to do nearly all the childcare. Passing Eric back to her when he needed to answer his phone. Thinking about how to word a report or what time to book his next flight as his little boy's words washed over him.

He'd been so convinced his work was more important. More important than his wife. His family.

"Frances, I've just been googling hedgehog highways," Tara said. "You can get these darling little surrounds to put around your hedgehog holes. Look at this one; it's got an Egyptian feel to it. Very classy. I'm sure my landlord won't mind holes in his fences if they're surrounded like that. I'm going to order one now."

Ryan tuned Tara out. In his mind he was back in his old sitting room, Eric bouncing on his lap, holding a book out to him. "Read to me, Dad. Read to me!"

Him, dodging both the book and the boy, trying to read something on his iPad, keeping tabs on the latest developments in some war zone or other. "I'll read to you later on, son. Daddy's busy at the moment."

Well, he wasn't busy now, was he? Only Eric didn't want to be read to any longer. Ryan didn't even know what books his son liked these days. Whether he read at all, apart from the books he had to read for school.

Ryan would like to take Jess's husband aside and tell him to pay his wife more attention. Share his pitiful story. Maybe the bastard could learn from it. Somebody had to learn from it. It couldn't all be for nothing.

Ryan looked up to see Jess shifting carefully on her flowerpot, trying to ease her obviously numb bum whilst not disturbing the sleeping boy.

"D'you want me to get you a chair?" Ryan asked. "I'd offer you mine, only I sort of need it." *Ha ha. Pathetic attempt at humour, Ryan.* "You can put him on my lap if you like. It won't hurt me. I hardly have any feeling in my legs."

Her eyes asked him questions. *What happened to you? How has it affected your life? What are you planning to do next?* Questions he might happily have answered had Toby not begun to stir at that moment, opening his eyes and looking fearfully around him.

"Mama?" he said, using it as a question. "Mama?"

"Thanks," she said, struggling to her feet. "But I think I'll take him home. It was nice talking to you."

"Likewise. Maybe my son and I will see you in the park with your puppy? Eric likes dogs."

Did he? He thought so, but really, he had no idea.

Jess gave a strained smile. "Dogs aren't allowed in that park. I'll have to take him further afield. Anyway, bye, Ryan."

"Bye, Jess."

He watched her go, the boy clinging to her front, dirt from the plant pot on the seat of her trousers.

"Michael, I'm taking Toby home. Keep an eye on Stella, won't you?"

"Sure. Want us to come with you?"

"No, it's all right. See you later. Thanks, Frances. Sorry I have to hop off early."

Suddenly, Ryan didn't want to be there any longer either.

"Poor thing. D'you think she has any idea she has mud on her behind?"

Tara of the overly strong perfume and jingle-jangle bracelets. Tara, with the bottle of innocent-looking water he'd seen her "dilute" her lemonade with.

"I don't think she'd care if she did," he said, hands on his chair, ready to wheel away, intending to say his goodbyes to Frances.

Only at that moment, his mother made a grand entrance, like a duchess arriving late to a garden party, and he changed his mind.

"Good timing, Mum," he said. "We've just been saying the parish council would love to get behind the hedgehog-highway project. It's such a great educational opportunity, don't you think? I bet you could get the local schools involved too. Win-win, all round."

If Ryan hadn't been subjected to so many looks of disapproval/ dislike from his mother over the years, he might have thought he'd imagined it, her expression was so fleeting as she looked in his direction. Then the very next moment she beamed her toothy smile at all and sundry.

"The library could get involved as well," Helen said. "I was just saying to Michael, libraries aren't just about books these days. We're very keen to get involved with community events too."

"Darling, you're not boring people about your work, I hope?" Justin said.

Ryan watched the light go out of Helen's eyes as her husband spoke. The colour rise to her face. *Bastard.*

"My wife thinks the whole world revolves around books. If she had her way, every wall in our house would be lined with bookshelves. Including the downstairs cloakroom."

As Ryan watched the man smiling around the group, inviting their laughter, a pain started up in his back. A pain exacerbated no doubt by the fact that he hadn't done his exercises yet. A fact that his physiotherapist would be very displeased about, should she find out.

When it came, the pain was sudden, severe, and unignorable. He could only ease it with strong painkillers, stretching exercises that made him literally scream with agony, and rest.

It was definitely time to go.

"Frances, those cameras I ordered online should arrive in the next few days. I'll come round and help you set them up."

"Oh, thank you, Ryan. You are good. And you'll write your piece?"

The pain was making him sweat. He could feel beads of it on his forehead. "I'll write my piece, yes."

She bent to kiss him. "You son's an absolute wonder, Irene. You must be so proud of him."

Yeah, right. Ryan didn't bother to check his mother's expression. People had been trying to tell her things like that for as long as he could remember. Teachers, lecturers, scout leaders. Even Annie, when they were first married. Nothing made any difference. For some reason, his mother had decided he didn't measure up when he was born and had never changed her opinion since.

And now, of course, with his career and life in ruins, her opinion of him was confirmed. He was a disappointment, just as she'd always thought.

On his way past Justin, Ryan couldn't help stopping his chair to speak his mind. That was one advantage of being at rock bottom, he supposed. Literally nothing mattered.

"Do me a favour," he said.

Justin blinked. "Of course, old chap. Of course. Do you need me to push you back home?"

Ryan shook his head. "No, I can manage, thank you. But maybe don't mock your wife's job in public? Books are important. Essential to knowledge and development. Books are one of the things that have got me through these last miserable months of my life. So maybe show her a bit of respect? Eh, old chap?"

He hadn't even reached the garden gate before he heard his mother swooping in. "I do apologise for my son, Justin."

"No, no, it's quite all right. Difficult for him to keep a sense of humour at the moment, I should think, with all that's happened."

"It's no excuse. No excuse at all."

Jesus. He really had to move out. Find an accessible flat. Sign the divorce papers so he and Annie could sort out their finances. She'd been asking him to do it for weeks. She was right. It was time. Life was hard enough without living with someone who sometimes felt like an enemy.

17

Two days later, they had the motion-capture cameras set up in Frances's garden. Ryan couldn't install them himself, so he'd paid a guy from the company that had supplied the cameras to do the job, and she hadn't questioned it. He couldn't afford to be so altruistic for much longer if he wanted to move out of his mother's house, but he didn't mind for now. The hedgehog project had given him an interest, and he was going with it. And so what if it distracted him from the harsh realities of his situation? Distractions were good. Essential, even.

Luckily, Frances had a laptop. An ancient one that took about five hours to fire up, but a laptop, nevertheless. And she had internet. Turned out her husband had had it set up before he died, and Frances had been shelling out for it every month since then without using it. When Ryan realised this—that, contrary to the shabby appearance of both Frances and her house, she had sufficient funds not to notice those monthly payments going out of her bank account for all those years—he briefly regretted not passing the charge for the installation of the cameras on to her. But then he put it from his mind and forgot about it. At least the hedgehog feeding stations hadn't cost him anything. He'd cleared his stuff from some plastic storage boxes and cut out an entrance with a Stanley knife. Turned upside down with a brick on top and strategically placed next to one of the cameras at the rear of the patio just where Frances's jungle of a garden started, they were ready to go, their food and water bowls temptingly full of the cat biscuits their research had told them were suitable for hedgehogs to eat. All they needed was some customers.

"I can't wait until it's dark," Frances said. "Will you come back to see?"

"Of course."

"The hedgehogs might not come tonight, though, I suppose. With it all being new."

"True. Though they have a strong sense of smell, don't they? They ought to be able to sniff out that food, I'd have thought. But we can test the cameras ourselves. They work by detecting movement. You can go out there and wave to me."

Frances practised waving. "Then will you go out there and wave to me, so I can see too?"

"All right." He paused. Then casually said, "Maybe once the feeding stations are established and you're getting regular visitors, I could bring my son to have a look sometime? If he's interested, that is."

"Of course. I'm sure he will be. Interested, that is. We can invite the other children too. That strange girl who likes bashing things with a stick. Hermie. And Jess's children. Though that one she's adopted is a noisy little thing, isn't he? Might scare the hedgehogs away."

"He just needs to settle down, that's all."

"I suppose so. Oh, why is nighttime so far away? I want to see all this working!"

18

Autumn had well and truly descended when Jess trudged back up the hill from a doctor's appointment, though she was in no mood to notice the gold-and-crimson silhouettes of the trees against the bright blue of the sky as she pushed Toby along the pavement. The doctor had been running late, and by the time her name was called, Toby had become restless, distracting Jess as she'd tried to explain how she was feeling. Jess had left the appointment with a prescription for antidepressants she wasn't yet sure she'd use. The same doctor had prescribed tablets for her after her miscarriages, and they'd just given her stomach pains and made her feel sick.

Besides, tablets wouldn't magically make Stella enchanted with Toby, would they? Or stop the dog from scratching and howling when she left him alone for more than five minutes. These days, Jess seemed to exist in a cacophony of noise—a toxic blend of yapping and wailing that made her head threaten to explode. What she wouldn't give to be one of Frances's hedgehogs, getting ready for a three-month hibernation, rolled up for winter in an oblivious ball in a nest of cosy leaves.

Jess had read about hibernation in the hedgehog leaflet Frances had given her. How amazing to hardly have to breathe at all. Not to have to exert the energy it took to draw a breath in and out, or to think constantly about what you're going to eat. Living off your fat, oblivious to the cold, cold world. Absolute bliss.

Perhaps she ought to have asked the doctor for sleeping tablets instead. Or at the very least, told him the last tablets he'd prescribed had made her feel ill. She was pathetic. But at least Toby wasn't crying at the moment, which was something. He was fast asleep in the buggy, a bubble of snot inflating and deflating in one nostril as he breathed in and out. Toby had a cold, poor little sod, and she probably should have kept him at home instead of dragging him out to a waste-of-time doctor's appointment.

"Hi there."

As Jess turned into Hilltop Place, Tara was just getting out of her car. "How are you? Sorry, I can't remember your name. Don't take it personally; I'm rubbish with names." Tara gave a little laugh and held up several expensive-looking carrier bags. "Except for designer names. I remember those, no trouble."

"I'm Jess."

"Of course you are. And I'm Tara."

"Yes, I remember." Jess hadn't meant it to sound like a rebuke but realised it probably had. So she added, "It's a pretty name. That's why it stuck in my mind."

Tara smiled. "Why, thank you. Though it wasn't so great at school. *Ta, Tara* to say thank you. *Tara, Tara* to say goodbye. Bloody hilarious. Not."

"Kids can be a nightmare, can't they?" Jess glanced down at Toby, still asleep in his buggy. "Though they're very angelic when they're asleep."

She wondered whether Tara had failed to see the snot bubble. Surely not. It had turned into more of a frothy stream by now.

"Fancy a coffee?" Tara asked. "We could sit outside so you don't have to disturb your son."

Conversation. With someone older than four years old. Jess felt like crying with gratitude. "That would be lovely, thanks."

"Great. Come round; the gate isn't locked. I'll put the coffee machine on."

Five minutes later, they sat at an attractive patio table together with Toby—mercifully—still asleep.

"So you've been clothes shopping in the city?" As a conversation starter, it was pretty lame, because clearly Tara had been shopping. Still, at least the topic wasn't connected to children. Jess didn't want to talk about children. Or even to think about them.

"Yes," said Tara. "Nothing like a spot of clothes shopping to lift the spirits, don't you think?"

Maybe she ought to have gone into the city instead of to the doctor. Although she'd have had to drag Toby around with her, so it wouldn't have been the same at all. But no, she wouldn't think about that.

"Mind you," said Tara, "I really shouldn't have done. My credit cards are completely maxed out now. I'm going to have to get a job."

She said it as if getting a job were akin to a root canal treatment or a colonoscopy. Jess was intrigued. "What work will you look for?"

Tara shrugged. "It will have to be something that fits around Hermie, I suppose, which probably cuts out anything the least bit interesting. I used to do bar work, which was quite good fun. But that's no good now, is it? Perhaps I could find a role as a professional shopper, eh? That would suit me down to the ground."

Jess looked at her. Tara was immaculate. Perfect makeup, stylish, coordinated clothing. She could work at a makeup counter in a department store, perhaps. Although those jobs were probably full-time and few and far between.

"Could you make videos?" she suggested instead. "You know, be one of those social media influencers, dispensing your tips and tricks for style and makeup to the world. Although it would take a while to get enough followers to earn any money, I suppose."

Tara's smile emphasised her perfectly applied plum-coloured lipstick. "I would love to do that. It's exactly me. Except for the tech side of things. I'm hopeless with it all. Ridiculous, I know, for someone my age. Hermie despairs of me."

"Maybe she could help you?" Jess suggested. "The videos don't need to be live, do they? You could make them in the evenings or at the weekend."

"I guess I could." Tara nodded. "Thank you, Jess. It's a great idea. I'll give it some thought."

Jess smiled and drank some of her coffee—far too bitter; she should have thought to ask for it to be milky—gratified to have been of use. It made a bloody change from feeling like a failure twenty-four hours a day, anyway.

"How about you?" Tara asked. "What did you do before you had kids?"

Jess shrugged. "I worked for a few different charities in a variety of roles. Typing to begin with, then a bit of fundraising and marketing. It was good to feel I was doing something really worthwhile."

"I'm not sure bar work was quite as worthwhile as that, although I suppose I helped a fair few people feel less lonely. You don't work now, though, do you?"

"I was just about to apply for a promotion when I fell pregnant with Stella."

"So you got pregnant by accident too?"

"I suppose so, but we were both delighted."

Tara pulled a face. "I wasn't. I always knew I'd be a car crash of a mother, and I wasn't wrong. When Hermie hits her teenage years, I'm leaving home, I swear." She laughed. "Only kidding. I love Hermie to bits, of course. I'd just like a break now and then, that's all, and you don't get that if you're a single parent."

"It sounds tough. Was it?" These past weeks, with Toby refusing to allow Michael to help out with him in any way, had shown Jess exactly how tough coping on your own could be.

"Yes. Especially when Hermie was a baby. Oh, her father was still around then, but Tony was totally useless. It was a relief when he left, really. I honestly don't think Hermie's missed out, though. My dad wasn't in the picture when I was growing up either, but I was never bothered. Mum made him sound like a total jerk. What about yours? Was he around when you were a kid?"

Jess nodded, feeling suddenly emotional. "Yes. We were very close. He died before I met Michael, sadly. He'd have loved being a grandfather."

"Where did you and Michael meet?"

"At university. On our very first day, actually."

"Ah, that's cute."

Jess smiled. "I suppose it is."

"Must make it so much easier if you can just leave the kids with someone." She sighed. "Don't you sometimes wish you could do exactly what you want, when you want?"

Yes.

"Going back to the subject of work, though, there are plenty of jobs that fill me with absolute horror. A teacher, for instance. I can't honestly think of much worse, trying to keep thirty kids in order. I'd rather go on the game, I think. At least I'd be using my natural talents."

Jess gaped, causing Tara to burst out laughing. "You should see your face! Don't worry, I don't have any current plans to become a prostitute. Not unless my finances get really tight. The hours wouldn't really suit, anyway, would they?"

Jess had no idea what to say to that, so she lifted her mug to her lips to hide her embarrassment, taking another sip of the disgusting coffee.

Opposite her, Tara glanced at her watch. It was a smartwatch. How did that work for a technophobe? Maybe it was just for show.

"I've got a handyman coming round soon. Not that that means you have to go. Though I guess he might wake your little boy up, sawing and hammering. He's going to make some holes in my gate and fences for Frances's hedgehog highway. I ordered some of those darling little entrance surrounds. So cute. I'll go and get them, shall I? To show you?"

Without waiting for Jess to reply, Tara left, scraping her chair back on the paving slabs and causing Toby to jolt awake. By the time she returned, package in hand, Jess was wheeling the buggy round the patio, trying unsuccessfully to get him to settle again.

"Sorry," said Tara. "Was that my fault?"

"He was probably about to wake up anyway," Jess said. "I'd better get him home and give him some lunch. Thanks for the coffee."

"You've hardly drunk any of it."

"Sorry, I . . ."

"Now, why do I think you're one of those women who apologises too much?" Tara said.

From somewhere, despite Toby's spiraling cries, Jess managed a smile. "Sorry," she said.

Tara laughed. "Touché. Look, pop round whenever you like, okay? And if your little girl ever wants to play with Hermie, she'd be very welcome."

Jess suddenly felt like crying. It really was time to go home. "Thanks. I appreciate that."

19

"Can you show me again from the beginning?" Frances asked Ryan. "I want to make sure I can do it when you aren't here."

"You can always video call me if you get stuck. I'll talk you through it."

"How would I do that?"

"Just with your smartphone. You know, FaceTime, WhatsApp. Wait a minute, you don't have a smartphone, do you?"

"Of course I don't, Ryan. Don't be silly."

Ryan smiled. It was his third consecutive day round at Frances's house. The first day, he'd supervised the installation of the cameras and set up the software on her laptop. The second day, he'd shown her how to view any footage. And this, the third day, he'd taught her everything all over again, because she'd forgotten it all. He supposed she'd gradually get the hang of it, though her IT instincts seemed to be practically zero, so there was no guarantee of that. He didn't mind, though, not really. In fact, not at all. Frances's enthusiasm and gratitude cheered him. Made him feel useful.

"All right, well, give me a pen and some paper, and I'll write the steps down for you."

"Like an idiot guide, you mean?"

He smiled. "You said it, Frances, not me."

"I'm well aware of my limitations," Frances said, slapping the pen and paper down in front of him. "As all of us should be."

Yes, indeed. Especially if those limitations had suddenly increased a hundredfold.

"This double-clicking thing throws me off right away," Frances complained. "Why do I have to click twice? Why won't one click do the job?"

"Well, the guy who invented the mouse wanted the button to work for several different functions, and . . ."

"Blimey, Ryan, I do hope your idiot guide isn't going to be written in that kind of technical speak. I'll never be able to follow it. Here, give me that mouse thing, so I can practise double-clicking."

But try as she might, Frances just couldn't get the hang of it.

"Come on, Ryan," she said. "You do it. I want to see whether I had any visitors. Well, I know I did, because the food's gone. But I want to make sure it wasn't a cat that ate it."

"The brick we placed in front of the feeder will have stopped any cats getting in," said Ryan, taking back the mouse and wondering whether he'd have to come round every day to help Frances access her footage.

"Oh, I know you say that, but cats are very supple, aren't they? Bendy."

An image of the horribly stiffened and definitely unbendy body of Jess's cat suddenly filled Ryan's mind, but he soon dismissed it when Frances squealed with delight as he successfully double-clicked on the footage. There, straight away, was a hedgehog—a large one, snuffling around the feeding station with surprisingly speedy movements.

"Look, Ryan, he's going in!" said Frances. "He's going to eat!"

As she spoke, someone knocked on the front door. Frances didn't look away from the screen. The knock came again.

"Aren't you going to answer that?"

"No, it'll only be someone trying to sell me new windows or something."

That wasn't unlikely. Frances's windows were in a right old state with their peeling paint. They looked distinctly drafty. And as for her guttering . . .

The knock came again. Ryan wheeled himself over to the front window to take a look. "It's Tara. She's got her daughter with her."

"What on earth do they want?"

"Maybe it's something to do with the hedgehog highway. She seemed pretty keen at your meeting."

"She did, didn't she?" said Frances. "I'd better see what she wants, then. Stop the film going, will you? I don't want to miss anything."

Ryan went back over to the laptop and paused the black-and-white footage, just at the point where the large hedgehog left the feeding station, presumably having eaten its fill. Wait a minute. Was that another hedgehog just coming into the frame? He had a strong temptation to restart the video to check it out, but Frances was talking to Tara now, their voices reaching him through the half-open door.

"She's off school with a headache. Oh, no, don't worry, it's nothing contagious. Only, the thing is, I've got a job interview this afternoon, and I can't take her with me. I'd ask Jess to look after her for a couple of hours, but I think she has already got enough on her plate at the moment, don't you?"

The door opened wider and Hermie walked in.

"What are you watching?" she asked Ryan, sitting herself down on Frances's vacated chair and reaching for the mouse.

"Well," Ryan started to say, "Frances was watching that too, so we'd better . . ."

But he broke off, shocked by what Hermie's click on the video revealed.

"Fighting hedgehogs," said Hermie.

They were fighting. Or rather, the larger hedgehog was attacking the smaller hedgehog which had just appeared at the feeding station, attempting to drive it away.

"Shit," said Ryan, momentarily forgetting about Hermie. "The poor little bugger."

"Who's a poor little bugger?" asked Frances, coming into the room and taking a look. "Oh! Oh, no. That's awful. Make it stop."

"This happened last night, remember. You didn't see a dead hedgehog when you went out there today, did you? So it must be all right," Ryan said.

"Unless it's crawled off somewhere else to die. Animals do that. You didn't see a dead or injured hedgehog in your garden, did you, dear?"

Hermic shrugged. "I haven't been out there. I've been on my Xbox."

"Your computer? With a headache?" Frances frowned. "That doesn't sound very sensible."

"It's not that bad. Bad enough to be off school, but mostly I'm tired."

She looked it, Ryan thought. She'd probably been up late, gaming without her mother's knowledge. Those dark circles round her eyes caused by lack of sleep were all too familiar to him.

"I could go and check for the hedgehog in your garden," Hermie offered. "It might be asleep in all those weeds."

"Well, all right. But don't wake it up if you find it. Hedgehogs are nocturnal."

"I know."

"Confident child, isn't she?" Frances said wryly as they heard Hermie let herself out of the back door.

Ryan wasn't so sure. He thought Hermie's confidence could be born out of neglect. Or if not quite neglect, then from being left to her own devices more than most children of her age were. Which just about described his own childhood.

Ryan hadn't realised his mother was different to other children's mothers until he was around six or seven years old and school friends had begun to invite him round to their houses for birthday parties or for tea. Friends' mums smiled at him. Asked him what his favourite pizza toppings were. Gave him sweets or cakes as a treat. Didn't complain when he and his friends got a bit overexcited or made a mess. It had consecutively blown his mind and caused him to draw into himself even more than ever at home. If she'd noticed, his mother had never said anything about it.

"I don't know why she likes thrashing about at those weeds so much," Frances said. "I quite like them as they are."

"They'll soon grow back."

"I suppose so."

The video footage came to an end. Ryan thought about Hermie's obvious confidence around technology and had an idea. "Hermie would probably be able to help you play any footage you get," he suggested. "She seems very confident with computers." And she and Frances might be company for each other.

"Kids all are these days, aren't they?" Frances said. "Jess's little boy would probably make a better job of it than me. It's a good idea, though."

"What is?" Ryan smiled. "Jess bringing Toby round to sort out your computer problems?"

Frances tapped him on the arm. "No, silly. Me asking Hermie to help. Strange name, isn't it?"

"Probably short for Hermione. I think she'd be up for it. Everyone likes to feel useful."

Frances looked at him. "You've been very useful to me lately, Ryan."

Ryan thought he detected pity in her regard and started manoeuvring his chair back from the computer. "Good. But now I'd better go. Physiotherapy appointment."

"Is it doing any good, the physiotherapy?"

"Honestly? I don't think so, no."

Frances put a hand on his shoulder. Gave him a squeeze. "I'm so sorry."

He couldn't bear anyone to pity him. Not even Frances. "Me too. Look, about that hedgehog. It might be an idea to investigate possible rescue centres in case it turns up with an injury. I'm sure Hermie can help you google when she comes in."

"Good idea. See you soon, Ryan."

20

The puppy was tearing at full pelt around Jess's garden, weaving around plant pots, ducking behind the midlife-crisis motorcycle Michael had bought two years ago and never ridden again after a near collision with a lorry on the motorway. Ever since then, the bike had sat, covered in a tarpaulin, beneath which—unbeknown to Jess and her family—a mother hedgehog had successfully raised a litter of hoglets the previous summer. One of these hoglets—now a slightly underweight juvenile—was currently asleep in the depths of an overgrown laurel bush next to the fence. It was about to have its life significantly shaken up.

Having chased a blackbird from the garden with much barking, the puppy moved on to attempt to nip at the legs of Michael's favourite jeans hanging on the washing line. Jess had almost given up trying to stop him doing any of these things, although she supposed she should summon the energy to rescue Michael's jeans before Patch shredded them. But she didn't want to do anything to draw Toby's attention back to her, because for once, she wasn't the focus of his attention. The dog's antics were entertaining him. In fact, he was sitting on a blanket on the lawn, laughing his head off. Not crying, not holding his arms out for her to hold him, but actually laughing. It felt like a miracle.

"Oh, Jess, Toby's gorgeous," said her friend Gina, who had popped round for a cup of tea to meet him. "Almost edibly gorgeous, if you know what I mean, with those eyelashes and those dimples. I'm so very happy for you. It could easily have turned out differently, couldn't it?"

It was so good to see Gina—who was still mourning her mother—smiling, enjoying the sunshine, that Jess didn't feel she could mention how dead she felt inside. How her brain told her how cute Toby looked, sitting there on the blanket in his stripey T-shirt, laughing, but her icy heart stopped her from feeling much about it at all.

And if she couldn't tell her very best friend how she really felt, then who could she tell? "It's good to see you smiling," she said instead, and Gina's eyes instantly filled with tears.

"I haven't done a lot of that lately, have I?"

"I'm so sorry, I didn't mean to . . ."

"No, it's okay. Whenever I do smile, I remember Mum's gone and feel guilty. Which is ridiculous, because Mum wouldn't mind me smiling, would she? And she'd have adored this. She'd have loved to have been here to meet the newest member of your family."

Sudden tears filled Jess's own eyes. "She would."

"But maybe she's up there somewhere, smiling down on us."

Or maybe Sheila was up there somewhere, screaming, *What the hell's wrong with you, Jess?* For Sheila would have sensed something was wrong, had she been here. Though to be fair, so would Gina if she hadn't been submerged in her grief.

Maybe Jess ought to just say it. Tell Gina she couldn't seem to love Toby. Couldn't feel anything for him at all except despair and a strong longing to push him away. Send him back, like a rescued dog who's too much to cope with.

"Listen, I really have to go," Gina said. "I've got an appointment at the solicitors, and you know what they're like. About a thousand pounds an hour. Let me know if there's anything of Mum's you'd like. I know you always liked her little painting of the Norfolk Broads."

The sound of Gina's departing car had barely faded away before the puppy began to bark dementedly at something at the bottom of the garden. *Shit. What now?* Jess glanced down at Toby to see his smile vanish.

"Mama!"

He was safe in the middle of the lawn. For once Jess ignored him and carried on down the garden to investigate. And found the dog terrorising an obviously young hedgehog, which had curled up in a tight ball at the base of the laurel bush.

"Leave it, Patch!" Jess yelled at the dog, trying to yank it away.

The dog ignored her, attempting to pick the hedgehog up in its jaws.

"Leave it!" screamed Jess, aware of Toby's cries becoming louder. The hedgehog was going to end up dead. In desperation, she shoved the dog away, causing him to yelp. As he backed off, she picked the hedgehog up and instantly dropped it again, its prickles like needles on her fingers. *Shit, oh shit.* Toby was there now, gripping her skirts, crying loudly. He'd probably seen her push the puppy. *She'd hurt a puppy!* The thought brought tears to her eyes. She would never normally do something like that. And now Patch made another lunge towards the bloody hedgehog. She needed help. She bloody well needed help!

Jess scooped Toby up into her arms and ran up the lawn and out to the street.

21

Ryan had just returned home in a taxi from an appointment with his consultant, Mr. Harker.

"I'm not going to walk again, am I?" he'd challenged the man. "That's what you're trying to tell me."

Mr. Harker had steepled his fingers. "There was always only a slim chance that you would, Ryan. I think I was very clear about that. But now, given your lack of progress since your last review . . ."

"I'm fucked?"

Mr. Harker regarded him, his expression sympathetic but unruffled. "Ryan, giving patients the news that they'll never have the use of their legs again is the worst part of my job. Hearing how they're living their best life, despite having received that news, is the best part. There are still so many things open to you, so many things you can still do. Why not try and turn this into a new chapter?"

"What, the one where I become a gold-medal-winning Paralympian?" Ryan asked sarcastically.

Mr. Harker shrugged. "An ordinary guy taking pleasure from life would do me."

What was there to take pleasure from, really, though? The most interesting thing in his sodding life at the moment was helping a lonely woman watch videos of hedgehogs eating. *Jesus.*

"Take advantage of all the help available to you, Ryan. Join as many support groups as you can find. Learn all the tricks and techniques you can to help with life in a wheelchair. Use your insurance money to convert your car and adapt your home. You're a journalist, aren't you? You can still write, albeit in a different way. Find that way. Your way."

Christ, if Harker didn't shut up, Ryan was going to sweep all the neat papers off the guy's desk. Bellow like a cornered bear. Deliberately overturn his wheelchair in the hopes of leaving himself lying in a tangled mess on the pristine carpet.

He had to get out. Now. Except he'd never be able to make a quick fucking exit again, would he?

"Thank you for everything you've done," he said, backing his wheelchair up and turning it to face the door.

Mr. Harker sprang to his feet to open the door for him. From now on, people would always spring to their feet to open doors for him.

"Goodbye, Ryan, and good luck."

Luck? What did luck have to do with anything?

He'd got to the appointment via a prebooked taxi. The same chirpy driver ferried him home again, unloading the wheelchair from the boot when they arrived at Hilltop Place. "Want me to see you inside, mate?"

"No, thanks, I'm good."

It was a lie. The guy knew it was a lie. He wasn't *good* by any definition of the word. But he could get himself indoors without help, thank you very much.

"Okay, mate. See you again."

Not if Ryan could help it. "Yes, thank you again."

"No problem."

At last—at long last—the taxi driver departed, taking his unwanted cheer with him. But before Ryan could make a move towards the house, someone called out to him. Jess.

"Ryan. Ryan!"

She was clutching a bawling Toby to her, looking panicked. "Can you help me, please? The dog's got hold of a hedgehog in the garden, and I can't get him off. It's a really small one. I'm afraid he's going to kill it. Either that or injure himself on the spines."

"What good d'you think I'll be?" he wanted to say. Or, *"How the hell d'you expect me to sort it out from my wheelchair?"*

But Jess had already turned back towards her house, apparently confident he would help. So he found himself following her.

Inside the garden, the puppy was yapping and springing up and down in front of a bush at the far end of a narrow path Ryan couldn't access in his chair. Jess looked pale-faced and panicked, yelling ineffectually at the dog. Ought he to offer to hold her little boy while she dealt with the situation? No, that felt far too passive. Besides, Toby was already in a state. If Ryan held him, he'd become catatonic.

Ryan had never owned a dog, neither his mother nor his ex-wife being animal lovers, and with his work always taking him away. But he had befriended friends' dogs, and those he'd encountered while reporting abroad—even army dogs. He'd witnessed the techniques the owners of the dogs had used to train them. Food and enthusiasm seemed to be key. Though whether either of these would eclipse the lure of a hedgehog was another question. Still, it was worth a try.

Moving his wheelchair as close as possible, Ryan reached into his jacket pocket for the sandwich he'd taken with him to the appointment in case he was kept waiting—the sandwich he'd had no appetite to eat. He'd packed it in an old bread bag, and now he took it out and removed the ham and cheese filling, trying—and failing—to remember the dog's name. Then, thankfully, Jess saved him by using it, her voice filled with desperation.

"Leave it, Patch! Leave it!"

Patch. Of course.

"Patch!" he called loudly with as much enthusiasm as he could muster. "I've got something for you. Yummy cheese and ham! Come and see, boy! Here, Patch! Come here!"

He crackled the waxed bread bag for good measure as he spoke, redoubling his vocal efforts when the dog turned, waving the ham and cheese enticingly, and against all the odds, it worked. Patch left the hedgehog to come and see what all the fuss was about, and the second his collar was within arm's reach, Ryan grabbed hold of it and held on fast.

"Have you got a plant pot to put over the hedgehog until you can get this one on the lead?" he called to Jess.

"Oh, good idea," she called back, her voice barely audible over Toby's crying. And he saw her go off in search of one as Patch struggled to get out of his grasp to return to the hedgehog.

"*Shh*, boy," Ryan said, hoping the collar wouldn't slip over the dog's head. "You'll hurt yourself."

Soon Jess had successfully covered the hedgehog and returned with the dog's lead.

"Mama's going to put you down for just a minute, Toby," Jess said. "Just while she puts Patch's lead on."

She put the boy down on the grass. There was a moment's shocked silence as Toby registered what had happened; then he flopped down onto the ground, screaming.

"It's only for a moment, Toby, I promise," said Jess, looking as if she didn't know what to do first—see to her son, see to the dog, or check on the hedgehog.

"Perhaps it would be best to put Patch indoors," Ryan suggested. "I'll keep an eye on Toby."

"Of course," Jess said. "Yes. I won't be . . ."

"And maybe bring a box to put the hedgehog in if you've got one? And a pair of gardening gloves?"

"Right."

While Jess hurried off to carry out his instructions, Ryan tried using the same bright-voiced tactic on Toby he'd used on the dog.

"Hey, Toby, I just saw a big red butterfly. It nearly landed right on your nose! Want to help me find some more butterflies? I bet you can spot more than I can."

"No, sod off, you pathetic git," Toby's plaintive cries seemed to say. And soon Toby tottered up the garden path after Jess, slapping his hands against the closed back door.

Dog secured, Jess soon reemerged with a cardboard box.

"The gardening gloves are in the shed," Jess said. "Are you going to help Mama find them, Toby?" She headed for the shed, Toby trotting after her like a noisy shadow.

Ryan could do nothing but sit and watch, feeling completely useless.

Eventually Jess was back at the hedgehog's side, gloves on, box at the ready. "The poor thing's still rolled up into a ball," she said. "I can't tell if it's injured or not. Come on, Toby, let's take the poor little hedge-hog over to Ryan, shall we? No, don't pull at the box. We don't want to hurt the hedgehog, do we?"

Jess placed the box on Ryan's lap and bent to pick Toby up. "I can't see any signs of injury, can you?"

Ryan looked down at the spiky ball. "It's hard to tell with it curled up like that, but there's no blood on the cardboard, which is a good sign. It's very small, though, for this time of year, isn't it? It'll never survive hibernation if it stays that weight."

"Oh dear. What should we do, d'you think?"

"I think we need to take it to a rescue centre. It could have a virus or something. They say if they're out in the daylight, there's probably something wrong with them."

"Where's the nearest rescue centre? I haven't got a clue."

Ryan pulled his phone out of his pocket and did a search. "There's one about four miles away."

"Right," Jess said. "Well, if I'm taking it, I'd better do it straight away, so I can get back by the time Stella finishes school. Are you busy, or could you come with me to give me directions?"

Ryan stared at her, his thoughts suddenly scattered to the four winds, but Jess was too busy disentangling Toby's fingers from her hair to notice his scrutiny.

When she'd finished and he still hadn't answered, she looked at him. "You're busy, aren't you? Sorry, I didn't mean to assume that . . ."

That because he was in a wheelchair he had nothing to do. "Wouldn't you rather ask someone else?"

She frowned. "Who? Michael's at work, none of my friends could get here in time. I could ask Frances, I suppose, if you can't make it."

"No, I can make it. I mean, I'm not busy or anything." He looked at her, making up his mind, deciding to stop being suspicious that she was only asking him to go with her out of pity. "Sure, let's do it."

22

Jess would have liked to have curled up in a ball like the hedgehog, untouchable, safe. To wait until the coast was clear so she could make her escape. Instead, she was dashing to the rescue centre before the school run, in charge of three needy beings when she was the neediest of the lot.

No, that wasn't fair. Ryan wasn't really needy. Though she'd sensed a pile of vulnerability as he'd transferred himself from the wheelchair to the car seat.

She probably should have taken the hedgehog by herself. She wasn't sure why she hadn't. But then she was never really by herself any longer—Toby was always there, watching her, making sure she wasn't going anywhere without him. Maybe that's why she'd wanted Ryan along. As a distraction.

Instinctively, Jess liked Ryan. Despite the feeling that he was as prickly as the hedgehog currently in the box on the back seat of the car. But who wouldn't be prickly when their entire life had transformed in the blink of an eye? She'd like to know more about him. To sit down with him and ask gentle questions about what had happened. But questions were tricky. They were usually a two-way process. You asked a question, and the other person asked a question back. And if she started answering questions about herself, the whole flimsy-card-house construction of her current life would come crashing right down. And she didn't know how she'd deal with the fallout of that. Maybe it was the same for Ryan. No, it was definitely the same for Ryan. Perhaps that's why they got along.

"Thanks for coming with me."

"That's okay. At the risk of sounding pathetic, it's nice to get out."

"I know what you mean. Sometimes I think the kitchen, garden, and the route to Stella's school are my entire world. Oh, not forgetting the supermarket, of course. That's in there too, most days."

"Didn't you go to the Dinosaur Park the other week?"

Jess glanced quickly in Ryan's direction and detected a teasing sparkle in his eyes.

"Ha! Six hours of trying to get Stella to leave the splash area before she froze solid, and then comforting Toby because he was scared to death by fibreglass dinosaurs. How could I have forgotten that particular pleasure?" Jess heard her voice wobble at the end of the tirade. Felt Ryan looking at her.

"Mama?" said Toby, because she'd said his name, but at least he wasn't crying.

"Didn't you like the dinosaurs, then, Toby?" asked Ryan over his shoulder, but Toby didn't answer him. As yet, he hadn't spoken to anyone outside the immediate family.

"He did not. But I suppose they must be scary, mustn't they, if you're not quite two years old and you don't know about dinosaurs?"

"He'll probably grow up to be a paleontologist," said Ryan.

Jess laughed, then abruptly stopped laughing, because if that theory were true—that you became the thing that traumatised you as a child—then Stella would probably become a social worker or a psychotherapist, some profession where she could draw on the trauma of being usurped by an unwanted brother.

"Are you all right?" asked Ryan.

"Better not ask me that when I'm driving," she said. "Not if you want to get there in one piece."

"Okay," he agreed. "But anytime you fancy chatting over a cup of the disgusting cheap coffee my mother insists on buying, I'll be happy to listen. If you think speaking to an embittered ex–foreign correspondent who's coming to terms with being paralysed for good would be of any help to you."

"Is it definite now, then? The paralysis?" she asked. "Have they told you so?"

"Yes. This morning, actually."

"God, Ryan, I'm so sorry."

What right did she have really to feel so sorry for herself when people like Ryan were going through things like this? Compared to never walking again, her problems were nothing.

Except, they didn't feel like nothing to her.

There was a sudden sound in the car like a drawn-out fart. At first Jess assumed it had issued from Toby, but when she glanced quickly in Ryan's direction, she found him looking hugely embarrassed.

"Apologies, I'm afraid my colostomy bag makes noises every once in a while. There's absolutely nothing I can do about it."

She shrugged. "Then there's nothing to apologise for, is there? I think the turning's near here, isn't it?"

"Yes, you need to take the next turning on the right. Then there's a track on the right shortly afterwards which leads to the sanctuary."

They saw cats everywhere as they drew into the sanctuary car park. Cats in the sunshine, cats on top of fences and gates, cats up trees.

"Think she's got room for hedgehogs?" said Ryan.

"I hope so," Jess said, opening the car door, averting her eyes from a stripey ginger cat. Although it would be nice, wouldn't it, to believe that these were all spirit cats, and Stripey had found a contented home here?

"Hello there. How can I help you?" A blonde-haired woman wearing brown dungarees emerged from an overgrown path, wiping her hands on a towel.

"We've brought a hedgehog for you to take a look at. My dog got hold of it. We can't tell whether it's injured, and it's very small."

"Right. Well, let's have a look, shall we? I'm Miriam, by the way. Want to bring your son to see the little guy settled in?"

"Yes, please. But is it accessible for my friend's wheelchair?"

Miriam's face fell. "No, I'm terribly sorry, it's not. It's barely accessible for anyone, to be honest. The path's overgrown, as you see. And stacked with old hutches and bags of feed. We're always too busy with our rescue work to do much sorting out."

"It's okay," Ryan said from inside the car. "I'll wait for you here."

Jess thought about protesting, but something about the set of Ryan's jaw stopped her. "All right. I can't be very long, anyway, because of getting back for Stella."

"Sorry, love," Miriam said into the car to Ryan as Jess unclipped Toby from his car seat.

"It's fine," Ryan said, but his voice sounded flat, and Jess felt bad as she followed Miriam down the winding—and yes, crowded—path, carrying Toby.

"I'm really sorry about your friend," Miriam said over her shoulder. "If he ever feels like volunteering here, we'd make sure the paths were cleared for him. Tell him I said so. We're always on the lookout for volunteers. Now, let's take a look at this little chap, shall we?"

She put on a pair of tough-looking gloves, reached into the box, and expertly pulled the hedgehog out, placing him on the examination table.

When Toby stretched out a hand towards the creature, she said, "No, sweetheart, we don't want to touch him, do we? He's got very sharp prickles. Fly strike too, by the looks of him."

"Fly strike?" Jess asked.

"Yes. See those things round his eyes like grains of rice? Those are fly eggs. If we don't get them off, they'll hatch into maggots. And we don't want that, do we? He's got ticks as well, poor thing. He's infested."

Jess held Toby tightly, trying not to think about the eggs hatching into maggots. Wondering whether Patch had picked up some of the ticks. She'd better add checking that out to her list of things to do. "How will you get the eggs off?"

"Good old-fashioned tweezers. That and some saline solution. That's the best way. Takes a bit of time, though."

"Will he be all right after that?"

"I think this one might be a she, actually. And yes, I don't see why not. She needs feeding up before she goes into hibernation, but I'll get plucking, and then she can join the other hedgehogs in the rehabilitation centre. Want to take a look while you're here?"

Jess thought of Ryan waiting for her in the car. "Well, maybe just a quick look," she said.

The rehabilitation centre was housed in a long, low shed next door to the examination room. It consisted of around fifty animal carriers stacked on top of one another, each containing a hedgehog, some newspaper, and some bowls for food and drink. It was pretty smelly, and Jess could only imagine how long it took to feed the hedgehogs and clean all the carriers out.

What must it be like to be a poorly hedgehog attacked by a dog, shut away in a box, and transported by car before being prodded and poked and placed into an animal carrier, surrounded by the smells of so many other hedgehogs? Standing there holding Toby, trying to remain unaffected by the ripe smell and the overwhelming sorrow of underweight hedgehogs, orphaned hedgehogs, and hedgehogs with missing limbs due to accidents, Jess thought she knew. It reminded her of all the pictures of children in the adoption materials she and Michael had received—all those hopeful faces waiting for forever homes and new starts they shouldn't have to make. A shopping catalogue of children.

Jess would have given them all a home, had she been able to.

Miriam was speaking, saying something about how often they had to feed the babies. How it led to a lot of sleepless nights, and that was very familiar to Jess too. She hadn't had a full night's sleep since Toby's arrival.

"Can we come back?" she asked. "Or call you? To find out how our hedgehog is doing?"

"Of course you can. And if you know anyone who'd like to volunteer, bring them along too. The more the merrier. We have all sorts of roles going begging—feeding, cleaning out, handyman jobs, fundraising. You name it."

"I'll see if I can think of anybody," Jess promised. "Thank you."

She'd almost reached the car when she realized she ought to have left a donation. But it was too late to go back now. She was already running late. She'd send something in the post.

"How was it?" Ryan asked as she clipped Toby into his car seat.

"Moving. Smelly. Look, I'm afraid I don't have time to take you home first before collecting Stella from school. I'm really sorry."

"That's okay," said Ryan. "Although your daughter hates me."

"She doesn't hate you. You just remind her of Stripey Cat, that's all," Jess said, starting the car and looking carefully for cats before she reversed out of the parking space.

"Patch hasn't helped her forget that at all?"

"Not entirely. She does like Patch, I think, but Toby also likes Patch, and Stella doesn't want to be like Toby in any way." She forced a smile. "But it's early days. I'm sure they'll get there. Just like our little hedgehog. Which is a girl, by the way, not a boy."

"Hilary Hedgehog?"

Jess's smile became easier. "Hortense?"

"Hannah."

"Hildegard."

Ryan laughed. "Hildegard it is."

In the end, Stella was late coming out of school. And then her new friend's mum had brought their dog with her again, and Stella had to go over to pet it. Aware of Ryan waiting in the car and wishing her daughter had as much enthusiasm for Patch as she did for the cute dog she was petting, Jess tried and failed to imagine bringing Patch on the school run.

"Come on, Stella. Sweetheart, we need to get home."

Perhaps the dog's owner picked up on the tone of a desperate mother trying to keep her voice calm when she felt close to exploding, because she told her daughter they had to go too.

"Can Jasmine come and play soon, Mummy?" asked Stella as they finally walked away.

"Of course," said Jess, her heart sinking at the prospect. "I'll speak to her mummy to sort it out."

"Jasmine hasn't got a daddy," said Stella. "She's got two mummies."

"Is that so?"

"Yes. And the dog's a girl, so that's four girls."

"That's nice."

"Before Toby and Patch came, we were two girls and two boys," Stella said. "Then Stripey Cat got run over, so Daddy was the only boy. But now we're two girls and three boys."

"Good maths," Jess said, her hip on fire from having Toby resting on it. If she put him down to walk, it would take even longer to get back to the car, but she didn't think she had much choice.

"Are you going to walk now, Toby?" she said, attempting to put some enthusiasm into her voice, remembering how Ryan had lured Patch away from the hedgehog.

She set him down on his feet. Instantly he began to wail. "Up, Mama. Up!"

"I wish it was still just you, me, Daddy, and Stripey Cat, Mummy."

Jess suddenly wished that too. So badly she wanted to sit down on the pavement next to Toby and bawl her eyes out. And because that made her feel guilty as hell, she snapped at Stella. "Well, you need to stop wishing that, don't you, Stella? Because Toby is part of this family now. And Patch."

Stella looked shocked. Then she began to cry and ran off towards the car park.

"Stella, wait!" Jess shrieked, thinking of the dangers of moving cars. Of blind spots and people who double-parked, restricting vision. "Wait for Mummy!"

But Stella flew on, her plaits streaming out behind her, so Jess snatched a still-bawling Toby up and ran after her, the pain in her hip forgotten.

When she reached the car, Ryan had his door open, his legs swiveled outside as if he'd tried to make chase.

"She went behind that minibus in the corner."

"Thanks. Will you hold Toby for me?" She thrust Toby at him, not giving him the chance to reply, running across the car park.

Stella was indeed behind the minibus. Crouched down in the dirt, crying. When she saw Jess, she wriggled even further away, pushing herself back between the vehicle and the brick wall which formed the boundary of the car park. Clearly, she didn't plan on coming out anytime soon. Stella could only hope Ryan would be okay with Toby, whose protests she could hear from the other side of the car park.

She'd been a good mother once. The type of mother who listened to her child. Took the time to explain things gently, in words that were easily understood. That was the type of parenting Stella was used to. The type she responded to. The only problem was, it was very time-consuming. You had to be very on the ball to do it effectively. Not weary beyond belief, staring into an abyss of guilt and desperation.

Jess squatted down on the tarmac, her back against the wall, and closed her eyes for a moment, trying to reclaim control and calm. She had been that gentle, patient mother very recently. She could be that mother again.

"Stella, sweetheart, Mummy's very sorry she shouted at you."

Stella had her arms locked around her legs, her face pressed into her knees. She didn't respond.

"I know things haven't been easy for you lately, baby. They haven't been easy for Mummy either. Or for Daddy. Or Toby. But they will get better, I promise."

They'd better.

"We'll get used to each other very soon. Toby will settle down, and then . . ."

Stella looked up. Her face was ravaged by tears. Her mouth was a mutinous line, her eyes—so like Jess's own sometimes it was like looking in a mirror—flashing with fury. "No! I hate Toby. I want him to go away."

Patience. Understanding. Deep breaths.

"That's not very helpful, is it, sweetheart? I know, let's think of something nice for us all to do together this weekend. How about a picnic in the garden? Daddy could put the tent up. Or maybe we could drive somewhere. The seaside, perhaps? You love the seaside, don't you? And I don't think Patch has ever seen the sea before."

Stella started to look interested. She'd always adored going to a beach. "Can we leave Toby at home?" she asked.

"No, of course we can't leave Toby at home."

Mutiny returned to Stella's face. "Don't want to go, then."

Patient Jess vanished like a popped balloon. "Right, then, none of us will go. We'll stay at home all day. And there'll be no television for selfish girls."

She got to her feet. "If you don't come out of there in ten seconds, Mummy won't be inviting Jasmine to play either, understood? I'm going to start counting now. Ten, nine, eight . . ."

Stella came out from behind the minibus at three, tears pouring down her face again, a picture of misery.

"Please, Mummy," she kept saying as they trooped back to the car, her voice wobbling as she struggled to keep up with Jess. "Please."

Jess wasn't sure whether Stella was begging for Jasmine to be invited, for TV, for the trip to the seaside, or all three. She only knew that she felt ashamed of her outburst, and that if Toby hadn't still been screaming his head off, and if Ryan weren't so obviously struggling, she would have taken her distraught daughter into her arms and hugged her close. Cried along with her. Told her she was sorry.

But instead, she just opened the car door and told her, "In you get, Stella. Now. We need to go home."

Then she took Toby from Ryan's arms and clipped him in too. Got into the car herself. Gripped the steering wheel with both hands while she waited for Ryan to lift his legs back into the car, one at a time, the children's cries blasting her from the back of the car.

"I'm so sorry about this, Ryan."

"It's no problem, Jess," Ryan said.

But he was wrong; it was a problem. Because on the way back, a lorry was double-parked, unloading a delivery of bread to a convenience store, combining with the school-run traffic to create a jam. And then, when they finally reached Hilltop Place, she had to get the wheelchair out of the boot and folded down. Ryan's transfer from the car to the chair to supervise. All with Stella and Toby still both crying in the back of the car.

Jesus. It was a living hell.

At last, he was in the wheelchair. "Thanks, Jess."

She wasn't sure what for. She'd dragged him out, made him wait for her in the car twice, forced him to hold her bawling son. She was pretty sure it couldn't be described as a fun afternoon out. "Thank you for coming with me."

"No problem."

"See you soon."

Not if I see you first, she could imagine him thinking. *Not if I see you first.*

23

Frances picked up the telephone receiver—she still had the old-fashioned type of phone with the curled-up cord—and dialed the number for the library where Helen Hedges worked.

A man answered. Frances hadn't been to the library for years, yet she still knew who he was. Could picture him exactly because of what she thought of as his hot-chocolate voice—a rich, velvety voice which would surely have suited him for a career as a voice-over actor, better than that of a librarian. Goodness, he must be long overdue to retire. But lucky Helen, hearing that voice every working day. Must make a very welcome change to listening to that twit of a husband of hers.

"Hello," said Frances, "this is Frances Mathews. May I speak to Helen, please?"

"You certainly may," said Hot Chocolate. "Right after she's finished bidding the babies from the Baby Bounce and Rhyme Hour goodbye. Are you able to hold for a moment?"

I'd hold on for more than a moment if it was him I was holding on to, Frances thought, only realising she hadn't answered his question when he asked, "Hello? Are you still there?"

"Yes, I'm still here. And yes, I can wait. I want to speak to her about hedgehogs, you see. It's very important."

"That is important," Hot Chocolate said. "They're such wonderful creatures."

She didn't detect a hint of *"Daft old bat, better humour her"* in his voice, and Frances sincerely hoped he wasn't patronising her and wishing he could get back to his book-shelving or cataloguing or whatever it was librarians did now that they didn't have to actually issue and date-stamp books any longer.

"They really are, aren't they?" she gushed. "I've got cameras set up in my garden to watch them feed. I put food out for them, you see."

"How wonderful. You're really doing your bit for conservation. Oh, I see Helen is free now, so I'll just get her attention before someone else claims her. Good luck with your hedgehogs. I wish you many fulfilling sightings of them."

"Thank you."

Frances waited, feeling cheered by the encounter, trying to remember how far away the library was. Perhaps she ought to get herself down there. Find out whether Hot Chocolate was married, and whether he'd be interested in coming round to view her hedgehog footage sometime.

"Frances? It's Helen."

"Oh, Helen. Hello. Sorry to interrupt you at work."

"That's okay. We never seem to see each other at home, do we? How can I help?"

"I was wondering whether you'd decided to support the hedgehog-highway project."

"Well," Helen said, sounding awkward, "if it was left to me, I'd support it one hundred percent. But Justin likes everything to be neat and tidy, you see, and as he says, we did pay rather a lot of money to have our fences replaced, so we're not keen to make holes in them. So I'm afraid . . ."

"My husband was a bully too," Frances blurted out in a rush. "Just like yours. Never let me do anything I wanted to do."

"Well, I . . ."

"I had to find ways to do things behind his back. It wasn't easy, I can tell you. But at least you've got your job. And Hot Chocolate."

Helen sounded confused. "Hot Chocolate?"

Frances thought it best not to explain and surged on. "It was different when I was first married; you were expected to just get on with things, no matter how unhappy you were. Lie in the bed you'd made, so to speak. But you don't have to do that these days."

There was a pause. "Thank you for your advice, Frances," Helen said eventually, with cool dignity. "But getting back to the hedgehog project, as I said at the meeting, I'm more than happy to support it in any way I can through my work. In fact, I've got a meeting next Wednesday lunchtime to discuss how the library and the primary school can collaborate on the project."

"Have you? That's wonderful."

"Yes, isn't it? I have several ideas to discuss with them. I'll let you know how it goes."

"Yes, please. And in the meantime, you will stop that husband of yours from putting out anything nasty like slug pellets, won't you? They're lethal for hedgehogs. And they've been made illegal now."

"Well, Justin certainly isn't the type to do anything illegal, Frances, so I'm sure you have no worry on that score."

Frances wasn't so sure herself. Justin Hedges probably had a stash of slug pellets in his garden shed, purchased before the ban came into operation. In fact, he was probably the type to increase his use of slug pellets if he was asked not to use them. That's certainly what Frances's husband would have done, anyway. Why did people have to be so nasty? So controlling? It made her so tired sometimes, it really did. When it wasn't making her so angry that she wanted to cross the road and key Justin Hedges's bloody car.

24

"You look so tired, Jessica. D'you want me to fly over?"

It was very tempting to say yes. To know that at the end of this video call, her mum would get busy booking a flight and arranging care for Derek, Jess's stepfather. Would be here within days to take over the reins. And that when the kids were in bed, maybe Jess could actually speak to somebody about how she felt. Somebody who loved her unconditionally and who wouldn't judge.

But she couldn't let her mum do it. Her stepfather's needs were so very much greater than her own, and her mother would need to find somebody she trusted to look after him. That wouldn't be easy at such short notice. Derek already lived such a limited life since his stroke only a year after he and Jess's mother had retired to Spain. He didn't deserve to be cared for by strangers. Or to lose the sunshine of her mum's company, no matter how much Jess might want to bask in that comforting warmth herself.

"No, Mum, I'm fine, honestly. Or I will be once things settle down. If worse comes to the worst, Michael can always ask his mother to come and stay."

Her mother's expression at this joke said it all. Michael's mother was a miserable human being who had always disapproved of Jess. Any visit from her was a depressing experience, and asking her to come now would make things a hundred times worse. She had frowned on their adoption plans from the start, and Jess didn't want her and her I-told-you-so attitude anywhere near Hilltop Place.

"I don't think that's a good idea, is it?" Jess's mother said now, looking even more worried, and Jess forced herself to smile.

"Just kidding, Mum. I'm not going to ask her to come. As far as she's concerned, everything's going swimmingly. And there's no need for you to worry, honestly. Like I said, I'll be fine."

But her mum still looked worried. Time to change the subject. "Did I tell you about the hedgehog-highway scheme we're setting up in the close?"

By the time Jess ended the call, the puppy was fast asleep in her lap, curled up nose to tail.

"You don't look like a vicious hedgehog persecutor like that, do you?" Jess said, stroking the fluffy softness of Patch's fur, delaying her return to the sitting room, because she could hear Toby crying and Michael doing his best to soothe him. Let him try for a bit longer.

The woman at the rescue centre had said Patch had done the hedgehog a favour, drawing their attention to it. That it might have died without intervention. Maybe Patch was a detector dog with the ability to sniff out illnesses?

"Is that it?" she asked Patch out loud. "Do you know when things are sick?"

Patch opened one cute eye to look at her, then closed it again.

Jess smiled. Against all the odds, the dog appeared to have wormed his way into her heart. He felt gorgeously warm against her, a super-soft hot water bottle, his body moving soothingly as he breathed in and out. Jess wasn't sure why it felt as if he were giving her a gift by choosing to sleep on her lap. Why, when Toby fell asleep on her, it felt as if he were taking from her. Her warmth. Her time. Her energy. Robbing her until she was spent.

Poor little sod.

Next door, his crying had grown louder.

Jess sighed. "Sorry, Patch," she said. "You'll have to come off. Duty calls."

She carefully picked him up, smiling at the cute whimper he made as she disturbed him, and placed him in the corner of the sofa, snuggled up to a cushion. Then she headed next door, where she found Stella scribbling all over a drawing she'd done, Toby crying in a corner, and Michael texting on his phone, apparently oblivious to the carnage.

"Michael," she said grumpily, picking Toby up, "can't you put that thing down?"

~

Sometimes, in the week that followed, it felt as if Patch's cheerfulness was the only thing that kept her going. That without his demands to be played with, let out in the garden, fed, or stroked, she might have gone back to bed after dropping Stella off at school. Toby wouldn't have minded if she had. He liked her being in bed—his captive playmate, right there where he could see her. When she was in bed, he brought her books to read to him. Toys to play with. Bounced up and down so she jiggled. Then he settled down to fall asleep in the crook of her arm.

Oh, yes, Toby would love it if she stayed in bed all day. But Jess felt so very tired she was afraid that, if she fell asleep, she might sleep right through school pickup time. So it helped to have the dog and his demands to keep her up and about. It was just a shame that Patch seemed to be at his worst behaviour when Michael came home from work, Stella was tired from school, and Jess was trying to cook tea. Five thirty always seemed to be the time Patch decided to chew a shoe or Stella's favourite toy, or once, to Michael's fury, the remote control for the TV.

"D'you think we need to take him to obedience classes?" Michael asked, searching online on his phone for a replacement for the remote.

"I'm sure we do. Though I don't know when we're going to fit that in, do you?" Jess had managed to ask civilly when she'd really wanted to yell, *"You bloody take him to obedience classes! Getting a dog was your stupid idea!"*

So the week lumbered on with, if anything, Toby becoming even more fretful than ever. From being relatively easy to please foodwise—a definite plus point Jess appreciated, even in the depths of her regret and despair—he suddenly became a picky eater, leaving most of his food on his plate, squirming like a colicky baby when she tried to feed him.

By Thursday morning, when Michael left early for a meeting, Jess was so exhausted she didn't wake up until nine fifteen. Fifteen minutes after Stella ought to have been at school.

As soon as she saw the time, Jess threw herself out of bed and dragged on a robe. Pulled it off and got dressed instead, reaching for the clothes she'd taken off the previous day.

"Stella," she called, running out onto the landing, "it's time to get up. We're late!"

When she received no reply, Jess went into Stella's room and dragged open the curtains. "Stella, you need to get up. We're late for school!" she shouted. Then she dashed into the bathroom to have a wee—because even useless, late mothers needed to have a wee—before going to get Toby up.

Why hadn't he woken her the way he always did? The way he'd done every day since his arrival. Why choose a school day to suddenly sleep like the dead?

"Toby? It's Mama. Time to wake up. We need to get you ready very quickly this morning because Stella is late for school. Toby?"

She pulled the curtain and saw Toby lying in bed with his mouth open, the bedclothes thrown off him, his face bright red.

"Toby?" Suddenly terrified, Jess lunged across the room to place a hand on his forehead. Jesus, he was burning up.

"Toby?" she said urgently, giving him the smallest of shakes. "Toby, can you hear me?"

He whimpered, but his eyes didn't open, his chest rising and falling rapidly as he breathed.

Wet flannels. She needed wet flannels. *No!* What was she thinking? She needed to call for an ambulance. And as soon as possible. Something was seriously wrong.

As she flew out of Toby's room, Stella's door opened. "Mummy?"

"Get dressed, Stella," she yelled. "Quickly. Toby's not well. I've got to take him to hospital."

But by the time she reached the bottom of the stairs, Stella still stood at the top, looking down at her, crying.

"Please, Stella, be a good girl for Mummy. Go and put some clothes on."

As she ran to get her phone from the kitchen, Patch jumped up at her, thinking it was a game.

"Get off, Patch!" she yelled, brushing him away, desperately trying to find her phone, moving drawings and washing-up gloves, wondering what to do with Stella. Michael would have to come home, take her to school. But where could she take her to wait? For she had to go with Toby, didn't she? She had to. He was likely ill because of her. She must have missed something while she'd been sleepwalking around, thinking only about herself. Some vital symptoms.

Her hands shook so badly they would barely function, but at last she managed to find the phone and tap the numbers out. Nine, nine, nine.

"Emergency. Which service do you require? Fire, police, or ambulance?"

"Ambulance. Quickly. Quickly."

"Just putting you through, madam."

Upstairs, Toby began to scream. Not the sorrowful wailing of the past few days—a wailing she hadn't read anything into, because he had cried so regularly since his arrival—but a real scream of distress.

"Ambulance. Which number are you calling from, please?"

For a moment, Jess's mind went blank. Then the number popped into her head, and she recited it.

"Can you give me your address, please, madam?"

She did so, impatiently, with a sense they were wasting time, though, of course, they would need her address.

"Is the patient breathing, madam?"

"Yes, but not very well. It's my son. He's burning up. He's almost two years old. I couldn't wake him at first, but now . . . Please come quickly. Please."

After she'd finished the call, she ran back up the stairs, then came down again to shut Patch away and open the front door, leaving it on the latch. Went back up the stairs, tripping over her own feet, smashing her knee on the banister, ignoring the pain as she forged onwards to get to Toby. She found him distraught, his face redder than ever, his little body arched upwards as if contorted by pain.

"Toby," she said. "Toby, it's Mama." But when she tried to hold him, her touch seemed to hurt him, his screams becoming louder still.

Sobbing, she remembered the cold, wet flannel she'd thought of five minutes previously. Picked Toby up and carried him out onto the landing, heading for the bathroom. Stella still stood in her bedroom doorway, wearing only a pair of knickers. "Get dressed," she said. "Please, sweetie. Please."

"Is Toby going to die?" Stella asked, and for just a moment, Jess wondered whether Stella wanted that.

"No," Jess said, hurrying to the bathroom. "He isn't going to die."

But Toby's body was so hot now she could feel it through her T-shirt, and a part of her thought that he might do just that—he might die.

He was struggling so much in his distress that it was difficult to hold him safely while she ran a flannel under the cold tap. And then, when she placed the wet flannel on his hot skin, he shrank away from it.

"Please, Toby," she said, "let Mama put it on you. It will help." Though she didn't know really whether it would help, and Stella still wasn't dressed, peering at them through the half-open bathroom door.

"Clothes, Stella!" she screamed, trying once again to press the flannel to Toby's face.

But he moved convulsively and was suddenly violently sick.

"Oh, God," she said. "Poor little boy. Poor little boy." She used the flannel to try to clean him, almost sobbing with relief when she heard a siren approaching. The ambulance. Thank God.

"Come on, Stella!" she cried, taking Toby carefully downstairs. By the time she reached the hall, the paramedics had let themselves in. The gravity of Toby's condition was obvious from their expressions.

"I've just got to take my daughter to a neighbour's house," she said, calling to Stella.

The little girl was still only wearing her knickers and a T-shirt, so Jess grabbed some leggings and socks from the floor, took her hand, and ran out of the front door. The ambulance had brought both Tara and Frances to their front doors to see what was happening.

"Will one of you take care of Stella?" Jess cried. "Toby's ill. I have to go with him."

"Sure," said Tara. "I can take her to school. Come on, Stella."

"Go on, darling. Mummy will see you later."

Stella went, sobbing and looking over her shoulder all the way. And all the way to the hospital in the ambulance, even as Jess watched the paramedic working on Toby and answered his questions as best she could, she couldn't stop thinking about Stella's tragic face. The appeal in her heartbroken blue eyes. *Don't leave me, Mummy. Don't leave me.*

25

From her mattress on the floor beside Toby's bed, Jess heard a trickle of soft voices drift in from the nurses' station. A stifled laugh. Footsteps squeaking on the linoleum. Other parents turning on their mattresses, fruitlessly seeking enough comfort and peace to sleep.

Toby was oblivious to it all, his slight body chock-full of drugs. Michael had spent most of the day with them, only leaving at 4:00 p.m. to collect Stella from Tara's house and to take her to his mother's fifty miles away. But now Jess was alone. Alone with only her conscience for company.

She had done this. Michael could say what he liked, the doctors and the nurses could repeat over and over again that bacterial meningitis can strike quickly, without warning. But whatever anybody said, it made no difference. Jess knew she was responsible. *She* hadn't noticed. *She* hadn't checked. *She* hadn't even bloody well cared. She'd been so busy resenting Toby's neediness that he had slid into this illness on her watch. A little boy who had done nothing more than want her, depend on her—no greater crime than that—and she had been so busy holding him at arm's length, even while he snuggled close, she could barely survive the crippling guilt of it.

As she'd done once before, she thought about Toby's drug-using parents, her imagination taking her to a squalid house and to Baby Toby in his cot, hungry and lying in his own filth, his cries unheeded. If his beginnings had truly been like that, then perhaps a sense of abandonment had been hardwired into his DNA. Was it any wonder he constantly searched her face? Not only for reassurance, but maybe also expecting to have his very worst fears confirmed?

And they had been. Because although Jess had held him, she had often done it against her will. And Toby must have sensed that, poor little sod. No wonder he'd cried; it was all he knew to do. He was a precious gift, this boy. A gift she'd longed and longed for. And ever since his arrival, Jess had chosen to exist in the past, lamenting the loss of the babies who hadn't lived. Constantly comparing their imaginary personalities with Toby's.

She had failed him so utterly and completely, and now it might be too late to do anything about it. He might die before she could give him an adoring smile and a loving hug.

Tears began to slide down Jess's cheeks. She wished she had someone she could call. Someone who would understand and accept her deepest guilt and shame. But she had no one. Not even Michael. If she tried to speak to Michael, she knew he'd just brush her fears and dark thoughts aside. Tell her nobody was perfect, that she was doing her best, that it wasn't easy, that nobody could have foreseen this. Anything to avoid an encounter with the dark, boiling pit of inadequacy she was floundering in, because to acknowledge it would require him to claim some of it for himself.

She couldn't pour it all out to her mother either, not while she was so far away in Spain, tied up caring for Jess's stepfather. And she couldn't confide in Gina while she was still grieving.

Briefly, as she lay there on the unyielding mattress, Jess thought of Ryan. Somehow, out of all the people she knew, it was easiest to imagine confiding in him. Probably because in him she recognised someone else who suffered. Someone else floundering in a mess of negative, self-blaming emotions. But it would hardly be fair to dump more darkness on him. And so, reluctantly, Jess let thoughts of speaking to Ryan slip away into the not-quite darkness of the hospital ward, to inhabit the unbearable loneliness of herself again.

The thin pillow beneath her head was damp. The temptation to give in to proper tears was strong. But she mustn't. Couldn't. Apart from anything else, it would disturb the other parents in the ward, and they were all suffering too. So she pressed her face into the pillow, stifling any shudders and trying to calm her breathing, praying to she knew not who. *Please. Please.*

Suddenly, she heard a movement in Toby's bed. Toby's legs, rustling the sheets. Toby's head, turning towards her.

"Mama?" he said in a small, weak voice.

"Toby?" she said, sitting up, going to him. "Sweetheart? I'm here. It's Mama; I'm here."

And suddenly, all at once, it happened, the way it had four years previously when she held Stella in her arms for the first time. Love. Swooping into every sinew and pore of her.

"Oh, Toby," she said, holding him, sobbing without restraint now, not even thinking about who might overhear, thanking someone—anyone—for this second chance.

Nurses came. Vital signs were checked. Caution was quietly advised, but their smiles said it all. Her boy was out of danger. There was room for hope.

In the days that followed, Jess felt as if she were walking a tightrope, waiting to see whether Toby had suffered brain damage or hearing loss, sleeping on the mattress beside his bed, showering only when she was sure he was fast asleep, her heart singing with her newly awakened feelings. Michael came as often as he could, offering to sleep at the hospital so she could go home to get a good night's sleep. But Jess declined all his offers of help, superstitiously believing that if she went away, the tide might turn on Toby's recovery again. Besides, Toby wanted her, not Michael. The two of them would need to work on that when she brought Toby home, but not now, not when he was still so weak.

In the evenings, Jess spoke to Stella on the phone, every phone call preceded by a hateful conversation with Michael's mother.

"The boy continues to make progress, then?"

The boy. Honestly. The woman spoke as if she were in a costume drama.

"Yes, Toby's recovering steadily now, thank you, Audrey. How's Stella?"

"She's all right. We've made good progress at teaching her to tidy up after herself. And she can hold a knife and fork properly now."

Jess pictured Stella receiving stern looks across the dinner table. Of Michael's mother saying, "We don't put our elbows on the table when we're eating, do we, Stella?"

"Michael and I are very grateful to you for having her at such short notice."

"I could hardly refuse, could I? She is my granddaughter. And none of this is her fault, after all."

Bloody bitch.

"Can I have a quick word with her please, Audrey?"

"I've just run a bath for her, actually. The water will be getting cold."

"I won't keep her very long."

"All right. Stella, it's your mother on the phone. Come and talk to her."

"Hello, darling, it's Mummy. How are you?"

"When can I come home, Mummy?"

"Daddy will come and fetch you on Saturday, sweetheart, okay? Grandma says you've been very good. I'm so proud of you."

"I don't like it here, Mummy. I want to come home."

"You'll be home very soon. I can't wait to see you. We'll do something very special when we're back together again, okay? Now why don't you go and have your lovely bath? I bet it's got bubbles and everything."

"Grandma doesn't have any bubbles. And there's nothing to play with."

Stella sounded tearful now, and Jess felt completely helpless, speaking to her from such a distance when really only a cuddle would make her feel better.

"Oh, sweetheart," she started to say, but then Audrey took the phone.

"It might be best if you didn't phone again this week, Jessica," she said. "It only seems to upset Stella, and her bath is getting cold. Let me know what time Michael's going to arrive on Saturday, won't you?"

Jess returned to Toby's bedside, reassuring herself that Stella would soon be home. That a few days of Victorian-style parenthood wouldn't traumatise her daughter for life.

Toby was breathing easily now, while he slept, his temperature almost back to normal. He was such a gorgeous little boy. Dark hair, dark eyes, long eyelashes. Having been so desperate to get away from him, now Jess could spend hours just gazing at him, drinking him in. In a way, so long as he continued to get better and he had no future complications, it had almost been worth his getting ill for her to wake up. It was awful to think such a thing, but somehow it felt true.

26

Michael was just getting into his car when Ryan hailed him from the drive. "I was so sorry to hear about Toby."

Michael nodded, hands on hips. "Thanks, it's been tough. He's on the mend now, though, thank God. I'm just on my way to the hospital, actually."

Ryan could see Patch scratching at the front window, barking his head off. Poor bugger. "If I can help out in any way with the dog, let me know."

"No offense, mate," said Michael, "but you can hardly take him for a walk, can you? And you can't stop him chewing everything in the house up. The bloody thing's just destroyed my best pair of trainers." He shook his head. "Jess was right. It was an idiotic idea to get a puppy. I think we'll have to give him up. But thanks for the thought, anyway." He looked at his watch. "I'd better get going. Jess will be wondering where I am."

Ryan wanted to say, *"Tell Jess . . ."* But what did he want to say to Jess? *"I hope Toby's all right? I hope you're not blaming yourself? I hope you don't mind your prick of a husband getting rid of your puppy?"*

Michael didn't wait to hear what he—a useless fucker in a wheelchair—had to say, anyway. He got in his car, turned the music on full blast, and waited for Ryan to move so he could drive off.

Ryan wheeled himself out onto the pavement and watched Michael reverse out, hating himself for responding when Michael waved. God, he was such a useless shit. Michael may have been offensive just now, but he was right. How the hell did he think he could take a lively dog like Patch out? It would have been much better if that land mine had finished him off. How, exactly, did he contribute to anything? What was the point of his existence?

"Ryan, come and see the latest footage! It's so exciting." Frances stood at her front door, dressed in her nightdress and a pair of green wellington boots.

She saw him looking. "Oh, don't mind this get-up. I've just been refilling the food bowls. Haven't bothered to get dressed yet. Hungry blighters, those hedgehogs. All of it gone—every scrap. Well, don't just stand there. Come in, come in. I can't wait for you to see this footage." She smiled. "If you're very lucky, I might make you a cup of coffee. I'll even wash up a cup. How about that for a deal?"

Against all the odds, Ryan found himself smiling. Only Frances could get away with telling him not to just stand there when he'd never stand anywhere in his life again. "You've managed to work out how to play back your footage, then?" he asked, propelling himself up her drive.

"Yes, Hermie showed me how to do it. Oh, I know you showed me, but Hermie doesn't mind showing me over and over again."

"Are you calling me impatient?"

"Wouldn't dare to insult you, Ryan. No, Hermie's taken a poor old lady under her wing, that's all. Says I could be an influencer, whatever that is. Sounds like an illness, doesn't it? She reckons I could make videos about what I'm doing to help save the hedgehogs. Spread the word, that sort of thing. Anyway, you go round. I'll bring your coffee out."

An influencer. Yes, Hermie might be right. Frances could never be anything but herself. She'd be a refreshing change from all those "Hi, guys" kids with their toothy smiles.

The coffee, when it came, looked like mud, but at least he didn't see any visible stains on the cup. Ryan took a tentative sip.

"Have you heard from the rescue place about how the little chap you took there is getting on?" asked Frances.

"No, Jess went inside with him, so they've got her details."

Frances nodded. "Poor Jess. Got so much on her plate, hasn't she? Meningitis. Serious, that. Let's hope the poor little boy makes a full recovery. There can be long-term complications with meningitis. Anyway, take a look at this footage. Move your chair a bit closer so you can see."

Ryan did so, on autopilot, saddened at poor little Toby being dismissed by an awkwardly double-clicked mouse. Pretty much the way he'd dismissed his employer's plans for his future with the company recently.

"We're not getting rid of you, Ryan, not at all. This research work is important, and you must know you can't remain in the same role you had before . . ."

Ryan stared at the footage of a hedgehog entering one of the feeding stations, without really seeing it, the feeling of uselessness back with a vengeance. He could do the research work they'd offered him from his desktop, as befitted someone confined to a wheelchair. He could already tell it would be mind-numbingly dull.

He put his cup of coffee down on the desk, suddenly desperate to be on his own. "Sorry, Frances, I've just remembered something. I'll have to go. I'm really glad you're able to watch the footage now, though."

Frances's voice followed him. "Ryan? Is everything all right?"

But he kept right on wheeling away.

~

He found a note from his mother waiting for him when he got home.

Annie rang. Eric can't come on Saturday.

What the . . . ? Fury swiftly descending, Ryan phoned Annie.

"What d'you mean Eric can't come on Saturday? Christ, Annie, I barely get to see him as it is. I've got things planned." He hadn't, but he would have tried to think of something by the time Saturday came round.

"Hey," Annie said, sounding angry herself, "before you go off on one, didn't your mum tell you why he can't come?"

"Mum's out. She left a note."

"Eric's been picked for the football team. They've got an away match on Saturday."

Ryan was stunned, the wind taken out of his sails. "Eric's been picked for the team? Why didn't he tell me?"

"Well, he hasn't seen you to tell you, has he? But he's thrilled about it, obviously."

Of course he was. Eric loved football. "Well, that's . . . Where's he playing?"

"Cromer. Look, he can come and see you on Sunday, if you like."

"All right," Ryan said, wishing he could find a way to get himself to Cromer to watch the match.

"But, Ryan, can you try to think of something constructive to do with him? I realise things aren't easy for you at the moment, but I'd rather he didn't just sit about and watch TV all day."

"He doesn't just sit about and watch TV when he comes here," Ryan protested, trying and failing to remember what they'd done last time Eric had visited.

Annie sighed. "If you say so. Anyway, I've got to go. I'll bring him round about ten o'clock on Sunday morning, okay?"

When she ended the call, Ryan tossed his phone onto his bed, irritated. Frustrated. Annie said she understood things weren't easy for him at the moment. But how could she? She'd never had her spinal cord shot to hell. Hadn't witnessed him struggling into his clothes. Hadn't heard him screaming when he did his exercises. Though she obviously understood that Cromer might just as well be the moon for him because she hadn't suggested he go there to see Eric play in Saturday's match.

God, what a self-pitying git he'd turned into. Jealous of a bloody football match. Taking it out on Annie. It was hardly her fault his mum had written the bare minimum on the note she'd left for him. And Annie was right about him needing to make more of an effort when Eric came round. If he wasn't careful, Eric would stop wanting to come at all. It was scarily easy to imagine his boy saying, *"Mum, do I have to go to Dad's? We never do anything. It's boring."*

If Ryan wanted to sustain a relationship with his son, he needed to stop acting like a sulky kid and really start working at it. Starting with thinking of something interesting for them to do together on Sunday.

Maybe he could take Eric round to Frances's house to watch some of the hedgehog footage? She'd said he could, that time he'd asked her. Better still, maybe he and Eric could make a hedgehog house for Frances's garden. Yes, that might be a worthwhile project. He'd watched a few videos about making them, so he had an idea of how to do it; it was relatively easy. And if he told him what to do, he was sure Eric could do anything Ryan couldn't handle himself.

Yes. He'd pop round to Frances's house now. Apologise for being such a tit earlier on. Put the idea to her.

Frances was thrilled by the idea, flapping a dismissive hand when he tried to apologise.

"You're not a saint, Ryan," she said. "Well, I assume you're not. You certainly don't look like one, anyway."

"How d'you know I don't keep my halo in a box in my bedroom?"

Frances laughed. "Well, for one thing, if you kept a box lying around the place, your mother would be sure to tidy it away. And for another, you're far too grumpy to be a saint. But you've got a very kind heart, I'll give you that. I'd love you and Eric to make a hedgehog house for me. What do you need me to get for you? Tea and biscuits I can do, but materials, I'm not so sure about."

"Well," said Ryan, thinking back to one of the videos he'd watched, "there are lots of ways to do it, but the simplest way I've seen uses an old plastic storage box and a bit of plastic drainpipe. It's a more elaborate version of the feeding station I made."

Frances frowned, thinking. "There's an old plastic drainpipe by the side of my house, I believe. But I'm not tidy minded enough to have a storage box."

"I've got one I can empty out."

"There's tools in Trevor's old shed if you need them. That's if they haven't rusted up. I've not been in there recently. Belonged to Trevor's grandfather, they did."

"We'd only need a knife and a pair of scissors. Oh, and some strong tape. Mum might have some of that."

"The scissors and knife I can do. I'll have a clear-up in the shed for you, so you can get your chair in there. Oh, and I'll look out for a saw. I don't imagine the hedgehogs want to walk down a ten-foot bit of drainpipe to get to their bed, do they?"

Ryan smiled, surprising himself. Half an hour ago, he hadn't expected to smile about anything anytime soon. Frances might be eccentric as hell, but she did him good.

"See you on Sunday, then."

"I'll look forward to it," Frances said.

"Me too," Ryan replied, meaning it.

~

"How many spiders d'you reckon live in this shed?" Ryan asked Eric on Sunday morning.

The shed was dark inside—mostly because the single window was coated with over ten years' worth of grime. Frances had cleared the workbench and the floor space for them, but she'd done nothing at all about the cobwebs festooning the ceiling. Very likely she hadn't even noticed them, knowing Frances.

Eric took a look around. "About thirty-eight or thirty-nine," he said.

Ryan laughed. "Sounds about right to me. I hope that doesn't put you off?"

"Nah. I'm not scared of spiders."

"Me neither," said Ryan, although he did hope one wouldn't drop into the mugs of tea Frances had insisted on making for them. "Okay, can you bring in the drainpipe, please? That's it, prop it on the workbench so we can saw a piece off. We need a piece about forty-five centimetres long."

"Shall I measure it?"

"Sure." Ryan handed his son the tape measure and a Sharpie, amused to see Eric's tongue protruding slightly from his mouth the way his own did when he concentrated on something.

"So," he said, "football was good yesterday, then?"

Eric shrugged, replacing the cap on the Sharpie. "Would have been better if we'd won."

"Oh, well. Next time, eh? They can't keep losing, not now they've got you on the team."

Eric gave him a look. Ryan suspected he'd overdone it. Which might be why he suggested, "D'you want to do the sawing?"

Eric's face lit up. "Can I?"

"Sure. As long as you're careful."

Under Ryan's instruction, Eric managed to saw off the length of pipe without incident. Then Ryan cut a hole in the storage box with a knife, and they worked together to put tape around the perimeter of the opening to prevent hedgehogs from injuring themselves.

"Okay, slip the pipe in, and we can put the house in position before we make it homey."

Frances had told them where she wanted it—next to the fence, behind a large, overgrown shrub. Eric carried it carefully over there and placed it on the ground.

"That's it," said Ryan. "Now, if you can take the lid off and go back for some of those newspapers in the shed? We can put some in the bottom and then pile lots of leaves on top to make a nice cosy nest."

With a couple of bricks on top of the closed lid to fix the house firmly in place, and with as many twigs, logs, and leaves as Eric could find scattered about the garden piled on and around it, the hedgehog house soon looked as if it had always been there.

Ryan smiled at his son. "I reckon that's a job well done, don't you?"

"Yeah," agreed Eric with a nod. "How will we know if they're using it or not?"

"I'll order another camera. Set it up on the trunk of that tree."

"Cool." Eric approved. Then, as they made their way back to the shed to tidy up, "Dad?"

"Yes?"

"That was great. But can we watch TV now?"

Ryan wasn't sure whether to laugh or frown. "Is that what you really want to do?"

Eric nodded.

Ryan smiled. "All right, then. But don't tell your mother. Okay?"

27

"Where doggie? Toby see doggie?"

Two weeks back from hospital, Toby's stunted vocabulary had begun to blossom like a tightly furled bud opening in the sun, probably because Jess had been talking to him so much.

Most of the time in the hospital it had just been the two of them. Towards the end of his stay, they'd celebrated Toby's second birthday together with a card, a cake, and balloons. And Jess had entertained him by chatting about what they could see out the window and the animals in the wall murals.

She read to him a lot too, finding a picture book about a lost baby hedgehog amongst the toys in the children's area. Though as the little hoglet searched for her mother in piles of leaves and through a dark forest, Jess soon regretted picking that particular book. Although it had a happy ending—the hoglet's mother had been looking for her too, and the pair were reunited beneath a full moon—the story felt too close to the bone.

Back at home, Toby seemed more settled, except that he kept looking for Patch.

Michael had broken the news about Patch at the hospital when Toby was drifting in and out of sleep, opening his eyes every now and then to make sure Jess was still there before closing them again. Jess had just updated Michael on his progress—out of immediate danger, but a long way to go before he was completely out of the woods—and then the two of them sat side by side next to Toby's bed, trying not to listen to other hospital visitors' conversations.

"Oh, I took the dog to a rescue centre," Michael said suddenly, in a by-the-way kind of a voice, and Jess stared at him, unable to believe what she'd just heard.

"Patch? You took Patch to a rescue centre?"

"Yes, that one off the A11. They were confident he'd soon find a new home."

Jess shook her head, tears in her eyes. "I can't believe you did that without asking me first."

Michael laughed disbelievingly. "You went on and on at me about getting him. You told me it was a stupid idea to get a dog."

"It *was* a stupid idea to get a dog," Jess said in a quiet hiss, aware that if they could hear the other visitors, then the visitors could certainly hear them. "But you did get one. And we got to know it."

"And it chewed our shoes, attacked a hedgehog, and pissed on the floor. It's been absolute chaos since he came to us."

"Yes, it has. Yes, he did. But we've come to love him anyway." Jess gestured towards Toby's sleeping form in the bed, a tear running down her cheek. "He adores Patch. Michael, you have to ring the rescue centre first thing tomorrow and get him back."

"I don't believe this," said Michael.

She gripped his sleeve. "Promise me you'll call in the morning. Promise."

"All right. But there's no guarantee they'll let us have him back, is there? And even if they do, how am I supposed to look after him while you're here with Toby?"

"We can sort something out. Get a dog walker in or something. Please, Michael."

He sighed. "All right."

But when he came the next day, it was with the news that it was too late. Patch had already been adopted.

28

Male hedgehogs are not a monogamous, romantic breed. They aren't interested in being lifelong partners, and they don't help with nest building or hoglet rearing. Their role in the furthering of their species consists of having sex with as many females as possible, which requires fighting rival males and always includes a great deal of noise during the sex act. Then, seed sown, they scurry off to replenish their energy levels with some juicy worms or crunchy beetles before moving on to the next lucky lady.

With male hedgehogs, it's all about satisfying an urge, wielding power, and not giving a fig for the consequences. And any cute, vulnerable offspring resulting from those encounters had better give them a wide berth if they don't want to get trampled, or worse still, eaten.

For the human males of Hilltop Place, it was somewhat different, although not entirely. Justin Hedges was certainly convinced he held all the power in his relationship with his wife, Helen. Even if Helen didn't initially agree with his plans, suggestions, or assumptions, she inevitably came round to his way of thinking or tucked her dissatisfaction away somewhere Justin could no longer detect it. Over the years, Justin had found that a newspaper held in exactly the right position in front of his face, combined with a confident, self-assured tone of voice, worked wonders.

Yes, one way or another, he could easily bring Helen into line.

In hedgehog terms, Jess's husband, Michael, was something of a failure. He wasn't macho, and he cared about his family. That was, he adored his little girl, Stella, and was perfectly prepared to adore his adopted son, Toby. The only problem was, Toby did not adore him, and nothing Michael tried seemed to change that. Every *"Mama, Mama"* that echoed around the house seemed to tell Michael to *"Get lost, get lost."* And with Jess so wrapped up with Toby, so needed by Toby, Michael was in fact beginning to feel exactly that. Lost.

As for Ryan, before that life-transforming terrorist attack, he had wielded power without even being aware of it, bustling about his business like a male hedgehog intent on his purpose. But now, with his injuries and his broken marriage and the aftermath of all that violence to deal with, he was more like a vulnerable hoglet baby, curled up, spine not yet hardened enough to protect him. A vulnerable hoglet in a fully grown, male body.

And Tara's lover/landlord, James? Oh, he was a male hedgehog, through and through. Including the need for children to give him a wide berth if they knew what was good for them.

Returned from his holiday, James popped round to Hilltop Place. He didn't really have time; he was flying between two meetings, with a stack of work waiting for him on his desk. His visit to Tara was scent marking, pure and simple. Maybe he could release a bit of the tension that had built up during the three weeks away with his family, if Tara's kid wasn't around. And she shouldn't be around, should she, as it was a school day?

But when James put his key in the lock and pushed the door open, he heard laughter. Tara wasn't lounging on the sofa with her skirt attractively ridden up or emerging from the bath in a loosely knotted silken bathrobe, as he'd imagined she would be. She was entertaining. And by the sound of it, there was a kid in the house. And a young kid at that.

James had a strong desire to pull the front door closed and to disappear before Tara detected his presence. But it was too late.

"James? Is that you?" Tara called out, forcing him to go and stand in the doorway to the lounge, looking in on the chaos of a child's playtime—plastic blocks scattered around the floor, a plate with a dismembered sandwich and pulverised potato crisps which had shed like dandruff onto the coffee table, an upturned tin used as a drum by a snotty-looking boy wielding a wooden spoon.

"Hello, Tara," James said. "I just popped in to assure you I haven't forgotten about the boiler servicing. I'll book it in the next few weeks."

The boy stopped drumming and turned to consider James with huge, dark eyes. "Man," he pronounced. "Man."

The dark-haired woman seated on the carpet—quite pretty, or she would be if she took a bit more trouble with her appearance—lit up as if the boy, presumably her son, had come up with a magical formula to cure cancer forever.

"Yes, Toby, it is a man, isn't it? Clever boy!"

Christ.

Tara got to her feet and sashayed over to him. At least she was wearing makeup. And the blue, figure-hugging dress he particularly liked her in. God, if she didn't have company—*Why did she have fucking company, today of all days, when he'd been away for weeks?*—he would have thrown her over the arm of the sofa and pulled that dress right up. He and Cressida had only had sex three times the whole time they'd been away.

"He is a man, Toby," Tara said, slipping her arms around his neck. "He's my man."

She pulled him in for a kiss. Instinctively James pulled away.

Tara laughed. "It's okay, darling, I've just been telling Jess here all about you. Jess lives next door."

"Hello," said Jess.

"Hi," he responded awkwardly, wishing he'd never given in to the impulse to come round. "I can't stay, I'm afraid. I'm on my way to a meeting. I just wanted to let you know I was back."

"And to let me know about the boiler servicing?"

"Well," he said, aware of the dark-haired woman—Josie? Jane? Something beginning with *J*—appraising him.

Tara removed her hands from behind his neck. James took a step back into the hall. "I'll come back soon."

"Do that," Tara said. "The boiler isn't the only thing in need of a service."

Christ, he loved it when she spoke like that. His wife never spoke to him like that. "I could manage five o'clock," he said, although he supposed the kid would be back then.

"Five it is," Tara said. "Can't wait."

~

Remembering Tara's disgustingly bitter coffee and her obvious dislike of young children, Jess had been hesitant at first when Tara had invited her round. She and Toby had been on their way home from the park when Tara had pulled into her drive and invited them in. But in the end, Jess accepted—she wasn't sure why. She'd only intended to stay for half an hour or so, to be polite, but Tara had surprised her by producing the building blocks from somewhere—*"I have a friend with a child Toby's age"*—and had then chattered on entertainingly about her continuing quest to find halfway interesting work. *"I suppose somebody has to work in a call centre, but it isn't going to be me, I can tell you that, darling."*

Jess was interested and gratified to hear that Tara had tried her suggestion to become a social influencer. It had been one of her better ideas, she thought. She could still imagine Tara being good at it. Not that she seemed to have done very much about it yet. Too much time wasted, waiting around for James to put in an appearance, perhaps.

Now, with the sound of James's car driving quickly away, Tara said, "You look a bit shocked."

Jess felt a flush rise to her cheeks. Michael always said she was too transparent for her own good. "No, not at all."

"It's all right; people have always disapproved of me. I'm used to it."

"How did you two meet?"

"Through my ex, Tony. Hermie's father. You know, the world-record-holding one-night stand? Useless father and a bit of a shit? Tony and James were good friends before I came onto the scene. But you can't help who you fall for, can you? Anyway, as I say, I'm used to people disapproving of me. Even people in Hilltop Place. Take Irene, for example. Lovely Ryan's mother. I'd bet any amount of money she's got me labeled as a scarlet woman who should know better, and Frances as a poor eccentric widow woman who's going slightly batty."

Like Frances as she did, Jess thought that was a fairly accurate assessment of her neighbour. Curious, though, that Tara thought Ryan was lovely. She hadn't realised Tara knew him particularly well.

"What d'you think Irene thinks about me and my family, then?"

Tara shrugged. "I'd say the jury's out right now with you lot because of the adoption. She's probably waiting to see which way that goes. But generally, my guess is she's marked you down as rambling, disorganised, and misguided."

Jess flushed some more.

"Sorry, but you did ask. And it's not me who thinks that about you, it's Irene. And it's only my guess."

It was probably a pretty accurate one, though. But weren't most parents rambling and disorganised? Anyway, what did she care about what Irene thought? From the few things Ryan had let slip about her, the woman seemed really cold.

"As for Justin and Helen, I'd guess Irene thoroughly approves of them. Professional, neat, and tidy, conformists through and through, both of them. Although I rather think Justin's got hidden depths. Helen's not right for him at all. He needs someone who can stand up to him, not a mouse. I can imagine a good ding-dong and a spot of rebellion turning him on. And he's got some very nice suits."

Jess had never noticed Justin's suits. And she definitely didn't want to think about Justin being turned on. "What about Ryan? What d'you think Irene thinks of him?"

Tara frowned. "Now that is a bit of a mystery, isn't it? All the evidence seems to suggest she thoroughly disapproves of him. What the poor bugger's done to deserve that, I have no idea. I intend to find out, though. Listen, I've told you before, if your little girl ever wants to come round to play with Hermie, she'd be very welcome. I know there's an age difference, but they seemed to get on all right together at Frances's house, didn't they?"

"Thanks. I'm sure Stella would love that."

Toby was bashing the bricks gleefully and very noisily on the table. Jess saw Tara flinch. Time to go. "But now I'd better get this one home. It's almost time for his nap."

She stood to gather her things together. Toby abandoned his brick bashing and held his arms out to be picked up.

"Don't you ever miss your work?" Tara asked.

Jess thought back to the days when her work had thoroughly absorbed her between the hours of nine and five o'clock—often very much more than that when the charity was running a campaign or was bidding for a funding pot. She'd enjoyed the sense of achievement when things went well. Not that they always had. The public could be fickle, and too many sad tales about world starvation caused their eyes to glaze over. She'd liked coming up with new ideas to get people's attention, though.

"Sometimes, yes. But it was quite a high-pressure job. I don't miss that. Look, I'd better get off. I think—actually, I'm sure—Toby needs a clean nappy."

"God. Rather you than me," Tara said with a wince. "I absolutely loathed all that. Look, put my number in your phone. Then you can shoot me a text, and we can sort something out for our girls."

When she left Tara's house, despite what she'd just said about Toby's nappy, she headed on impulse for Irene and Ryan's house instead of going straight home.

"Mummy just wants to tell Ryan the good news about the hedgehog, and then we'll go home, okay, Toby Bear?"

It was a relief to see that Irene's car wasn't in the drive, and acting on impulse again, Jess pushed the buggy round the side of the house and onto the patio. And instantly came face-to-face with Ryan, who was sitting in the open doorway, staring out at the garden.

"Jess!" His expression had looked utterly bleak before he saw her, but now he smiled.

"Hi. Sorry to disturb you. I hope you don't mind me coming round the back like this? Only you mentioned you had this room, and I thought . . ."

"Not at all. If you'd rung the doorbell, I'd probably have ignored it. How's the little chap?"

The little chap was rubbing his eyes and kicking his legs. "He's in need of a nap, but he's fine, thanks. Made a full recovery, I'm relieved to say."

How very inadequate words were sometimes. She looked down at Toby's squirming body, tears filling her eyes. "I really thought at one point we were going to lose him. You can't imagine."

She looked up, wiping away a tear, and saw from Ryan's face that he absolutely could imagine what those long, dark lonely hours of despair had been like for her. Of course he could.

"It's great that he's come through, Jess. I'm so glad."

She looked back down at Toby, pulling herself together. "Me too. Oh, I came to tell you about the hedgehog we rescued—she's fully fit now too. They're bringing her back to release her in our garden next week. They wouldn't normally release her in a garden where there's a dog, but we don't have a dog any longer. You heard about Michael taking Patch to the dog rescue centre, I suppose?"

"I did hear that, yes."

"Doggie," Toby said. "Where doggie?"

Jess sighed. "He keeps asking for him."

Toby's eyes filled with tears. He began to wail. Jess kicked herself. Why on earth had she mentioned Patch? "Look, I'd better take him home for his nap. I just wanted to let you know about the hedgehog."

"Well, thanks for doing that, Jess. It's good to see you both."

"Are you sure about that?" she asked with a smile, speaking over Toby's increasingly loud crying. The sound didn't make her panic the way it once had, and that felt like a miracle. Now it sounded like a full-bodied, full-lunged complaint—something to celebrate rather than something to worry about.

She began pushing the buggy towards the side gate, then realised she hadn't asked Ryan anything about himself and turned back, remembering the bleak expression she'd seen on his face when she appeared on the patio. "Would you like to come and witness the big hedgehog reintroduction?"

He smiled. "I'd love to. Thanks."

"Okay, good," she said, raising her voice to be heard over Toby's cries. "Eight o'clock on Thursday."

"I'll look forward to it."

"Goodbye, Ryan."

"Bye, Jess."

Toby fell asleep almost as soon as Jess had changed his nappy and was still fast asleep when it was time for them to leave to collect Stella from school. Jess stood gazing down at him in his cot, delaying the evil moment when she would have to disturb him. He looked so gorgeous asleep, with those long black lashes, his breathing soft and steady—oh, the joy of those soft, steady breaths after days and nights of listening to snatched, laboured breathing, Toby's face flushed red, his lashes batting against his closed eyes as he dreamt feverish dreams. Jess could watch him sleep like this for hours. Except that she couldn't because she was going to be seriously late to collect Stella.

Very gently, she reached into the cot to lift him out. Toby stirred and whimpered slightly, then carried on sleeping, allowing her to strap him into the buggy, not noticing as they went out the door and began to make their way to the school.

When they got there, Jess was surprised to see Stella's teacher waiting with Stella. "Could we just have a little word, please? It will only take a few minutes."

Jess's heart sank. "Yes, of course."

She tried to catch Stella's eye as she pushed Toby's buggy after the teacher, but Stella didn't look up, her lips pressed together in the mulish expression Jess had become all too familiar with lately. Hell, and she'd been having such a nice, sociable day.

"I'm afraid Stella's behaviour hasn't been quite what we hoped it would be today," the teacher said as they sat on ridiculously small chairs around a very low table. "You got very cross when I asked you to share your crayons with Jemima, didn't you, Stella?"

"I had the yellow first."

"But we need to learn to share, don't we, Stella? The crayons are for everyone to use. Jemima was very sad when you tore her lovely picture up, wasn't she?"

Oh, hell.

"You didn't do that, did you, Stella?" asked Jess, aghast. Her daughter had always been so easygoing and generous. Tearing up somebody's painting didn't seem like the sort of thing she would do at all.

"It was a silly picture," Stella said, still sounding mutinous, but now with a big fat tear streaking down her face. "The sun had a face on it. Suns don't have faces."

Stella never had liked to give the sun a face. Or sunrays. In terms of artistic development, she was streaks ahead of other children her age. But not, it seemed, in terms of her actions.

"I know you don't like the sun to have a face, sweetie, but Jemima can give her sun a face if she wants to, can't she? You mustn't tear people's artwork up. How would you feel if somebody did that to one of your lovely paintings?"

Stella immediately turned her tearstained face towards Jess. "But they do, Mummy," she said. "All the time."

"Who does, darling?" Jess asked.

Stella glared in Toby's direction at the exact same time as he began to stir, pointing an accusing finger at him. "He does. He tears them up and he treads on them, and he uses my things, and I hate him, Mummy. I really hate him. I wish he'd never come. I wish he would go back." So saying, Stella exploded into racking sobs.

Hearing them, Toby began to cry too.

"Oh, Stella," said Jess, teetering on the brink of tears herself, aware of the teacher's scrutiny.

"Well," the teacher said, "I just thought you ought to know. I'm sure it won't happen again. Tomorrow's another day, okay, Stella? You can say you're sorry to Jemima, and it will be as if nothing happened."

"But I'm not sorry," Stella said. She pressed her face into her arms on the table, and the words came out very muffled. But everyone heard them, nevertheless.

"Come on," said Jess, suddenly feeling exhausted. "Let's get you both home."

29

It was motivating to have a plan, Ryan thought as he got up early to wash and shave—the first shave in a while, so he had quite a lot of accumulated beard to hack off. He was outside ten minutes before the taxi was due, thankfully half an hour after his mother had gone out so he didn't have to fill her in on where he was going.

As he waited there by the kerb, a blue car drove into Hilltop Place. Ryan looked up, expecting the taxi, but saw that it wasn't. The car toured the road slowly, the driver obviously checking out the house numbers. A delivery driver, perhaps? Then Ryan's taxi arrived, and he forgot about the car as he concentrated on transferring himself from the wheelchair.

"Where to, mate?" the driver asked after Ryan had safely belted himself in, the wheelchair stowed in the boot. Ryan gave the address of the dog rescue centre. It was only as they pulled away that he noticed the blue car had parked outside his mother's house, its driver staring out the windscreen in Ryan's direction. Oh well, if it was a parcel delivery, the man would just have to come back later.

"Thinking of rescuing a dog, are you then, mate?" the taxi driver asked, then proceeded to rattle on about his own rescue dog for the rest of the journey.

Not wanting to talk himself, Ryan encouraged him with repeated murmurs of "Oh?" "Is that so?" and "Really?" until they'd arrived at their destination. After the whole palaver of paying, he transferred back into his wheelchair and pushed himself up the slope to the—thankfully—accessible entrance. He gave his name to the friendly receptionist, then waited, listening to the yips and barks of the dogs outside in the kennels, trying—stupidly, he knew—to pick out Patch's bark.

"Mr. Tindall? I'm Jane, one of the resettlement workers."

"Hello." He shook her hand.

"Thanks for coming in today. I understand you're looking for a dog?"

"Well, yes, one particular dog, actually. A border collie pup, about four months old? He was brought in a few weeks ago. Patch. I live on the same road as his owners, you see, so I got to know him quite well, and I thought . . ."

Ryan's voice trailed off. He was making a complete mess of this. Blathering on like an idiot.

"Oh, I'm so sorry. Patch was rehomed almost straight away, I'm afraid. Puppies usually are. But we have lots of other dogs, so I'm sure we can find one to suit you. A border collie may not have been the best choice for your circumstances, anyway, if you don't mind me mentioning it. They're such lively dogs, aren't they? Especially puppies. I gather that was partly why his family brought him to us."

Ryan felt sick. He could hear Toby's voice in his head. *Doggie. Where doggie?"*

"Who did he go to?" he heard himself ask.

Jane looked slightly taken aback. Ryan realised belatedly he might have spoken a bit aggressively.

"Well, obviously that information has to remain confidential, but I can assure you Patch has gone to a good home, so you don't have to worry on that score. Shall I leave you to complete an application form? If you complete the details, I'll come back in ten minutes, and we can discuss things further."

She gave him a pen and a clipboard with a form attached to it and departed, leaving Ryan feeling like a total failure. It was too late. He'd failed. But the only surprising thing about that was the fact that he'd expected anything else. Dashing over here like some idiotic white knight on a charger—or as close to one as a paralysed git in a taxi can get. What had he been thinking? Even if Patch had still been here, it was highly unlikely they'd have let Ryan take him. Jane's casual reference to his circumstances and the liveliness of border collies was enough to tell him that, even without the questions on the application form.

What type of property do you live in? Answer: my mother's.

Is there an enclosed garden? Yes, but she'd never put up with a dog shitting and pissing everywhere, and I'd probably find it tricky to scoop its poop by myself.

How often would you be able to exercise a dog? Once a day, at best, because everywhere but the park is at some distance away, and the fucking council won't let dogs into the park.

Do you intend to move in the next six months? Probably not, worst luck.

On and on, until it became clear to Ryan that the only breed they'd likely let him adopt would be a waddling Pekinese that wanted to ride on his lap, and which only put its paws on the ground to relieve himself. An old dog with halitosis and a tendency to lick its arse frequently.

Despite the turmoil of these bitter thoughts, Ryan found himself completing the form anyway, giving answers that showed himself in the best possible light—given the circumstances Jane had alluded to—to become the owner of a four-month-old border collie pup. You never knew—another dog like Patch might come on the scene, and somehow, despite everything, the memory of Jess's expression when Toby asked, *"Where doggie?"* wouldn't quite go away, pushing aside his self-pitying apathy.

"Okay, Ryan, thank you very much for this," Jane said after she'd returned and gone through the form. "As I say, we've no dogs that fit your bill currently, but we do get new dogs coming in all the time, so I'll let you know if anything changes. Then we can arrange to come round for a home visit."

A home visit. Which he would surely fail. Unless—*radical thought here, Ryan*—unless he managed to change his home circumstances. Get a place of his own, suitable for a dog. Somewhere he and Eric could spend quality time together. He'd worked in war zones, for God's sake. Survived a terrorist attack. How hard could finding a suitable property and moving house be?

30

It was December, and the hedgehogs were hibernating, waiting out the winter in a state of suspended animation, barely breathing, their body temperatures so low it beggared belief. They were oblivious to the fact that it was almost Christmas, or that this winter was nothing like the kind you see on Christmas cards with powdery snow and rosy-cheeked children gleefully making snowmen. It was a wet, windy winter of constant, driving rain and bare tree branches clattering together like skeleton bones. Rivers burst their banks and homes flooded, though thankfully not the homes of the residents of Hilltop Place, because Hilltop Place perched at the top of a hill, several miles from the nearest river.

No, the residents didn't need to worry about their belongings getting swept away or their carpets getting ruined, but they still felt the effects of such a sodden, miserable season. Forced inside and left to their own devices too much, it was difficult to stay optimistic and resourceful.

Even Frances—who had got into the habit over the past few years of not going out very much—found this winter difficult. The hedgehogs had given her an interest and a purpose—keeping the feeding bowls topped up, checking for video footage first thing every morning, smiling at their antics. But now the cute creatures were all tucked away, hibernating, and there was no footage to view. Nothing to liven her day. She still kept the food bowls topped up, just in case, but there were never any takers, so gradually she stopped checking.

She watched TV for something to do, for company, telling herself every day that she ought to go out—perhaps to the library—but somehow never getting round to it.

Jess still had to venture out, of course, inclement weather or not, to get Stella to school. She'd come to dread the afternoon trip, though, not only because of the rain penetrating her clothing, Toby's buggy, and her spirits but also because increasingly frequently, Stella's teacher wanted to speak to her at the end of the school day about some misdemeanour or other that Stella had committed—children's arms pinched, belongings stolen, activities stubbornly and vociferously refused, food thrown. Jess often felt as if she pushed Toby's buggy to the school empty—apart from the precious, joyful cargo that was Toby—and returned with it laden down with extra weight that she couldn't manage to carry on her shoulders. Stella's cold hand would be clamped in hers—or not, if Stella refused to let her hand be held—and Jess sometimes felt like a jailor or a prison guard. They talked of bringing in an educational psychologist, but there was a long waiting list. Besides, everyone knew what was wrong with Stella. They just didn't know what to do about it.

Jess and Michael had long, whispered discussions about the situation at night when they were both tired and really ought to be snuggled up, cementing their relationship in the few moments they had without the children.

From time to time, Michael would make a suggestion like, "I really think it would help if you spent some time alone with Stella at the weekends, just the two of you. How about I take Toby to the castle for the afternoon, and you and Stella do something nice together? You could take her to that plate-painting place on the Unthank Road. She'd love that."

Stella *had* loved that. She painted a lovely picture of a family of three right in the centre of her plate. "That's you, me, and Daddy," she told Jess, just in case Jess hadn't already got the message, and when Jess gave a sad smile and said very gently, "It makes Mummy a little bit sad that you haven't painted Toby too," Stella threw the plate onto the floor with such force it smashed into about a hundred sharp pieces, one of which cut the leg of a little girl busy painting a cute picture of a teddy bear on a plate for her grandma.

Weekends were a lot more successful when Michael took Stella off somewhere, but for some reason Michael had taken it into his head to volunteer to be the lead for a new client account, and the client seemed to assume it was perfectly acceptable to hold meetings at weekends, for goodness' sake, so he was often absent for hours at a time.

Left alone, doing her best to satisfy the demands of two combative children, Jess stared out the window at the puddles collecting in the road and wondered bleakly how the other residents were getting on. Wished with all her heart she could skip Christmas. Christmas, with all its hype, hopes, and expectations, felt like a disaster waiting to happen with the current tinderbox atmosphere of her family. She'd like to hibernate like a hedgehog and emerge in the New Year when it was all over. But the juggernaut of the festive season continued to loom unstoppably closer, and still Jess hadn't done any food preparation or present shopping.

31

Christmas Day dawned. Ryan had yet to move out of his mother's house. The insurance company was dragging its heels, and although he had signed the divorce papers, nothing was finalised yet. But none of that mattered now, because Ryan was waiting for Eric to arrive. Eric was joining them for Christmas lunch.

This fact had been a hard-won victory. Over the past few weeks—it had felt more like years—Ryan had been on his best behaviour, thoughtful and acquiescent whenever he spoke to his ex-wife about the arrangements, not verbalising his frustration when she and her new partner bought Eric the exact same gift, a Nintendo Switch, that Ryan had planned to buy for him.

He'd done his best not to annoy his mother too, asking her politely how various committee meetings had gone, complimenting her cooking, even when he could have killed for a curry instead of meat and two veg. All this so that Annie would indeed drop Eric off as promised and he, Eric, and his mum could share a civilised Christmas meal around the dining room table together.

In place of the Nintendo Switch, Ryan had bought a fully functioning replica of an engine they could work on together, father and son, the way they'd worked together to make Irene's hedgehog house. Ryan had cleared a table in his room so they could spread the pieces out away from his mother, who would no doubt be irritable by then, forced to clear up after the meal herself, even though she had cooked it.

Eric must have a wonderful Christmas. He must return to Annie and Jimmy's house full of tales about how cool his dad was and how they'd made an actual working engine, and wasn't that amazing?

So Ryan sat, wearing a new Christmas jumper, waiting for Eric's arrival. The turkey had been in the oven since 9:00 a.m., and the house was filled with the smell of Christmas. Or, at least, it had been before it was eclipsed somewhat by the stink of his mother boiling up turkey innards to make "proper" gravy.

The potatoes were peeled. The brussels sprouts only his mother would eat had been neatly prepared the way she liked them, with a little cross cut into the end of each trimmed stalk. Christmas music played on the radio—the sort that played constantly and drove you to despair by the seventh of December—but which Ryan, having done all his shopping online, hadn't heard at all so was confident he could tolerate for a few hours.

By the time Annie arrived—ten minutes late, but heck, it was Christmas Day, so he would keep smiling anyway—Ryan was hot and clammy in his Christmas jumper. His mother refused to turn the heating down—*it was her house, and she would keep it at the temperature she wanted it, thank you very much*—and Ryan was regretting his second cup of coffee because he'd need to empty his catheter soon, which would leave Eric alone with his grandmother when the poor kid had only just arrived. But he could hold on for a while; he was sure he could. At least until they'd opened their presents.

A large pile of presents waited for Eric under the Christmas tree—sadly an artificial tree, not the real tree Ryan had wanted to have. But obtaining and decorating a real tree had been beyond him, so a ready-decorated pop-up Christmas tree it had to be, and it still looked festive.

The stage was set. All that was needed was the principal player. And now here he was. Ten minutes late, but here.

"Hello, son, happy Christmas!"

"Hi, Dad."

"Happy Christmas, Ryan. Happy Christmas, Irene. Now be a good boy, Eric. Remember what we talked about, okay? I'll see you at three o'clock."

They'd said four o'clock, hadn't they, for Christ's sake? They'd never finish the model by three. And what did she mean, *"Remember what we talked about?"*

"Bye, Mum."

"Well, come along in, then, Eric." His mother bustled about. "Don't just stand there by the door."

"Yes, son, come into the sitting room. There's a heap of presents for you under the tree."

Ryan began to propel his chair along the hall, aware of Eric following on behind, trying not to think about the fact that Eric had already experienced the excitement of opening presents earlier that morning back at his mother's house.

"Ta-da!" Ryan said, moving out of the way so Eric could see the present stash, smiling at the excitement on his boy's face. Thank God. It had all been worthwhile, after all. All the preparation, all the effort to keep his temper and frustration reined in. Just for this moment.

Unfortunately, the moment lasted all of five minutes. In a very short time indeed, Eric had unwrapped all the presents, the gift wrap discarded on the floor. He'd politely said thank you for each and every one, but now the gifts were stacked up in a pile next to the fake, tacky Christmas tree with the engine construction kit right at the bottom, and Eric was playing on his new Nintendo Switch, his feet tucked beneath him on the armchair.

"We don't put our feet up on the furniture, do we, Eric?" Ryan's mother said. "And could you help me to clear up this mess, please? Your father can't get about in his wheelchair with all this paper strewn everywhere."

God, why did she have to use that cold tone of voice? And why did she have to be right? He couldn't easily move his chair with the wrapping paper everywhere, and he needed to attend to his catheter.

"Thanks, mate," he said. "I'll be back in a few minutes."

"Okay, Dad," Ryan said, but he'd already sat back on the armchair, staring at the console, uncomfortably hunched forward so his feet could touch the ground.

By lunchtime, Ryan had given up trying to interest his son in anything but the Nintendo on the proviso that he'd put it away after lunch while the two of them built the engine together. Ryan had already opened the box and laid out all the pieces and the instructions on the table in his room, ready to start.

"Shall we say grace?" his mother said, after she'd set the steaming plates of food in front of them. It looked good; he'd give her that—Christmas dinner was a plain cook's dream—but grace? Since when did they say grace, for crying out loud?

"For what we are about to receive, may the Lord make us truly thankful. Amen."

"Amen."

Ryan picked up his knife and fork, trying not to notice how Eric immediately pushed his vegetables to one side, willing his mother not to comment on it, wondering whether the atmosphere could be any drier and duller, then suddenly remembering the Christmas crackers he'd bought. Some corny jokes, tacky plastic gifts, and stupid paper crowns were exactly what they needed to lighten the mood.

"Hey, we forgot the crackers, Mum," he said, backing his chair up, pushing himself over to the dresser to fetch them.

"Your dinner will be getting cold," she said as he returned to the table and began picking at the plastic wrapper.

"It will be fine. We can't have Christmas dinner without crackers, can we? It wouldn't be right."

He had the box open—finally—and delved into it, pulling out a glossy red cracker for Eric, a silver one for his mother, and another red one for himself.

"Come on then, link arms," he encouraged them. So they all crossed their arms in front of their chests, one hand holding their own cracker, the other holding their neighbour's cracker, and Ryan began the countdown. "One, two, three, pull!"

The crackers all went off at slightly different times—*bang, bang, bang*—like machine-gun fire, shifting Ryan without warning to the smoky aftermath of the explosion. Lying in the road with a piece of the exploded vehicle pressing him down into the dust, a terrorist patrolling round, picking off any survivors.

Bang, bang.

Play dead, Ryan. Play dead!

Cold sweat drenched Ryan's Christmas jumper. He shook so much that his cutlery was clattering. The cranberry sauce on his plate had morphed into blood and gore, the turkey carcass into torn-off flesh. All around him he could hear the cries of the wounded, those innocent passersby caught by the explosion.

The mingled smells of singed flesh and rotten eggs was so strong he felt sick. The terrorist was getting closer and closer, his boots kicking up clouds of dust. *He mustn't cough. He mustn't cough.*

More cries. Good. That would draw the terrorist's attention away from him. A hand shook him. He flinched from the contact.

"Ryan, stop it, you're frightening Eric. Ryan!"

Ryan came to, or almost to, to find his hands clutching the table. He could still smell burnt flesh. Still hear that machine gun. *Bang, bang, bang.*

His mother tossed her napkin down onto the table. "Whoever is that at the door on Christmas Day? Pull yourself together while I answer it, Ryan."

Eric was staring at him. Ryan did his very best to pull himself together. To smile. But the smile came out like a grimace, and he could do nothing about the shaking.

"Sorry, son," he managed. "I . . ."

But Eric got up from the table and hurried past him.

"Eric!" Ryan called after him, but Eric was gone, into the sitting room.

He ought to go after him, but he wasn't sure he was capable of it. His whole body felt like liquid. He didn't think he'd have the strength to propel the wheelchair. So he waited, trying to block the images out, instead filling his mind with the memory of Eric's face as he saw the pile of presents. With Jess and Toby, in their matching bobble hats when he saw them on the other side of the park on the only dry day recently. Him and Eric laughing about spiders in Frances's shed. Anything to push those other images out.

Tears streamed down his cheeks. As he reached up to wipe them away, he heard his mother's voice in the hallway.

"I told you in my letter. I want nothing to do with you. I'm sorry if that's hurtful, but I made my decision a very long time ago. Now, please, I'd like you to leave."

Whoever was it at the door?

The front door closed. He heard his mother's footsteps approaching the kitchen. But she didn't come in. Instead, she went quickly up the stairs. He ought to find out who'd knocked at the door, what was going on, but he was more interested in Eric. Making sure he was all right.

Weakly, Ryan managed to summon the strength to get himself to the sitting room, where he found Eric bent over the Nintendo again.

"Sorry about that, son," he said, intending to explain.

But Eric quickly said, "That's okay," and carried on playing his game, and somehow Ryan couldn't find it in himself to say that they ought to carry on eating their dinner or to ask Eric to go upstairs to check on his grandmother.

So when a second knock came on the front door, that was where they still were—Eric playing on his Nintendo, Ryan in his chair, watching him and focusing on getting his breathing back to normal, and his mother still upstairs, doing whatever she was doing up there. Christmas Day in ruins.

But then Eric got to his feet, taking his Nintendo with him, passing Ryan on his way out to the hall.

"Eric? Son?"

Ryan followed just in time to see Eric open the front door to his mother.

"What are you doing here?" asked Ryan, baffled to see her.

Annie wrapped a protective arm around her son. "Eric called me to ask me to come and collect him. You frightened him. You need to get some help, Ryan, you really do."

And as Eric left the house without a backward glance, his gifts abandoned beneath the tacky, bloody awful Christmas tree, Ryan knew she was right.

Miserably, Ryan steered his wheelchair to where his jacket hung from a peg in the hallway, desperate for a cigarette. It wasn't until he'd started fumbling in the pockets that he remembered he'd decided to give them up—that it would be a great plan to end a thoroughly miserable year on a positive note so he could start the new one in a healthy frame of mind.

Great idea, Ryan. Great idea.

32

A hedgehog's favourite foods include beetles, earwigs, slugs, and earth-worms. A noisy eater, the hedgehog consumes these delicacies with lip-smacking, chomping relish and likes nothing better than rooting around in leaves and loose soil to find them.

When pickings are rich, a hedgehog will ignore any offerings humans leave for it, even if by doing so, it may be turning its back on the opportunity to star in a TikTok or YouTube video. But when times are hard, a hedgehog will gratefully eat any food humans leave out for it, which can be highly dangerous if the humans in question are ignorant about the foods hedgehogs should and should not eat. Some foods—tasty as they may be for hedgehogs—can do them significant harm.

One spring afternoon when Hermie returned from school, she regaled her mother about a trip her class had taken to the local library that day, for a talk by a lady from a hedgehog charity.

"D'you know, Mum," Hermie had said, sounding outraged, "some people are so stupid they actually give hedgehogs milk to drink."

"That's okay, isn't it?" Tara asked, and Hermie rolled her eyes.

"No, Mum, hedgehogs are lactose intolerant. Milk gives them diar-rhoea, and then they get dehydrated and die! People are so stupid!"

And after Hermie was safely ensconced in her bedroom, playing *Plants vs. Zombies* on her Xbox, Tara quickly sneaked outside to remove the saucer of milk she'd placed on the patio earlier that day.

Food intolerances can be tricky to accommodate at the best of times, as Tara had recently discovered. When her tummy first began to stick out, she was terrified she could be pregnant again. After a panic-induced race to her local pharmacy for a pregnancy testing kit that gave her the all clear, Tara consoled her frayed nerves by sharing a giant pizza with Hermie, and suffered severe bloating as a consequence. She no longer seemed to fit into the body-hugging clothes James liked her to wear, and sometimes, when they made love, she was so busy trying not to pass wind she had to fake her orgasm to hurry things along a bit.

When Tara described her symptoms to her GP, he suggested she try a gluten-free diet, which meant no bread, pasta, pizza, or a myriad of other foods Tara loved. It also meant a great deal of fuss and planning, and Tara, who'd never taken an interest in cooking, found the whole thing extremely tedious and not at all sexy. What could possibly be less sexy than an embarrassing excess of wind and a growing tendency to have to dash posthaste to the toilet? It was only a matter of time before someone noticed. Only so far an open window or an air-freshener spray would go.

Tara's new dietary requirements weren't the only thing getting her down over the winter. She'd planned to enlist Hermie's help to become a TikTok star and YouTube vlogger—to become such an overnight success, she'd get sponsorships and free beauty products and achieve a level of fame that would negate the need to look for a proper job. Hermie had never been that keen on the idea, although she did go along with it at first, helping her mother to set up the camera and lighting to do her makeup demonstrations, and to show off various outfit combinations.

But Hermie soon got bored when Tara ignored her advice about using hashtags and trending tunes, as well as interacting with other vloggers and TikTok users. The truth was, Tara wasn't a natural in front of the camera. She came across as self-conscious, self-important, and superior, and it was not a winning combination. She also refused to upload any videos which showed her skin in anything but a flawless, perfect light, and since she was now pushing forty-five, this was a tall order.

By the time spring arrived, Tara had become despondent and discouraged, her plans for internet fame largely abandoned, the blame apportioned largely to Hermie for not being sufficiently supportive. Especially when Hermie began to spend several hours a day—the cheek of it—with Frances instead, helping her to make videos about hedgehogs. Videos which received more likes in a matter of days than Tara's received over several months.

What the appeal was, Tara couldn't fathom. Frances remained her normal scruffy self—she didn't put on any makeup, and she didn't change out of her rag-bag clothes. Whenever she smiled, the gaps where she'd had teeth extracted were clearly on display, and it was all hedgehogs, hedgehogs, hedgehogs. Tara may have installed her pretty-bordered hedgehog hole surrounds, but that had mostly been because she liked shopping. In reality, she couldn't really see the appeal of hedgehogs at all.

When she challenged Hermie about the amount of time she spent helping Frances, saying, "If you'd put in this much effort to help make my videos a success, things might have turned out very differently," Hermie didn't even bother to reply.

~

Frances's motivations for making videos were entirely different from Tara's. Frances didn't give a hoot about becoming a celebrity; the very idea was ridiculous. She simply wanted to spread the word about hedgehog highways and to inform the public about the real threats the creatures faced.

Every day when Hermie arrived after school, Frances greeted her with a chocolate bar and buckets full of enthusiasm, keen to put the ideas she'd had during the day into practice. But first, she always asked Hermie about her day, because she might be old, but she still vividly remembered her preteen school days. All the insecurities, the friendship snubs, the gathering pressure of schoolwork. Besides, young as she was, Hermie was now a friend. So Frances asked Hermie about her day, and after a while, Hermie stopped giving a shrug and saying it had been fine and began sharing titbits of information. *"Kerry called me fat. Jaden pulled the chair away when I was about to sit down. I hate history. Who cares what some boring old king did years ago? I don't understand why we need to learn about that stuff."*

Frances made sympathetic sounds and suggestions and then, gripes dealt with, chocolate bar devoured, the two of them would enjoy a happy hour or so, making their videos.

The hedgehogs were beginning to emerge from hibernation, and every morning Frances had new footage to watch. It was like receiving a daily gift, and Frances was starting to distinguish between the different hedgehogs. They all had their individual characters, and Frances named them accordingly.

"I call this one Miss Hopoff," she told Hermie one afternoon.

"Miss Hopoff? Why d'you call her that?"

"Because she's got all these males interested in her, and she's not interested in them. Not at all. Look, she's telling them all to hop off."

Together they watched the footage of a male circling round and round, a disinterested, feisty female hedgehog who suddenly lashed out with her nose to give him a shove.

"Isn't she a character?" Frances said fondly. "She's saying no and meaning no."

"My mum's more Miss-Come-On-In than Miss Hopoff," Hermie said.

"Is she, dear?" Frances asked sympathetically, but Hermie was busy searching for the perfect piece of music to accompany the footage, and the moment passed.

The finished video, which combined music, a voice-over from Frances, and the shove by Miss Hopoff repeated over and over, quickly went viral, and each one of the likes it received gave Frances a glow of satisfaction, making her feel connected to the world. Made her feel useful too, as more and more people commented on her videos and learnt about the importance of hedgehog highways.

One afternoon when Hermie was at her house working on a video, Frances heard her singing. "What's that you're singing, dear?" she asked. "You have a lovely singing voice."

"Thanks. It's just a little song to go with a video."

"Well, sing it for me, then."

"Happy hedgehog highway, Happy hedgehog highway, da-da-da-da, da-da-da-da."

Frances laughed. "That's really catchy! I'll have it in my mind for the rest of the day. It's the conga tune, isn't it? 'Let's all do the conga, let's all do the conga, da-da-da-da, da-da-da-da.'"

Hermie shrugged. "I just heard it once and thought it would fit."

"Well, it does, doesn't it? It fits perfectly. Come on, then."

"What?"

Frances held out her hand, ushering Hermie over to her. "Sing your song, and we'll do the conga to it."

Hermie went over doubtfully but was soon giggling away as the two of them toured Frances's dining room, then went through the kitchen and finally into the garden, singing and kicking their legs out to the side—first to the right, then to the left. "Happy hedgehog highway, Happy hedgehog highway, da-da-da-da, da-da-da-da."

Finally, back in the kitchen, Frances collapsed, puffing, on a kitchen chair. "Goodness, I'm too old for that kind of thing. Pity there wasn't anyone to film us, because I don't think I'll be able to do that again."

"I did film some of it," Hermie told her, replaying the footage she'd captured of them on their way through the dining room.

Frances burst out laughing. "What an old goose I am," she said, and got up to put the kettle on, not thinking any more about it.

The hedgehog project filled Frances with nothing but joy. Occasionally, after she'd watched the most recent footage when she got up in the morning, Frances would sit out on her weed-bound patio with a cup of tea and reflect on what her husband would have made of it all.

It wasn't difficult to imagine, since he'd always been intent on snuffing out any little bit of joy that entered Frances's life. The magpie nest in the hedge destroyed, the greeny-blue eggs smashed on the ground. *"We don't want to encourage corvids, Frances."* New recipes she'd tried out, barely tasted. *"Stick to what you know, Frances. Good plain cooking."* How he would have hated the buzz of the pollinators, collecting nectar from the weeds and flowers growing on his beloved bowling-green lawn. *"There's a bloody bees' nest in the attic. Better get the exterminators in."*

But Frances didn't often think about her husband. The miserable old git had spread unhappiness through her life for far too long as it was. She wasn't going to let him do it now.

Then one day Frances received a message from a local hedgehog charity, complimenting her on her videos and asking whether she'd be interested in volunteering for them. They needed people like her to take in sick or injured hedgehogs for rehabilitation. Would she like to come round to find out more and take a look?

Would she like to? Yes, she bloody well would. The glow of excitement in Frances's belly reinforced what she already knew—that it was high time for her to come out of her own hibernation. She'd barely gone anywhere or done anything these past few years. It was time to go back into the big wide world again.

33

It was Ryan's cap that caught Jess's attention—Hogs Rule, emblazoned above an image of a feisty-looking hedgehog. That, and the wheelchair.

She called to him across the street. "Ryan?"

He looked up, and for just a moment, Jess thought she'd made a mistake. The man with the bleak expression didn't look like Ryan at all. But then he recognised her and smiled and became the man she knew again. "Hi, Jess."

"I'll cross over," Jess called, and waited for a van and a bike to pass before pushing the buggy across the road and joining him on the pavement.

Then once she arrived, she wasn't sure what to say. It had been months since she'd last seen him.

"How are you, Jess?" he asked, recovering his social skills before she did. "And this little chap? Looking very good in your stripey jumper, my man."

Something about Ryan's face didn't quite match his jaunty cap and bright tone of voice. Jess had a sense that she'd interrupted something.

"I'm—" she started to say, but broke off when a man with a walking stick emerged from the community hall behind Ryan.

"See you next week, Ryan."

"Yes, see you, Chris."

Chris was followed by a couple who looked to be in their late thirties, holding hands.

"Are you sure we can't give you a lift home, Ryan?"

"Thanks, Jean. My taxi should be here any minute."

He must have felt Jess looking at him, wondering what event he'd just been to in the hall.

"They're from the support group I go to. For people with PTSD." He jerked his head towards the hall entrance. "It's every Thursday. I've been coming for a few months now."

Jess felt shocked, though she wasn't quite sure why. She did, after all, know that Ryan had been injured when a land mine exploded. "I didn't realise you had PTSD."

Ryan shrugged. "I hide it well, I guess. Except for when I can't."

"I'm so sorry. Is coming to the group helping?"

Ryan sighed. A weary sigh that spoke of the draining effects of the session. The poor guy was obviously wiped out, and here she was, making him talk about it. "I think it will help, given time. It already has in some ways, I suppose. It puts things into perspective, if nothing else. Honestly, the things some of these people have been through, Jess. It beggars belief, it really does."

She met his eyes, wanting to tell him not to think his own experience didn't compare with everyone else's. That she may not know exactly what had happened to him, but she could see its effects. That what he felt was legitimate. But now, here, wasn't the place to talk about such things.

So instead, she said, "Look, I know you're expecting your taxi, but we're parked just up the road if you'd like to come back and have a coffee with us? Toby's had quite enough of shopping for one day, haven't you, Toby?"

She thought for a moment he might refuse. But then he said, "I'd like that. Thanks. I'll just give the taxi company a call to cancel."

When they got back to Hilltop Place, Jess remembered that she'd left the house a mess. That she'd need to move shoes, a pile of library books waiting to be returned, a ride-on Thomas the Tank Engine, and Stella's abandoned roller skates, just so Ryan could get to the sitting room after he'd negotiated getting inside from the patio. This was what he had to put up with all the time, she supposed, this level of difficulty just to get about. How long did it take to stop comparing how life was now with how it had been before? Did you ever just accept it? You'd have to, surely, if you didn't want to get bitter.

Toby was becoming fretful, stretching his body stiffly and flailing about in her arms. "Toby's worn out, poor little chap. D'you mind if I put him down for a nap before I make us a drink?"

"Of course not. Go for it."

Toby only put up a token resistance before slipping into sleep.

Jess crept downstairs.

"Gone down okay?"

"Yes, bless him. We've got about half an hour. An hour, tops. I'll make us some drinks. Coffee okay?"

"Perfect, thanks. Black, no sugar." When she returned, taking a seat on the sofa opposite him, he said, "I like this room."

"It's a bit of a mess," she said.

"That's why I like it. If I leave one dirty cup next to the sink, my mother washes it up straight away. It's hardly a relaxing way to live. This is homely."

"Thanks. But sometimes I wish I could be just a bit more like your mother—"

"Trust me," Ryan interrupted. "You don't want to wish that."

"I just mean, sometimes I wish things weren't such a mess. Not only the house, but life. Me."

She hadn't planned to say all that; the words had just gushed out of her. Something about Ryan—she wasn't sure what—seemed to make her say exactly what she felt.

"I'm sure that isn't true."

Tears pricked her eyes. "It is, though. I couldn't bond with Toby when he first arrived. I couldn't love him. Now I love him too much, or at least, that's what Michael thinks. I'm a mass of contradictions, honestly. I don't love; I do love. I don't want a dog, then I'm heartbroken when Michael gets rid of it. I want to be there for my children so much it hurts, and at the same time, I really miss my job, making a contribution to society. Oh, and my daughter hates me."

"Now, I know *that's* not true."

"It is lately, sometimes. You should see the way she looks at me. Everything's a constant battle." She sighed. "But it's all so trivial compared with all the dreadful things going on in the world, isn't it?"

"You're bringing up human beings. There's nothing trivial about that. And in any event, it's not a case of comparing who's got it hardest, is it? What you feel is what's important."

She looked at him. "You can hear yourself, right? That's exactly what I wanted to say to you when we met just now. You feel the other people in your group have it harder than you, don't you?"

"Well, they have. I was just a cocky git who thought he was invincible. I thought everything I did was so important. Most important. That time would stand still while I did what had to be done. But what really happened was my wife ran off with a work colleague who didn't abandon his family at a moment's notice to go and see his friends blown to bits in front of his sodding eyes."

He swiped tears from his cheeks, and Jess went to sit next to him, reaching out a hand to squeeze his shoulder.

"Sorry," he said with a sniff before she could say anything. "You must think I . . . ."

"What I think is that you need to talk. To let it all out."

"That's the whole point of going to the group. *You* don't want to hear it, believe me. Shit, I really am sorry. It's just that sometimes . . . sometimes it all feels so recent, you know? As if it's only just happened. I can't go anywhere without being noticed these days, and I hate that. I used to be able to look people straight in the eyes, but now I'm in this chair, and I have to look up to them, as if I'm Eric's age all over again. And sometimes . . . when I'm asleep, I dream I can still walk. It's no big deal in the dream, I'm just walking. Then when I wake up, I have to accept the way I am all over again."

There was a pause, while she absorbed it all. Then she said, "Look, it's strange advice to give to a journalist, but have you tried writing about it? They say it helps, don't they?"

He sighed. "I've tried, yes, but I can't. At least, I haven't been able to yet. What about you? Have you tried writing out your feelings about everything?"

"No. Perhaps I should."

He smiled. "I will if you will."

She smiled back. "Deal. Writing therapy, it is. And I'm going to take some other action too. Starting with doing what Frances has done. I'm going to put some cameras up near our hedgehog feeder. I thought Stella might like to get involved with it. That it could be our special project. Though it will probably have to wait, because Michael's so busy with work at the moment it'll likely take him an age to do anything about it."

"I can help you with it, if you like?" he said. "Get the company in I used for Frances's cameras. I could even make you a hedgehog hotel like the one Eric and I made for her garden. It wasn't difficult. We could do it together."

She smiled. "I'd really like that. Thank you."

~

"I'm so excited," Jess said after they'd finished the next day. "You'll have to come round to watch the footage."

He needed to tell her. She'd find out soon enough anyway. But for some reason he was reluctant. Who was he kidding? He knew exactly why he was reluctant to tell her. "Actually, I'm going to be moving out of Hilltop Place soon."

"Are you?"

Was he imagining that her face had fallen when he'd said it? "Yes. I can't live with my mother forever, can I? Not unless I want one of us to commit murder. I need my independence. A place Eric can come to. Not that Eric wants to come and see me at the moment. I had . . . an episode at Christmas, and now . . . Well, I think he's a bit afraid of me. Not that I blame him. It was all pretty grim. My ex-wife doesn't really trust me to have him any longer."

"But you're attending the group. You're doing something about it."

He wasn't really, though, was he? He might attend the group, but he hadn't spoken much about what had happened that day yet, not really. He'd let the odd thing slip, spoken about his experience of having flashbacks—which were becoming increasingly frequent—but he hadn't talked about seeing the driver with part of his face missing. Johnny the cameraman's cries of agony. The thought of saying such things out loud made him feel physically sick. Every week, he sat there in the circle, psyching himself up to talk, and every week, he chickened out. He'd done it again, just now, with Jess. Though somehow, he could imagine talking to Jess about it, but it would hardly be fair to dump all that horror on her when she was dealing with shit herself.

"If I can ever help out with Eric, let me know, won't you?" she said. "I realise a four-year-old and a two-year-old aren't the best company for him, but maybe we could go to the zoo or something during the school holidays. He'd like that, wouldn't he?"

Ryan was ashamed to say he had no idea. That he didn't know whether Annie took Eric to the zoo regularly or whether Eric already thought he was far too cool for such a place. But he would like it himself, he did know that. And far more than he ought to.

"Thanks, that's kind."

"No problem."

"I'm not moving very far away," he said, suddenly needing her to know that. "I'm buying one of those flats at the bottom of Wall Road. It's specially converted for a wheelchair user, and there's a garden of sorts."

Jess smiled. "I'm so glad you won't be far away," she said, and just for a split second he felt a connection between them—a spark that made Ryan's heart slam inside his chest.

Then Toby began to cry upstairs, Jess got to her feet, and the moment was over.

"I'd better just go and . . ."

"Yes, sure."

34

As spring turns into summer and the daylight hours stretch into the evening, a hedgehog has less time to find the food it needs. Sometimes it has to risk venturing out before the sun has completely set, or staying out after the sun has begun to rise. At such times, it's a distinct possibility that people with motion-activated cameras installed near their hedgehog feeding stations will wake up to find some thrilling colour footage of the hungry creatures.

But there can be side effects to this joyous viewing. Life-transforming ones in some cases. And one such life-transforming side effect was just about to play itself out in Hilltop Place.

It was late May, the first day of the Whitsun school holidays. Frances was up early—nothing to do with it being the school holidays; Frances was always up early, keen to view any hedgehog activity recorded overnight.

Frances had another reason to feel excited that week. She had decided it would be the week she'd get herself to the hedgehog rescue place to have a look around. She'd been meaning to go for a while, but had, for some reason, felt nervous about it and kept putting it off. But some recent, full-technicolour footage of two hedgehogs at her feeding station had finally inspired her to do it. One of them—the one she'd named Gloria—looked fatter than the last time Frances had seen her. Could she be about to retire to her nest to give birth? It might well be Gloria's final prebirth feed-up!

It was all so thrilling; Frances didn't want to wait for Hermie to post a TikTok video. She wanted to share her joy and excitement right away. Surely she could make a video herself? She'd watched Hermie do it so many times.

To Frances's joy, she did manage to make a video—not up to Hermie's standards, but a video, nevertheless—of herself speaking passionately about Gloria and the chance that there might be the patter of tiny hoglet feet soon, followed by a clip of the footage of Gloria at the feeding station.

After she'd posted the video, Frances had such a sense of achievement that she punched the air and did a celebrational robot dance out on her patio, inspired by a TikTok video she'd seen the previous day. And after she finished the robot dance, she gave a loud *whoop* and laughed out loud, speaking to the garden, the sky, the trees. "What d'you think about that? I did it all by myself!"

Frances's upbeat, confident mood lasted for about an hour or so, until she'd had some breakfast and checked to see whether her new video had scored any likes. It had—*yippee!*—several hundred. And there were comments too. Smiling to herself, Frances clicked through them. They started off well—So cute! Baby hedgehog vids please! Et cetera. But then they changed. Somebody called @tastesnap had left several comments. Loads of comments. And they were all nasty. In fact, they were vile.

Ugly bitch.

We're here for the hogs, not the ugly owner.

Did you get your hair advice from a scarecrow?

How old is that jumper? It's disgusting. I bet you've got fleas—caught them from the hedgehogs maybe. No wait, bet you gave the hedgehogs fleas!

On and on. *Bloody hell.*

Leaving the computer on, Frances traipsed out into the hallway, her worn mule slippers slapping the soles of her feet. She rarely looked in the mirror, but now she took a long, hard look at herself. At her wild and unbrushed hair, sticking out on one side. @tastesnap was right— she ought to have brushed it before she made the video. Come to think of it, had she brushed it the day before? She couldn't remember. And the jumper was ancient, it was true, saggy and bobbly from the wash. But she didn't think it was dirty. Well, not really. Certainly not dirty enough to harbour fleas. And anyway, wasn't it what was inside your clothes that mattered? The person you were. Whoever had left those messages was obviously just an unpleasant human being.

A shaft of light suddenly streamed in through the glass panel in the front door, picking out the lines on Frances's face—the furrows carved by age, experience, and sorrow—and instantly the remainder of her positivity was snuffed right out. Who was she kidding? @tastesnap was right. She was nothing but a ridiculous, aging woman, making an utter fool of herself, thinking she could make videos the world wanted to see. She ought to give everyone a break and pack it in.

But first, she'd go back to bed.

～

The footage picked up by Jess's new camera was also in colour. (It was also of hungry Gloria, but Jess had no idea about that, not being familiar yet with the different hedgehogs or the names Frances had given them.) All Jess knew was that she couldn't wait to watch it with Stella. Maybe, just maybe, this plan to get closer to her daughter again would work. Even despite the trauma of the previous evening.

Jess had taken Stella to a funfair the night before, just the two of them, with Michael staying at home to take care of Toby. It had been an evening of fairground rides, far too much sugar, and lots of laughter. Jess had even won Stella a giant teddy bear on the firing range. They'd driven home, singing songs and trying to think of an appropriate name for the new bear, only to arrive back to find Toby crying the house down. He'd refused to let anyone but Jess comfort him, and as she'd scooped him up into her arms, she'd witnessed Stella's face change from happy back to jealous, resentful, and mutinous. Next thing, the carefree girl who had beamed and waved at Jess while she rode on a pony on the carousel was kicking over Toby's ride-on Thomas the Tank Engine and hurling one of her roller skates, shattering one of the glass panels in the kitchen door.

The noise of the breaking glass had been terrifying. Stella had burst into tears, even before Michael had begun shouting at her, and what with clearing up the broken glass and calming both Toby and Stella down, they'd all got to bed late, so Jess hadn't got round to saying anything to Michael about Ryan helping her to install the camera near the hedgehog feeding station.

But today was a new day, and the new camera had filmed a hedgehog in their garden. Jess knew she really ought to wait to watch it with Stella, but Stella had been so exhausted after last night's drama, who knew when she'd wake up? And Stella wouldn't know Jess had already watched, would she?

Feeling only slightly guilty, Jess clicked to play the video and was soon grinning from ear to ear. The hedgehog was so cute! And so hungry. She could hear it snuffling about and crunching the cat biscuits she'd left in the feeder. Wow. She hadn't expected the sound quality to be so good. And to have colour images like this. It was fantastic. Stella would be thrilled. Which would hopefully lead to them all having a better day.

There were more videos to watch, but Jess placed the computer in sleep mode, deciding to wait to watch them with Stella when she woke up. It would be good to do it while Toby was still asleep, though, just the two of them. Jess crept upstairs to take a peek round Stella's door but found her starfished in her bed, still dead to the world. Unfortunately, quiet as Jess had been, Toby heard her anyway and began jumping up and down in his cot, calling out for her. So Jess whisked him downstairs for breakfast, leaving Stella to sleep.

In the end, Jess didn't manage to watch the videos with her daughter until ten thirty, after Stella was up and fed, and Jess had managed to distract Toby with a fishing game—or almost distract him, because Toby kept wanting Jess to join in with his celebrations every time he caught a fish, or to answer him when he said, "Where fishy, Mama? Where fishy?"

Jess was looking down into the cardboard fish tank when the second hedgehog video began to play, and Stella said, "This one's all dark."

Jess glanced up. "Yes, it's nighttime now, darling. The camera is a special camera that can film when it's dark."

She looked down again, carefully moving Toby's red plastic fishing rod so that its magnet would make contact with one of the magnets on the side of a fish.

"There's just feet and legs on this video, Mummy."

"Are there, darling?" Jess said vaguely, glancing up and expecting to see hedgehog feet and legs, but seeing two pairs of human feet and legs instead. *What the . . . ?*

There were voices coming through the speakers. Whoever the feet and legs belonged to, they were having a conversation. Had the camera caught would-be burglars? Maybe they had been burgled and she just hadn't realised it yet?

Jess glanced fearfully around the room to check that everything was still there but was quickly drawn back to the video footage when Stella said in an excited voice, "It's Daddy talking, Mummy. It's Daddy."

"What?"

Bored with trying to catch fish, Toby bashed the top of the cardboard fish tank with his fishing rod, and Jess leant forward to turn up the volume on the speaker in time to hear the unmistakable sound of her husband's voice.

"I've missed you so much. When will you be able to get away properly again?"

"I'm not sure. I'm running out of excuses. It wasn't easy to get away this evening. I had to pour the milk down the sink and say I'd forgotten to buy any."

Was that Helen from across the road? It sounded like Helen. But it couldn't be, surely?

Suddenly a noise like a giant vacuum cleaner roared inside Jess's ears. Her mother's instinct made her reach forward to switch the speakers and the computer off. She thought she might be sick.

"No, Mummy. I want to see Daddy on the computer!" Stella protested.

"Not just now, darling," Jess said as Toby began to climb up her leg and onto her lap as if she were a climbing frame.

And that was enough to send Stella into an absolute raging tantrum, throwing herself down onto the floor, kicking and screaming like a toddler, whereupon Toby started bawling too. Jess felt like joining in with them both. To give in to her feelings instead of sitting there frozen with shock, her fingers tingling with pins and needles, her mouth numb. Was it really possible that Michael was having an affair with Helen Hedges from across the road? The idea seemed absurd. Ridiculous. Yet she had heard what she had heard, hadn't she? She needed to hear it again. To see what else they said to each other. To confirm that she really had seen and heard what she thought she had. But to do that, she'd have to find some way to get the kids out of the room, even if that meant barricading them temporarily in their bedrooms.

~

Frances stayed in bed for thirty minutes before throwing the covers back and returning to her computer. Maybe she'd imagined how bad the comments were? She took a look. No, they were every bit as vitriolic as she remembered. But she had to scroll back quite a long way to find them now, because plenty of other people had left comments after @tastesnap had left hers—encouraging, enthusiastic comments. And her video had received another hundred likes.

Sod @tastesnap. Whoever they were, they were just a vicious human being with nothing better to do than try to destroy people's days. If Frances wanted to carry on making videos, then she bloody well would. Though maybe she'd make sure she brushed her hair next time. And perhaps she'd wear something smarter. What about makeup? Or would that be going too far? Frances hadn't felt confident about wearing makeup ever since her husband told her she looked like a clown with it on. But perhaps Hermie's mum could give her a bit of advice? She was into makeup and outfits, all that kind of stuff. Yes, maybe she would ask Tara whether she could spare an hour or so, to teach her how to use makeup.

And today, she was bloody well going to phone for a taxi and get herself down to the rescue centre. She still felt nervous about it, and if she waited until she had an appointment, she might never do it. If they were too busy to show her round, she'd just come back another day. At least she'd have taken a first step, and it would be easier next time.

Before she could change her mind, Frances booked the taxi, then wondered whether she ought to change her clothes. No, no need. Everyone at the centre would be dressed in old clothes, focused on the animals rather than their image. She would be fine as she was.

She checked her purse to make sure she had enough money to pay for the taxi and stood in the open doorway to wait for it to arrive. Outside in the road, everything was calm and peaceful. Birds were singing in the trees. Somewhere nearby, hedgehogs were no doubt curled up, fast asleep. Gloria, perhaps, having a last nap before giving birth, her belly pleasantly full up from her feast at Frances's feeding station.

A car pulled into the road. But it was a blue car, not a taxi. She watched it park outside Irene's house. Frances couldn't see inside, but whoever was in the car didn't get out.

Another car turned into the road. Her taxi this time. Frances's stomach lurched. @tastesnap's comments suddenly rushed back into her mind, reminding her of her husband. Robbing her of confidence. *"Get a job? You?"* he'd said once when she'd thought of doing something to take her out of the house. *"Who'd want to employ you? You're neither use nor ornament."*

The voice inside her head sounded so real that Frances wouldn't have been surprised to turn to find Trevor behind her. Shakily, she reached out to hold the doorjamb for support. The taxi stopped outside her house. The driver waited, engine running.

Frances did her best to replace her husband's mean voice inside her head. *Go on, Frances. Think of all those hedgehogs at the rescue centre, waiting for you to help them. It doesn't matter what you look like. Or what anyone thinks about you. You can do it. You can.*

But she couldn't.

The driver finally got out and said, "Taxi?"

Frances took a step backwards, into the dimness of her hallway. "No, sorry, I'm not well. I won't be able to travel today, after all," she said, then pushed the door closed.

She heard the taxi drive away. This was why she hardly ever tried to do new things, because it hurt so much when you let yourself down. When you were thwacked in the face yet again with evidence of what a failure you were. A pathetic, useless failure. @tastesnap was right about her. Her husband had been right about her.

"Bloody hell, Frances. And you ask me why I won't want us to have children. You can't even look after yourself, let alone another human being. The poor kid would end up lost or starved to death while you were busy with one of your pathetic paranoias."

Outside the window, Jess hurried past, carrying Toby on her hip, clutching Stella's hand, dragging the little girl along. Curiosity cut through Frances's despondency. Where could they be going in such a rush? Frances craned her neck just in time to see Jess turn up Tara's drive. Minutes later, Jess returned, minus Stella. She must have dropped the little girl off at Tara's. Frances hadn't realised the two of them were on such close terms. Shortly afterwards, Jess's car backed quickly out of her drive and roared up the road. Goodness, something definitely wasn't right. Jess was clearly upset about something. But what?

~

At Tara's house, Tara was asking herself the same question. Jess had basically just turned up and dumped her kid on her without so much as a by your leave. Okay, so Tara had said Stella was welcome to come round and play with Hermie sometime, but a bit of notice would have been good, and at a time that suited Tara, which was not before she'd taken a shower and put her makeup on. And if you were going to dump your kid on someone, then surely they deserved a bit more of an explanation than *"I wouldn't ask, but there's something important I've got to do. Something I can't do if I have Stella with me."*

Tara supposed she ought to be grateful that Jess hadn't tried to dump Toby on her too. Though she'd have put her foot down about that, no question.

"Where's the girl?" Stella asked.

Her hair looked like a bird's nest, and she appeared to have breakfast cereal in it. There also seemed to be what looked like yoghurt down the front of her T-shirt. Had Jess dressed her in yesterday's clothes?

"D'you mean Hermie? She's still in bed, being lazy. Shall we go and wake her up?"

"Yes, yes, yes!"

Bloody hell.

"All right, you go up first. It's the first door you come to. Go straight in and jump on the bed. Give Hermie a nice surprise."

At least it wasn't raining. The two of them could go and play in the garden, to give Tara some peace.

Hermie was predictably grumpy at first, not appreciating the rude awakening. But she soon came round when Tara threw together a picnic—mostly consisting of sweets and unhealthy stuff, but what the hell—and set the girls up in the garden with a picnic blanket and a pop-up tent. Listening to the giggling coming in through the window, Tara felt quite pleased with herself. Maybe she wasn't so bad at this mum stuff, after all.

All still seemed well when she'd finished applying her makeup and fixing her hair—the girls had emerged from the tent and were practising dance moves on the lawn. Well, Hermie was practising dance moves, and Stella was copying her and not doing too bad a job of it. Hermie seemed to have become the kid's idol, and was soaking it up. Which was a very good thing, because just then a car pulled up outside and Tara saw it was James, which was fantastic, because she hadn't expected to see him. Though it was less than fantastic that she had not one but two children on the premises.

Hurrying to the back door before he could knock, Tara hesitated for just a second before turning the key. Not that she would keep the girls locked outside; of course she wouldn't. But the sound of the rattling handle would serve as an early-warning system, giving her time to put some clothes on. For she fully intended to take some off.

"Hello, you," she said to James, opening the door and pulling him into the hallway by his tie.

"Is the sprog around?" he asked, casting a wary eye about.

"She's out in the garden with a friend. Don't worry; they won't disturb us. Not for a while, anyway." And she proceeded to unbutton her blouse right there in the hall, licking her lips suggestively as she did so, exposing his favourite black lace bra and an abundance of cleavage to his hungry eyes.

"Come on, then," he said, the bulge in his trousers a testimony to her instant effect on him. "I've got a meeting in an hour."

∼

Across town, Jess parked her car on a double yellow line and bumped Toby's buggy up the steps to Michael's office building. She would have preferred not to confront Michael in front of Toby, but leaving him in

Tara's care was unthinkable, and she couldn't—simply couldn't—wait until Michael got home from work to confront him. She tried really hard to be a good mother, she really did. But she was not superhuman. If life as she knew it was about to be blown sky high, then she needed to have it confirmed as soon as possible.

Michael's personal assistant said he was in a meeting. Of course he was. In films, unfaithful husbands were always in meetings when their spurned wives came to confront them.

"Jess? I'm sorry, you can't go in there."

Personal assistants always said that in films too.

In movies, spurned wives did not normally have to back their buggies into meeting rooms to confront their husbands, but when Jess actually got into the room and turned round, the reception she received was exactly like a scene from a film. Everyone seated around the boardroom table in their dull business clothes swiveled their heads in her direction. The speaker halted in the middle of her PowerPoint presentation. The unfaithful husband—Michael—got to his feet and said, "Jess? What are you doing here?"

But there the similarity to the movies ended. Because instead of accusing Michael of infidelity in front of his boss, his colleagues, and Melissa Freeman, Michael's rival for promotion, Jess began to cry—great, ugly, shuddering, gulping sobs involving a lot of snot and extensive mascara trails.

"How could you, Michael?" she managed through her tears, while everyone sat staring at her with a combination of horror, embarrassment, and open curiosity, especially as Toby, witnessing her distress, began to wail too.

Only after Michael had managed to steer both Jess and a now-deafening Toby from the boardroom and into his office did Jess's anger manage to resurface, this in response to Michael having the temerity to say, "That was so embarrassing, Jess. What were you thinking?"

Jess literally growled at him. "Don't you fucking *What were you thinking*' me! What were *you* thinking, shitting our marriage down the toilet?"

Michael went pale. "What are you talking about?"

"I'm talking about you and Helen. And don't bother to deny it. You were caught on camera." Jess impersonated the voice she'd heard in the video. *"I've missed you so much. When will you be able to get away properly again?"*

Michael sank back into his ergonomic chair. "What camera?"

"It doesn't fucking well matter what camera, Michael. I saw you. I heard you. That is all."

Jess's fury ebbed away as quickly as it had arrived. She began to cry again, bending to unfasten Toby's harness to scoop him from the buggy, tears dripping into his hair as she held him close.

"Mama," he said, looking up into her face.

She kissed his forehead, a wave of grateful love for him sweeping through her. Shit was going to continue to hit the fan. The coming months would be bleak as hell. But she had Toby, and she had Stella— her gorgeous children. They would get her through.

"You're a complete bastard, Michael," she said, and walked out, leaving the buggy where it was so she could make a quick exit.

~

When somebody began to scream back in Hilltop Place, Tara didn't hear it. Or, rather, she did, but she was building up to orgasm and doing quite a lot of moaning and screaming herself, so her brain failed to compute it.

But Frances's brain did. The screaming was so loud, so horrified, so cop show / crime drama, she rushed to her front door and pulled it open to find Helen standing on her drive, obviously in a state of high distress.

"What is it?" Frances called across the street. "What's wrong?"

"There . . . there's a hedgehog. I . . . I was doing the strimming Justin told me to do, and suddenly it was just there."

Frances quickly made her way down the garden path, only pausing briefly to clutch at the gate post as she asked, "Is it injured? Have you hurt it?"

"I think . . . I think I might have cut one of its legs off. I . . . I'm not really sure. I couldn't look. I just dropped the strimmer and ran. I'm not very good with blood and stuff. Can you come and see?"

"Where is it? Show me."

She followed Helen—still blathering on about not meaning to do it and how she ought to have checked the long grass before she started strimming—round the side of the house and down to the bottom of the garden to the scene of the incident to find a hedgehog, lying inert in blood-splattered grass, its twitching nose the only sign of life.

Tears filled Frances's eyes. She blinked them quickly away. Tears would be no help at all. This wasn't about her. Or hand-wringing Helen. It was about the injured creature on the grass.

"Poor little thing," Frances said, bending over to take a proper look. Helen was right, she thought. One of its legs had definitely been severed. "Have you got a box or something to put it in? We'll have to take it to the hedgehog rescue centre."

"I . . . I think so. I'll go and look." Helen scuttled off towards the house like a primary-school pupil charged with an important errand by their teacher.

Alone with the hedgehog, Frances spoke to it. "You poor thing. We'll get you sorted out; I promise you we will."

Then, suddenly, as she knelt there, Frances heard a squeaking sound coming from the corner of the garden. *Oh no, please don't let the hedgehog have babies. Please.* She got up, her knees protesting, and went to take a look, carefully parting the leaves of a shrub.

"Oh," she said. "Oh." For there, partially concealed by fallen leaves, were four tiny, extremely cute, and incredibly vulnerable hoglets. She glanced over at the prone hedgehog, tears once again pricking her eyes. "You must be Gloria. Oh, darling, you must be Gloria."

Helen came running back across the lawn with a cardboard box. "I found one!" she said triumphantly, then stopped. "What? What is it?"

"She's got babies. We'll have to take them to the rescue centre too. Quickly, there's not a moment to lose. Go and find another box!"

"I'm not sure I've got another one."

"You must have," said Frances, the tears making her voice harsh. "Go and look."

Helen soon returned with a fancy-looking round box. "I'm going to my friend's wedding next month. I took my hat out of this."

Frances didn't care whether the box had contained a wedding hat or a pack of toilet rolls. It was a box, and it would do. Besides, she was busy ripping her cardigan off to create some cushioning for poor, broken Gloria to nestle in. No need to put the lid on the box—Gloria wasn't going anywhere.

When she'd settled the injured hedgehog as comfortably as possible, she turned her attention to the babies.

"Get some of that grass to put into the box," she told Helen, pointing to the grass that had been cut by the vile strimmer. "And some of those leaves. The babies will feel more secure with somewhere to hide."

Finally, finally, they were on their way—Frances carrying the hatbox, Helen the cardboard box containing the babies. Frances knew the way to the rescue centre—she had researched it often enough. She had so wanted to go there, but not like this. Not on a dreadful do-or-die, lifesaving mission for poor Gloria. Gloria, who had been so full of life in the video footage the other day.

"You need to turn right here," Frances told Helen when she looked as if she might drive straight on and miss the turning.

"Oh, sorry," Helen said, indicating at the last minute and earning a blast on the horn from the driver behind her.

A lorry zoomed past, making the windows shake. Traffic seemed to come at them from every angle as they waited to turn at the busy junction. Never a very good passenger, Frances felt suddenly dizzy but pushed the feeling away, refusing to acknowledge it, focusing instead on Gloria. She was so still. Would she survive? And what of the hoglets? They were so very tiny. So vulnerable.

"Why didn't you check the grass before you started your blasted strimming?" she snapped bitterly. "I gave you that leaflet. I bet you didn't even bloody read it."

Helen sounded tearful. "I did, Frances. I promise you, I did. Only Justin went on and on about that part of the garden being a mess. He can be really . . . Well, anyway, I just wanted to stop him complaining about it. I didn't think. I'm so sorry."

Frances, recognising the real distress in Helen's voice, sighed. "You really shouldn't let that man order you about the way he does, you know. It's the twenty-first century."

There was a gap in the traffic. Helen moved the car forward. "I know I shouldn't. And actually, I am doing something about it. I'm . . . I'm not going to put up with it forever, I promise you."

"I'm very glad to hear it."

~

One of the reasons Ryan had decided to buy the flat on Wall Road was because it was close to Hilltop Place—close enough for him to return whenever he liked on his newly purchased mobility scooter.

Not that there was any particular need for him to return to Hilltop Place—his mother had popped round on a few occasions, and Hermie was helping Frances with her hedgehog filming, so he wasn't needed there. But you didn't only see friends when they needed you, did you? And Frances was very much a friend now. Which made visiting all the more important now that he had no chance of running into her by accident. No chance of running into anyone from Hilltop Place by accident.

As Ryan steered his scooter up the hill, he thought about Jess, about the moment his gaze had connected with hers when they'd had coffee together at her house. It wasn't the first time he'd relived that moment. He'd thought about it pretty much every day since. Even more since he'd moved house. That was what this trip today was really about—not to collect some forgotten item from his mother's house. Not for a casual catch-up with Frances and her hedgehogs. But for the possibility of running into Jess. It was foolish, he was an idiot, no good could come from it, et cetera, et cetera, but there you were. Ryan couldn't help himself.

He had his excuse ready, should he find the courage to knock on Jess's door. He'd ask her how her writing therapy was going, whether it was helping her at all. He hoped it was, because it seemed to be helping him. Stupid that he—a journalist—hadn't thought of it himself. Every day now, first thing in the morning, he sat down to fill three pages or more with stream-of-consciousness writing—word after word about his frustration of not seeing Eric as much as he wanted to, his despair as he finally began to accept that he wouldn't walk again. His loss of identity without the focus of his work. And Jess. Oh yes, Jess had definitely featured in his outpourings.

He didn't plan on anybody ever reading any of it. And maybe it was a mistake to write about his feelings for Jess, because it made them very much harder to ignore. Maybe . . . no, certainly, he should focus on the one topic he had so far avoided writing about—the terrorist attack.

The new mobility scooter had certainly extended the range Ryan could travel. But sometimes he missed the physicality of propelling his old chair along—hands pumping, biceps straining, working up a sweat. When you passively sat, you had more time to think. And sometimes you arrived at places before you were mentally prepared to.

Steering into Hilltop Place, Ryan slowed down. His mother's car wasn't in the drive—surprise, surprise. Lover boy's car was parked outside Tara's house, so he must have honoured her with a visit, and there was a random blue car parked opposite—the one he'd seen once before, maybe?—but no Jess. She must be out. Maybe if he popped round to see Frances, Jess would return by the time he'd had a cup of tea and a chat.

But Frances didn't answer when Ryan knocked on her front door, and when he cheekily went round to the back of her house, there was no answer to his knock there either. Frances was never out. And yet today, she was.

Disappointed, Ryan returned to the street. A man was getting out of the blue parked car. Caught up in his thoughts, Ryan paid him little attention at first. Not until he crossed the street and said to Ryan, "Excuse me, are you Irene Tindall's son?"

Ryan frowned, looking the stranger up and down. He was tall with dark hair, nice clothes. About five years older than he was. There was something familiar about him, though Ryan was pretty sure they'd never met before. "I am."

The guy, whoever he was, looked at Ryan every bit as intently as Ryan looked at him.

"This is a bit awkward," the stranger said eventually. "Actually, there's probably no easy way to say it, so I'll just come right out with it. I think you're my brother."

~

Up in Tara's bedroom, in Tara's bed, Tara and James lay in the afterglow of amazing sex, Tara's head on his chest. These were Tara's favourite moments, before either she or James began to speak and the magic of what they'd just created together still bonded them. No thoughts of work, of his family, the intrusion that was Hermie. Nothing but liquid legs and gratitude, his hand absentmindedly stroking her back.

Outside in the street, Tara could hear male voices. It sounded like Ryan speaking to someone, she couldn't tell who. It didn't matter. She didn't care. It was just background noise, the way the girls playing in the garden would be background noise if Tara could hear them. But they must be absorbed in whatever game they were playing because Tara couldn't hear them at all, thank goodness. No girlish chatter or giggling to pull James out of his mood. Though he would pull himself out of it soon enough, she knew.

"I adore your nipples," Tara said, exploring the closest one with her tongue.

There was a gratifying rumble of laughter from his chest. "What a perfectly ridiculous thing to say," he said, but Tara could feel his body responding to her twirling tongue.

"You're always so up for it, aren't you?" he said approvingly.

Tara laughed. "Always," she said, kissing him, moving the fullness of her breasts against his damp nipple.

He groaned, his tongue thrusting greedily into her mouth, hands jamming her against him. As he did so, Tara heard a car screech into the close.

"Jesus! You fucking maniac!"

Kissing James deeply back, Tara couldn't help but hear Ryan's shout through the open window.

As James's hand reached down between her legs, Tara heard the squeal of brakes. The sudden silence as the car engine was switched off. The slam of a car door.

"You're going to kill someone, driving like that!"

High heels clip-clopped up Tara's path. Tara had a sudden bad feeling in the pit of her stomach. By the time whoever it was began to pound on the front door, James was already getting out of bed.

"James! I know you're in there!"

"Shit, it's my wife," James said, searching for his boxer shorts in the bed, almost falling as he accidentally tried to put both feet into the same leg hole.

Heart sinking, Tara reached for her robe. She'd always known this day would come; she just hadn't thought it would be today. How had his wife found out about them? And was it necessarily a bad thing that she had? Maybe it would propel them into divorcing, which would leave James for her.

"Where the fuck d'you think you're going?" James hissed at her as she padded across the carpet.

"To open the door before she bashes it down."

"She mustn't fucking see you, you stupid cow," he snarled, pulling up his trousers and thrusting his arms into his shirt.

Seconds later, he thumped down the stairs. A pause—presumably while he put his jacket on—then Tara heard the front door opening. "Darling, what are you doing here? I just popped round to collect some rent arrears. Hey, what are all these tears? Come on, sweetheart." The front door slammed shut.

~

"Wait, Jess, I can explain."

Jess straightened from strapping Toby into his car seat to watch Michael attempt to negotiate the exit doors of the office building with the buggy. He wasn't doing a very good job of it. The doors kept closing on him, bashing into the buggy handle, catching his hand once, causing him to cry out.

Jess hoped it hurt. A lot. She hoped the wind took the door and slammed it onto his hand so bloody hard it turned it to pulp. Then she thought of the kinds of things the hand had very likely been doing to Helen recently and started crying all over again.

"Sweetheart, honestly," Michael called, walking towards her now, "there's no need for this. It meant nothing. Honestly."

Jess thought about shy, skinny Helen. Voluptuous, pouty Tara was the type you could say "It meant nothing" about, not Helen. If you got involved with someone like Helen, it definitely meant something. Helen just wasn't the have-a-fling-with type.

Michael reached her with the buggy. She grabbed it from him, aiming an expert kick to fold it down, and slung it into the car boot.

"Let's see whether Helen agrees with the it-was-nothing angle, shall we? I'll go straight round to the library right now to ask her."

"She's not . . . ," began Michael, giving away his knowledge of Helen's work schedule.

"Not at work today?" Jess finished for him. "All right, I'll go round to her house, then." She wrenched the car door open.

"Please, Jess . . ."

"Please what? 'Please don't be nasty to my girlfriend'? 'Please don't be angry'? 'Please pop back in fucking time and don't decide to install a camera in the garden'?"

"Jess . . ."

"Fuck off, Michael."

And with that, Jess got into the car and drove away.

~

The rescue centre was incredible. Frances had never seen anything like it. After turning off the road and heading along a track through woodland, they'd been greeted by cats—everywhere, seated on fence posts, on roofs, in trees. And when Helen had parked the car and they walked together to the centre entrance, carefully carrying their precious charges, feline eyes watched their progress every step of the way.

"Goodness, d'you think they all live here?"

Frances spotted a cat with a missing tail. Another with only one eye. "I do, yes. That's an awful lot of cat food to buy."

An old ship's bell hung next to the gated entrance. Frances carefully placed the hatbox down on the ground and rang the bell, the resulting peal echoing around the trees. Shortly afterwards, a woman wearing Wellington boots and a T-shirt emblazoned with the words Rescue and Protect emerged from a long ramshackle building and came towards them. She had her hair pulled back into a scruffy ponytail and a pair of glasses perched on top of her head. She didn't look like somebody who watched and commented on TikTok videos, but then Frances did, so who knew?

Frances explained why they were there, showing the woman—who introduced herself as Miriam—the contents of the boxes, thinking it best not to mention that Helen was the strimmer-wielder, a decision which Miriam ratified as she let them in through the gate and they followed her towards the building.

"If I had my way, there'd be an outright ban on strimmers. And I'd set a legal requirement that all gardens should give over at least fifty percent to nature. We're far too fond of being neat and tidy these days, and wildlife is suffering as a result."

Frances wholeheartedly agreed, though a sideways glance at Helen walking beside her with her eyes guiltily lowered like a prisoner at the dock made Frances sigh. Even if Helen agreed with Miriam's views, she couldn't act on them with Justin at the helm of their marriage. And sadly, the world was full of Justins.

When they entered the building—the obvious control centre of the rescue operation—Frances instantly forgot all about Justin and Helen because the place was crammed full of hedgehogs. Shelf after shelf, containing crate after crate of them, many snuggled into old woolen hats for warmth.

"Oh, my goodness, you have so many."

"We do. Hedgehogs with mites, hedgehogs with worms. And, unfortunately, victims of accidents like this little girl here."

"Will she be all right?"

"Hopefully, since you got her to us straight away. She's in shock at the moment, of course. We'll have to keep her in while her injuries heal. Unfortunately, she won't be able to be released into the wild after that, though."

Frances was alarmed. "What will happen to her, then?"

"We have a few volunteers with secure gardens; I'm sure one of those will take her."

The opposite of a hedgehog highway, then. Poor Gloria.

Helen's phone began to ring. "Sorry, sorry," she said, taking it out of her pocket. "I'll have to take this." And she left the building.

"What about the babies?" Frances asked. "Will they be all right?"

Miriam sighed. "We can but hope. They're very young, so they'll need round-the-clock care. I've got a volunteer who'd be willing to help with that, though."

"I'd like to volunteer myself," Frances said. "I'm on TikTok. You liked some of my videos about the hedgehogs that visit my garden."

Miriam smiled. "That will probably have been Otis, one of our younger volunteers. I'm afraid I haven't got a clue about social media. But good for you, getting stuck into all that yourself. I'm sure we can find something for you to do. Fill out the application form on our website, and we'll have a chat. In the meantime, I'd better sort these guys out. Thanks so much for bringing them in."

Frances was on cloud nine as she walked back to the car. She would fire up the laptop and fill out the application form as soon as she got home. Maybe she'd even get to help take care of Gloria's hoglets.

Helen was in the car, waiting for her. She looked as if she'd been crying—obviously, the phone call had upset her for some reason.

Frances sighed, reluctant for her mood to be sullied. "Bad news?"

Helen nodded. "D'you mind if we go straight home?"

Frances clipped on her seat belt. "Of course." Then she had a thought. "Actually," she said, "if you don't mind, could you drop me off at the library on your way back? I've been meaning to go there for ages."

"Of course."

Helen was silent for almost all the journey back to the city. Then, about two miles from the library, she suddenly asked Frances, "Was it very hard for you to get used to your husband not being around? You know, after he disappeared?"

It was such an unexpected question that Frances's head whirled round. Why on earth had the woman asked her that out of the blue?

"Sorry," Helen said quickly. "I shouldn't have asked. It's none of my business."

"No," said Frances, "that's okay." She paused, considering how to answer. In the end she said, "My husband wasn't a very nice man. It was a very long time until I felt safe."

"Oh," said Helen, "I didn't realise."

"People so rarely do, do they?" Frances said, turning away to look out the car window again, and the subject was dropped.

~

Tara had returned to bed after James and his wife left.

The day had started so well—James unexpectedly turning up, amazing sex. He'd been almost loving afterwards too. But the way he'd spoken to her when Cressida had arrived! If she'd been fooling herself that James might voluntarily leave Cressida for her, then that tone of voice had certainly dispelled any such romantic thoughts.

Of course, they might divorce after this. But was that really what Tara wanted? To be a default choice? After all, she wasn't getting any younger. James would soon cast around for someone younger to have a bit on the side with.

A bit on the side. That's what she was, what she'd been for years. Wasn't it time for a little more self-respect? To forge a better life for herself? And for Hermie too, of course.

Hermie. She'd better go and check up on her and Stella, she supposed. But she'd take a little nap first. This morning's events had quite worn her out.

35

It was true; it had to be. Ryan had no idea how or why, but this man definitely had to be his brother because looking at him was like looking at a middle-aged version of Eric. As if Eric had found a time machine and propelled himself forward thirty-odd years.

The guy had been telling Ryan something about how he'd found this address—Ryan hadn't listened properly; he was too shocked—but now he paused. "I'm sorry," the guy said. "I don't know your name."

"Ryan."

"I'm Jonathan."

The guy looked as if he were about to hold out his hand, like they were strangers meeting at a party. *Bloody hell.*

"You'd better come in." The words sounded ridiculous in their ordinariness. Necessary, though. They couldn't just talk out on the street. What if someone came out? What if Jess came out? *"Hi, Jess, good to see you. This is Jonathan, the long-lost brother I never knew I had."*

Without saying anything else, Ryan led the way round the side of the house. But when he tried his key in the french doors, he found they'd been bolted from the inside. "We'll have to sit out here, I'm afraid. I can't offer you tea."

"It doesn't matter."

Of course it didn't. It was the last thing that mattered.

In the absence of any chairs—Irene invariably kept them locked away in the shed—Jonathan perched on the wall at the edge of the patio. "I'm sorry to turn up here and throw a bombshell at you."

Ryan shrugged. "Don't worry about it," he said dryly. "I'm used to bombshells."

Jonathan's eyes moved down to his legs. Ryan spoke quickly to head off any sympathy or questions. "You came here before, didn't you? On Christmas Day."

It wasn't a question; it was a statement. Despite the Christmas crackers, the flashbacks, Eric phoning his mother begging to be collected early, Ryan could still remember the knock at the door. His mother's rebuff. The way she'd gone upstairs afterwards.

Jonathan nodded. "Yes. Stupid day to pick, I know. I don't know what I was thinking. Or if I was thinking at all, or just . . ."

"How did you say you found us?"

"Through our shared DNA. I think you registered yours?"

Of course. He'd done it after his marriage had broken up, when he'd felt so lost. It had been a whim, really, to try to find his father, but when the search proved unsuccessful, he'd decided to leave his DNA results public, just in case. And now here was Jonathan, the result of that decision.

"Look," Jonathan said, "don't get me wrong; I had a fantastic childhood. I've always felt really loved and supported by my adoptive parents. Very much so. They're amazing people. But even so, there's always been a part of me that's wondered where I came from, and for whatever reason, the need to know has got stronger and stronger lately."

"I knew nothing about you. Mum . . . she's never mentioned anything."

Jonathan nodded, a sad, resigned movement of his head. "I'm not really surprised. I was found in a phone box, and I suppose . . ."

"Wait a minute. You're a foundling?"

Another nod. "Yes. The phone box was right near a hospital, and she'd wrapped me up well, but . . . yes."

213

"Good of her to wrap you up." Ryan hadn't thought his opinion of his mother could sink much lower, but here it was, getting the remaining life choked right out of it.

"Look, I didn't come here to try and wreck your relationship with your mother."

"Don't worry about it. Mum and I have never been very close. There's not much to wreck. How old are you?"

"Thirty-eight."

"She had me five years after she abandoned you, then."

The sun kept going in and out of the clouds, spotlighting the familiarity of his brother's face, then smudging it again like a child playing peekaboo.

"Look, my mother's not exactly the maternal type, mate. You haven't lost out, believe me."

She could have been, though, couldn't she? After this? After abandoning one child for whatever desperate reason, she could have poured extra love onto the child she'd chosen to keep. Only she hadn't.

"I'm not entirely sure she's capable of loving anyone, not properly," Ryan said. "She even keeps my son at arm's length."

Jonathan's face brightened. "You've got a son? I have one too. Charlie. He's eight."

Ryan stared at him. "My God. My son's eight too. Eric."

They smiled at each other for a moment, but then Ryan realised that Eric and Charlie might have known each other from birth if only he'd known about Jonathan's existence, and he shook his head. "I can't believe this. It's surreal. Yet at the same time, it feels exactly right. As if you've handed me a piece of a puzzle I didn't even realise I was missing."

"I'm sorry," Jonathan said, and Ryan shook his head.

"It's not your fault, is it?"

Jonathan sighed. "My mum warned me about this kind of thing. Said I might stir things up. Hurt people. She's not insecure about it or anything herself; she knows how much I love her. That nobody will ever replace her. She's just worried I'll get hurt or end up hurting others."

Ryan experienced an uncomfortable, squirming feeling in his belly. He realised he was jealous. No, not just jealous, jealous as hell. His brother, abandoned in a fucking phone box, had had a happier childhood than he had.

But that wasn't Jonathan's fault. He hadn't come here to grind Ryan's face in the dirt. He'd come to discover the truth. To make connections.

"Tell me about yourself," he said to Jonathan. "Where d'you live? What d'you do? Are you married?"

When Jonathan began to talk, it occurred to Ryan that he'd have to reciprocate, share some facts about himself. But maybe his mother would return before he had to do that. Maybe a showdown to beat all showdowns would eclipse the need for him to talk about the failure that was his life. Or maybe, just maybe, it would be good to talk about it all? To his brother?

God, how many times during his childhood had he longed to have someone to talk to and to play with? Maybe whatever happened when his mother came back, he and Jonathan could build something from this mess?

36

Jess parked her car in the drive and got Toby out of his car seat. He whined slightly, no doubt stirred up by her confrontation with Michael. Helen's car wasn't parked in her drive. Just as well. Jess needed to calm down before they spoke, otherwise that tasteless garden gnome by their front door might end up crashing through Helen's front window. Did smug Justin have any idea his wife was having an affair? Somehow Jess couldn't imagine it. Maybe she ought to wait to confront Helen until he got back from work.

She would collect Stella from Tara's. Then what? Go home and carry on with the day as if nothing had happened? Yes, probably. What other choice did she have?

It took Tara a while to open the door.

"Hi, Tara. Thanks so much for looking after Stella. I really appreciate it. I'll take her out of your hair now." Jess's words came out in a rush because she needed to collect Stella quickly before the tears came. She had to hold it together until she got home. Otherwise, she might blurt the whole ugly mess out to Tara, and although she and Tara had become friendly recently, she wasn't yet a friend the way Gina was a friend.

"It's not a problem," Tara said. "They're outside, playing in the garden."

Jess followed Tara inside, closing the front door after her. When they reached the kitchen, she was surprised to see Tara turning the key to unlock the door.

"Wait a minute," Jess said. "Have you locked them out?"

Tara looked shifty. "Only for a moment while I was busy doing something. I put a tent up for them. Gave them a picnic. They've been having the time of their lives."

The defensive note in her voice made Jess panic. Quickly she stepped past Tara to open the back door, her stomach squelching. "Stella?" she called. "Stella? It's Mummy. Time to go home."

There was no answer.

"They'll be in the tent," Tara said.

But when they went to look, the tent flap wafted about in the wind, and the tent was empty. Then Jess saw the gate leading to the woodland standing open.

Tara noticed it at the same time. "They'll have gone to the park. You know what children are like. It's fine."

Jess stared at her for a moment. "My daughter is four years old. How can it be fine for her to go to the park on her own? What's wrong with you?"

She ran across the lawn with Toby bobbing up and down on her hip, his cries of distress loud and plaintive as he caught her mood. It would be so much easier to leave him with Tara, but there was no way she would ever leave either of her children with Tara again. The woman had locked Stella and Hermie out of her house. Actually locked them out.

"Stella!" she cried. "Stella!"

The woodland was wild, untamed except for the narrow, self-made track to the park, and as Jess wound her way through the tangle of ivy and twisted trees, it was difficult to avoid the clinging, thwacking branches. By the time she reached the gap in the fence, Toby was bawling even louder, holding one small hand over a scratch on his face, and Jess was sweating, her clothes clinging to her, her heart hammering in her chest.

"It's all right, baby," she said to soothe him.

But it wasn't. It wasn't all right at all.

"Stella!"

In the park, Jess stood for a moment, frantically looking around, finally picking out Hermie in the distance, climbing up the grass mound to the top of the slide.

Relief turned Jess's legs to liquid, but somehow she ran anyway, Toby bouncing and screaming in her arms. If Hermie was there, Stella couldn't be far away.

Finally, she reached the bottom of the mound. "Hermie? Where's Stella?"

Unbelievably, the girl shrugged. "Dunno. She was here, then she wasn't."

"What d'you mean?" Jess pounded up the mound as she spoke, grabbing Hermie by the shoulder the minute she reached her. Giving her a little shake. "Where is she? Where's Stella?"

"I don't know." Hermie was tearful now, flinching from her.

Suddenly Tara appeared. Jess let Hermie go with a whimper of distress, her eyes once more darting desperately about, searching for Stella. What had she been wearing that morning? Her yellow dress? Her blue T-shirt? Jess couldn't remember. Couldn't think what colour to look out for. Everything between seeing the video and confronting Michael at his office was a grey, scrambled mess.

"Listen, Hermie," Tara said, "this is very important, okay? Where were you playing the last time you saw Stella?"

"In the sandpit. She was cross because I knocked her castle down. But it didn't even look like a castle, Mummy. And she wouldn't stop crying, so I came up here."

Jess didn't hear the rest. She was already running towards the sandpit. But when she got there, she found nothing except a pile of sand. No other sign Stella had ever been there.

37

After Helen dropped her off, Frances walked up the path to the library entrance behind a young couple. Their toddler was fast asleep in her buggy, which was just as well, because the couple were having a blazing argument. Or at least, the man was, his angry face pressed far too closely to his wife's for Frances's liking, his tone unpleasantly aggressive. "What the bloody hell have you done with that library book, then? They'll make us sodding well pay for it now."

The woman made no reply, just went on grimly pushing her daughter into the library, eyes cast downward.

"Money down the bloody drain, Jennifer. Again. It's not rocket science, is it? Keeping track of a bloody library book!"

Frances waited to let them get further ahead, her heart suddenly beating nineteen to the dozen, torn between a desire to run after Helen's retreating car to get a lift home and wanting to confront the man, to tell him not to speak to his wife like that. Ask the poor woman whether she was okay. Coming so soon after Helen's question about Trevor, the man's aggressive tone of voice brought back a rush of bad memories of Trevor speaking to her in exactly the same way. As if she were a useless nothing that deserved to be stamped from the face of the earth.

A rushing sound engulfed Frances's ears. When she swallowed to try and clear it, the paving slabs seemed to move beneath her feet. She took a few deep breaths to try to control it. This was stupid. All in her head. Trevor wasn't around to bully her anymore, to tell her reading was a waste of time or to demand that she *"get her head out of that bloody book and do something useful."* She was free to do as she liked. Be who she liked.

"Excuse me. Can I get past, please?"

Frances realised she was blocking the library entrance. "Oh, I'm so sorry. Of course."

She shifted to one side to let another woman with a toddler in a buggy pass, then took a deep breath and forced herself to step forward. She would go in like a normal person, and she was bloody well going to take some books out. And then she would bring them home and take as long as she liked to read them. *So there.*

But once she was inside, Frances found the library far from the peaceful, studious sanctuary she had expected. Instead, it was a noisy blur of parents and children—young children Toby's age. Younger, some of them. All of them squawking or crying or bashing plastic instruments or shaking bells, their mothers and fathers laughing, singing, chatting, cooing. One older child was slapping a bongo drum. To Frances, it sounded like a hand striking a cheek. The clashing cymbals like saucepans clattering noisily to the floor from the pan rack.

Oh, God. This had been a mistake.

"Hello. Welcome to the library," said a voice.

A man came into focus. Hot Chocolate himself.

"Er . . . thank you," said Frances.

Hot Chocolate frowned. "I say, are you all right?"

"Yes," said Frances uncertainly. "I just . . . felt a little faint for a moment. I'm all right now."

"Are you sure? Perhaps you ought to sit down for a moment. Would you like me to get you a glass of water? Or a cup of tea, perhaps?"

Frances took in a shaky breath, gradually pulling herself together. Hot Chocolate was one of the reasons she'd wanted to come to the library in the first place, and now here she was, making a complete and utter fool of herself in front of him.

"That would be nice. Thank you. I didn't know you could get tea in a library."

He twinkled at her. "It's a new thing. Part of our campaign to tempt people across the threshold. That and the free internet. How do you like your tea?"

"Strong with two sugars, please."

"A strong tea with two spoons of sugar it is. Back in a jiffy."

After he'd gone behind the library counter and into the staff area, Frances sat quietly, allowing her unpleasant memories to retreat into the past and the smiles and the laughter and the sounds to become just that—smiles and laughter and sounds. Just a music session for mums and babies, the type of event that would never have been held in a library in a month of Sundays when Frances had first married.

She thought of herself back then in the hopeful days when she still thought she and Trevor would have a family. Before she'd fully realised what a cruel, vindictive bastard she'd married.

"Here you are," said Hot Chocolate, returning. "One cup of strong tea."

"Thank you." As Frances reached to take the mug from him, she felt a tear run down her cheek. Saw him notice it.

"Are you sure you're all right?"

Frances sniffed. "Yes, quite sure. I'm so sorry to keep you from your work."

"Oh, don't worry about that. I find I'm largely superfluous during Baby Bounce and Rhyme Time. Is there anything else I can help you with? Any particular books you came in for today? Books, I can do. Baby Bounce, not so much."

His eyes were very twinkly. It was a long time since Frances had been twinkled at.

"Well, I'm interested in wildlife. Hedgehogs, in particular. I'm trying to encourage everyone in my street to take part in a hedgehog highway."

"I think we spoke on the phone," he said. "You're Helen's hedgehog lady. Frances, if I remember rightly?"

"Yes, that's right," she said, pleased he remembered her, deciding not to say anything about Helen and her strimmer. Let Helen confess to that if she wanted to.

"Well, we have a whole section on how to encourage wildlife into your garden, but I don't imagine you need that, do you?"

"I'd very much like to see it anyway. Wildlife of all kinds gives me so much pleasure."

"Then come right this way, Frances. Browsing heaven awaits you."

Frances wanted to giggle. Browsing heaven. It probably ought to sound ridiculous; she could well imagine the caustic words Trevor would have used, had he heard the phrase. But sod Trevor. She was sick of thinking about what he would have said or thought about anything. Browsing heaven sounded like exactly what she needed. And with Hot Chocolate bringing her books, it sounded as if that was exactly what it would be. Heaven.

38

Ryan heard a car come into the close. His mother's car. "She's back."

Opposite him, Jonathan went suddenly pale. "Our mother?"

Ryan nodded. "Yes."

Together they sat, listening as the car engine cut and she got out of the car. Let herself into the house.

"She'll probably ask me to go."

"She'll have to speak to you sometime, now that I know. But if you want a sympathetic ear afterwards, come round to mine. I'm just down the road. Flat Seven, Heath Heights, Wall Road."

He waited a moment, then moved to bang on the french doors. After a while, his mother appeared, frowning, and reached up to fiddle with the locks. Jonathan, sitting to the left on the wall, was concealed from her view.

The door slid open. "Ryan?" she said. Then her gaze moved on, beyond him. "Oh."

Bitter words sought to spew from Ryan's mouth. *"When were you going to tell me I had a brother? How could you do that to anybody?"* And, most pressingly, *"What is wrong with you?"*

But this wasn't about him. His thoughts and feelings weren't the priority right now. He needed to shut up and make sure Jonathan was okay.

So he said, "The two of you need to talk. I'm going to go home and leave you to it. Come round anytime you like, Jonathan. I'm looking forward to getting to know you."

Then he turned to his mother. "Do the decent thing, Mum. Talk to him."

He moved off, along the side of the house, down the drive and into the street.

Jess's car was back, but there was no sign of her. For a moment he considered knocking on her door but decided it wouldn't be fair to inflict himself on her right now. What would he say, anyway? How would he begin to explain what had just happened? No, he'd go home and wait to see if Jonathan came.

But when he got out onto St Clements Hill, he saw a woman running up the hill from the park entrance, carrying a child. It looked like Jess. Was it Jess? Whoever it was, she was shouting at the top of her voice. When she got closer, he heard what she was shouting. "Stella! Stella!"

Ryan moved the scooter quickly down the hill to meet her. "What is it? What's happened?"

Jess looked frantic. "It's Stella. She's gone missing from the park. I left her with Tara, and she let them go there on their own. We've searched everywhere. I came back this way to see if . . . Oh, God. I must get home in case she's gone back there."

Shit.

She began to hurry on. He shouted after her. "She'll turn up, don't worry. Let me know if there's anything I can do . . ."

Not surprisingly, Jess didn't answer, and Ryan ignored his instinct to power after her, heading instead down the hill to the park. It was empty—no Tara, no Hermie, no one at all. Just an innocent space with no evidence of recent trauma. Nothing.

39

At the rescue centre, while her hoglets were being hand-fed and warmed up by hot-water bottles, Gloria, the injured hedgehog, was snuggled up in her bedding of torn newspaper, recovering from her ordeal. She wasn't thinking about her babies at all. She was fast asleep, disconnected from the feelings of terror that had so recently driven her motherly instincts into oblivion.

As for Jess, pacing up and down at home, waiting for the police to arrive, trying unsuccessfully to get through to Michael, she was crushed by fear, whimpering out loud as her mind supplied increasingly awful scenarios about what might have happened to Stella. Her beloved girl.

Desperately, she tried Michael again. Still, he didn't answer, no doubt assuming she wanted to give him more grief about his affair. She sent a text instead. Come home. Stella missing. Police coming. A children's animation was on the TV, the wildly inappropriate upbeat music filling the room. A babysitter for Toby.

Jess sat down and put her face into her hands. One minute had passed since she'd last looked at the clock. How long would it take the police to arrive? Should she have stayed in the park instead of coming home? Where was Michael? One of them needed to be here, and one of them needed to be in the park. Oh, God, what would she do if anything had happened to Stella? How would she ever bear it?

She ought never to have left her with Tara. For goodness' sake, hadn't she seen firsthand how casual Tara could be about parenting?

Hermie had probably been going to the park on her own since she was Stella's age. Stella hadn't been herself since Toby's arrival; all her acting up and bad behaviour were a way of expressing her unhappiness. She probably felt neglected. Even replaced. And that was Jess's fault too, because adopting Toby had been her idea.

Toby himself giggled in front of the TV, amused by the ridiculous antics of a cartoon mouse. He turned his face in Jess's direction to share his delight with her, and despite her utter despair, she smiled briefly back. She couldn't regret Toby. He was adorable. But she needed to help him fit into their lives better. When Stella came back, that would be her priority. When Stella came back. Oh, God, where was she?

~

Ryan had a hunch. He'd had them all the time in his working life; if they drove on a few miles, they'd get to the real story. If they followed the dodgy-looking guy with the torn shirt, they'd discover who was behind the real operation. It usually paid to follow his hunches. Too bad no hint of a hunch had arrived to help him the morning the shell had gone off. But that didn't mean his hunches were now null and void, and Ryan had a hunch that Stella was still in the park.

So he carried on down the road to the park and stopped on the brow of the sloping path, searching the hillocks, trees, gullies, and shrubs—all the likely hiding places for a small girl. Then he thought about what he knew about Stella. It wasn't much, really. Whenever he was with Jess, she was the full focus of his attention—the stupid, hopeless crush he had on her—a crush doomed to failure, but irresistible, nevertheless.

Stella, Stella. She liked painting pictures; he knew that. Her paintings hung everywhere in Jess's house. What else? She was horribly jealous of her new brother. Ryan's gut told him this was what her disappearance was about—a punishment. And suddenly he remembered something else. Stella loved cats. And was, no doubt, still grieving for Stripey Cat.

Mind made up, Ryan set off along the path that ran beside the shrubs, calling, "Here, kitty, kitty, kitty." A fool of a man calling for a nonexistent cat, or a genius laying down bait to lure a lost girl from her hiding place. It didn't much matter; there was no one there to see him. It was just him and his gut, and, hopefully soon, Stella.

No response from the bushes. With his old wheelchair, that would have been it—he'd have been forced to abandon his search. But the scooter could deal with rougher terrain, and he sped towards a bamboo grove, the stems swaying about in the breeze. Or was it more than just the breeze that was making them rustle and sway?

"Here, kitty, kitty, kitty."

A movement. Yes, definitely a movement. A patch of blue amongst the green. With great self-control, Ryan managed to ignore these signs, calling out again for the imaginary cat. "Here, kitty, kitty, kitty."

Then, suddenly, a voice. Stella's voice. "You haven't got a cat."

And there she was in her blue T-shirt, her head poking out of the bamboo stems. Safe and well.

Ryan looked at her calmly, careful not to show relief. "I'm practising for when I get one. In case she comes over here and I can't find her."

A hint of a smile. "That's silly."

He smiled back. "I suppose it is, a bit. But I'm just afraid of losing her."

Stella's smile slumped. "I lost Stripey Cat."

"I know. I'm sorry."

Stella nodded, her thumb finding her mouth. Then, after a moment, "You shouted wrong."

"Did I? How should I shout?"

"Like you're happy, not scared. Mummy put happy in her voice when she called Patch."

Ryan felt a glow inside, remembering how he'd done the same when they'd been trying to get Patch to leave the hedgehog alone. "I see," he said. "Will you show me?"

Stella smiled and took a deep breath, shouting excitedly, "Here, kitty, kitty, kitty!"

Ryan smiled. "Oh, yes. I see the difference. That would definitely make a cat come out if she was hiding. She'd want to know what fun she was missing."

Stella's face fell. She bent one of the bamboo stems over until it snapped. "Mummy was calling me."

"Was she? And what did she sound like? Happy or scared?"

She poked at the grass with her shoe, not looking at him. "Scared."

"Is that why you didn't come out?"

She shook her head. "She loves Toby now."

"Is that what you think?"

Stella nodded, her bottom lip wobbling.

"Well, I think your mummy still loves you very much, you know. I think that's why she couldn't use her happy voice when she was calling for you. She had to use her scared voice because she was afraid she wouldn't see you again."

Stella began to cry. Ryan risked moving a little closer. "I tell you what. Why don't you hop up here and I'll give you a ride home. You can tell your mummy how you're feeling, and she can tell you how she's feeling, and then everything will be all right again."

"Okay."

As Stella clambered up, he looked at her. "Is it all right if I phone your mummy to tell her we're on the way?"

Stella nodded.

"Thank you."

Ryan took his phone from his pocket and dialed. "Jess? I've found her. She was in the park. We're on our way home now."

He could hear Jess sobbing on the other end of the line. A snatched-in breath. Michael's voice, asking Jess a question. Then Jess said, "Oh, thank you, thank you . . ."

He smiled. "See you soon." He glanced down at Stella. "That was your mummy's happy voice," he said, propelling the scooter towards the park gates.

"But she was crying."

"Sometimes, when you're really, really happy, you do cry."

He expected Stella to say how silly that was, something like that, but she didn't. Instead, her thumb went thoughtfully into her mouth, and she leant back against his shoulder, the most precious weight Ryan had felt in a long time—perhaps the most precious since the day Eric had been placed into his arms at the hospital as a baby.

~

Frances saw the police car outside Jess's house immediately as Hot Chocolate—Frank, she now knew—pulled into Hilltop Place.

When Frank offered her a lift home during his lunch break, she hadn't hesitated to accept. They'd got on like a house on fire during Baby Bounce and Rhyme Time, and she even confided in him that she hadn't been out of the house much in recent years.

"My wife got like that," he'd said. "She was ill for some years before she died, you see, so she got a bit too used to being indoors. It can really knock your confidence."

Frances had agreed, delighted that he'd confided in her. Frank lived a few miles away, by the river, and had actually had otters come into his garden. Otters. Hedgehogs were very special, but otters! "You ought to get cameras set up in your garden," she'd told him, and he'd said that maybe he would.

But they'd arrived back in Hilltop Place now, and the pleasant interlude was about to come to an end.

"I hope nothing's wrong with Jess or her family," she said. "Jess is such a lovely girl."

"It's always alarming when you see a police car parked near your home, isn't it?"

Frances knew all about that. "The police came here when my husband went missing," she said.

Frank looked at her, his handsome face furrowed with concern. "Goodness, Frances. That's awful."

"It's a long time ago now. Fifteen years or more."

"Even so . . ."

She nodded. "Yes, it's been very hard."

Frances remembered the long years of waiting for the police to discover Trevor's whereabouts. The constant feeling when she was at home of being watched, of thinking she'd turn round and Trevor would be there, waiting to make her life a misery all over again.

"Did they never find him?"

"No, they never did. In the end, the police closed the case. He was pronounced dead five years ago."

Frank shook his head. "I can't imagine how difficult that must have been for you. To never know what happened . . . At least with my wife, I knew. I was at her side when she died." He shook his head again. "It's no wonder you . . ."

"No wonder I'm a fruit loop who's pretty much forgotten how to go out? Well, all that's going to change. From now on, I shall get myself to the library regularly."

"I'm very glad to hear it."

"And if you ever want advice about setting up motion-activation cameras to film your otters, you only have to ask."

"Thank you very much, Frances. I'll definitely do that."

Frances nodded, smiling back at him, pleased by her own boldness. She opened the car door. "Thank you for the lift home."

"It was my pleasure. Until the next time."

"Until the next time," she agreed, swinging her legs out.

"Oh, and Frances," he said.

She looked back. "Yes?"

"For the record, I don't think you're a fruit loop at all. And my days at the library are Tuesdays, Thursdays, and Saturdays."

She grinned. "Got it. Bye, Frank."

"Bye for now, Frances."

~

Stella's face was dirty when Jess reached her on the corner of St Clements Hill. She had bits of twig in her hair. But oh, the utter joy of scooping her from Ryan's lap and into her arms. Pressing her face into her soft hair, against her sweet skin. Stella was crying, and Jess was crying, both of them clinging to each other, and Jess felt such a sweet, exhausting relief, holding her baby safely.

"Oh, Stella," Jess said, her voice cracking. "What would Mummy have done if she hadn't found you?"

Stella's sobs increased. "You . . . love Toby." The words were shuddered against Jess's chest. Jess only heard them because the two of them were melded together so closely she wasn't sure where Stella ended and she began.

"That's true," she said. "But Mummy only knows how to love Toby because she loves you so much."

She held her little girl close, feeling her trembling. "I loved you straight away, from the moment I could feel you swimming in my tummy. And when you arrived, you were so perfect I couldn't stop looking at you. And you looked at me too, as if you were puzzling me out. Like this."

Jess wiped away a tear and screwed her face up, her eyebrows almost meeting. Stella pulled back to look and giggled through her tears. "I didn't, Mummy."

"You did. I could see you thinking, *'Who are you? Oh, yes, you're my mummy.'* And I said, *'Hello, little one. Welcome to the world. I love you. I will always love you.'* And I do, Stella. I always will. Even if fifteen Tobys came to live with us in our family, I would always love you."

"Where would we put fifteen Tobys, Mummy?"

Tears dripped down Jess's cheeks. "Well, five in the attic, five in my room, and five in yours, I suppose."

Stella put her thumb into her mouth and cushioned her cheek against Jess's chest again. "I was first, wasn't I, Mummy?"

"You were, darling."

"And I was in your tummy. Toby wasn't in your tummy."

"That's true. Toby was in another lady's tummy. But that lady isn't here now, so Toby needs us very much, okay? He needs you to be a big sister to him and to show him what to do, now that he's in our family. Can you do that, Stella Bella? To help Mummy?"

Stella made no answer, but Jess thought she felt the slightest movement of her daughter's head against her chest. That would do, for now.

Jess glanced over at Ryan, who was sitting quietly, observing her reunion with Stella while pretending not to. His face was impassive— for her sake, she knew—as if he knew how much it was taking her not to howl with relief. To take hold of Stella and bawl, *"Have you any idea how scared I was? Don't you ever dare do anything like that again!"* Only his mouth was soft, a giveaway to the fact that he was, actually, moved. And Jess wondered whether that's how he got through the repeated slaps of witnessed trauma in his work, by switching a switch, sliding down a barrier, pulling up a mask.

She held Stella on her hip and reached out a hand to curl it in his, hoping her fingers would convey her gratitude better than the words *thank you* would ever be able to do. But she said it anyway. "Thank you, Ryan, thank you so much."

He smiled, squeezing her hand. "Sure."

"That girl showed me the gate, Mummy," Stella said when Jess let go of Ryan's hand and held her close again.

"Hermie?"

Now there was a definite nod. "She smashed my sandcastle."

"Never mind. We can go to the seaside soon. Make a proper sandcastle. But we'd better get home now, hadn't we? Daddy and Toby are waiting for us. They're very worried about you."

Beside her, Ryan pushed the throttle control of the scooter, and they moved forward side by side, Stella heavy in Jess's arms. It would have been much easier to place her back on Ryan's lap, or ask her to walk, but even if Stella hadn't clung to her, Jess wouldn't have wanted to let her go. Her body needed to catch up with her brain's knowledge that Stella had been found, and skin-to-skin contact was the only way to do that.

At the top of the hill, when it was time for Jess and Stella to turn left for Hilltop Place, Ryan said he was going back to his flat.

"Thanks for helping me with my cat-finding practise, Stella."

Jess had no idea what he was talking about, but as Stella smiled and slid down her body to stand on her own two feet, another wave of gratitude swept over her. She didn't want Ryan to go, didn't want Stella's saviour, her friend, to be anywhere other than Hilltop Place. She wanted him to be only a few houses away.

"I don't even know your new address."

"Flat Seven, Heath Heights, Wall Road. You'll remember that, won't you, Stella? Until your mummy can write it down?"

Stella nodded seriously, and Jess knew that she would. Even though she wouldn't need to. "Thank you again, Ryan."

He nodded. "No problem."

"We'll see you soon."

"I hope so."

~

Jess could hear Toby crying, needing her, two houses away from home. She glanced down at Stella to see if she'd noticed, but of course she had—she could tell by the way she gripped Jess's hand tighter. She squeezed Stella's hand, about to distract her by mentioning the police car, when Tara's door opened.

"You found her all right, then?"

"Yes." It was all Jess could manage to say. She guessed that some-time in the future she might be able to speak civilly to Tara. But for now, anyway, any filaments of friendship between herself and Tara had been severed.

The front door opened. Michael had Toby in his arms. Toby instantly reached out to Jess. She wanted to ignore the reflex-action impulse to take him into her arms but couldn't because Michael thrust him towards her so he could scoop Stella up.

"Oh, Stella, Daddy's been so worried. Don't do anything like that again, okay? Promise me you won't do anything like that again."

And suddenly they were both sobbing in the doorway—broken but fitting together—and Jess moved past them with Toby to speak to the police officers. To find lucid, rational words that would never sufficiently express her emotions, but which would serve to send them on their way, incident over.

Both children were so worn out by the events that they fell asleep midafternoon. Jess had to stop herself from going to check up on Stella every five minutes, to make sure she was still there. She mustn't. Shouldn't. She might disturb her, and Stella needed to sleep away the trauma of her day. And it occurred to Jess that good parenting could be as much about not doing things as it was about doing the right things. And that sometimes it could be harder—much harder—to hold back.

Michael hadn't gone back to work. And while Jess suspected she might have wanted to contract-kill him had he disappeared the minute he discovered Stella was safe, it felt odd, having him in the house, sitting in his usual chair, just as if nothing had happened. As if the whole awful series of events had been a dream or a figment of her imagination.

Yet, at the same time, those horrific thirty minutes when she hadn't known where Stella was or whether she would ever see her again had put things into perspective. Jess no longer wanted to rail and shout at Michael—she had neither the energy nor the enthusiasm for it. But she did need to ask him questions.

"Is Helen going to leave her husband for you?"

Michael ran an agitated hand through his hair. "Jesus, please, Jess . . . do we really need to speak about this now?"

"Just tell me."

"I don't know. We haven't talked about it yet."

"Do you want her to?"

His face reddened. "I think . . . Yes, I think I do. I'm so sorry."

She wanted desperately to curl up on the sofa to go to sleep, the way she'd done in the evenings when Stella had been a baby, taking the opportunity for oblivion before the 11:00 p.m. feed, in the optimistic hope that Stella would sleep right through the night.

Only back then, she would have laid her legs across Michael's lap, and he would have massaged her feet to help her drift off. And it occurred to Jess that he might never again give her a foot massage. That if they split up, there would be two folders for Stella's paintings—one kept here, as always, and another wherever Michael went to live.

"How could you, Michael?"

He put his face in his hands. Sighed. Looked up. "I don't know. I real-ise what a cliché it is, but it just happened. I certainly never intended . . ."

"How did you meet? Just here, in Hilltop Place?"

He shook his head. "No, we ran into each other in the city during our lunch break. We started off talking about the hedgehog project, actually. Then we found out we were both heading to the same food stall in the market, so we walked together."

"The falafel stall?" Jess asked, not sure why she wanted to know, yet thinking of all the times they'd gone to that stall together.

He nodded. "Yes."

"Flirting over falafels," she said bitterly.

"It wasn't like that."

"Fondling over falafels, then. *Fucking* over falafels. Was it more like that?"

"No! At least, not at first. Helen was just easy to talk to, that's all. She listened to what I had to say. Made me feel interesting."

"And I don't?"

He sighed. "There's no time for either of us to be either interesting or interested here, is there? It's all kids and the humdrum ordinariness of life."

Jess's laugh lacked even a shred of humour. "I've seen Helen put her bins out. She wears rubber gloves to do it. Everybody has to do humdrum ordinary tasks, Michael, and in case you haven't noticed, life's been a bit fraught lately, dealing with Stella and Toby."

"Of course I've noticed. That's the point. Spending time with Helen was a reprieve from all that. A way to get some peace. Or at least, at first it was, anyway. Until Helen and I started speaking, I don't think I even knew how unhappy I was. And Helen's not been happy either, with Justin. He treats her like—"

"I do not want to dissect Helen's marriage, thank you."

"Well, all right. All I'm just saying is that we had things in common. And we both needed someone to talk to."

What about her, dealing with Toby's neediness? The tense interviews with Stella's teacher every week? She'd bloody well needed someone to talk to as well. Suddenly Jess felt exhausted. What was the point of continuing this conversation? It wasn't going to change anything. Whether Michael and Helen got together permanently or not, Jess's relationship with Michael was over. It was mind-boggling that she could have woken up with no clue that her marriage was about to implode, and now, a mere six hours later, she was about to give Michael his marching orders. It was unbelievable, but true. She would never trust him again, and what was a marriage without trust?

"I think you'd better go," she said.

For a moment he looked as if he might protest. There were tears in his eyes. He opened his mouth as if to speak. Then he closed it again and nodded. "I'll pack a bag."

He went upstairs, leaving Jess remembering herself after her mum had dropped her off at university, her dad dead for only four months. She'd been excited about starting her course, yes, but the reality of not having her beloved dad there to wish her luck was a physical pain in her stomach. Swamped by utter loneliness, Jess had left her room the second she heard someone in the communal kitchen. The occupant had been a boy—a boy with curly hair and a friendly smile, standing waiting for the kettle to boil. Michael.

God. Had the two of them really got together in the first place because she was lonely and grieving her father? Surely that hadn't been the only reason. They'd been happy together. They had.

Until they were not. And until just now, she hadn't realised how much Stella had been the glue that kept them bonded together. How that glue hadn't been strong enough to hold up against the uproar Toby's arrival had caused.

No, it was definitely over between them. Which meant a future of weekends without Stella while she spent time with Michael wherever he ended up living.

And Toby? How did he fit into this picture when he and Michael had never bonded? *Shit.* What were they going to do about Toby?

40

Irene's gaze roamed around Ryan's living room, ostensibly taking in his new TV, his largely empty shelving unit, and the framed photo Frances had taken of him and Eric in front of the hedgehog house they'd made for her. Anywhere but at his face.

She clutched a mug of tea, but had yet to drink any of it. If she was waiting for him to break the ice, she'd be waiting a long time. *She* was the one with explanations to make.

As Ryan made himself sit quietly to wait it out, the faint sound of traffic reached him through the double-glazed windows, and he remembered other times when—as a journalist—he waited for someone to speak. The mother of a slaughtered hostage victim. A young man who'd seen his best friend sucked into a drug gang. The parents of a little girl undergoing cutting-edge cancer treatment. All of them hesitant at first, sizing him up. Judging whether or not he was worthy of their trust. All of them vulnerable.

Was his mother vulnerable? He'd never thought so before. But you'd need to be desperate to abandon a baby in a telephone box, surely? So maybe she was as deeply vulnerable as all those others. Unless she was just completely heartless.

"You never met your grandparents," she said at last. "My mother and father."

It wasn't how he'd expected her to start. He shook his head. "I didn't."

She sighed. "They were country folk. Farmers. They believed in hard work, not dreams. When I wanted to go to university, they were scornful at first. But then I won a scholarship, and they gave in and let me go." For just a moment, her eyes glittered with remembered excitement. "I couldn't wait to leave that bleak life behind me. And it was so very bleak, Ryan. Not a life I would wish on anyone." She sighed. Met his gaze. "Which was why I was glad to hear that Jonathan had a happy childhood. He wouldn't have if he'd stayed with me, you see. I would have been constantly reminded of what happened."

Ryan frowned. "What did happen?"

She looked at him square on. "Are you quite sure you want to know? I didn't say anything to him. I never will do. If I tell you, then you'll have to carry the secret too."

They considered each other in silence. Ryan knew that if he never learned the truth, he'd always wonder. That it would be there between them always, another obstacle to prevent their crossing the divide that had always separated them.

He nodded. "Yes, I want to know."

She sighed, looking down, away from him. "It wasn't how I'd imagined it would be, university. I'd led such a sheltered, isolated life, you see, back home. I had no idea how to behave or what to do or say. How to speak to people. It wasn't that they were unfriendly to me; they were quite happy for me to tag along. But I was completely out of my depth. So I drank a lot to help me feel more confident. And it worked to a certain extent. But then . . . I made the mistake of trusting somebody I shouldn't have trusted, and he . . . well, he attacked me."

"D'you mean he raped you?"

She flinched at the word. "Yes."

"Jesus. Did you tell the police?"

She shook her head. "No. I was too ashamed. I thought they'd take his word over mine. When I . . . realised I was pregnant, I went home on the train to tell my mother what had happened. But she didn't believe me. Said I must have led the man on. Called me . . . well, awful things.

Told me I was on my own, that no daughter of hers was going to be an unmarried mother."

"Oh, Mum." He stared at her, stunned by what she said, wishing with all his heart they had the kind of relationship that would allow him to reach out to her. "That's just awful."

"Yes." She swallowed. "It was, a bit. At the time, doing what I did with Jonathan seemed the only possibility. Only afterwards . . ." She swallowed again, fiddling with her sleeve. "I couldn't stop thinking about him. Wondering where he was, whether he was being well cared for. When I met your father a few years later, I tried my very best to put the past behind me, to bury myself in our relationship. But the spectre of the attack was always there, like a cancer. And when I fell pregnant with you, it was as if the whole thing was happening all over again. Your father left before I could tell him about you. I don't blame him; I imagine I drove him away with my coldness and strange behaviour."

Ryan thought about his unknown father; the man wasn't even aware he existed. At some point in the near future, maybe he would ask his mother about him. Restart his efforts to track him down. But not now.

His mother had a distant look in her eyes as she relived the past. "So there I was, once again alone with a baby. I didn't know how I was going to get through it. I only knew I couldn't have two unknown fates on my conscience."

"So you decided to keep me."

She nodded. "Yes."

Suddenly, Ryan felt he understood. Guessed that the memories and questions hadn't stopped when she made that decision. That somehow, for some twisted reason—maybe because she'd had to build a fortress around herself in order to survive—she'd kept him at a distance. Stopped herself from loving him with her whole heart.

It wasn't so surprising. Ryan had seen it time and time again with victims of war or terrorist attacks. The disengaged facial expression. The cold determination never to feel joy again so they could never feel pain.

He'd even tried to do exactly the same thing himself since the attack, withdrawing from the world, ignoring professional advice.

The difference with him, though, was that all those evasion tactics had failed. No matter how much cold, empty space he tried to place between himself and the world, people and events kept getting in the way. Dead cats. Squashed hedgehogs. Eccentric old ladies. Jess with the sunshine in her hair, her face lighting up when she spoke about her children. Even the small quirk of Eric's mouth when he moved up to the next level of a computer game. All of it dragging him out of his enforced solitude and tempting him to feel again.

"I'm so sorry that happened to you, Mum," he said, and saw the hastily controlled wobble of her mouth.

"Well, worse things happen at sea, don't they?" she said, using one of her favourite sayings. "Things eventually settled down, and I got the job working for Mr. McArthur. He was very good to me, over the years."

Ryan thought back to all the times after school when he'd sat quietly with a book in a corner of his mother's office, waiting for her to finish off her typing. How Mr. McArthur had sometimes come out of his office with a bag of sweets for him. He'd seemed ancient to Ryan back then, but he'd probably only been ten years older than his mother. Ryan could remember him saying, *You get off, Irene. Go and cook that boy of yours some tea. Those letters will get typed tomorrow.*

"Was Mr. McArthur in love with you, d'you think?" he asked, the idea suddenly occurring to him.

His mother set her tea aside, placing it on a newspaper on the coffee table so it wouldn't leave any heat marks. "Well, if he was, he never said anything to me, thank goodness. I wasn't interested in having a relationship with anyone ever again." She picked up her handbag from the floor. "Anyway, now you know. I won't turn Jonathan away if he wants to see me, but I don't intend to actively try to build a relationship with him. He already has a mother, after all. But you must do as you see fit." She looked at him, her smile grim. "But then you always have done that, haven't you?"

"I've just tried to do my best, I suppose," he said. "Isn't that all anyone can do?"

"I suppose it is, yes," she said, and reached out to pat his hand, taking him by surprise. Then she got to her feet. "Right, I'll be off, then."

Listening to the door close quietly behind her, Ryan's mind reeled with everything he had just learned. He wanted to weep for the young, vulnerable teenager attacked before she'd been able to enjoy her taste of freedom. Deeply regretted the fact that she was so closed up they couldn't console each other about the shit hands life had dealt them both. As far as she was concerned, the subject was done and dusted. There would be no follow-up questions, no repeat interview. She would very likely remain as unreachable as a balled-up hedgehog, spines turned out against the dangers of the world. It was such a waste. And he saw only one way to make sure he didn't become like that himself.

"Shit," he said out loud to himself. "I'm really going to have to talk about the terrorist attack, aren't I?"

41

Tara learned that her relationship with James was over, and that he was putting the house up for sale, in a straight-to-the-point phone call.

"You bastard!" she screamed, already thinking about getting Hermie to help her spray-paint graffiti all over the walls—some sorely needed mother/daughter bonding time after the screaming match about Hermie taking Stella to the park.

"You locked us out!"

"Only for a few minutes!" (A lie.)

"You always let me go to the park on my own!"

"Not with someone else's four-year-old child!"

"How was I supposed to know that? I've been going to the park on my own since I was four!" (Also true.)

"Come on, Tara, you've had it good for years. It always had to end sometime," James said.

"*I've* had it good? What about you, getting sucked off whenever you feel like it, popping in here between your fucking business meetings? You've got someone else, haven't you? That's what this is about."

"You're being hysterical, Tara. There is nobody else. Our relationship has run its course, that's all. Now, I've arranged for the estate agent to come round on Friday morning to measure up and take photographs."

"If you expect me to cooperate while you sell my home from under me, then you've got another think coming."

"If you don't, then I shan't be able to make the handsome payment I'd planned to make into your bank account."

"How much?"

"Ten thousand pounds."

"Twenty."

He sighed. "You always were greedy, Tara. All right, twenty. Half now, and half after you've moved out."

Tara let the estate agent in. But she didn't bother to tidy up. To hell with it. The property listing could damn well include photos of her clothes all over the bed and the bottle of vodka she'd made inroads into the previous night.

But while the estate agent picked his way across the detritus on Hermie's bedroom floor to take measurements, and Tara stared moodily out the living room window drinking a cup of coffee, a drama began to unfold outside. A very intriguing drama, between Justin and Helen.

Helen had come out of the house carrying a small holdall, which Justin was attempting to wrest from her hands. Surreptitiously, Tara opened the window to hear what they were saying.

"Don't do this, Helen." Goodness, the man was begging. That was most un-Justinlike. "Don't go. Please."

And Helen answered, "I have to, I'm sorry. I just don't love you anymore. I love him."

Bloody hell! Who?

"You don't. You just think you do. I won't let you do this."

Justin redoubled his efforts with the holdall and managed to get it out of Helen's hands.

"Fine," Helen said. "Have it. I'll leave with nothing. All I need is my love anyway."

And with that, she climbed into her car and drove away.

Well, well, well. Tara almost felt like applauding Helen. Except that Justin stood there on his drive, broken and weeping, still clutching the holdall, and another, more attractive thought suggested itself to Tara.

Seconds later, she had shoved her feet into a pair of delicate, furry mules and crossed the road, the silk fabric of her robe billowing in the breeze to reveal her skimpy nightdress and a generous helping of cleavage.

"Justin, you poor man," she said. "I saw what just happened. Come over and have a cup of coffee with me. Tell me all about it."

And Justin, still in a state of shock, having had no idea about either his wife's affair or her ability to stand up to him like that, allowed himself to be led. And after the estate agent had left with his measurements and unsatisfactory photographs, Justin found himself in Tara's bed with Tara doing utterly incredible things to him, and both his mind and his male member felt as if they might explode at any moment.

When, later, Justin emerged from his sex-scented trance and started to wonder how all this had come about, Tara began ministering to him once more, reawakening his tired, bewildered, and intensely grateful body all over again.

Later still, when violent sounds like machine-gun fire began to penetrate his afterglow and he frowned and asked, "Whatever is that?" Tara replied, "That's my daughter, playing her computer games." And when Justin said, "Isn't the volume a bit loud?" there was a steely edge to Tara's voice as she replied, "It is quite loud, yes. But after all, this is her home, isn't it? She can do as she likes, so long as I say it's okay." Whereupon Justin hastily agreed that yes, it was, and of course she could. And Tara relaxed in his arms, point made, feeling like a proud mother sticking up for her daughter's rights. Like someone who never intended to be an underdog with absolutely zilch power ever again in her entire life.

42

"Your mother will soon come round, I'm sure of it," Jonathan's wife, Alice, said the first time Ryan met her.

They were at Ryan's flat, Alice squeezed close to Jonathan on the sofa. "Who wouldn't want to get to know gorgeous you?"

"I think you might be just a tiny bit biased, darling," Jonathan said.

Deluded, more like, thought Ryan, although he had to admit that if anyone could get his mother to melt, it might be Alice, with her huge smile and her direct way of speaking. She'd soon won him over, anyway. Something told him it would take a lot to offend Alice, that it just wouldn't occur to her to be offended. She'd see any standoffishness as a juicy challenge.

"That's a wife's prerogative," she said to Jonathan, turning to smile at Ryan. "But I'm sure Ryan can give me some pointers. What's your mother interested in, Ryan? What are her passions? People always want to talk about their passions."

The minutiae of planning applications? What was his mother passionate about? Ryan was quite glad when a knock came at the door and he didn't have to answer Alice's question. "Oh, sorry," he said. "Excuse me."

It was Jess. Standing on his doorstep twirling a strand of her long hair around her finger, looking nervous. Warmth washed over him. He smiled. Then remembered the last time he'd seen her—after Stella's disappearance—and checked her expression. "Jess! Hi! How lovely. Where are the kids?"

"My mum's looking after them. She's visiting from Spain, so I . . . just thought I'd pop round and see if you were in. Make the most of my freedom, you know. And to thank you again for last week." Another uncertain smile. "But you're probably busy. I probably ought to have phoned first."

"No, it's fine. It's great to see you. Come in. Come in."

He couldn't stop smiling. She smiled back, crossing the threshold.

"Go on through. There are some people here I'd like you to meet, actually. Jess, this is my brother, Jonathan, and his wife, Alice. Alice, Jonathan, this is Jess."

Jess looked awkward for a second, then stunned. "Hello, good to meet you." She glanced round at Ryan. "But I didn't know . . ."

"You didn't know Ryan had a brother?" Alice finished for her.

"Neither did he," said Jonathan. "Good to meet you, Jess. I turned up out of the blue last week."

"Jonathan was adopted," Ryan explained. "I knew nothing about it until last week."

"Goodness," said Jess. "That's incredible. You're so alike."

"Aren't they?" said Alice. "And get this, our son is the same age as Eric."

"Wow, that's amazing." Jess turned to Ryan, her eyes searching, asking him, *Is it amazing? Are you okay?*

Ryan reveled in the silent communication, hoping his eyes were telling her, *Yes, it's okay. I'm okay. All the better for seeing you.*

The moment went on. Ryan wanted to reach out to touch her.

Behind them, Alice mumbled something to Jonathan, and they got to their feet. "I think we'll head off now, Ryan. Charlie's probably starting to get bored at his grandmother's, and . . ."

Ryan cranked his gaze away from Jess's to find Alice smiling broadly at him.

". . . and I think you and Jess have things you want to say to each other."

Jonathan clapped him on the shoulder. "We'll see you very soon, mate. I can't wait for Charlie and Eric to meet."

"No, me neither. I'll call you. Set something up."

"Great. Good to meet you, Jess. Hopefully, we'll see you again very soon."

They left, and suddenly it was just him and Jess. Alone. And Ryan had no idea what to say to her. What do you say when everything you wanted to say was off-limits?

"A brother, eh?" she said. "That must have been a shock."

"Yeah, just a bit. But a good one, I think."

"It's a lot to take in. I can't believe your mum's never said anything."

Ryan sighed. "You have met my mum, haven't you? She doesn't talk about personal stuff. And to be fair, it's not something you think to ask about, is it? You don't think to say, '*Mum, have I got any brothers and sisters you haven't told me about?*'"

"I guess not."

They were silent for a moment. Then Jess said, "I'm going to be completely open with Toby when the time comes. He has a book Social Services made about his origins. I thought I'd add to it."

"Of course you will. Because you're a great mum. How are the kids? How's Stella after her ordeal?"

Jess perched on the arm of the chair. "She's all right, I think. Or at least, she is at the moment. But . . ." She broke off, suddenly looking upset.

Ryan wheeled closer to her. "What is it? Has something else happened?"

Jess nodded. "Michael and I have split up."

Ryan was stunned. "Bloody hell. Why?"

"He's having a . . . well, relationship with Helen. I asked him to leave."

Now Ryan really gaped at her. "Helen of Justin and Helen?"

Jess nodded. "Yes."

"God, Jess, I'm so sorry. I can't believe it. I thought Helen was completely under that idiot's thumb."

"Me too." Jess got up from the chair and walked over to the mantelpiece, picking up a trophy Ryan had won for his writing years ago, putting it back down again. "Maybe Michael didn't want the responsibility of another child," she said. "Or maybe I've become boring and provincial. Who knows? I don't."

"There's nothing boring about you, Jess. If Michael thinks that, he's deluded. Either that or having a midlife crisis he'll regret forever once he's come to his senses."

Jess was looking at the floor. "The thing is, I know I should be upset. And I am. But to be honest . . . Well, I'm not as upset as I probably should be, you know? I mean, I realise there's going to be a whole lot of pain and disruption. I *hate* what all this is going to do to Stella. She adores her daddy so much. Toby's okay; it hasn't affected him, really, because he and Michael never became close. We've got a meeting with the social worker next week to bring her up to speed with what's happened. We're going to tell her Michael's not going to be in the picture with Toby."

"He's agreed to that?"

She nodded. "Yes. I think he was relieved, to be honest."

"God, this is such a lot for you to deal with. Are you all right?"

"I wasn't, at first. But now . . . if I'm really honest, the main feeling I have about it all is . . . well, relief, I think. Things haven't been right between me and Michael for a while. If I hadn't found out about him and Helen, we'd probably have split up anyway, in the end. We never really recovered from trying to have another baby, I don't think. My grief about it all."

"Just as long as you're not blaming yourself. None of this is your fault."

"No, I know." She smiled sadly. "When big life things happen, it can really put the spotlight on the state of your relationship, can't it?"

Ryan thought back to his time in the hospital after the land mine exploded. Knew that if he and Annie hadn't already split up, his helplessness would never have been enough to save them.

He took Jess's hand. "So really you're okay?"

"I'm getting there. It's all a bit daunting, that's all. It's like . . ."

"What?"

"Well, a bit like when I lay a new sheet of paper down on the table for Stella to paint on. All the colours and the brushes are at one side, ready, and I have no idea what she'll paint."

"And then she just makes a start and comes up with something incredible?"

"Exactly." A single tear slid down her cheek. "Yes. Only it's a bit scary if you look at that white paper for too long. You start thinking about whether the marks you make will turn into an amazing picture or whether it'll just all be a muddy mess."

"Well, I think Michael's a complete idiot." He could hear the emotion in his voice. Saw her tears begin to fall harder. "And I also think you should come over here so I can hug you."

She smiled, her tears dripping onto the carpet. Came to kneel beside his chair, placing her head on his shoulder. As he gave her a side hug, his mouth finding her hair, she began to weep properly, her shoulders shaking.

"Hey," he said softly, hating Michael for hurting her. Despising the kernel of hope that unfurled inside his body. The coiled spring of longing. It wouldn't be right to act on his feelings when she was feeling so vulnerable. Jess had just got rid of a selfish, unfaithful pig of a husband. Why would she want a useless, miserable bastard in a wheelchair?

She sniffed, moving back slightly, wiping away the tears. "Would you mind . . . ," she asked hesitantly. "Would you mind if I kissed you?"

Ryan looked at her. "Are you sure that's what you want?"

"Yes. Unless . . . unless you don't want me to?"

He reached out to stroke her face. "Oh, I do. I definitely do."

He turned as far as he could to face her, his mouth finding hers, the sweetness of the kiss diluted by his frustration at not being able to reach her with both arms.

He drew back.

"What?" she asked. "What is it?"

He sighed. "I can't walk, Jess. All these weeks of going to the support group, and I still haven't managed to speak about what happened to me. I've no idea how to get back to my work or even what work I want to do now that everything's changed. I'm going through a divorce, my son thinks I'm a freak, and what else? Oh, yes, my long-lost, formerly unheard-of brother's just turned up out of the blue. I'm a mess. And you deserve so much more than that."

She stroked his hair back from his face. The tenderness of the gesture gave him the courage to look up.

"You're kind. Funny. And so resourceful. God, you found Stella when I thought she'd been abducted, that I'd never see her again. You really care about people, Ryan. Yes, you're in a wheelchair, but so what? You can be very hard on yourself sometimes, and I know you feel bitter about what happened to you. But you can work on those things. And if you do, your wheelchair will just be another thing about you, like the colour of your eyes."

She was right. It really was time to ditch bitter, unaccepting Ryan. To come to terms with who he was now. Decide who he wanted to be. To make new marks on that sheet of white paper.

"Besides," she said, "you're sexy as hell."

He swallowed back the tears crowding his throat. Grinned. "Come here," he said, patting his lap, and she smiled back, getting to her feet.

"I won't hurt you?" she asked as she climbed up, watching his face.

It didn't hurt at all.

"You won't hurt me," he said, and began to kiss her again. Properly. His hands tangled in her hair, the sweet scent of her in his nostrils. Heaven.

Much later, his phone began to ring, vibrating in his shirt pocket.

"I'll leave it," he said, but she shook her head, taking the phone out and handing it to him.

"It might be important."

And it turned out that it *was* important. It was the dog rescue centre, calling to tell him that Patch had been returned to them. That the family who adopted him hadn't been able to cope with his hyperactivity.

When Ryan told Jess, she squealed with excitement. "Oh my God! Let's go and get him now! You see? I said you weren't useless, you amazing man, you!"

And Ryan laughed and told the woman on the other end of the line they'd be over to collect Patch right away.

"I was convinced they'd filed my application to adopt under *U* for *Unsuitable*," he said, snatching up his door key on the way out.

"I'm going to talk about what happened to me," he promised Jess as she drove to the rescue centre. "I'm going to find ways to deal with it. Get work that has value. Focus on my fitness so I can be as self-dependent as possible."

"All that sounds good, Ryan," she said with a quick glance in his direction. "But do it all for yourself, not just for others."

He thought about that for a moment. "Can I do it for you too?" he asked. "And for Eric?"

She grinned. "And for Stella and Toby. Yes, you can. You can."

43

It was July, and England was experiencing a heatwave. For the past few weeks, the residents of Hilltop Place had taken to wearing loose, floaty clothing, eating a great many salads, and finding it increasingly difficult to get to sleep in the sticky air of their bedrooms. At night, the hedgehogs drank thirstily from bowls of water left out for them and depended on humans for their food more than they usually did because the baked earth made digging for worms difficult.

One Monday afternoon, on the outskirts of Norwich—in Frank's garden, to be precise—Frances arrived to find a table set out for two on the big sweep of lawn that ran down to the riverbank. Tablecloth, dainty china teacups, teapot with a tea cosy, the lot. The lawn was a vast, impressive expanse of striped green, worthy of a manor house, and there were roses everywhere—huge, gorgeously scented roses that looked as if they ought to win a prize in a flower show.

"Crikey," Frances said, her arm linked in Frank's. "Do you employ a gardener?"

"No," said Frank, "I do it all myself. Got one of those ride-on thingamabobs. Even so, it generally takes care of my Sunday mornings."

Frances, who disapproved of overly tidy lawns anyway, considered that a right royal waste of a Sunday morning, especially since Frank worked at the library on Saturdays, but refrained from saying so.

"This looks lovely," she said when they reached the table. "Thank you for going to so much trouble."

Frank pulled her chair out for her, and Frances sat down, feeling scruffy in her shorts and T-shirt. The surroundings definitely warranted a dress. Maybe even a hat.

"Not at all, not at all. Now, what can I get you first? A scone or a sandwich?"

Frances settled for a scone, deliberately not asking whether he'd baked them, since she already felt quite inadequate enough, focusing instead on enjoying the crunch of the crisp exterior and the soft, warm centre, the ooze of the jam and cream blending together in her mouth.

"Delicious," she pronounced, and he smiled.

"Jolly good. My wife's recipe."

Ah.

Silence reigned after that, filled only by the rustling leaves of the poplar trees and some ducks quacking on the river.

She'd seen a photograph of Frank's wife inside the house—chic grey bob, perfect makeup, smart dress. Admittedly it had been taken at their son's wedding, but Frances knew she'd never looked that smart or put together herself in her entire life.

A blob of jam suddenly dripped from the scone onto her T-shirt, quickly followed by a splatter of cream. "Oh, hell!" she exclaimed. "What a clumsy cow I am."

Frank got to his feet. "Not at all. It's my fault for not offering you a napkin. I'll go and fetch a damp cloth. Won't be a tick."

As he hurried off, Frances gazed morosely across the lawn to the river, suddenly swamped by a hundred and one memories of similar incidents. Her mother's favourite teapot, smashed when she tripped over the edge of the rug. A hole burnt in the brand-new carpet by an ember from the fire. An incinerated stew, the blackened meat welded to the saucepan. Moth holes in her favourite sweaters. Her one and only online purchase turning out to be dollhouse furniture, rather than the full-size dining room table she'd thought she'd ordered. Disaster, over and over again.

And every time, even after he was gone, the disparaging comments from her husband in her head. *"Clumsy bitch. For Christ's sake, Frances, can't you do anything right? God, give me strength. They broke the mould when they made you. At least, I fucking well hope so."*

"Oh, my dear, whatever's the matter? You aren't crying because of a bit of spilt jam, are you?" Frank was back, damp cloth in hand, hovering over her with concern.

Frances grabbed one of the previously unproffered napkins from the centre of the table and used it to blow her nose. "My husband wasn't a very nice man," she said.

Frank knelt down beside her, putting his cream trousers at risk of grass stains. "Wasn't he, darling?" he said. "I'm so very sorry."

Frances looked at him. This kind, handsome man who worked part-time at the library because he wanted to, not because he needed to. They'd only known each other a matter of weeks. Ridiculous, really, to already feel so much. "Why are you so good to me?"

"Why wouldn't I be? I think you're marvellous. Championing hedgehogs the way you do, overcoming bad memories with such courage."

"Some would say it was stupid of me to have stayed in such an unhappy marriage for so long."

"Well, I would tell anyone who had the temerity to judge you in that way to go to hell, quite frankly. Nobody's walked in your shoes, have they? Nobody but you has the first clue what you've had to deal with."

Frances sniffed. "I bet your wife wasn't such a hopeless case as me, though."

"Ah," he said, "let's leave old Philippa out of it, shall we? I don't want to get into any comparisons. There's no need for it. My marriage to Phil was one thing, and you and I are something else. Something different. Now, are you going to mop down your T-shirt, or would you prefer to come inside and choose something of mine to wear?"

Frances lifted her head, unsure of his meaning. Was he suggesting . . . ? Surely not. But then again, his eyes were definitely twinkling, so maybe . . .

Goodness, it was a very long time since she'd had sex of any kind, let alone sex in the afternoon. A lot longer still since she'd actually enjoyed it.

"I think," she said, mentally preparing herself to be disappointed when he took her to his bedroom and showed her his T-shirt drawer, "I'd like to come in and choose something of yours, please."

He smiled. "Excellent decision. Come along, then. I'll stick the cream pot in the fridge. We can carry on where we left off here afterwards."

When they emerged from the house an hour and a half later wearing matching robes, fresh from a shared, postcoital shower, Frances very much enjoying the softness of the grass beneath her bare feet, they found a pair of ducks on the table, tucking into the abandoned sandwiches.

"Blasted things," said Frank, clapping his hands.

The ducks flapped away, quacking, sending the teacups toppling onto the lawn, and Frances burst out laughing. Perhaps she wasn't the only shit show in town, after all. And even if she was, Frank had just shown her in no uncertain terms that he couldn't give two hoots about it. That he liked her exactly the way she was. And Frances could never—ever—remember anyone thinking that about her before.

Life was definitely on the up.

44

Ryan was going on an outing with Colin from the PTSD Support Group. Seated in the front of Colin's car, Ryan had part of a model aeroplane balanced across his knees, the overspill from the back seat and the boot of the car, which was jam-packed, not only with Ryan's wheelchair but also with other planes, flight controllers, metal boxes containing LiPo batteries, a fold-up stand for the models, a canvas chair, a picnic basket, and extra clothing in case the weather changed.

They were headed for a former air base twenty miles away to fly Colin's planes. Ryan had recently discovered that Colin belonged to a local model aeroplane club and had expressed an interest in seeing him fly his models sometime.

Colin was a chatty man, around twenty years Ryan's senior, who had lost his wife and daughter in a car crash ten years previously. All these years later, he still relived the accident—an uninsured driver competing in a reckless race with a friend had ploughed into Colin's car at high speed—but as he'd shared with Ryan and the rest of the PTSD group, he had finally let go of the guilt and despair at being the only member of the family to survive. These days, Colin only attended the PTSD Support Group meetings very occasionally, and Ryan counted himself fortunate to have met him. The two of them had hit it off straight away.

It was good to have a new friend, especially one who accepted him as he was. So many of his old friends had connections to journalism;

they'd found it difficult to know what to say to him after he'd been injured, especially when it became obvious he wasn't going to be able to go back to work. Then there were the friends he'd shared with Annie, but most of them had sided with her following their split. Either that or slunk away, never to be seen again, as if their impending divorce were somehow contagious.

Yes, it was definitely good to have a new friend.

"The other club members won't mind you turning up with me, will they?" Ryan asked as they arrived at the air base gates and drove towards the security barrier.

"The guys? Nah, they won't mind at all. They're a good bunch. Difficult to be miserable when you're with them. We have a right laugh."

Colin produced a toggle which he waved in front of a sensor, and the security barrier lifted up.

"Ever been here before?" he asked as they took a road that led towards two huge aircraft hangars.

"I haven't."

"It's an interesting place. Important during World War II, of course. Lots of businesses here now, everything from a sculptor to a guy who collects old cars for use in films. Oh, and one of the old bunkers is used to house the council's archaeology archive. You get a lot of nature here too—larks, birds of prey, rabbits."

They passed between the aircraft hangars and drove on the old runway.

"Some of the guys like to drive really fast along here," Colin said. "I might be able to do that myself one day, but not yet."

He turned slightly to smile grimly at Ryan. Ryan knew he was thinking about his lost family and nodded his understanding, then Colin slowed to go round a bend, and Ryan saw some parked cars and a group of guys. Colin parked and got out, calling out greetings, and Ryan opened his door, feeling suddenly self-conscious. But then Colin returned, took his wheelchair from the boot, and waited for Ryan to transfer himself from the car to the chair before they headed over to the group of men to make their introductions.

On the way, Ryan had just enough time to get a quick impression of the weirdness of their surroundings—the runway stretching away into the distance. Brambles and long grass dotted with concrete blast walls left over from the Cold War. Then they reached the group, and Colin said, "Guys, this is my mate Ryan," and proceeded to reel off lots of names—Ray, Grant, Steve, Andy, and two guys called David, who introduced themselves to him as David One and David Two.

"I think I've seen you on the telly," said one of the Davids—Ryan couldn't remember whether he was One or Two. "Heck of a job. If you can report from war zones, you can fly a model plane. You aren't a gamer, I hope? You know, computer games?"

Ryan frowned. "No. My son is, but I'm not, really."

"That's good, because gamers often get confused when they start flying models. You have to move the joystick in the opposite direction to the way you move one on a games controller, you see. Does their heads in."

"Right. Well, I've only come to watch Colin fly, really."

"Rubbish, mate," said Colin. "You're definitely having a go."

Ryan was worried. "What if I crash one of your planes or something?"

Colin shrugged. "Then I'll repair it. You saw the back of my car. I'm not exactly short of models. Anyway, one of the lads can lend me their controller, and we can buddy up. That way, if anything goes wrong, I can take over."

And so, after Colin had talked Ryan through the controls and launched a model glider with alarmingly large-looking wings, Ryan found himself in charge of steering it around the sky. At first, it was absolutely terrifying—the controls were so sensitive. One minute the plane was flying okay; the next, it was diving towards the ground.

But Colin was there every time disaster threatened, taking over the controls, his voice calm and reassuring. "Just the very slightest movement on the joystick. That's it."

Soon Ryan found that he pretty much had it. And each time the plane responded as he wanted it to respond, he experienced a sense of achievement he hadn't felt since he'd stopped working.

Turning his head to follow the plane's course across the sky, Ryan caught a glimpse of the huge aircraft hangars and imagined the airfield during the Second World War. All those young Royal Air Force pilots, taking off to fight the enemy over the English Channel during the Battle of Britain. Stalwart. Brave. Focused. Confident they could do their job, because if they weren't confident about that, they didn't stand a chance up there.

He'd been confident like that once. Would he have carried on working in the field if he'd survived the shell explosion and the terrorist's bullets uninjured? Yes, definitely. He'd loved his work. But maybe it would have knocked his confidence. Maybe he wouldn't have been quite as good at his job as a result. There had to be something else he could do now, something equally fulfilling, perhaps in an entirely different way.

"Watch out, mate," Colin said, interrupting his thoughts. "Don't lose your concentration. Never a good idea to fly in front of the sun."

"Sorry," said Ryan, correcting the plane's course.

"No worries. You're doing really well."

Ryan smiled, but didn't turn his head to acknowledge Colin's words, directing his focus back to the sky.

After a while—only around ten minutes, Ryan was surprised to learn; the flight had seemed to last forever—Colin said they needed to land before the battery ran out and took over the controls, bringing the plane effortlessly down onto the tarmac.

"You're a natural," David Two? One? told Ryan.

"Thanks." Ryan grinned. "It was fun."

"He's got the bug, Colin!" said one of the other guys.

"It looks like it, doesn't it?" said Colin. "We'll have to get you down to the model shop, mate."

Ryan smiled back. "Sounds good," he said, then settled back to watch the experts fly for a while, dipping in and out of the banter that flew as thick and fast between the men as the planes, enjoying the sound of the skylarks in the skies high above him.

"We often get buzzards over here," Ray said, positioning his fold-down chair next to Ryan and sitting. Ryan remembered his name because he was by far the oldest of the group. "Sometimes they get a bit too close for comfort, if you know what I mean."

"Who normally wins between a buzzard and a model plane?"

"It's touch-and-go. Normally us if we hold our nerve." Ray looked at him, nodding towards Ryan's chair and his useless legs. "How d'you cop for that, then?"

Everyone else—Colin included—was standing further away along the runway, crowded around an expensive-looking, jet-powered plane preparing for takeoff.

"Sorry," Ray said, when Ryan didn't reply immediately. "Don't mind me. I'm always putting my foot in my mouth. Ask anyone."

"No," said Ryan, "it's all right. I was working as a foreign correspondent in Syria. A land mine went off."

"That's bad luck."

Either bad luck or bad judgement. Ryan had acted on a hunch, driving up that particular road to follow that particular story, and the film crew had gone along with it. The worst decision any of them had ever made. The last decision they'd ever made.

"It wasn't the explosion that put me in the chair, though," Ryan carried on.

"No?"

He shook his head. "When I came to—I don't know, probably only a minute or so later—there was a piece of the wrecked vehicle lying across my legs. But instinctively I knew I was all right, you know? Cuts that needed stitches, a few broken ribs, but ostensibly okay."

"So what happened, then?"

Ryan looked out across the runway towards the tangle of a bramble patch. "There was a gunman, making sure we were all dead. I could hear him, the crunch of his boots as he patrolled around, picking us all off, one by one. My cameraman—Johnny—he was screaming out in agony. Then suddenly the gun went off and he stopped."

"Jeez. So then he came for you?"

Ryan nodded. "I tried to play dead. Guess I'll never be up for best actor at the Oscars. The bastard sank three bullets into me—one into my shoulder, and two that shattered my spinal nerves."

Suddenly, there was the sound of boots on the airfield tarmac, a lot like the terrorist's boots.

"Everything all right?" Colin asked as he approached, concern in his voice.

Ryan made himself look up. Gave a quick nod. "Ray here was just asking me how I ended up in this chair."

Colin frowned, giving Ray an annoyed look.

Ryan held up a hand. "It's fine, honestly. It's high time I started talking about it all if I want to move on. And I have started to, a bit." He smiled at them. "To quote one of my mother's favourite expressions, there's light at the end of the tunnel. All I have to do now is sort things out with my son, and my life will be well on the way to being good. And I never bloody well thought I'd say that six months ago, believe you me."

Ray grinned. "Your life'll be even better, now you've discovered model aeroplane flying! And us lot, of course."

And Ryan, who was inclined to agree, smiled back.

∼

The taxi dropped Ryan off outside Annie's house at 5:00 p.m. the next day. It was the first time he'd been there, and he spent a few moments to take it all in. A new-build in the centre of a meandering estate, constructed on what had once been agricultural land, the house was part of a small terrace of pale brick houses situated opposite a children's play area. Comfortable, anonymous, no doubt with a small square of fenced-off lawn at the back. Definitely not hedgehog heaven.

But as he registered that Annie's car wasn't parked on the drive, Ryan wasn't thinking about hedgehogs. His thoughts were wholly with his son and the conversation he was about to have with him. If Eric wasn't home, as appeared to be the case, he'd wait. It had to be now, today, while he had the courage.

Suddenly the front door opened. Jimmy looked out. "Ryan?"

Ryan pushed his chair forward. "I didn't think anyone was in."

"Annie isn't back from work yet. She'll be another half an hour or so. Eric's here, though."

"Can I speak to him, please?" Asking Jimmy for permission to speak to his own son really stuck in his craw. But it wasn't the guy's fault, was it? And he probably wasn't too bad, if you could look beyond the designer track suits and the glint of a gold chain around his neck. In fact, it would be a whole lot better for Ryan to believe the guy was a properly sound person, since Eric spent so much time with him.

"Sure. He's on his PlayStation. I'll let him know you're here." Jimmy looked doubtfully at Ryan's wheelchair.

"I'll wait out here," Ryan said quickly, before Jimmy invited him inside and they had to address access issues.

"Right."

As Jimmy turned and ran quickly upstairs, a distant part of Ryan's mind registered that at one time, probably very recently, he'd have experienced a feeling of black, boiling bitterness in his belly as he watched the ease with which his ex-wife's new man took the stairs two at a time. Now he no longer cared. It didn't matter in the scheme of things, not compared with sorting things out with Eric.

He heard a rumble of voices, and then suddenly Eric appeared, coming downstairs towards him with Jimmy following behind. Ryan tried his best not to search for signs of wariness or reluctance in his son's body language, concentrating instead on giving him a big smile.

"Hi, mate. I thought we could go to the park for a bit. If that's all right with you, Jimmy?"

"Sure, I'm cooking tea for when Annie gets back, but it won't be ready for half an hour. If that's cool with you, Eric?"

Eric shrugged. "Yeah, that's okay."

Then, after Jimmy closed the door and as the two of them made their way across the road towards the park, Eric said, "It's mostly baby-ish stuff in here, though, Dad, apart from the climbing wall."

"That's okay," said Ryan. "To be honest, I mostly wanted to talk to you about something. But first of all, show me how fast you can do the climbing wall."

Eric smiled. "Will you time me?"

"Sure," said Ryan, setting the timer on his watch, praying Eric wouldn't fall, injure himself, or do anything else at all that might require a trip to Accident and Emergency and earn Annie's undying hatred and resentment.

Ten high-adrenaline minutes later, a breathless Eric came to sit on the bench next to where Ryan had parked his wheelchair.

"That was fast, mate. Really fast."

Eric grinned. "I've been practising."

"It shows."

Ryan took a deep breath. "Listen, I'm sorry I haven't been there for you much this year, what with everything that's happened. I know it's been hard on you, having to get used to a whole lot of new stuff."

Eric shrugged. That shrug. Ryan wanted to pull him in close for a hug but held back, sensing it was too soon.

"The thing is, some of those changes, well, most of them, actually, are going to be permanent. Me and your mum, me in this wheelchair. You see, I went to see my doctor recently, and he told me that . . . well, I'm definitely not going to walk again. This is it, from now on. But . . . I really don't want that to change things between us, okay? I might not be able to play football with you, but we can do other stuff. I'd really like you to teach me how to play some of your computer games. Of course, I won't be very good at it at first, but . . ."

He broke off. A smile spread across Eric's face. "I'll thrash you, Dad," he said.

Ryan smiled back. "That's fine. I expect I'll cope. And just you wait until I get good at it." Then he did what he'd wanted to do all along and pulled Eric to him, holding him close and planting a kiss on top of his head for good measure. "We're all right, you and I, aren't we, mate?"

Eric didn't answer, but his head bobbed up and down against Ryan as he nodded, and that was all the reassurance Ryan needed.

"I'm so proud of you, son. I love you more than I can say."

He pulled back slightly to look at Eric. Both of them had tears in their eyes. "And I want you to know that it's fine for you to like Jimmy. It's not going to make me jealous if you do." It would, but he would try his very best not to show it. "Mind you, if he ever does something you're not happy about, just tell me and I'll sort it out, okay?"

"Okay, Dad."

A car pulled up behind them.

"Mum's back."

Ryan nodded, pulling Eric in for another hug before letting him go. "Yes. You go inside. I'll just have a quick word with her."

Eric stood, looking at his father doubtfully. "How will you get home, Dad?"

Ryan took the brake off his wheelchair and began to propel himself towards the park exit. "I'll call for a taxi. Don't worry about me, mate. Don't ever worry about me, okay? I'll be just fine."

Eric nodded, then ran off to join his mother, who was waiting for him by her car. "Hi, Mum."

She ruffled his hair. "Hi, Eric. I'll be in in a minute."

Eric nodded. "Bye, Dad."

"Bye, son."

As Eric went indoors, Annie stayed by her car with her arms folded. "Everything all right?"

It was his fault she looked so defensive. God only knew he still felt some bitterness about the way she'd given up on him, but it was perfectly possible he'd been so selfishly driven by his work that he'd given her very little choice. Something to explore in counseling, perhaps. No, definitely something to explore in counseling if he wanted to make sure he never made the same mistake again. Make sure he didn't do anything to stuff things up with Jess.

He nodded. "Yes, all good. Me and Eric just needed a little chat."

She waited, expectantly. The old Ryan might have told her to mind her own business. The old Ryan had been difficult and revengeful, unaccepting, and bitter as hell about the circumstances he found himself in.

"I told him I'm not going to walk again. I didn't want him to . . . well, harbour any unwarranted hopes that I would be able to."

"I'm really sorry, Ryan."

He sighed. Attempted a smile. "To quote my mother, it is what it is."

She smiled back. "You must be glad to be in your own flat now."

"I am, yes. Though Mum has done a lot for me since . . . well, since it happened. I appreciate that. Look, I'm glad I've seen you. I wanted to say . . ."

She looked suddenly wary. "What?"

"Well, that I'm sorry. For not being there for you when Eric was young. Being so obsessed with work."

Her eyes suddenly glittered. "It was very hard, sometimes. Lonely too."

"I know. I ought to have cut my hours back a bit. Stopped acting as if having Eric in our lives should make no difference about where I went and what I did. It's . . ."

He broke off, wondering how helpful—at this stage of their relationship—it would be to try to explain how compulsive reporting from war zones could be. How the constant witnessing of people's horror and despair could almost invalidate your own life, make you feel that taking a personal joy in anything felt like a betrayal to those who suffered. That reporting from dangerous places and getting the word out about it could give you such an adrenaline rush it was almost like an addiction.

"Well, anyway, I'm sorry."

She nodded. "Thanks."

He nodded. "Anyway, that was all I wanted to say. I'll get off, let you have your tea. What are you having?"

"Burgers and chips, I think."

"Great. Well, see you, then."

"Goodbye, Ryan. Take care."

45

Hedgehogs normally sleep fairly soundly, recharging themselves throughout the daylight hours in piles of old leaves and sticks after a busy night foraging for food. In the same way that human beings can tune out the sounds of trains on nearby railway tracks or the drone of nighttime traffic when they're in their beds, the hedgehogs in the belt of woodland between the park and the houses on Hilltop Place could tune out the happy laughter of children playing, and even the occasional sound of Tara and Hermie chatting as they cut through the trees to their garden gate.

But when the men from the council arrived one day to measure up the strip of woodland between the houses and the park, hacking back branches and undergrowth in order to make progress, it was quite a different matter. The hedgehogs awoke, startled, blinking as they sniffed the air, trying to identify the sound of the men's clumping boots and the alarming whine of unfamiliar machinery. And as time went on and the interlopers drilled and hacked, taking soil samples and investigating drainage, the hedgehogs rolled up into terrified balls, hoping the noise would soon stop.

Tara was out in the garden when the men began their work. She barely used the garden, but since it was a sunny day and she had no guarantee that James would pay the electricity bill now that he'd given them their marching orders, she was hanging a load of washing on the line instead of bunging it into the tumble dryer the way she usually did.

When she first heard voices coming from the trees, she, like the hedgehogs, was alarmed. Then she decided to go and investigate.

"Excuse me, madam," one of the council workers called out to her as she entered the woodland, eyeing the gate to her garden with a frown. "You're not allowed in here. This is private property."

Tara smiled her best smile, wishing she were wearing something slightly more appealing than her fluffy dressing gown and the bright-pink flamingo head slippers Hermie had given her as a joke present the previous Christmas.

"I was just wondering what you were up to," she said, ignoring both the look and the comment. "We're not used to hearing anything but birdsong coming from these woods."

"We're carrying out a land survey," the man told her. "The land is being put up for sale."

Tara was taken aback. "But whoever would want to buy it? It's just trees."

"On the contrary, with the trees cleared, it's prime development land, madam."

"You mean, whoever buys it may build houses here?" Tara asked, aghast.

"Provided the survey suggests the land is suitable for housing, yes," said the man, his patience exhausted. "Now, if I could ask you to leave the area, please? It's unsafe for you to be here while we're carrying out the work."

He turned his back on her, and Tara scuttled straight round to Frances's house to break the bad news to her and Frank.

Frances was outraged. "They can't do that!" she yelled, making for the door. "We have to stop them!"

46

"Frances, wait!" Frank called after her, but there was no stopping her. By the time he emerged onto the close, Frances had vanished.

"She's probably gone through my garden to get to the gate," Tara said. "Come on."

Frank followed Tara along the street and up her drive, the necks of her ridiculous flamingo slippers bobbing up and down as she hurried along, his own feet crunching on the gravel. Even from here, Frank could hear Frances shouting. He couldn't make out her actual words, but he could hear her outraged, angry tone of voice and hoped her blood pressure was up to it. Come to think of it, he had no idea about the state of Frances's health. Which was ridiculous when you thought about it. He of all people ought to know that health issues can strike a person down completely without warning.

"The gate's just over there," Tara said. "I won't come with you if you don't mind. Those workmen have already copped an eyeful of me like this. I need to go and get dressed."

Frank didn't mind whether Tara came with him. Suspected he would barely have noticed if she'd been stark naked apart from the ridiculous slippers. Every part of his consciousness was focused on trying to make out what Frances was saying and what the workmen were saying back to her.

But, being Frank, he shot Tara a brief smile. "Thank you for the use of your gate."

He couldn't see Frances immediately, once he was in the woodland. He could still hear her, though, and he could see the fluorescent-green jackets of the workmen she was shouting at, so he headed in that direction, ducking to avoid the twigs and branches that sought to gouge his eyes out, lifting his feet to step carefully over tree roots and fallen logs, the soles of his leather brogues sliding about in the mud. Frances must have been propelled along by her fury and indignation to have gone so far so quickly.

"Frances?" he called, drawing the attention of the two burly workmen his way, and then, as they turned towards him, he saw exactly where Frances was—halfway up a spindly tree, high enough up to look down at the top of the workmen's white safety helmets.

"Hi, Frank," she said, as if it were perfectly normal to be clinging on, up there like that. "I was just telling these men I'm staying put up here until they rethink the atrocity of their plans. Wildlife habitats such as this must be protected at all costs. Hedgehogs have no voice, so we must speak out for them." She punched her fist into the air, wobbling a little on the tree, causing Frank's heart to skip a worried beat. "Help hedgehogs! Save our woodland!"

The taller of the two workmen—the foreman, Frank guessed—addressed him. "As we've tried to tell your wife, sir, this is private council property. If she doesn't come down from that tree, I'll be forced to call the police."

Frank wavered, uncertain what to do. On the one hand, he adored Frances with pretty much every fibre of his being and would support her to the ends of the earth and back. On the other, he suspected that this stern foreman would do exactly as he threatened, and Frank didn't like the idea of the authorities dragging Frances from the tree in handcuffs. Apart from the humiliation and potential scratches from all this overgrown undergrowth, Frances's arrest would serve no purpose whatsoever because the general public currently had no idea what was at stake. No, the time for protests should come later, after all other possibilities had been exhausted. For surely there must be another way to deal with this situation? Something more constructive?

"Frank?" Frances called to him, obviously wondering why he was just standing there.

"Well," said the foreman, "are you going to get your wife down from there, or am I going to have to call the police?"

Frank looked at the man, registering two things simultaneously. One, that he would very much like to slam his fist into the odious man's overlarge hooter, and two, it felt jolly good to have Frances described as his wife.

"Perhaps I could have a word with my wife in private?" he asked, managing to keep all hint of potential violence from his voice.

The foreman glowered for a moment. "Two minutes," he said. Then he and his companion clumped away in their big boots, twigs cracking and breaking beneath their feet, causing Frank to pray that no hedgehogs had chosen to sleep in their path.

"You called me your wife," Frances said when they were alone. "You aren't going to propose, are you?"

Frank swallowed a momentary hurt, well aware that Frances's pig of an ex-husband was very likely behind any negative view of marriage Frances might hold. "No, darling, not just now."

"Oh. Well, are you going to come up here with me, then?"

Frank shook his head. "I'm not sure that tree is strong enough to support us both. I think you should come down and we should call a meeting for all the residents of Hilltop Place, to let them know what's happening. But don't worry, darling, we won't let them get away with this, I promise. I think I've got an idea. A plan."

"What plan?"

"Can I possibly tell you about it tonight, darling? After I've done a bit of research and fine-tuned the details?"

Frances huffed. "All right. But what if this plan, whatever it is, doesn't work? What, then?"

He smiled up at her. "Then I promise I'll buy us both the very best quality chains and handcuffs, and I'll join you up there."

Frances's eyes gleamed at him. "You don't mean the pink, fluffy sort of handcuffs, I hope, Frank?"

"Not unless they're the type you want, no. Now, come on down, darling. You've got a meeting to organise."

After securing Frances's promise that she wouldn't climb any more trees in his absence, Frank, having sent his son and daughter a message that he urgently needed to speak to them both, drove home.

Arriving at his house ten minutes before the arranged call, he had just enough time to sift through the pile of post that had accumulated on the doormat and to make a cup of coffee with his expensive coffee maker and to drift out into the garden to drink it. The lawn looked very neglected—overgrown with weeds sprouting vigorously up here and there. Frances had persuaded him not to mow it quite so often for the sake of pollinators. She'd spoken at length recently about starting a campaign to persuade the council to do the same with the verges that ran alongside roads too, though Frank wasn't sure how successful they'd be at persuading the authorities to change their mind about either the verges or the woodland. He supposed they would have to consider the effect on wildlife as part of the environmental considerations attached to the planning process. However, whether they would really care about their findings was quite a different matter. No, much better if the decision didn't rest on their conscience or their view of how important wildlife and its habitat were in the scheme of things.

Jason arrived on the call first, fresh from the shower and half an hour in his home gym by the look of him, dressed in a suit and tie, ready for work, even though it was only just 7:00 a.m. in New York. Jason had lived and worked in New York for the past five years, and every time they spoke, he sounded more and more like a native New Yorker. Frank supposed it was inevitable.

"Hi, Dad. I can't talk long; I've got an important board meeting this morning. Everything's all right, isn't it? You aren't ill or anything?"

Frank smiled. "Hello, Jason. No, no, nothing like that. Just a spot of news, that's all."

"What news?"

"Well, shall we wait until your sister gets here?" Just then, his daughter's yawning face appeared on screen. "Oh, here she is now. Hello, Meryl, darling."

Meryl had moved to Melbourne, Australia, around the same time Jason had moved to New York, and like her brother, showed no signs of wanting to return to the United Kingdom.

"What's up, Dad? I'm just on my way to bed. I've got an early start tomorrow."

His two impressive children with their high-powered careers and their busy lives. For just a moment, Frank remembered them as toddlers, tumbling about together on the living room rug, playing a game they'd invented, called Tigers. The two of them had been inseparable, and now they lived over ten thousand miles away from each other.

"Dad?"

At Jason's prompt, Frank blinked, pulling himself from the past. "Sorry, yes, I'll get straight to the point. I'm thinking of putting the house up for sale. In fact, I—"

But Jason interrupted him. "You're *what?* Don't be ridiculous, Dad. You love that place. I can't believe you're even considering it. Besides, the market's terrible at the moment."

Meryl, meanwhile, looked tearful. "You can't do it, Dad," she said. "You lived there with Mum. I cannot believe this."

Oh dear, this was not a promising start.

"What's put this ridiculous idea into your head, anyway?" asked Jason.

"Well, to be honest, I'm hardly ever here these days, and—"

"I knew it! It's her, isn't it? Whatshername. That woman you're seeing. She's put you up to it."

"Not at all," Frank started to say, but Meryl cut him off.

"If you sell the house, Mum will be completely lost to us. All those memories will have gone."

Frank swallowed, remembering all the months before her death when Philippa had longed to see her children. Even before they'd emigrated, they'd never visited much, and Philippa hadn't liked to nag them, not wanting to make them feel guilty. It had taken a terminal illness, in the end, for them to show up.

They were both talking at Frank now, making it impossible for him to say anything, making him think he might have to resort to typing his reasons for the house sale into the chat box. In the end, he put his hand up—both his actual hand, and the little yellow hand the technology provided him with.

"Firstly," he said, after they had finally paused long enough for him to speak, "Frances has nothing to do with my decision. In fact, she has no idea whatever that I'm considering selling the house. And secondly, I must say, I don't appreciate your negativity towards somebody you've never met. Somebody who has, quite frankly, transformed my life, made me happier than I've been in a very long time. Frances is a lovely woman, and the least mercenary person I know. I realise it's probably difficult, seeing me move on; honestly, Meryl, darling, I do see that, I really do. But I truly believe your mother would be happy for me."

In her Melbourne sitting room, tears ran down Meryl's face. Frank reached out to touch the computer screen, the closest he could get to giving his daughter a hug.

"Oh, please, darling, don't cry. You know how hard it was for me, losing your mother. I'm not trying to replace her; honestly, I'm not. But I really don't think she expected me to live the rest of my life feeling sad and lonely."

Jason cut in, clearly tired by all the emotion. "Look, I haven't got long, as I said. Can we please park the discussion about your love life and get back to the matter of the proposed house sale?"

Frank nodded. "Of course. Well, the truth is, I want to buy a piece of land that's come up for sale."

Jason frowned. "What land? D'you mean development land?"

Frank stifled a sigh. "No, actually, the complete opposite. I want to save the land from development. It's a piece of woodland, an important wildlife habitat, and—"

"You want to use our inheritance to save a few deer and squirrels?" Jason cut in disbelievingly, his voice raised.

Frank licked his lips, wondering whether his son spoke to his employees in the same scathing, dismissive tone of voice. The same tone of voice Jason had used when he'd first heard about Frank's job at the library. *"You've only just retired! Whyever d'you want to work in a library when you could take up golf?"*

Meryl was still tearful. "I don't understand why you're doing this to us, Dad. I really don't."

"You can't stand in the way of progress. People need housing, and that means getting our priorities right. People are more important than a few trees and animals, end of story. *Family* is more important."

"Mum would hate to think of you wasting our inheritance, Dad, you know she would," Meryl said.

Frank's heart sank. She was right. Philippa had always put their children before anything and everything else.

"I wasn't thinking of using all the money from the house sale," he said. "Just some of it."

"How much is this land you want to buy?" asked Jason.

Frank watched his own dawning embarrassment on the screen. "Actually, I'm not sure."

Jason looked outraged. "You don't even know?"

"Well, the land isn't officially on the market yet, which is why I wanted to get in quickly, before—"

Jason had obviously had enough. "Look, Dad, I have to leave for work. At the end of the day, it's your money, and your conscience. You must do as you think fit. Speak soon, Meryl, all right?"

Then he was gone, leaving Frank alone with his tearstained daughter.

"Meryl, sweetheart," Frank began to say, but Meryl leant forward to click on End Meeting too, and suddenly Frank found himself in the chat room alone, neither of his children having said goodbye.

Well, then.

Sighing, Frank closed the computer down and wandered back outside into the garden. What had he expected, though, really? He hadn't thought what to expect, that was the trouble. And Meryl was right. Philippa might not mind him downsizing, but she would want any profit from the house sale placed in a trust for their children. A high-interest bond that would yield as much income for them as possible.

So, no buying the woodland outright, then. He had some savings, but he'd need to keep some put by for a rainy day, and he doubted whether what he had left would be anywhere near enough.

Bugger. He'd so wanted to turn up at this evening's meeting like the cavalry. To present Frances with evidence that the land was safe, that he'd saved it. He could still picture her expression of delight, the way she would have thrown her arms around him. But alas, that was not to be.

He'd have to think again.

47

Because of the children, the meeting was held at Jess's house. By six thirty, everyone had assembled in Jess's sitting room—even Ryan, though he was no longer officially a Hilltop Place resident—and Frances briefly outlined the council's plans.

"So I'm sure you can see, we cannot possibly allow this to happen. That piece of land is vital to wildlife. It's an integral part of our hedgehog highway. We mustn't let it be destroyed just to boost the council's coffers."

"It's the council that owns the land, though, isn't it?" said Justin from his seat next to Tara on the sofa. "And it's the council that says yea or nay to planning applications. Ergo, I don't rate our chances of changing their minds."

Trust Justin, thought Jess, meeting Ryan's eye. *Straight in with the bad news.* Although, sadly, he probably had a point. But it didn't mean they had to accept the plans to develop the land lying down.

Frances obviously felt the same way, because her cheeks flamed as hotly as if Jess had lit a fire in her fireplace. "That's defeatist talk!" she said. "If it comes to it, I, for one, will be chaining myself to the trees. Organising a march on Parliament. Throwing eggs at politicians!"

"Let's hope all that sort of thing isn't necessary, Frances," said Irene with a shiver.

Jess suspected Ryan had been surprised to see his mother when he arrived. He hadn't got round to telling her about the two of them yet, but he'd told Jess only the previous evening that he would do so soon. That if he and his mother were ever going to have a different kind of relationship, he'd need to get used to opening up to her more. Jess agreed. She just hoped that Irene would unbend a little and start to respond in kind.

"I'll do whatever I can to help, Frances," Ryan said. "I've got several colleagues in the media who report on this type of thing. I'll contact them first thing tomorrow."

"I don't mean to be defeatist," said Justin. "Merely realistic. Presumably the council is only selling the woodland because it needs the money, and unfortunately, there's a plethora of property developers waiting to snap land up. Sites like that are rare opportunities."

Frances looked as if she might burst into tears. Either that or throw her mug of coffee at Justin. In fact, Jess suspected that if they'd been at her house, Frances might have done just that.

"Frank says he has a plan," Frances said instead, turning to look at Frank.

Frank cleared his throat. He looked uncomfortable. No, more upset than uncomfortable. "Well, I thought I had a plan. I thought . . ." His head dropped. "I thought I could buy the land myself when it officially comes on the market. But unfortunately, it seems as if . . . well, I was a little naive. It turns out that, much as I'd like to do so, on reflection, I wouldn't be able to afford to."

"Oh, Frank," said Frances, squeezing his hand.

While a part of Jess's mind registered that the two of them were clearly in love and how sweet and utterly heartwarming that was, another part was busy searching for a memory—a situation she'd come across similar to this when she was involved in charity work.

Suddenly, it came to her, and she smiled. "What if we all bought the land?" she said.

All eyes turned in her direction. "What d'you mean, Jess?" Ryan asked.

"Well, if we were to get the local neighbourhood on board somehow, spread the news about the proposed plans, emphasise the noise factor as well as the effect on wildlife—the strain on local services, that sort of thing—then we could establish a community group. Persuade the council to agree to an asset transfer. Maybe even organise a fundraiser. I came across a group that did something similar through my work once. I think, if we handled it right, people would really want to get on board."

Ryan beamed. "That's an amazing idea, Jess," he said. "I think I've heard about those sorts of schemes before. It wouldn't be easy, but I certainly think it's possible. We'd need to really get ourselves in the public eye, but if we work together, we could make a go of it. What does everyone else think?"

Frances took Frank's hand and lifted it into the air. "Let's do it!" she cried, her gaze sweeping over the rest of them. "Who's in?"

One or two hands shot into the air. Other hands rose more slowly. But finally, everyone agreed, and Operation Save Hilltop Place Woodland was born.

48

Hedgehogs weren't the only creatures living in the woodland between the park and the houses on Hilltop Place. Apart from the insects, there were mice and voles. A fox family, and an occasional deer. Birds, too, of course. Lots of them. And a bird flying from the treetops into the skies above Hilltop Place one Saturday afternoon a month or so later would have witnessed a hive of activity taking place below. In one corner, a local TV crew had just finished setting up, and an interviewer was speaking to Eric and his newfound cousin, Charlie. Having quickly become friends, the pair sat next to the elaborate hedgehog model they'd made together, talking to the camera about their "Guess the number of spines on the hedgehog" activity.

Jess was with her kids at the art-and-craft table, finishing off organising the paints and the balls of soft modeling clay, bundles of sticks, and googly eyes for messy hedgehog fun. Conservation and wildlife experts sat at tables, ready to hand out leaflets and to explain statistics and hedgehog facts. Justin and Tara, wearing hedgehog-themed aprons, were in charge of the cake stall, which was laden with hedgehog-themed cakes baked by members of the local community and Hermie's TikTok friends. Frances and Frank were running the refreshments stall and currently filling Hilltop Place with the delicious smell of frying sausages and onions for hot dogs.

As for Ryan, he was busy circulating, ostensibly checking that everyone had everything they needed and all was ready, but in reality going over the speech he would shortly deliver and trying to deal with his growing nervousness. It had been a while since he'd made a speech of any kind, and this was the first time he'd ever done so from a wheelchair, and his stomach felt sticky and bubbly at the same time.

Jess's table drew him like a magnet. Jess. How the hell had he ever managed without her in his life? He simply couldn't imagine. This past month, Ryan had spent increasingly long periods of time at her house, even sleeping there with her occasionally on the sofa bed in the sitting room. They'd discussed him selling his newly purchased flat and moving in with her. Getting a stairlift installed. Converting the bathroom into a wet room. When his mother warned against "jumping out of the frying pan and into the fire," Ryan had done his best not to feel impatient with yet another well-worn phrase, but instead to appreciate what she likely considered care and concern. Then he'd done his best to explain how sure he was about Jess and their future together. He wasn't so sure he'd done a good job of that, though, because what he had with Jess felt like a miracle, and throughout history, it had never been very easy to explain a miracle.

When he reached Jess's side, she reached over to kiss him. "We did it," she said, waving her hands to indicate everything they'd set up. "We actually did it. I can't wait until people start to arrive."

Ryan nodded. "Even if we don't get the go-ahead to buy the land, we won't have completely failed. We'll have raised awareness about hedgehogs and brought this community together."

Jess picked up the demonstration clay-and-stick hedgehog model she'd made and placed it in front of her face, making it speak for her.

"We're not going to fail, Ryan, okay?" she said, putting on a daft voice.

When he laughed, she took the model away, saying, "How can we possibly fail? If all the people come who've said they will, the council will be the most unpopular council in the land if they turn our offer down. Hermie's TikTokers would see to it."

Hermie's TikTokers had really got behind the Operation Save Hilltop Place Woodland campaign, taking the internet by storm with videos of themselves making hedgehog cakes—the crazier the cake, the better, and all accompanied by Hermie's "Happy Hedgehog" song.

"I love you, Jess Crawford," Ryan said, kissing her again.

Within minutes it seemed, Hilltop Place was packed. The only person missing was his mother, but Ryan refused to let that discourage him. If she came, she came; if she didn't, she didn't. It was her choice.

But he really hoped she did.

~

Over at the cake stall, Justin looked at Tara with concern. "Are you all right? You're very pale."

Tara felt pale. Nauseous, even. She didn't answer Justin straight away—her mind was too busy calculating dates. *Bloody hell!* She couldn't be, could she? No, she must have eaten something with gluten in it without realising it. Surely? But scrabble for another explanation as she might, some instinct in Tara's currently besieged stomach told her that, yes, she was indeed pregnant. *Shit.*

"Tara, sweetheart?" Justin persisted, one hand stroking her hair. "Do you want me to get someone to stand in for you?"

Tara looked at him and slowly shook her head. She'd been a stand-in herself, with James. Maybe it was time to play a starring role.

"Don't worry," she said with a smile. "I'm okay. But something tells me we need to have a little chat after we've finished here."

"Oh, all right," Justin said doubtfully. "Of course."

Justin's anxious frown boosted Tara's confidence. It showed he cared about her. The only time James had looked at her with an anxious expression like that was when he'd thought she was about to demand more of him than he was prepared to give.

"It's nothing bad," she said, wanting to reassure him. "Honestly."

Justin smiled. "Oh, good. You had me worried there for a moment."

With Justin's arm around her shoulder, Tara looked over at Jess's craft table. "Justin, d'you you mind holding the fort for a sec? I just want to have a quick word with Jess about something."

"Sure, sweetheart. No problem at all. Two pounds a slice for the cake, and a pound for a cupcake, right?"

She stretched up to kiss him. "That's it. And remember not to cut the slices too big. Smaller slices means more profit."

"Small slices. Got it."

She gave his arm a final squeeze and began to push herself through the crowd, spotting Hermie laughing with a couple of her friends. It was good to see her daughter happy; it lit up her whole face when she smiled like that.

Trying not to inhale the fumes of the frying sausages, Tara wondered how Hermie would react to the news that she was to have a new sister or brother, if that proved to be the case. Actually, Tara thought Hermie might be quite pleased about it. Provided she remained front and centre, not shunted aside the way little Stella had perhaps been when Toby arrived in the Crawford household. But that had all turned out okay in the end, hadn't it? By the looks of things, it had, anyway. At one time Stella wouldn't have even sat at the same table as her new brother, and now she appeared to be helping him paint a picture. If you could use the word *painting* to describe what Toby was doing. Crikey, how could a child get so much paint on himself? It was a wonder there was any on the paper at all.

For a moment Tara paused, her hands resting on her stomach, thinking of all the mess and chaos that would soon enter her life if a pregnancy test proved to be positive. *Bloody hell.* Could she really do it all again?

Hermie materialised in front of her. "Can I have a hot dog, Mum? Oh, and Marcie said to ask if you can show her how to do makeup. I told her you haven't even shown me yet. Can she come round for tea so you can show us both?"

Tara felt a little glow in her heart. "Of course, darling. I had no idea you were interested in makeup."

"Er, duh," said Hermie as if her mother were a complete idiot. "Can I have one, then?"

"What?" said Tara, still thinking about makeup.

"A hot dog!"

"Oh, yes." Tara reached into her bag for some money and handed it over.

"Thanks, Mum."

Hermie ran off, leaving Tara standing in the crowd, feeling emotional. *Oh, God.* Was this what being pregnant was going to be like? One kind word and she transformed into a soggy mess? *Hell's teeth.* It was hardly like her, was it? She was tough, resourceful. Ready and able to ride the crest of any storm.

Jess looked up, catching her eye. Frowned. No big surprise there after what had happened with Stella. Thank God the kid hadn't been abducted from the park. Why had Tara thought it was a good idea to come over to speak to her? She and Jess would never be bosom buddies, bonding over babies and having playdates together, after what had happened. She'd go back to Justin, see how he was getting on with the cakes.

But before she could turn away, Jess waved her over. Tara took a deep breath and went.

"Hi, Jess, isn't this going marvellously? You must be so thrilled."

"I am. It's wonderful. Whatever happens, it's great to have this sense of community spirit. How are the cakes selling?"

"Very well. Justin and I have managed to restrain ourselves from eating too many slices. Got to save the stock for the punters!"

Jess smiled. "That's great."

Tara gestured towards the children. "They seem to be having fun. What are they painting?"

"Hedgehog footprints. Can't you tell?"

Tara recognised that she was being teased and felt a swell of hope. "Well, now you point it out, of course I can."

"We found hedgehog footprints in the garden," Stella told her without looking up. "In the earth where Mummy buried Stripey Cat."

"Oh," said Tara, unsure what the correct response to that was. "That's, er . . ."

"It was interesting, wasn't it, Stella? They were very cute footprints."

"Er . . . good."

"I'm going to paint Patch next. I wanted him to come with us today, but Mummy wouldn't let him."

"I told you, sweetheart," Jess said. "It's too busy here. He'd be scared. He's quite okay at home with the new bone we bought him, isn't he?"

Tara thought Stella didn't look very convinced, but she carried on painting hedgehog footprints anyway.

There was a pause; then both Tara and Jess spoke at the same time.

"I just wanted to say—"

"Actually, I was going to—"

They both broke off. Jess indicated that Tara should speak first.

"I just wanted to apologise to you again, Jess. I should never have—"

Jess lifted a hand, silencing her. "There's no need, Tara. Honestly."

Tara nodded, wanting to say more, knowing there was no way Jess would ever leave her children with her in the future and unable to imagine the two of them planning trips to the park together. But Jess's attention was diverted back to the painting table, where Toby had just knocked over the paint water, and the moment passed. Oh well. If she was pregnant, she'd have to find mum friends and occasional childcare elsewhere. Justin would pay for it, she supposed. Or maybe she could even—horror of horrors—join some baby groups? Make some new friends? It might not turn out to be quite the hideous experience she anticipated it would.

Last time around, with Hermie, she'd been dealing with so much crap, what with Tony refusing to accept Hermie was his until the paternity test proved it, and the hassle from her landlord when the rent was late. Life had been unspeakably hard and lonely. It was no wonder she hadn't made friends with other first-time mothers. But now, with Justin in the picture, surely it would all be different. Justin was reliable. Dependable. He was there for her. It was all very grown-up and completely unlike the exciting relationships she'd always yearned for in her youth, but somehow it was exactly right for her now. Besides, it never paid to make your relationship your everything in life.

And as Tara smiled a goodbye in Jess's direction and drifted back to Justin and the cake stall, she pictured herself with a trio of other mums, giggling as they took sneaky sips of wine from innocent-looking plastic cups in a park while their offspring entertained themselves. Yes. Maybe this time around, things would be okay.

~

Frances and Frank soon had something of a production line going for their hot dogs. Frances did the frying, and Frank took orders and assembled the dogs, as well as serving teas and coffees. They made a good team, and Frances couldn't help smiling to herself as she turned the sausages, feeling, as she did almost all the time these days, as if she'd won the lottery.

Her newfound happiness had taken a bit of getting used to after her shit of a husband, but she was beginning to believe that this was going to last. That Frank truly wanted to commit to her. He'd even put his house on the market, despite his children's objections, so he could move in with her. Every morning, when she woke up to find him next to her in bed, she almost had to pinch herself, she felt so happy. Frank still appeared to love her exactly as she was—which was definitely a first. He didn't seem to want to change her or her house or her garden. Which was just as well, because Frances had no intention of changing anything. Except perhaps for the front garden. Yes, Frank was obviously so talented at growing roses, she'd let him indulge his passion for them at the front of the house. Irene would certainly approve of that.

As Frances placed a new batch of sausages into the pan, she saw Tara and Justin kissing at their cake stall and smiled. Tara had recently shown a new side of herself to Frances. When Frances had cautiously asked Tara to recommend a good hairdresser, Tara made an appointment for her with her own stylist. What's more, she came by to drive Frances there and stayed during the appointment to chat.

"This is my neighbour Frances," Tara introduced her. "She's a wonder with hedgehogs, and she's just got herself a very handsome new beau. She wants an easy-to-maintain hairstyle suitable for her lovely life. Does that sound about right, Frances?"

Frances glowed. "It does, thank you, yes."

"No problem." The stylist beamed. "You have beautiful hair. It just needs reining in a bit."

Looking at her reflection at the end of the appointment, Frances couldn't believe the difference. Her long hair now reached just below her shoulders and had been tamed with layers which made it shine.

"Thank you," she said, patting its softness. "It looks fantastic."

The stylist smiled. "A new hairstyle deserves some new clothes to go with it. You should let Tara take you on a shopping trip. She's so good with clothes. And colours. She'd help you pick out exactly the right shades and styles to suit you."

Frances had liked that idea. Tara had too. They were due to go shopping very soon. Frances was looking forward to it. She'd never thought she and Tara could be friends, but somehow they were. Justin had turned out to be a bit of a surprise too. She'd had him down as a dyed-in-the-wool bore, but since he'd got together with Tara, he'd definitely changed for the better.

With Tara's house snapped up days after it had gone on the market, she and Hermie had moved in with Justin, and he had turned out to be such a good father figure, helping Hermie with her homework, giving her chores to do, making her earn her Xbox time. And against all the odds, Hermie had lapped up all this discipline and structure, instead of resenting it. She seemed not only to welcome boundaries but also to thrive on them. And it was working both ways, by the looks of things. If Justin encouraged discipline and self-control in Hermie, then Hermie and Tara had helped Justin to relax just a little. He'd even agreed not to mow his lawn so often. And from what Hermie said, he'd allowed some areas of the back garden to be set aside for wildlife habitat.

The frying pan felt heavy in Frances's hand as she moved it from side to side to separate the sausages. She ought to have borrowed a pan from Jess instead of using hers; it always had been a useless thing, more ornamental than functional. How furious she'd been when Trevor had turned up with it for her as a belated birthday present. A present he hadn't given her on her actual birthday because he'd been off who knew where with his fancy woman—no explanation, no note, no message—driving Frances to report him missing.

"What the hell did you do that for, you stupid fucking cow?" he'd asked, seated, legs splayed, on the kitchen stool, with every expectation that they'd resume their lives together as if nothing had happened. Telling her what to do, doing as he liked, deriding her, and giving her a slap after a few drinks. *"You knew I'd be back."*

But Frances hadn't known. As the days and the weeks had passed, she'd begun to hope. To start to anticipate a new, happier future alone. And now, there he was, back again, and nothing had changed. Would never change. He didn't even respect her enough to buy her a decent present for her sixtieth birthday. Who buys their wife a frying pan for her sixtieth birthday, for goodness' sake?

"Stupid bitch," he'd said, turning away to reach for his cup of tea.

And that was when Frances had brought the solid cast-iron frying pan crashing right down onto his hateful head, putting every second of all those years of misery, abuse, and hatred into it, sending him flying from the stool and into the corner of a worktop, slicing his head right open.

There was blood. A lot of it. He was unconscious, at first. Frances stood there, staring down at him, waiting for the horror and panic to set in. It never did. So after a full minute of waiting, Frances left the kitchen and closed the door behind her, the frying pan still in her hand. When she went back several hours later, Trevor was dead.

What Frances had told Helen on the way back from the animal rescue centre had been true, or at least, partly true. She'd lived with fear for years after reporting Trevor missing to the police, waiting for them to knock on her door with a search warrant to dig up the garden. But they never had. And so after the requisite number of years had passed, Frances applied to have Trevor pronounced dead.

Until today, the pan had hung, largely unused, in her kitchen, a reminder that she had stood up for herself. That she was worth standing up for. That her views counted for something. But she no longer needed such a reminder, because Frank showed her those things each and every day. After this afternoon's event was over, she would throw the pan out for the bin men to take the following morning. Decades into the future, no doubt someone less enlightened about pollinators and hedgehogs would clear the tangled jungle of her garden. And if they did any digging, no doubt they'd discover Trevor's body where she'd buried it.

But she and Frank would be long gone by then. They'd live their lives out happily here, and while they were around, nobody would be any the wiser about what had happened in her kitchen all those years ago. Not even Frank, bless him.

~

Jess's heart swelled with pride as she watched Ryan up on the stage constructed by Frank and Justin. What a difference he'd made to her life. Stella adored him—he was her rescuer, after all—and Toby seemed to really like him too. Which meant Jess could leave the two of them together sometimes to spend an hour or two alone with Stella—precious time, now that Stella stayed over at Michael and Helen's flat every other weekend.

It had been difficult at first, dropping Stella off with her weekend bag. Both she and Stella had been tearful. It hadn't helped that Helen was there, lurking in the background, but Jess avoided looking at her. What was there to say, after all? The woman had stolen her husband. No doubt time would take the awkwardness away, and thankfully Stella seemed to like Helen well enough. Even though she didn't have children herself, Helen was obviously used to them through her work. Yes, everything would turn out all right. Ryan made it right.

Despite what he'd said about being nervous, Ryan's voice was calm and controlled as he began to speak, and the entire assembled crowd—apart from Stella and Toby, who were busy with their hedgehog paintings—hung on his every word.

"The humble hedgehog has to focus on its own survival because it needs to eat around eight percent of its body weight every day in order to thrive. That's the equivalent of an adult human eating around thirty baked potatoes in a night. Yes, that's right—thirty. That, I'm sure you'll agree, is a lot of food. It's no wonder hedgehogs are solitary creatures. They haven't got time to be sociable, for one thing, and for another, other hedgehogs are rivals, hungrily searching for the same food sources.

"In these frenetic, no-time-for-anything times, it's easy for humans to keep themselves to themselves too. Even when times are difficult. In fact, especially when times are difficult."

Jess felt tears prick her eyes as Ryan built up to the most personal part of his speech. The part she knew he worried would make him lose control and give way to emotion.

"It doesn't matter if you do," Jess had told him in bed the previous evening. *"Everyone will understand. People respect us when we share our deepest feelings instead of trying to keep a stiff upper lip. You taught me that."*

"When times are tough, it's easy to shut other people out, to be too proud, too hurt, or too suspicious to accept help. That was me, this time last year, after a terrorist land mine put me into this wheelchair. There was plenty of help out there if I'd troubled to look for it, but I wanted nothing to do with it. As far as I was concerned, my life, as I knew it, was over. And if it hadn't been for one remarkable, committed woman in Hilltop Place, I might still be that angry man, balled up in my room with my spikes on display like a frightened hedgehog. I'm speaking, ladies and gentlemen, about Frances Mathews. Frances, for those of you who don't know, is an amazing champion for wildlife, and for hedgehogs in particular. When I first found out from Frances how difficult we were making life for hedgehogs with our fencing and our pristine gardens and our slug pellets, I was inspired to do something about it. And I wasn't alone. With Frances's influence, we set up a hedgehog highway in Hilltop Place. It was a huge success. Thanks to our efforts, hedgehogs can now easily get from garden to garden to eat their thirty-baked-potatoes'-worth of food every night."

A ripple of laughter came from the audience.

"Word about what we've achieved has spread. All over social media, people have started to share their own hedgehog-highway success stories. Many of those people are here today. Thank you so much, all of you, for all your efforts. It means the world to all of us."

Somebody cheered. Others clapped. Somebody started to sing, *Happy hedgehog highway, happy hedgehog highway, da da da da, da da da da*, which led to more laughter and cheering.

Ryan waited for everyone to settle down before continuing. "So everything was going fantastically well. Then the council decided to put the woodland backing onto Hilltop Place up for sale, and the hedgehogs were facing yet another battle for survival. Frances was determined we should fight the sale and any subsequent development plans. She organised a meeting, and at that meeting, another amazing resident of Hilltop Place—Jess Crawford—had the idea of approaching our neighbours with a view to a community purchase of the woodland. It turned out to be an amazing idea, because we've been out and about, meeting and talking to all of you, meeting the strangers behind all those walls and fences, and the hedgehog highway we established has grown tenfold as a result. So even if our campaign to save the woodland doesn't turn out to be successful, which, of course, we very much hope it will be, then—"

Suddenly, Ryan broke off, staring towards the end of the street. Jess, along with pretty much everyone else in the crowd, turned to see what had caught his attention. By stretching up onto her tiptoes, Jess could just about make out Irene, making her way through the crowd with a piece of paper held aloft.

"Mum?" said Ryan, as Irene climbed the slope to the stage.

"I have news," Irene said, handing Ryan the piece of paper.

He looked at her for a moment, searching her face. Then he unfolded the sheet of paper. Read it. Flung his arms triumphantly into the air. "The council has accepted our offer! We've won! The woodland is safe!"

A huge cheer went up from the crowd. Stella threw her paintbrush in the air, splattering people nearby with paint. Toby copied her, splashing even more people. Jess looked up from dealing with the situation to see Ryan and his mother hugging each other. The next moment, she snatched Toby up into her arms. "Come on, Stella," she called, and the three of them rushed up onstage to join Ryan.

When the TikTokers suddenly burst into the "Happy Hedgehog" song, everyone began to sing along, and soon a giant conga line formed around the square. As Jess and Ryan finished kissing, Jonathan rushed up onstage to grab hold of the handles of Ryan's wheelchair. "Come on, mate," he said. "You have to join in."

"I can't, can I?" protested Ryan, but he was smiling, and he didn't protest too much when Jonathan didn't listen to him.

"Yes, you bloody well can," Jonathan said. "You do your arms, and I'll do my legs." And he trundled the wheelchair down the ramp to join the line.

Smiling, still holding Toby in her arms, with Stella clutching her skirt, Jess held out a hand to Irene. "Are you coming to join in, Irene?"

"Oh," said Irene, "I don't think—"

"Please," said Jess. "I could do with some help so that Stella can join in too."

Another moment's hesitation, then Irene nodded. "Very well."

Irene didn't exactly kick her legs out to the side like the rest of the people doing the conga around the close, but she did point her feet and give a little hop. And at one point, as Ryan and his brother laughed and played the fool together like a couple of kids, Jess could have sworn she saw Irene smile.

~

After the conga was over and the TV crew had wound up their interview with a social influencer who—much to Hermie's delight and excitement— had ventured down to the event to lend her support, one of the reporters came over to speak to Ryan.

"This is all so impressive," he said, offering his hand for Ryan to shake. "Bill Hislop."

Ryan recognised him from the local early-evening news. "Thanks, Bill. It was a hundred times more successful than we thought it would be. We appreciate your coming down."

"Our pleasure. It's great to meet you. And your hedgehogs are really safe now, then?"

Ryan smiled. "It would seem they really are, yes."

"That's so cool. Listen, I think this would make an excellent in-depth report. You know, something to follow on from what we've filmed today. Would you be up for doing that if the powers that be are interested? Go to some rescue centres to interview the people on the front line, show us some cute babies being hand-fed? That sort of thing? I'm thinking there's quite a nice parallel with your own story, if you get what I mean. You know, the whole getting-a-second-chance thing. Especially as you're already so well known for your news reports." Bill looked closely at Ryan. "God, sorry, I hope that doesn't offend you."

Ryan looked at him, remembering how he couldn't access the rescue centre when he went there with Jess that time. Thinking about thousands of people watching him on TV in his wheelchair as he compared the rescue and rehabilitation of hedgehogs with his own circumstances. He could be proud and stagnate, or he could go for it and let the TV company worry about the accessibility issues. It wasn't as if one TV report for a local news station had to be the beginning of a new career if he didn't want it to be. And who knew? It might even be fun. It would certainly raise more people's awareness about the need to help hedgehogs.

"I think it's a great idea, Bill. Thank you. Yes, do suggest it."

Bill gave him a relieved grin and shook his hand again. "Excellent. Will do. And congratulations again. This really was fantastic."

49

And so, the land between Hilltop Place and the park was saved, which was good news for all the birds and animals that called it home—not that they'd ever known it was at risk.

Ryan made a five-minute feature for local TV news, on the strength of which he was commissioned to film a two-part documentary showing how—in setting out to help hedgehogs—he had gone a long way to saving himself. The project had him touring the UK to visit various hedgehog welfare projects and returning to Syria to revisit the scene of the terrorist attack which had so changed his life. It also involved a great deal of public—and highly moving—soul-searching.

Afterwards, when he'd returned home and had time to process everything, Ryan felt that his meetings with all those passionate hedgehog saviours—those inspirational people who cared for rescued hogs in their garages and spare bedrooms, getting up every two to three hours during the night to feed broods of motherless hoglets—had been every bit as therapeutic for him as flying back to Syria. Not only had they restored Ryan's faith in human nature but they'd also gone a long way to reinstate his *can-do* attitude to life. The documentary went on to win a BAFTA.

While Ryan was away filming, Frances and Frank became hedgehog saviours themselves, volunteering at the rescue centre and caring for recovering hogs in Frances's own garage. Their efforts over the years saved hundreds of prickly lives.

As for Jess, she put her charity-work experience to good use to fundraise for the rescue centre. She also had some of Stella's cute hedgehog paintings made into greeting cards. When these quickly sold out, she printed some more, and an important hedgehog charity chose one of the images for their new logo.

And while all this was happening, the hashtag for a hedgehog highway—#hedgehoghighway—grew in popularity, largely assisted by a trending social media challenge amongst musicians to come up with their own version of Hermie's "Happy Hedgehog" song. Soon there were thousands of versions on the internet, including a highly successful rap rendition which briefly reached the top of the charts.

So in a way, the hedgehogs of Hilltop Place became famous— international celebrities, no less. Although, of course, they were just as oblivious about this as they'd been about the near loss of their habitat. As they went about their snuffling, lip-smacking ways, they only knew they could always find dishes of food when there were no beetles or worms about, and it was easier to get around because holes had miraculously appeared at the bottoms of fences.

As for the humans of Hilltop Place, they carried on living their interconnected lives. Roses flourished and were approved of. Babies were born and siblings bonded. Mothers softened and found the courage to build relationships with grandchildren, and lovers held hands in the gathering twilight and drank wine on overgrown patios.

And when the moon was big in the sky and it was time for hedgehogs to turn their attention to the furthering of their species, the sounds accompanying their mating rituals were often echoed from within the houses.

All was well with the world.

Acknowledgments

Firstly, heartfelt thanks to my readers—without you, there'd be no point in writing. I'd probably write anyway, because I'm a bit obsessed, but it wouldn't be the same at all. So thank you!

My thanks, as always, to my agent, Carly Watters; and to Jo Ramsey, literary assistant, at PS Literary. You both rock!

To Alicia Clancy and Jodi Warshaw for your amazing enthusiasm and editorial insight: my characters are more well rounded due to your efforts. Thanks, too, to Danielle Marshall, Kyra Wojdyla, Adrienne Krogh, Rachael Clark, and the whole team at Lake Union. Also to Cassie Gonzales for a fantastic book cover! I love it.

To Ann Warner, who gives such useful feedback on my first drafts: I appreciate your input so much. Thanks, too, to members of the writing community who give me such great support, especially the Rubies and the LU Debuts. Writers need each other, and you're the best!

Thank you to all those who helped with my hedgehog research and knowledge acquisition, especially my fellow volunteers at Hodmedods Hedgehog Support: you do such valuable work to help hedgehogs in need; the hedgehogs and I are so grateful.

My thanks to the post-traumatic stress disorder (PTSD) sufferers who have been brave enough to speak out about their experiences, including the journalist Fergal Keane, whose writing and documentary really helped me to get into the mindset I needed to write about a character going through a similar ordeal. Also, to the journalist Frank

Gardner, who made a moving documentary about his life in a wheelchair after devastating injuries sustained while reporting from Riyadh, Saudi Arabia.

Lastly, I'd like to thank Graham, Alfie, and all my family, including my mum, who supported my writing with all her heart. You may not be here now, Mum, but I still see your face beaming with joy and approval every day.

Hedgehog Facts and Information

- The European hedgehog is native to the UK and Ireland, Western Europe, and Southern Scandinavia. In the 1870s, settlers introduced hedgehogs to New Zealand to make the country more like home. Today hedgehogs are considered a threat to indigenous wildlife there.

- The name *hedgehog* dates back to the Middle Ages and comes from *hyge* (*hedge*) and *hoge* (*pig*) because hedgehogs love hedgerows and make snuffling, grunting sounds.

- An adult hedgehog has between five thousand and seven thousand quills (spikes) to protect it from predators. Its face, legs, and belly are covered in short, coarse fur.

- When threatened, a hedgehog curls up into a spiny ball.

- Hedgehogs are nocturnal and depend mostly on their senses of taste and hearing.

- Hedgehogs eat a diet of insects, worms, beetles, slugs, caterpillars, earwigs, millipedes, birds' eggs, and anything meaty they can find. They can consume fifty to seventy grams of food a night and travel up to two kilometres to find it.

- Hedgehogs hibernate between December and March, when the weather is cold and food is scarce. During hibernation, a hedgehog's body temperature drops from 34 degrees centigrade to 2–5 degrees centigrade. Their heart slows dramatically, and they barely breathe at all. A hedgehog may occasionally wake from hibernation for a quick feeding foray, then return to its nest.

- A group of hedgehogs is called an *array*, but they are generally solitary creatures and get together to find a mate only between the months of April and September.

- The average litter size for a female hedgehog is between four and five, though it can be more. Hoglets are born blind and without spines. White spines appear a few hours after birth, and brown spines after around thirty-six hours. The hoglets will stay with their mother for between four and seven weeks before going off on their own.

- Currently there are believed to be just under one million hedgehogs in the UK. In the 1950s, the population was around thirty million. The dramatic decline in numbers is thought to be due to habitat loss for housing, removal of hedgerows in rural areas, and fatalities on roads.

- While numbers continue to decline in rural areas, there are signs they are increasing in towns and cities as hedgehogs adapt to living in gardens, parks, and cemeteries.

- Humans can help hedgehogs in a number of ways: (1) by establishing hedgehog highways, holes at the bottoms of gates and fences that allow hedgehogs to get about more easily to find food; (2) by leaving cat, dog, or hedgehog food and water out for them between March and December; (3) by leaving parts of their gardens wild with leaf and log piles for foraging and hibernation; (4) by making or buying a hedgehog house for hedgehogs to rest or hibernate in; (5) by ensuring any garden ponds have a slope or other easy way for hedgehogs to get out of them; and (6) by contacting a hedgehog rescue charity if a hedgehog is out in the day when it shouldn't be or seems ill or underweight before hibernation.

Q&A with the Author

1. **When did you first realise you wanted to be a writer?**

   I wrote my first novel straight after finishing art college. Unsure how I was going to make a living as an artist, I thought, *I know—I'll write a bestselling novel to support myself while I paint.* Ha ha! The reality was very different, of course. Success took much longer to come, but as soon as I submerged myself in the world of my characters, I caught the writing bug. Now, although I do still create art, it very much takes second place to my writing.

2. **What was the inspiration for this book?**

   There were so many inspirations! I'm a member of the Women's Institute here in Norfolk, UK, and through that I met some wonderful women who take care of sick hedgehogs until they're well enough to be released back into the wild. I also learnt about hedgehog highways, where neighbours cooperate to make life easier in all sorts of ways for hedgehogs, and since I've always loved the prickly creatures, I was really interested in the idea of a community working together in such a positive way. In my working life, I've seen how different personalities come to the fore when perfect strangers are thrown together, and I liked the idea of combining these two things—a quest to save hedgehogs and a group of very different people with different agendas and personalities trying to work together. How well do any of us really know our neighbours? It seemed like an ideal opportunity for secrets to come out. Hilltop Place is very much like the road I live on, but I hasten to add, none of the characters in the book are based on real-life people, and there's less drama here!

3. **Do you volunteer to help hedgehogs yourself?**

Yes, I'm one of a team of volunteer drivers who works for a hedgehog support charity here in Norfolk called Hodmedods Hedgehog Support. Hodmedods Hedgehog Support is one of many charities in the UK who work alongside other wildlife rescue organisations to help hedgehogs. (*Hodmedod* is a Norfolk word for *hedgehog*.) The charity runs a helpline, and I go to collect hedgehogs from people's gardens, sides of roads, parks, and so on when a call comes in about a hedgehog in need. Hedgehogs are nocturnal creatures, so if they're out during the day, there's often something wrong. Habitat loss, human gardening practices, and changing weather patterns have a lot to answer for. Once I've collected a hedgehog, I take it to one of the volunteer carers for them to work their magic. These amazing people sometimes take care of twelve or more needy hedgehogs at a time—often in a spare room in their home. They're prepared to feed hoglets (baby hedgehogs) at two-hour intervals through the night, and their dedication is incredible. Sadly, not all rescued hedgehogs survive to be released back into the wild.

4. **What part of the book was the most fun to write?**

    All of it! I really liked the mix of characters and the dramas that played out between them. But I did particularly enjoy writing what I call "the hedgehog bits." From time to time, an all-seeing narrator looks down on the community, almost from the point of view of the hedgehog residents. This was something new for me and great fun to do.

5. **Where do you prefer to write? Tell us about your writing routine.**

    My favourite time to write is early in the morning, sitting up in bed with a giant cup of coffee and my notebook. I check emails and do a word puzzle first; then after the caffeine kicks in, I begin writing—usually a line of dialogue to start with. I'll write for an hour or so, and after breakfast, I'll type this up and carry on writing on the computer. If I have a cat nap after lunch, I can usually carry on writing later in the afternoon. Cat naps play an important part in my creative life!

6. **Kitty Johnson isn't your real name. Why did you decide to write under a pseudonym?**

    No, my real name is Margaret Johnson, and I've previously been published under that name, as well as Margaret K. Johnson. My publishing history is fairly complicated; in another life I wrote a lot of fiction with simplified vocabulary and grammar for people learning to speak English. I have also self-published my own fiction. When I came to Lake Union Publishing, it made sense to start with a clean slate. I chose the name Kitty because it was the name I would have given my son had he been a girl.

7. **What's the best way for readers to reach you and to find out about your books?**

I always love to interact with readers, and I'm more than happy to come along to book clubs online, or in person if they're local. I have a newsletter that readers can sign up for via my website at www.kittyjohnsonbooks.com; I send out infrequent mailings about my books, any special offers and giveaways, my writing life, and basically anything I think my readers will be interested in! I also blog occasionally on Goodreads. My social media handles are below—do follow me or get in touch. I'd love to hear from you, and if you've read my book, it would be great if you could leave a review!

Website: www.kittyjohnsonbooks.com
Instagram: @kittyjohnsonbooks
Facebook: Kitty Johnson Books

About the Author

Photo © 2020 Graham James

Kitty Johnson is the author of *Five Winters*. She has an MA in creative writing from the University of East Anglia and teaches occasional creative writing classes. A nature lover and artist, Kitty enjoys walking in woodland and on the coast and makes collages and paintings from the landscape. She loves a challenge and once performed stand-up comedy as research for a book—an experience she found very scary but hugely empowering. Kitty lives in Norwich, Norfolk, in the UK with her partner and teenage son. For more information, visit www.kittyjohnsonbooks.com.